MAD WORLD

MAD WORLD #1

HANNAH MCBRIDE

Copyright © 2021 by Hannah McBride

MAD WORLD

Mad World Series, Book 1

Original Publication Date: October 2021

ALL RIGHTS RESERVED. This book contains material protected under International and Federal Copyright Laws and Treaties. Any unauthorized reprint or use of this material is prohibited. No part of this book may be reproduced or transmitted in any form or by any means, electronic or mechanical, including photocopying, recording, or by an information and retrieval system without express written permission from the Author/Publisher.

This is a work of fiction. Names, characters, places, and incidents either are the product of the author's imagination or are used fictitiously, and any resemblance to actual persons, living or dead, business establishments, events, or locales is entirely coincidental.

The Author acknowledges the trademark status and trademark owners of various products referenced in this work of fiction, which have been used without permission. The publication's use of these trademarks is not authorized, associated with, or sponsored by the trademark owner.

All rights reserved.

Cover Credit: Temptation Creations

For Mom & Dad
Thank you for a lifetime of support, laughs, and unconditional love.

AUTHOR'S NOTE

Hey, friend! If you're reading this, THANK YOU SO MUCH! But also, check this out:

Mad World is a completely fictional story that deals with some very real world (and heavy) issues including substance abuse, childhood sexual abuse, language, and has an alphahole that can be unsettling for some readers. If you're someone who might have a hard time with that, please stop here!

If you're one of my amazing family members here to support me... please skip to the acknowledgments. Seriously. You can read this note and that. Then you're done. Mmmkay?

PROLOGUE

"**Y**ou stupid *bitch!*"
His voice cracked through the empty hallway as I scrambled back several steps, as if I could actually outrun his fury.

I had seen him angry, but never directed at me. And never this out of control. His rage was its own entity as it swallowed up the air in the space and pressed around me from every side.

Terror dried my mouth to ashes, and I struggled to form words to calm him down.

"Just... take it easy, okay? We can talk about this." I held up my hands between us, but he lunged forward and grabbed me, hauling me toward his powerful body.

He wrenched my wrist to the side, and I cried out at the sharp sting of pain that blasted up my arm. My eyes flooded with tears, but I wasn't sure if it was from fear, frustration, or physical agony.

"I'm done talking."

I tried to pull away, but that only made him angrier. The haze of rage in his eyes was chilling.

"I can expl—"

He cut my words off with a backhanded slap that sent me stumbling into the side table and knocking it to the ground. Glass shattered as a picture fell.

A picture of *us*. Or, more accurately, what should have been us.

I raised a hand to my jaw, feeling the pulse of blood as it swelled and throbbed.

Fuck.

Someone had hit me before, but never with that much power or strength.

Maybe because I had never been hit by someone who truly *hated* me. Hated me in a way that I hadn't seen until it was too late.

Way too late.

I had made a mistake. A horrible mistake.

Believing him was going to cost me everything. The same way it had cost my twin.

I closed my eyes as the next punch he threw sailed toward my face.

Pain exploded in a riot of white pops of light behind my eyes as my legs gave out and I fell to the floor.

See you soon, Madelaine, my brain whispered as I surrendered to the dark.

CHAPTER 1

SIX MONTHS EARLIER

The end of my life started with my speech class final assignment for my junior year. It seemed easy enough on the surface: research an issue you're passionate about and create a presentation for how you would recruit potential investors.

By the time the last school bell rang, I had an idea of what to do. I went straight to the library, which was where I spent most of my evenings and weekends when I wasn't working or at cheer practice. It was easier than stepping around the empty bottles and ashtrays of the double wide I shared with my mom.

And it definitely smelled better.

Plus, we didn't have internet in our trailer. Or a computer. Even my cell phone was an antiquated brick that I filled up with minutes whenever I got a paycheck that didn't first go toward things like food or rent.

I smiled at Marge, the librarian I was on a first-name basis with despite her being old enough to be my grandmother, as I headed for the cubicle with the desktop that I had claimed as my own almost five years earlier.

Dropping into the wooden chair, I used my library ID to sign in and started my search.

World hunger charities.

I could have picked a harder topic, but I was going for the easy A to keep my average on track for the scholarships I needed to apply for in the fall. I didn't have many options since my funds were limited to whatever scholarships I could piece together and could finance on my own. Most of the money I made from my jobs went toward things like bills and food.

You know. Small stuff.

But I planned to finish my junior year with a perfect GPA to give me the best chance possible. I needed to focus all my attention on my upcoming finals. Speech was an easy class. It was the elective that filled up the fastest because it was widely known that the teacher, Mrs. Bryant, was willing to give you an A if you provided a halfway decent presentation.

She was a teacher who was a year shy of retirement and it showed. She knew the statistics of our school; half of the kids who entered freshman year wouldn't graduate. Another seven percent would be lost to the mindless violence that was everywhere in our county. Another fifteen percent would be hooked on drugs or dealing drugs. And that wasn't even touching on the rampant STIs and teen pregnancy cases that cropped up on a daily basis.

But that wasn't me.

That wouldn't be me.

Earlier this year I went to the local clinic and had an IUD implanted just in case. Not because I planned on needing it, but because I knew I didn't want to get caught in a situation where I needed to worry after the fact about birth control.

Sex wasn't so much my concern as the out of control sexual assault statistics in our city. Combine that with my mom's penchant for letting her dealers in our trailer for a party, and it was all the fuel I needed to make sure my uterus was locked down for visitors.

I was part of that elusive one-percent club at school. The kids who were determined to make it out. And, with my 4.0 average, a spot on our mostly cheerless cheerleading squad (considering our teams rarely won), a couple of volunteer stints at the local soup kitchen, and a kickass essay about how I'd managed not to be part of the other ninety-nine percent, I was angling for a scholarship to a Michigan state school that would get me out of this place.

Cliftown was only a few miles from Detroit, but it carried the same stigma, if not worse, than the larger city, with only a third of the population. I wouldn't let this town swallow me whole the way it had my mother.

I scanned the articles that popped up within a second of the search. There were thousands to sift through.

I groaned, regretting my decision for a second.

There were endless options, but the perfectionist in me wanted to find the absolute best articles to outline my pitch.

An hour and a hundred clicks later, I changed tactics and shifted the view from search to news. Maybe if I saw a recent event it would spark a direction to focus on. I clicked on the first link I saw.

Business Mogul and Philanthropist Pledges One Million Dollars to Little Angels Food Kitchen

I scanned the article, clearly a puff piece that painted Gary Cabot, the donor, as a hero who was single handedly saving hundreds of starving kids in California.

Because the volunteers and staff of the food pantry clearly did absolutely nothing at all.

Insert sarcasm *here*.

But, hey. It made Gary Cabot, a man with dark hair and sharp blue eyes, look like the benevolent king he was to the adoring public, dashing in to save the peasants as he smiled for the cameras.

I scrolled to the bottom and flicked through the images of the recent fundraiser, which had been held at a hotel in Los Angeles. It was easy to spot who the rich donors were and who the underfunded volunteers were by the way they dressed.

My finger clicked to the last picture of the slideshow... and my jaw fell open.

I stared at the girl with her arm tucked inside Gary Cabot's. A girl with *my face*.

Her blonde hair was twisted into an elaborate updo, and I knew the diamond studs in her ears and the diamond chain around her throat were real gems. Her gown was a stunning ocean blue that matched her turquoise eyes.

How the hell did my face get photoshopped on this girl?

It was the only logical conclusion, right?

I skimmed the caption beneath the photo.

Gary Cabot poses with his daughter, Madelaine Cabot.

Madelaine Cabot.

Frowning, I abandoned my search for a new one.

Madelaine Cabot.

"Maddie?"

A hand landed on my shoulder and I jumped and twisted around to see Marge looking down at me.

"I'm sorry, honey, but I called your name a few times," she apologized. "I need to lock up."

I glanced around the dark library and then at the clock. It was after nine.

Flashing Marge a rueful smile, I started to gather my things. "I lost track of time."

"Not a problem," she replied, waving a hand. "You know I like having you around. It makes my nights a little less lonely. I'm finishing up at the front, and then we can walk out."

I watched her leave. If I was around in the evenings when the library closed, I always made it a point to walk Marge to her car. Three years earlier she had been mugged outside in the dark.

Seriously, who robbed a little old librarian at gunpoint?

I couldn't stop a bullet, but there was safety in numbers. Plus, Marge would drive me home as a thank you. I was getting the better end of this deal. I might have saved her from walking alone a hundred feet to her car, which was parked around the side of the building, but she saved me the trouble of walking a couple miles or taking the bus.

I finished gathering my books into my backpack and waited until

Marge turned off the overhead lights before shutting down my computer.

The image of Madelaine Cabot's Instagram page flickered as the screen powered down.

"Ready?" Marge gave me a wide smile as I joined her in front of the main doors.

I waited as she let us out and then locked the doors, my gaze darting around the dimly lit street. The sound of glass shattering on the pavement echoed down the alley behind the library where the dumpsters were.

I couldn't help but wonder what Madelaine Cabot was doing right now.

Probably not standing guard in front of a library and wondering if the shattered glass was from a rat knocking something over or Homeless Harry on another bender.

Marge finished closing up and gave me a weak smile. We walked around the corner and she quickly unlocked the car so we could slide inside.

"What were you looking at that had you so enthralled?" she asked, pulling out onto the street.

I hid a smile at her word choice, wondering if *enthralled* was the word of the day from the calendar she kept at the front desk.

"Just research," I replied.

She nodded sagely. She was well aware of how hard I was working toward a scholarship. "Which class?"

"Speech." I focused my attention on her, shoving thoughts of my doppelganger out of my head for the time being.

"My Chester was always such a wonderful speaker," she replied with a heavy sigh.

Chester, her only child, had been killed in a drive-by nearly a decade earlier. But Marge kept his memory alive by working him into almost any and every conversation.

I settled into my seat as she reminisced about Chester and his grades. Who he would have been if not for being at the wrong party on the wrong night.

As usual, Marge was sniffling as she pulled up in front of the entrance to the Bright Woods Trailer Park. A single streetlight overhead blinked and hummed with static as it struggled to stay on and illuminate the rusted sign that welcomed all who dared enter.

With twenty trailers deep across four roads, situated on a plot of gravel and mud, the trailer park wasn't all that bright, and the only woods to be found was a scraggly little forest along one side of the chain-link fence that surrounded the area like a prison.

The car coasted to a stop, the brakes whining in protest.

"I'm sorry," Marge apologized, grabbing a tissue from the console compartment.

"It's fine," I assured her, reaching across the space between us to squeeze her hand in mine. Marge was the closest thing to a grandmother I had. I knew she was lonely, and I was happy to listen to her if it gave her someone to talk to.

"Such a good girl," she murmured. "Thank you, Maddie. Will I see you tomorrow?"

I swallowed. Even though tomorrow was Saturday, I had early morning cheer practice and then was working a split shift at the diner. But I needed to get back to the computer and find out more about Madelaine Cabot.

"I'll stop by after work," I promised, opening my door.

Her face brightened considerably. "Don't work too hard. You're too young to be so serious."

I could only smile as I closed the door and headed inside the park. Slipping through a gap in the fence along the side nearest my home to avoid the crowd of men hovering by the front entrance, I kept my head down while walking by another man chain smoking on his steps. His gaze crawled over me as I passed, so I hiked up my backpack and lengthened my stride.

Our trailer was the seventh one in the far-left line of double wides that backed up to the only waterfront property the trailer park had: a tiny little canal with more trash than liquid in it. It smelled like urine and brackish water and whatever trash the late-spring sun had warmed.

It was the reason I never opened my bedroom window, even in the stifling summer heat.

I frowned when I got to the front door and realized it was not only unlocked but also slightly ajar.

Great.

Stepping inside, I flinched at the loud, tinny sound coming from our television. Apparently drugs also meant your hearing was just another sense that copious amounts of drugs and alcohol distorted.

With a sigh, I closed the door and locked it before crossing the cracked linoleum to turn off the TV before my ears started bleeding.

Mom was sprawled across the couch, the glass pipe still dangling between her fingers. I pulled it away and set it on the end table beside the baggie of little pellets.

Once upon a time, I had tried throwing Mom's stash away in a stupid attempt to make her get clean. Like if I removed the drugs, the urge would vanish.

Instead, I wound up with a broken hand when she went completely off the rails and raged out on me.

I stared down at her, at the smudged mascara she still put on every morning. At the way her clothes hung off her thin body. The bruises, the sallow skin, and the track marks showed the roadmap to hell.

After grabbing the thin blanket from the back of the couch, I paused a second more to study her before I dragged it across her body and then headed into my room to get ready for bed.

But when I lay down, I couldn't stop thinking about Madelaine Cabot and the bed she might be lying in right now.

CHAPTER 2

By the time I finished my shift at the diner the next day, my skin felt too tight from all the anxious energy bottled up inside of me.

Cheer practice had been decent earlier that morning, but kind of pointless since our school didn't have a spring sports team to cheer for. It was mostly us keeping in shape for next year when football season started.

Work had been painful. I'd made it through the lunch rush and then most of the dinner crowd, but when a closer left early because one of her kids was sick, I got roped into an extra hour. I had a headache from dealing with customers and shrieking toddlers for the last two hours that we'd been slammed. It didn't help that I had messed up several orders and made the kitchen staff annoyed with me.

I was doing an awkward half-walk, half-jog to the library with only forty-eight minutes left until it closed, but I hadn't been able to get her out of my head all day.

Madelaine.

My thoughts were dangerously consumed by her. I needed to know who she was and why we looked exactly alike.

Shoving open the doors, I inwardly sighed in relief when I noticed Marge was helping someone else. That meant no one was in my way as

I headed for the back cubicle and jiggled the mouse to wake up the monitor.

It took only minutes before I was completely submerged in Madelaine's world.

Jealousy spiraled in my gut and I ground my teeth together while scrolling through pictures of her life.

Social media was designed for people to showcase the best versions of themselves and to make others envious of what they didn't have.

And what I didn't have compared to my mirror image was everything.

Her life looked like the type of fairy tale I would dream up at night when Mom's screaming kept me awake. Her paranoid bouts of drug-induced psychosis were infamous in our trailer park.

Last month she'd bitch-slapped a plastic flamingo for following her.

Rolling my shoulders to work out the knots, I enlarged a photo of Madelaine with a group of girls in matching outfits.

#AllStarCheer #KnightsCheer #EliteSquad

The black-and-white cheer uniforms were crisp and perfectly emblazoned with their school's crossed swords logo in stunning gold thread that glimmered in the sunlight as she grinned at the camera, flanked on either side by six girls who looked like models.

It was a far cry from the hand-me-down uniforms my squad wore.

But she was also a cheerleader, which was unexpected.

More photos scrolled by. The same groups of girls and guys kept popping up sporadically, but Madelaine was the focal point of every shot. I zoomed in on several photos, trying to spot what I could in the blurry backgrounds.

There were a few scattered posts of her with Gary Cabot at various functions, mostly red-carpet events that she sparkled at. But the entire page seemed dedicated to her social life, which she felt the need to share with the world.

I scrolled to the comments section, but every photo on her Instagram feed had removed the commenting option. The thousands of likes on every photo, though, clearly showed she had an attentive audience. Over ten thousand people followed her, stalking her every move and weighing in with a random assortment of emojis until she seemed to turn off commenting.

I'm sure it sucked to be so adored that the constant praise gave you a headache to the point of disabling their reactions.

My heart pounded as I paused on a photo of Madelaine and her friends celebrating her birthday. I looked at the time stamp, my heart pounding when I saw the date.

September 25.

We had the same birthday.

"Shit," I whispered to myself, leaning back in my seat and letting that sink in.

It couldn't be a coincidence, right? What were the odds that a girl who looked exactly like me—okay, albeit a tanner, richer, slightly skinnier version of me—would share my birthday?

I kept looking with wide eyes until the images seemed to blur together.

"Maddie?"

I startled and looked up, surprised to see darkness had fallen outside the windows and Marge was smiling expectantly at me.

"Hey," I replied with an exhausted smile. My eyes flicked to the clock in the lower right corner of the monitor, and I realized it was close to closing time.

"Ten-minute warning, okay?" Marge informed me before turning and heading back to the front counter and disappearing into her tiny office.

Ten minutes.

I still had so many questions. Too many questions.

Drumming my fingers nervously on the desk, I considered my options.

I could ignore it. I mean, what did I really think was happening here? I had a long-lost twin sister who lived like every bit the princess to my completely stereotypical pauper? That shit only happened in movies.

I could message her social media account, and probably sound like a super-obsessed fangirl or stalker.

I snorted to myself. Yeah, that would go great.

Or, I could ask the only other person I knew who might be able to shed light on my mystery doppelganger. That is, if she wasn't completely trashed and trying to make out with a pillow.

Because, yes, *that* had happened before. And drugs or not, it was fucking weird as shit.

Sighing, I made my choice.

I printed a couple of Madelaine's photos and turned off the computer before getting my stuff together and going to the printer. I lifted the pages and stared at them for a second.

This was ridiculous.

After folding the pages, I shoved them into the pocket of my backpack and walked up to the front counter to wait for Marge, trying to come up with a plan that would hopefully get Mom to open up.

THE DELIVERY GUY was pulling up in front of the trailer park when Marge dropped me off. I fished out enough money for the pie and tip, hating to be using my cash on something so frivolous, but I knew I would have the best chance at getting Mom to talk to me if I came bearing grease and carbs.

It was a good sign when I entered the trailer and saw that the couch was empty and the blanket had been folded into a painstakingly neat square and placed in the middle of the right couch cushion. My gaze slowly wandered around the open living room and kitchen, and I winced, seeing how clean everything was.

Great.

We had officially swung into the super energetic, manic phase of her addiction. Which meant she would be extra talkative, but keeping her on target would be a herculean task.

"You're home!"

The sharp, brittle pitch of her too-bright tone blanketed in a two-packs-a-day rasp was an auditory assault, but I smiled back.

"I brought pizza." I set the warm box on the edge of our small dining table. The yellow formica was chipped but clear of grime.

Mom flashed me a grin as she headed toward the box. "Smells wonderful, Maddie." She paused and pressed a cold palm to my cheek. "How did I get so blessed to have such an amazing daughter?"

I felt my smile start to slip, but I locked it in place by sheer will and years of practice. "I'll get you a plate."

Humming happily, she slid into her chair and opened the box.

By the time I made it back with plates and two glasses of water, she had inhaled one slice and was reaching for a second.

"This is wonderful," she managed around a mouthful of food. "Were you at work today?"

I nodded and took a slice for myself, picking off a pepperoni and popping it into my mouth.

"I had an idea," Mom started, then paused to take a drink. "We should think about taking a trip this summer. Maybe the ocean? We could drive to the East Coast for a few days. Get a cheap little motel room on the beach?"

I kept nodding, not bothering to remind her that she'd pawned her car last year and subsequently lost it when she'd failed to make the payments.

I was used to this, her sudden urge to be a mom. It never lasted more than a few days, a week tops. I was too old to let it phase me the way it had when I was a kid who lived with a lifetime of broken promises.

My whole life was a broken promise.

Or maybe it was just plain broken.

"Sounds great," I agreed instead of calling her on her bullshit.

I was still chewing my first piece of pizza when she finished her third.

"I guess I was hungrier than I thought." She laughed, the sound a brittle, hacking bark that made me flinch inwardly and wonder if she should see a doctor.

Looking at her, it was easy to see the beauty my mother had once been. If you added a healthy twenty pounds to her skeletal frame, a decent haircut, and erased the age lines that had been carved into her face, you could see the diamond in the rough.

Years earlier, I had found a few beauty pageant awards tucked in a box under her bed. Pictures of her with a brilliantly white smile, full cheeks, and sparkling blue eyes still haunted me. I'd never learned how or why she had fallen into the life she lived. How she went from Miss Sun Valley in a random town in California to vying for the top Junkie-of-the-Year spot.

All I knew was that once Angie Porter fell, she sank like a doomed ocean liner.

I had been taken away by a social worker when I was eight, thanks to the concerns of my second-grade teacher. I spent four months in a group home while Mom went to rehab and got clean, proving that she could be a normal parent.

Those first two weeks I had been back home had been weirder and scarier than when I was sleeping near strangers in a room of bunk beds that smelled like musty blankets and stagnant water.

Normal Mom wasn't *my* normal, and that was more unsettling than any bender I had watched her ride out.

Then, one day, I came home from school and she was passed out on the couch with a bottle of vodka, and life went back to normal.

Mom pushed up from the table and looked around, her fingers twitching as she tried to find something to clean. Her OCD was just as strong sober as when she was high. It was just a different fix she was searching for now.

I pulled in a deep breath and pushed my plate away. "Can I talk to you about something?"

She looked at me, surprised. "Of course, honey. Is it about college? Have you started applying?"

"Not yet." I wouldn't start applying until next year and only if I saved the money for the application fees. I would need to narrow down the schools I had the best shot with so I wasn't throwing money at pointless application fees.

A sad look shadowed her eyes, disappointment etching even more stress lines into her weathered face. "Oh, no."

I frowned quizzically at her.

She started wringing her hands. "I'll support your decision, no matter what, Madison." She sat down and reached for my hands across the table, her expression serious.

An amused laugh bubbled out of me as I realized what she was thinking. "Mom, I'm not pregnant."

Relief brightened her expression and she exhaled loudly. "Thank God. I'm too young to be a grandma."

"It's about my dad," I said slowly, carefully watching for a reaction. Any reaction.

She blinked several times before smoothing a hand down the front of her shirt. "Your father? Honey, I told you. I don't know who he was."

A one-night stand was the official explanation I had been given a decade earlier, when I'd had no clue what that even meant. It was the answer I'd received the four other times in my life I had brought him up. The last time I broached the subject was when I was thirteen. The fallout from that (a three-week bender where she'd basically disappeared) still caused me to question bringing this up again.

But now I had more information... and I *needed* to know.

"Right," I continued, reaching into my pocket and pulling out the folded pages. I unfurled the papers and laid them between us. "Can you tell me who this is?"

Mom glanced at the pages and something in her expression shifted for a split-second before she looked back at me. "It's you. Did you get new uniforms?"

I mashed my lips together. "That's not me, Mom. Her name is Madelaine Cabot."

Another owlish blink. Lines formed above her brow as she tried to concentrate. "Is this a trick? A joke? One of those photoshopping things you kids do?"

"Her dad's name is Gary Cabot," I added, not bothering to correct her.

At first she didn't move, but then Mom exploded from her seat with enough force to knock her chair over. I jumped back.

"What the *fuck* are you trying to do, Madison?" She jabbed a finger at my chest. "I told you—your father was a loser I met and fucked one night behind an eighteen-wheeler."

"Mom." I stared up at her, my jaw hanging open.

"What? You think you're some pretty little princess with a daddy who will rescue her?" Mom whirled around, lifting her drink and hurling it clean across the trailer. It shattered in a spray of glass and water.

"Mom!" I shot to my feet in alarm.

She rounded the table on me, her expression feral and dangerous. Enough so that I tried backing up, but there was nowhere to go. My seat was between the wall and the table with a window to my left.

"Shut up, Madison. Shut your selfish, bitchy little mouth. Fucking ungrateful brat," she spat. The unhinged glint in her eyes was familiar, but not normal when she was sober.

Somehow that made it scarier.

"I didn't mean—"

The crack of her open palm connecting with my jaw stunned me into silence a second before the burning pain flared across my cheek and toward my temple. My eyes watered instantly.

Shit, that hurt. It had been a while since she'd slapped me, and I'd forgotten how much it stung. Blood rushed to the surface of my skin as it started to throb.

"Look around, Madison," she hissed, her spittle dotting my face. "This shithole is your life. Fucking accept it."

She turned and stalked into the kitchen area, her entire body coiled tight with tension. With shaking hands, she reached into a cabinet and pulled out a bottle of tequila before storming into her bedroom and leaving me with even more questions.

CHAPTER 3

A week after Mom's meltdown, I was officially ready to label myself a stalker.

I was completely and utterly consumed by Madelaine Cabot. Not only had I turned the internet upside down seeking information about her, but I had scoured every article I could find for Gary Cabot as well. Then I moved on to the people in Madelaine's photos.

Friends, teachers, coaches. I created several dummy accounts to follow private accounts in hopes they would let me in so I could steal even more glimpses of her and her father. I had found the school she went to, even going so far as to take the virtual tour for potential new students at Pacific Cross Academy.

Pacific Cross had been around since the early 1900s, when the West Coast's elite needed someplace special to ship their children off to under the guise of a good education.

Okay, a *great* education.

It hadn't taken much to learn the history of Pacific Cross, which boasted an excellent curriculum that fed into every Ivy League school in the US and the United Kingdom. What started as a school had turned into a full-fledged institution one hundred years later, one that included ninth through twelfth grade *and* an ultra-elite university that set up its students for the grad school of their choosing. The sprawling campus was full of stone and glass buildings with state-of-the-art technology and the best of the best professors.

Senators, CEOs, lawyers, doctors, scientists, and a few presidents had attended over the last century and sent their heirs there to be shaped into the next generation of asshole leaders who would manipulate this country for their own bank accounts.

It was the type of school that didn't advertise the cost of enrollment, because if you needed to ask, you definitely weren't the type of person who could attend.

But... I was still curious and searched for the information to the point where I was wondering if there was a college curriculum for budding private investigators. Hopefully a local state school had it, because I sure as hell wouldn't be able to afford the education Madelaine was getting.

I hadn't been aware that an education could start at a base cost of seven-figures.

Every person who attended Pacific Cross came from money, and lots of it.

I knew Madelaine was rich. Hell, I'd known that since the first night I saw her picture at the charity gala. The lists of designers and stylists tagged in her photos weren't carried in department stores or generic chains that you could find at the mall.

She definitely had a thing for Louboutin and Cartier (and a whole bunch of other brands I couldn't pronounce).

But I needed *more*.

Now I knew she loved avocado on anything from pita bread to salad. I knew she had the same nonfat, caramel macchiato every morning. That she was captain of her cheer squad and had been in every homecoming, winter, and spring formal court at Pacific Cross since starting as a freshman, but she never attended with a date. Her love life was a mystery. Pictures of her with guys and girls flooded her social media feeds, and it was usually the same people, but nothing that suggested she was in a relationship. At least not one that went beyond a dance or event where she needed a plus one.

So, yeah.

I had become her stalker.

To the point where I knew this wasn't enough. I needed more. I needed to know who Madelaine was... and to see if she knew who I was.

Minutes before the library closed for the night, I finally summoned the nerve to do what I'd been debating for the better part of a week.

I tapped the message button on her Instagram and waited for the page to load.

I stared at the white screen, still trying to figure out how to say this. How to make it sound like I wasn't a total nutcase.

Eventually, I started typing.

My name is Madison Porter. I think we might be related.

I included a link to an article from our school paper earlier in the year that had a picture of my squad so she could see who I was, and I hit send.

And then I waited.

∼

IN THE THREE weeks that passed after I had sent Madelaine the message, I had run the gamut of emotions. Hope bled into anger; wonder morphed into irritation. The silence on the other side of the message frustrated me to no end, until I finally forced myself to move on.

The stupid message was tagged as having been read, but still all I got was a lot of nothing.

I threw myself into the last couple weeks of school, neatly sweeping my classes with straight As. I left school the last day of my junior year with a packet of potential colleges my counselor was encouraging me to apply to, provided I could come up with the fees needed to process the applications and find a few scholarships to keep me from a lifetime of student loan debt. I had the next three months to plan.

Summer vacation was a double-edged sword for me.

Yeah, it meant I got a break from studying and homework and cramming for exams to keep my grade point average as high as possible, but it also meant long days with little to do. Stretches of time where I had to invent ways to occupy myself. At least I had my job at the diner, plus a part time summer job at the library for extra income.

Whatever kept me out of the house and away from my mom, who hadn't slowed in her quest to destroy her liver before the age of forty.

I didn't even look up as a stack of books tumbled into the return bin beside me and someone slinked by the counter. I simply reached into the bin to start logging the books.

"Busy day," Marge remarked as she came up beside me. She pushed her glasses up higher on her nose as she looked around, seeming pleased with the full seats.

I didn't have the heart to tell her that most of the people were only in here for the free air conditioning and wifi. The sudden heat wave hitting our area was sticky and gross. People who couldn't afford air conditioning often sought sanctuary in the library.

Instead I smiled back at her. "Yeah."

Marge loved this place, and I loved her. I often wondered if she worked too much, but this place was her life. She had no family left, so she invested everything in being the head librarian in our town.

"Any plans for this summer?" she asked brightly, glancing around again before her gaze settled on me.

"Just work and here," I replied with a single shoulder shrug. She knew my home life wasn't the best, but she never pried.

Another reason I loved her.

A tiny frown further creased the wrinkles around her eyes and lips. "You work too hard, Maddie. You need to live a little. Maybe go on a date?"

I smothered a laugh. Dating in Cliftown was more like randomly hooking up and praying you dodged an STI bullet.

"I'll think about it," I answered after a beat, smiling.

"Have you thought any more about what you'll study when you go to college?" she asked.

I grimaced as the familiar sweep of uncertainty covered me. "I'm still not sure."

That was a lie.

I knew what I *wanted* to study.

Social work.

It was hard not to walk around the streets of Cliftown and see the need everywhere. Children huddled in threadbare clothing next to an adult who was trying to score from a corner dealer, who probably should have been in high school himself. Elderly people who had been rolled outside in a rusting wheelchair with watery eyes and bruised skin and then left for hours.

Social work wouldn't be the most glamorous career. Maybe I should have done something more financially sound like becoming a lawyer or a doctor, but I knew these streets. I saw how people were neglected and abused.

Yes, the system was overloaded and the people in it were overused and overworked. But I needed to try to make a difference. If I'd had more time, I would want to volunteer at a local youth center, but between school and the diner and the part-time hours I would work at the library in the summer... There simply weren't enough hours in the day.

Besides, first? I needed to get into a college.

Marge's shoulders slumped, but she reached out with a soft hand to stroke the ends of my ponytail. "I'm sure you'll figure it out. You're so smart. I see you doing great things, my girl."

"Thanks," I whispered, basking in her praise like a barren tree soaked in the golden rays of sunlight after a long winter.

I looked back out at the sitting area closest to the front desk and watched as a mother got up with three children. She stuffed a bag of garbage into the can on her way out, but the lid to the full bin barely closed.

"I'll get the trash," I told Marge, getting up from my seat and grabbing a new trash bag from the box under the counter before going out to change the liners.

Weaving through the stacks, I carried the trash out the side door to where the bin was located.

"Yuck," I muttered, getting a whiff of the dumpster we shared with the Chinese restaurant across the alley. The sweltering heat made the normal stench even worse as I flipped open the top lid and tossed the bag inside.

I slammed the lid back down and turned, my entire body jolting as I realized there was someone behind me.

"Holy shit," I started. "You scared the hell out of—"

The words died on my lips as the figure across from me removed the large sunglasses from her face. Bright blue eyes, identical to my own, stared at me.

"Christ," she whispered, her low tone amused. "It's like looking in a fucking mirror."

I stumbled back a step, taking in the girl before me.

Her blonde hair was pulled back in a simple yet elegant French braid. She was in jeans, artfully ripped and frayed in the right places. Supple leather boots encased her feet, and her plain white t-shirt was covered by a cropped leather jacket. She carried a large leather purse that she tucked the sunglasses into.

Who wore a leather jacket and jeans in the *summer*?

Her eyes rolled dramatically. "You can actually talk, right? I mean, you can type. At least, I'm assuming you sent me the message."

"You never replied," I responded stupidly, still barely treading water in the depths of my shock.

She arched her brow. "Because I was busy. Besides, I wanted to see if you were real for myself. It's Madison, right?"

I nodded slowly. "Yeah. And you're... Madelaine?"

She smirked, an angular hip jutting out. "Obviously."

Okay, she needed to dial back the bitch a little. My shock was wearing off and now I was getting annoyed at the surprise attack.

"Well, you came. You saw," I said shortly, folding my arms under my chest.

Her brows lifted elegantly. "Okay then. Guess I wasn't the one who got all the attitude in utero."

"Why are you here?" I demanded, looking around the empty alley. "I messaged you *weeks* ago."

Her nose wrinkled as her eyes followed mine. Disgust pulled down the corners of her mouth. "Believe me, I'm asking myself the same thing." She shook her shoulders and stepped forward. "Can we go somewhere and talk?"

"I'm working," I replied, gesturing to the door beside me. "I don't take out trash at the library for fun."

She frowned deeper and looked at the door. "Can't you tell your boss you need the rest of the day off? Tell them it's for family shit."

"Wow," I muttered, shaking my head. "First of all, no. That's not how having a job works. Second? You've ignored me for weeks, remember? You don't get to stroll up and start making demands."

"I was *busy*," she repeated emphatically, punctuating it with another eye roll. "And you seriously work here? It smells like a sewer."

Oh, my God.

"I work in the library," I snapped. "Not the alley."

"Smelly alley or musty library," she countered, pretending to weigh their value in her palms. She made a pained face. "Not seeing the difference."

"Yeah, I'm not doing this," I said curtly, turning away.

Did I want answers? Hell, yes. But I wasn't going to let this spoiled bitch come into my town and treat me like a science experiment.

"Hey, wait," she said softly, reaching out to stop me. She held her hands up in surrender as I twisted out of her hold. "I'm sorry, okay? Sarcasm is my default setting. My therapist says I use it as a coping mechanism when I get flustered."

I didn't bother hiding my smirk. We had that in common.

"Okay," I allowed after a beat.

"Let's try this again?" She smiled at me and held out a hand, dark purple nails sparkling in the sunlight. "Hi, I'm Madelaine. I'm your twin sister."

I hesitantly reached for her hand. "Twin?" The word rolled off my tongue as a stunned question as I let myself speak it aloud for the first time.

She rolled her eyes again but grinned at me. "Of course. How else do you explain that we're carbon copies of hotness?"

An unexpected laugh bubbled from my lips.

Her hand dropped to her side. "That," she added, "and I found some documents on our birth records." She patted her bag, and her expression melted into something more somber. "I brought them with me. I was really hoping we could talk. Figure this shit out or something."

I glanced back at the door. "I can't right now. I'm working, and I really need this job."

She puffed out her cheeks as she exhaled, clearly annoyed. "Okay. What time are you off?"

"We close at nine," I replied slowly.

Her mouth flattened. "Fine. How about if I send my driver for you then? He can bring you to my hotel. Does that work?"

It took a second for her offer to sink in, but when it did, I couldn't deny wanting to find out exactly what was in that bag. "Yeah."

"Want me to order dinner? My treat," she added quickly as I started to protest.

I managed a shrug. "Sure. I'm allergic to—"

"—peanuts?" she finished for me with a knowing smile. "Me, too."

"Oh." I bit my lower lip to try and stop from smiling. Hope fluttered in my chest, a dangerously foreign feeling.

"Nine o'clock," she confirmed, walking backward out of the alley. "If your mom won't miss you, you should spend the night. Like a sleepover."

Mom definitely wouldn't miss me.

"Okay."

"Awesome," she replied. "See you soon."

"See ya," I murmured as she exited the alley and turned the corner.

CHAPTER 4

When Marge and I exited the library hours later, a shiny black town car was waiting by the curb. A large man in a suit got out from behind the wheel and nodded to me before returning to stand sentry by the hood. His dark blond hair was slicked back, exposing the strong cut of his jaw.

I felt Marge tense, and I quickly guided her to her car in the opposite direction.

"Maddie?" she questioned, pausing at the open door to peer at the opening to the alley where she parked, probably expecting the guy to show up with a knife or something.

"He's waiting for me," I assured her, with a flash of a smile that belied the anxiety fluttering in my chest. "I'm meeting someone."

Her eyes widened with intrigue. "A new beau?"

Marge really needed to lay off the historical romance novels.

"A *friend*," I corrected, holding back a laugh. "But I'll see you later, okay?"

"All right," she replied, patting my hand before getting behind the wheel and starting the engine. I waited for her to pull out onto the main road before turning around and walking back to the person Madelaine sent to collect me.

"Hi," I said with a small, awkward wave as I walked up to the stranger.

He was huge and hulking, looking more like he should be guarding a celebrity than driving me around. His black jacket pulled tight across his wide shoulders, and he was wearing sunglasses that hid his eyes even though it was nighttime.

He opened the back door for me, and I saw the familiar flash of leather and metal at the holstered weapon tucked to his side. "Good evening, miss."

"Maddie," I said as I sat down on the leather seat, my anxiety ratcheting up a notch. Guns didn't really freak me out (much) anymore. I was used to seeing the glint of metal from people walking by on the street. But I'd never gotten in a car with someone carrying until now.

By *choice*.

"Is everything all right, miss?" he asked slowly, his head lifting and surveying the area around us.

I wasn't sure if he was looking for a potential threat or potential witnesses.

"I'm getting into a car with a guy who's carrying a gun," I blurted out.

I could've sworn his mouth tightened a fraction as he tried not to smile. "For protection only."

"Oh, good," I said, only half-joking. "I was worried you might be a kidnapper or something."

"That's not my job description tonight," he replied evenly.

I started to laugh until I realized he wasn't joining me.

"Shall we go? I'd rather not keep Miss Cabot waiting," he told me.

I nodded mutely with a rough swallow.

"Very well, miss," he replied blandly, closing the door behind me. He walked to the front of the car and got in. A second later, we joined the traffic on the road.

"There's water for you, should you like," he informed me, meeting my eyes in the rearview mirror.

I glanced down to see a glass bottle of water in the cupholder behind the center console. Who bottled water in *glass*? Was plastic too pedestrian? "Um, thanks."

"Of course, miss," he repeated.

I tried not to fidget, but the urge to run my hands across every surface in this vehicle was killing me. "You can call me Maddie."

His eyes met mine in the mirror. "The temperature can be controlled from the remote beside you, miss."

Clearly this was a losing battle, so I let it go.

"I'm good, thanks."

I let my hand rest on the buttery soft leather seat and traced the stitching with my index finger as the car drove through the night, leaving Cliftown and heading for Detroit. It wasn't a long drive, and there was hardly any traffic on the interstate as the car ate up the distance toward the smattering of twinkling lights ahead.

I tried to focus on the road, the lights, hell, even the construction work, but all I could think about was the person waiting for me ahead.

By the time we coasted to a stop in front of the imposing glass front of the Grandeur Hotel & Spa, my nervous butterflies had morphed into a flock of birds with talons and beaks shredding my resolve.

The driver got out and came around to let me out.

"Whoa," I murmured, looking up at the front of the building until my head was tilted all the way back.

"Miss Cabot is on the penthouse floor," he told me, drawing my attention back to earth.

I looked down to see him holding out a plastic key card.

"You'll need this to access the floor," he informed me, pressing the plastic into my hand.

"What's your name?" I asked.

He blinked, surprised at the question. "Evan, miss."

"Have you met Made—uh, Miss Cabot before?"

"I've been her driver for years," he confirmed stiffly. A curious muscle in his jaw ticked as his eyes moved away.

So he was someone my sister trusted, given she'd brought him with her from her home in California.

"What's she like?"

He gave me a droll look. "Impatient."

Okay, then.

"Thanks for the ride, Ev," I told him with a wide smile as I started for the front doors with the keycard clutched in my hand.

I was wildly aware of how out-of-place I looked as I walked through the grand lobby of the hotel. A massive chandelier that dripped crystals like tears hung from the ceiling. The bubbling rush of water in the fountain provided a soft white noise to the sterile silence of the open space.

I received a few curious stares, but no one stopped me as I walked to the elevator bank for the penthouse. When the golden doors opened, I stepped into the car with an older woman.

She pressed her keycard to the black square on the panel and the number 15 lit up. I did the same with my card and the letter P flashed before the elevator started to rise.

We didn't speak as the woman left the elevator on her floor and I kept climbing. I looked at my reflection in the mirrored glass around me, hoping the crazy fluorescent lighting was the reason I looked physically ill.

The doors opened with a chime, announcing my arrival as I stepped into the room.

My eyes went huge as I looked around the massive space with hardwood and marble floors. It looked like an upscale apartment, and nothing like I had imagined. Then again, my one motel experience when I was ten didn't give me a lot to compare it to. Mom had decided on an impromptu trip to Chicago for my birthday that collapsed when we got kicked out of the hotel after the first night.

Well, Mom got kicked out and I had to go with her. Apparently they were serious about not smoking in the room.

"You're here!"

I jumped as Madelaine appeared in front of me. A second later, her arms were thrown around my shoulders as she hugged me.

I slowly hugged her back.

After a beat, she leaned away and gave me a careful once over. "Sorry. Too much?"

"No," I said quickly. Maybe a little too quickly. "It's fine. This is all just... Wow."

Rolling her eyes, Madelaine twirled away from me and waved a hand. "I know, right? This place definitely needs some renovating. I mean, I'm pretty sure they haven't updated the hotel in a couple of years."

"Looks great to me," I said, almost grimly.

Madelaine winced. "Shit. I'm sounding like a spoiled bitch again, aren't I?"

"Maybe a little." I gave her a curious look. "I mean, I fly my personal chauffeur with me when I travel, too."

Her nose wrinkled. "Oh, that's a joke. Cute."

I snorted and shook my head. "Yeah. It's a joke."

"You know what's *not* a joke?" she whispered conspiratorially, her blue eyes glimmering. "This size of his dick."

My jaw dropped in surprise when she held out her hands for a crude measurement.

"You're sleeping with the guy who drives you around? Isn't he, like, old?" I asked hesitantly.

She rolled her eyes and sighed like I was too young for this talk. "Evan's like twenty-six? It's whatever. We've been hooking up on and off for a few years now."

"Isn't that illegal?" A few years ago she would have been fifteen and he would have definitely been over twenty. Pretty sure that was a no-no.

"Maybe? Probably? Who really gives a shit?" Madelaine gave me an indifferent shrug. "We didn't get serious until recently."

"Wow," I murmured. "That's... wow."

Her lips pressed together and I got the feeling she was annoyed by my concern. "Don't be a wet blanket, Madison. It's just sex. *Really* great sex."

I held up a hand. "I get the picture."

"Are you hungry?"

"I could eat," I admitted. Truthfully, I was starving.

She grinned and linked her arm with mine to pull me deeper into the suite. "Then I guess it helps that I ordered every item on the room service menu?"

My brows shot up.

"I wasn't sure if you'd eaten anything yet," she said, twisting her fingers together.

"Food would actually be good," I replied, meaning it. I hadn't eaten since breakfast.

Her expression brightened. "Fab. This way." She led me deeper into the penthouse suite and flicked a hand at the sideboard table, full of everything from salad to lobster to pizza.

"Have whatever you want," Madelaine announced, taking a seat in an oversized white chair and tucking her legs up.

"I can't eat all of this," I said stupidly.

She laughed. "Of course not, silly. The staff will throw away the leftovers."

"Throw it away?" I echoed, taking a slice of pizza and a cupcake and carrying the plate back to the couch. "That's a lot of food to throw in the trash."

She gave me an odd look. "It's just food."

Yeah, *just food*. But I knew too many people who went hungry that would love this food.

"Right," I muttered, taking a bite of the pizza to distract myself. "Did you eat?"

She nodded, her blue eyes studying me curiously. "So, how did you find me?"

I swallowed. "I was researching a topic and I came across a picture of you with your dad."

She tapped her nails on the tufted arm of the chair with an amused smirk. "What are the odds?"

"Probably about the same that they would name us Madelaine and Madison?" I asked wryly.

Madelaine made a face. "Yeah, definitely not original. And confusing."

"Do people call you 'Maddie', too?"

Her nose wrinkled. "I actually hate that nickname. They call me by my full name or Lainey."

"Lainey," I tested the name out on my lips.

She grinned at me. "Nice to meet you, *Maddie*."

"Thought you hated that name," I remarked.

She ducked her head. "Maybe I like it now, since it's my sister's name."

That warmed up a piece of my heart. I set my plate down on the coffee table. "You said you had proof that we're related?"

"Not just related," she corrected. "We're *twins*." She reached down into the bag beside the chair and pulled out a file before passing it to me. "Identical twins."

I opened the file and scanned the birth certificate inside. There was a matching one under it that simply referred to Baby Girl A and Baby Girl B. The next page was Madelaine's official birth certificate with her name.

But mine was... gone.

I glanced up at her. "My birth certificate isn't in here."

"I know. I'm guessing your mom has it."

I held in a snort. No telling where that document would be.

The last item was a picture, stapled to the back of the folder. Two wrinkly babies, swaddled in pink blankets, were sleeping in the same hospital bassinet.

"Is this..." I traced the tiny faces.

"Us?" Lainey grinned at me. "Yeah. Our first picture. We're pretty damn cute, if I say so myself. But thank God we grew out of that wrinkly phase. There isn't enough botox in the world to fix that."

I closed the folder and handed it back to her. "Where did you find this?"

She blinked at me, her expression unreadable. "In Daddy's office. He thinks I don't know the combination of his safe, but I have for years."

"And he never said anything about me?" Doubt crept into my voice.

"Did your mom say anything about *me*?" she offered in reply, her arch tone brittle. "Clearly it wasn't an amicable split."

I grabbed my plate from the table and took a bite of my pizza, trying not to groan at the burst of pepperoni, sausage, and gooey cheese hitting my taste buds. Pizza was the food of the gods. I would build a time machine for the sole purpose of going back in time to thank the creator of it.

"Mom told me that my dad was a one-night stand, and she wasn't even sure which night." I grimaced at the memory.

"I was told my mother died when she had me," Lainey said flatly. She crossed her arms, eyes narrowed in thought.

"I wonder why they never wanted us to meet," I mumbled, shaking my head as my stomach soured. I set the half-eaten pizza aside and stared back at the girl with my face.

Lainey had mastered the art of the poker face. Her gaze was entirely unreadable as she studied me closer.

"I have an idea," she said suddenly, leaning forward. Her pink lips curved into a secretive smile.

"Okay."

"We should switch places."

My brows shot up to my hairline, and all I could manage was a wheezing laugh. "You're kidding."

She rolled her eyes, which I was starting to think was her signature move. "Just for the summer or whatever. I can meet our mom and you can meet our dad."

My stomach twisted. "Yeah, I don't think meeting Mom is going to be everything you think it is."

Her face fell. "Look, I know you've had a hard life, Maddie."

"Guess I'm not the only one who stalked her twin," I muttered, shaking my head.

A smile creased her face, a dimple appearing on her left cheek that matched my own. "Look, I did my research before I came here. I know your mom has problems. I know your life isn't that great."

"So why would you want it for a day, let alone a whole summer?" I arched a brow curiously. It didn't add up.

Something like grief mingled with sadness softened her face. "Because I spent my entire life not having a mom. Even if she is messed up, I still want to meet her. I want to know her."

"And then what? We just trade back lives at the end of it?"

She beamed at me with a nod, her shoulders relaxing as I seemed to entertain the idea. "Exactly."

I paused for a second, running through all the outcomes in my mind. "It will never work."

Her eyes narrowed back at me, the stiffness creeping back into her spine.

"I work two jobs," I pointed out. "Have you ever waitressed?"

The unease on her face was telling. This girl was waited *on*, not the one doing the waiting.

"This is why it can't work," I pointed out with a sigh. "When you go back to your elite school and rich life, I'll come back *here*. I can't afford to not have a job that pays the bills when I come home."

Lainey licked her lips. "What if I supplement your income?"

"You want to pay me to be you?" I laughed.

"I want to help my *sister*," she corrected, leaning forward with bright eyes. "Look, you've learned about me. You know I have money. I could easily send you whatever you need to cover what you'd make at your jobs for the summer. Hell, for the rest of your senior year, Maddie."

"I don't need charity," I replied stubbornly. I had survived this long on my own, and the idea of just taking money—no matter how appealing—felt wrong.

Lainey held up her hands. "I'm not saying it's charity. I'm saying you got fucked over in this parental arrangement shit. Let me help you, since our dad clearly doesn't give a shit about it."

That stung more than it should. Why didn't he care? Did he know what Mom had become? What the life of his other child had become?

"And I have the funds to get our mother into rehab."

My head snapped back. "She won't go."

"I'll make her," Lainey replied, steel in her tone as her blue eyes took on a hard glint. "Money talks. I'll have her committed to the best rehab facility in the state. In the damn country. I'll get her clean and sober."

Hope washed over me, unexpected and almost paralyzing. "Are you serious?"

She smiled back at me. "Yes."

"It'll be hard to connect with her if she's in rehab," I pointed out softly. My eyes studied her, watching the unconscious roll of her tense shoulders. Something wasn't adding up.

Sighing heavily, Lainey grimaced. "Okay, truth? I could use a break."

"A break?" I echoed, eyeing her up and down.

What did she need a break from? Designer clothes? Her chauffeur/sex toy? Not having to worry about buying groceries or paying the water bill?

"I've been Madelaine Cabot my whole life," she started slowly, choosing her words carefully, "and while I am fully aware that I sound like a spoiled bitch right now, I could use a breather. All I've ever been is Lainey, and honestly? I don't even know who she is. I'm told what to do, where to go, and how to act. I'm constantly under a microscope, and I just want out for a little while."

That sounded like it sucked. My life wasn't easy, but I lived it on *my* terms, for the most part.

"Don't you think people will notice I'm not you?" I asked hesitantly. I gestured to my clothes. "I don't even know how to be you."

"I'll teach you," she said quickly. "I booked this room for the week. I'll tell you everything you need to know about my life. We can go shopping, and we'll get your hair done. The works. All on me."

It sounded too good to be true.

"And you'll have a chance to meet our dad," she added with a knowing smile. "Haven't you always wanted to meet him?"

Of course I had. What girl didn't want to know who her dad was?

My gaze swept the room, taking in the grandeur and the luxury. A chance to live as a princess for a summer?

I closed my eyes and nodded. "What the hell? Let's do it."

CHAPTER 5

It was pretty amazing what a few hundred dollars worth of hair and skin treatments could do for a girl. My blonde hair now had fresh highlights and felt a million times softer. My skin glowed even before I applied an artful bit of makeup.

"Easy," Lainey chided, reaching for the brush I wielded in my hand to apply highlighter to my cheek bones. "You want to look glowy. Not like you're stepping off a stripper pole."

I smirked at her reflection in the mirror, her heart-shaped face identical to my own. I took it in for a moment.

In the four days I had spent with Madelaine, my hair had gained extensions to match her length and my teeth had gotten a whitening treatment that bleached my smile the same brilliant white as her own.

We were perfect matches in almost every single way. The only difference was my sister—just saying that felt surreal—was a few pounds lighter and her frame slightly more willowy.

Probably because in the days we had spent together, I hadn't seen a single carb or gram of sugar pass her lips.

I, on the other hand, had a massive sweet tooth and I'd yet to meet a carb I didn't love.

Pressing my lips together, I refocused on the makeup tutorial

Madelaine was giving as I softly dusted the glimmering powder on my face.

"Perfect," she murmured, her voice soft and throaty as she watched me with approval. "We just might make you a Cabot yet."

I dropped the brush and turned to her. "Yeah, speaking of, when are we going to discuss exactly what being a Cabot means?"

Over the past days, Lainey had peeled back almost every facet of my life, exposing pieces I'd long ago buried and damn near forgotten. She was like Lois freaking Lane trying to uncover every detail about me.

She'd given me the basic rundown of her life, but she'd been really cagey about her own details. Details I needed if I was going to be her.

Her gaze shifted away. "Being a Cabot is a lot like being in a painting in a museum. Your job is to look pretty, make people want to study and dissect you, but ultimately never give them a clue as to what lies beneath."

I felt my eyebrows lifting. "That's cryptic."

"That's my life," she said flatly. "Yes, there's the pretty, gilded frame that cages the painting, but it's really about keeping people guessing and never letting anyone know what's really going on."

The sadness in her tone sent a pang of regret ricocheting in my chest. I reached for her hand and squeezed her fingers.

Lainey jumped as if surprised to find me touching her. She stared down at our connected hands.

"That sounds pretty awful," I told her gently.

She pulled her hand away with a sniff, lifting her chin. "Yeah, well, it is what it is. Besides, it doesn't all suck. Whoever said money can't buy happiness clearly didn't understand that money buys things that *make* you happy."

I laughed and watched as she got up from the chair beside me. She crossed the room, all fluid grace in heels, even on carpet. Lifting a glass bottle of some French named water, she took a delicate sip.

I blinked slowly as I watched, wondering how the heck I was supposed to emulate her for a few weeks with no one noticing a poser had taken her place. She exuded grace and sophistication.

Settling the bottle back on the side table, Madelaine gave me her full attention, and the result was striking. From the angle her hip jutted out to the lift of her chin, she didn't just draw the eye of anyone in the room, her very being demanded it.

I swallowed and sat back in my chair.

"Okay, you want the truth?" she asked me, almost daring me to say no.

I nodded slowly.

"My life is a fucking circus and everyone's just there for the show." Smirking darkly, she sank into the chair and artfully crossed her legs. "I'm Madelaine Cabot. My father is one of the richest men in the country. In the world, even. I weekend in Rome, Paris, London, and Dubai. My dad has homes on five continents. I'm the head cheerleader and queen of every formal at Pacific Cross. Everyone there either wants to be me or fuck me."

Unease prickled up my spine until I shivered. For someone who had it all, she looked pretty miserable.

Her gaze sharpened and she snapped her fingers at me. "What you just did? You can't do that if you're *me*."

"Well I'm not *you*," I shot back.

"You're going to be," she returned. "So, own it. Own who I am. Fuck, own who *you* can be, Madison."

"Forgive me if I wasn't born with a silver spoon shoved up my ass," I hissed, my fingers curling into small fists. She didn't need to point out how totally different our lives were.

"Try platinum spoon, Maddie," she replied evenly. "Silver is so eighteen hundreds."

I shot to my feet, sending a bottle of foundation toppling over. "You know what? Fuck this. And fuck you." I wasn't going to just sit here and let her keep insulting me.

She laughed, the sound not at all pleasant. "Fuck *me*? You couldn't afford me. Also? We're twins and incest is a crime." She got up slowly. "But that's the point, Mads. I'm going to make you *into* me."

"I don't want to *be* you!" I shouted at her, ready to head for the door.

"Don't you?" she challenged. "Don't tell me you didn't spend hours in the sad, little library studying my every move? Every single post, every single hashtag? Every article you could find about me?"

I flushed, hating that I couldn't deny it.

I had been fascinated by her. I still was. But I hadn't signed up for whatever caustic shit she was throwing at me now. Her mood changes were like changing tides in the midst of a hurricane; utterly unpredictable and wholly capable of wreaking devastation.

One minute she was trying to be my best friend and the sister I always dreamed of. The next I could feel every mocking word and disdainful look she tossed at the *poor* girl.

Fuck it.

I was so over her shit. I didn't need this. I had spent almost eighteen years living my life; I could handle it for another few months until I turned eighteen.

"You can't leave!" Her shrill voice cut through the air.

I whirled. "Watch me. You don't know shit about me, *sister*."

Lainey moved forward slowly, her speed that of a panther stalking its prey. "You think I don't have people who could pull up every keystroke you made trying to figure me out? I know *exactly* who you are, Madison. I'm trying to give you the chance at a life you only dreamed of."

"If it's such a fan-fucking-tastic life," I snarled, "why are you so eager to give it to me?"

Her eyebrows twitched. "Because I'm bored as fuck. You know what else comes with all those fancy trips and pretty pictures you see? A lot of responsibility that I'm sick of shouldering. The truth is what I told you that first night—I want out of my life so I can actually *breathe*."

"This had nothing to do with me, did it?" I asked slowly, staring at her. Who the hell had I spent the last four days with?

A bitter smirk twisted her pink lips. "Did I think meeting my twin sister might be cool? Sure. It's been fun, and bonus points to you for not being a total wimp, the way I originally pegged you. But I also saw this whole thing for the advantage it was. My chance to have a summer of freedom before my life is over."

"But you're Madelaine *fucking* Cabot," I ground out, letting the acid singe my tone. "Don't you have the picture-perfect life, princess?"

"Exactly. My father—*our father*—has my entire life planned out. Has since before we were born," she said bitterly, waving a hand. "You want to know why you're not part of it? Because he only needed one kid, and I'm still not entirely sure which one of us drew the short straw."

"What do you mean?" I demanded softly, my heart pounding in my chest at the revelation.

Madelaine rolled her eyes and blew out a hard breath. "Cabot money is old money. It started as a steel company back in the early eighteen hundreds and just kept growing. There's an insane amount of money that is held in a trust for the next generation so the current people in control can't fuck it up for everyone."

"Congratulations," I drawled sarcastically. "You're even richer than you told me."

"If it was that simple, do you think I'd be here? Don't be stupid, Madison. It isn't a cute look."

My eyes narrowed. "Then tell me, oh wise one."

With another long-winded sigh, she spun away from me. "The will is old, and the money is always distributed through the oldest male child. Dad's an only child, so he inherited stocks, money, and everything. But there's also a codicil."

"A codi-what?" I frowned.

She sighed as if annoyed she was having to explain this totally foreign word to me. "It's an amendment to a will. And the plot twist of this whole fucked up thing is that there's a completely *separate* account that our great-grandmother set up to protect the women of our family. Five percent of every dollar earned by a Cabot-owned business has to be held in a trust fund for a woman of the family to access. There haven't been any girls born in the Cabot family since then."

My jaw dropped. "None?"

Lainey's lips mashed together. "Well, that's not quite true. We had a great-aunt, but she died before she came of age. So it's just been a giant bank account with a shit-ton of money in it that keeps getting bigger and bigger."

"Damn," I murmured. "That's... I don't even know what to say."

"Unfortunately, the will also is pretty damn reflective of the times, and in order to access the money, the woman has to be married." Lainey leveled me with a stare.

"I'm sorry, did you say *married*?" I started to laugh.

"I did," she replied stiffly.

I stifled my giggles. "That's insane."

She leaned forward, her eyes meeting mine. "No, here's the insane part. To get that money, I have to be married before I'm nineteen."

My laughter died. "You're kidding."

"Don't I wish," she muttered.

"Why nineteen?" I frowned at her.

"Because back then arranged marriages were *normal*. Women were married when they were still, like, fifteen. The will is iron-clad, so there's no work around. Daddy had every lawyer he could find looking for a loophole."

"You could *not* take the money," I suggested.

"That's not an option."

"Okaaay—" I dragged out the word "—so you have to find someone to marry in the next, what? Fifteen months? Is Evan not up for the job?"

After a second of watching me, Madelaine stormed across the room and threw open the double doors that led to her bedroom. She was back a moment later, holding up a ring with an enormous diamond.

"Holy shit," I murmured, watching the light catch the stone and splay rainbows across the walls. "So, you're *already* engaged?"

"Yes." She tossed the ring onto the coffee table with a sneer.

Tossed. A. Diamond. Ring.

Like it was a bag of chips.

"To who?" I stared at her with some weird mix of horror and interest. "Is it Evan?"

She scoffed. "Please. Like Daddy would let me marry someone who drives a car for a living?"

"Okay." I gritted my teeth and tried not to let my temper flare up again. "Then who is about to be my brother-in-law?"

"The asshole son of my dad's business partner and oldest friend," she replied coldly. "It's a bad look to be planning to pass your daughter off as a child bride, so they've kept our childhood engagement a secret."

"Then say no," I told her. "Tell them all to fuck off."

"Oh, my God. You are so naive, it's almost painful, Madison." She turned away with a snort. "Don't you think I would if it was that simple? Ryan and I have been looking for a way out of this deal since we first met. But we're out of time and our relationship is finally public knowledge."

"Ryan?" I echoed.

"Ryan Cain," she said slowly. "Heir apparent to Cain International, Cain Financial, and my not-so-doting fiancé. Gorgeous, entitled, and a total fuckboy. I literally can't stand him."

"You're aware we live in a country where you can say no, right?" I stared at her. "If you two are so against getting married, don't get married. It's that easy, princess."

"Trust me when I say that the world I live in isn't like the one you live in," Madelaine retorted, ice dripping from her words. "It's easier to just go along with it. I tried fighting it for years, and it was more of a headache than I needed to deal with. One thing rich people always want more of? Money."

She sat back down, her expression stormy. "Besides, Ryan and I have an agreement. We'll get married and spend the rest of our lives living on opposite ends of the world with someone who is *not* our spouse in our bed. He can have a mistress in every city in Europe for all I care."

"That's sad," I said flatly. "It's truly sad."

"No, what's sad is living in a trailer with a junkie mom and working two jobs to save for a mediocre state-school education," Madelaine countered.

"Wow," I muttered, running a hand through my hair. "You're a bitch."

"I'm well aware," she replied evenly. A second later she sighed regretfully. "But I'm a bitch who is trying to help you out."

"Help me out how?" I demanded. "By throwing me into the very life you want a vacation from? By insulting me?"

Madelaine's features softened slightly, and she sighed. "Look, Maddie, I get it. I'm a world class bitch. But I can help you *and* your mom."

"She's your mom, too," I pointed out.

She waved a hand. "Whatever. I'll set her up in a cushy rehab. I'll get her clean with the best doctors. And when this summer is over? I'll make sure there's enough money in your bank account to fully fund your way through whatever school you want. I'll give you enough so you can get an apartment off campus and not have to work a single hour when you're in school."

The idea of taking her offer soured in my stomach. "I don't need your pity money."

"Maybe not, but it would make your life a lot easier. And if not for yourself, do it for your mom."

I stared at her in open disgust. "Or you could be a decent human being and help her anyway because, again, she's *your mom, too*."

Madelaine made a face and shook her head. "I could, but I won't. Maybe that makes me heartless, but you try growing up in my world, honey. I learned early on that life is one big negotiation."

"And that's all this is?" I ground out, hating that her true reasons for meeting me stung a lot more than I had expected.

"Yes." She leaned forward, her blue eyes glittering. "But I'll give you something no one else ever gave me. A little insight."

"Do tell," I said wryly.

"If someone comes to you looking for a favor? That means the deck is stacked in *your* favor."

I studied her for a minute as the meaning of her words sunk in.

Madelaine was coming to *me*.

She needed me more than I needed her. And that meant I had power.

"No one will believe I'm you," I finally said, shaking my head.

She smiled. "That's the beauty of it. It's summer vacation, and Daddy is hardly ever home. You'll have a mansion full of servants to wait on your every need. You can sit poolside for weeks, just chilling out before senior year. Get a manicure every day, go shopping with my credit cards. You'll have weeks to indulge in my life. It might be a cage, but it sure is pretty."

"And you're going to what? Live in my trailer?"

Her nose wrinkled. "God, no. I'll be traveling. I'm thinking I'll start in New York. Or maybe Paris. I plan on spending the summer having Evan fuck my brains out before I go back and slip into the role of Ryan Cain's fiancé."

I chuckled darkly, shaking my head. "This was never about meeting me or Mom, was it?"

Her lips thinned. "Meeting my birth mother? No. But I did want to meet you, Madison. You're my *twin*. You're part of me. And you also happen to be the only person who can help me."

"Yet again, it's all about *you*," I pointed out.

She let out a frustrated groan. "We can help *each other*. Don't you see that? And I really do want to help you."

"Won't it be obvious when the credit card bills show you in Paris *and* California?" I smirked at her, changing tactics to point out another flaw in her plan.

She gave me a knowing look. "Please. You think I haven't planned this out? I have plenty of cash to cover my summer abroad."

I hesitated. Part of me wanted to go. Wanted to embrace the chance to have the summer of my dreams. But another part of me could see only all the ways this would go wrong.

"What about your fiancé?"

She snorted. "Ryan? He's spending the summer in Japan or China or something. Probably building another well in Africa or whatever. Besides, we try to ignore each other as much as possible."

"And your friends?"

Something passed over her face, but then cleared almost as fast. "My friends all have their own plans. I told them I was taking the summer for self-reflection."

"Your dad? The people who live at your house?" I kept trying to stab holes in her reasoning.

"Mrs. Delancey is the only one you have to worry about, and I told you she pretty much keeps to herself. The staff doesn't really notice us. They stay out of the way. And Daddy is traveling. He's working on something big right now in Asia, so he and Uncle Adam won't even be home until the end of summer," she insisted.

My brows shot up. "I have an uncle?"

She tensed and slid her gaze away. "He's a friend of Daddy's. I just always called him that."

I folded my arms, watching her closely. "So, you weren't going to tell me that I dad I was hoping to meet won't even be in the same country?"

She flinched at being caught in the lie. "He might wrap things up early, but no. He'll probably be home right before I leave for school."

Snorting, I rolled my eyes. "Awesome. God, do you even know how to tell the truth? What is it exactly that you want, Madelaine?"

Her lower lip trembled just a bit as she looked at me with more raw vulnerability than I'd seen. "Look, Maddie, I'm drowning, okay? Between school and cheer and my dad's expectations and *Ryan*... I just need a break. Maybe it's not fair that I'm putting this on you, but you're literally the only person I can ask to help me." Her eyes searched mine, begging me to understand. "I just want a normal summer with my boyfriend, preferably on a nude beach, before my life goes to shit."

I could feel my resolve starting to crack.

"I need a fund set up for my mom, too," I said slowly, wanting to make sure I covered all the bases. "I want her to be able to move out of the trailer park and into a better neighborhood. One where drugs aren't being sold outside her door so she has a chance at staying clean."

"Done," she agreed quickly. "Hell, I'll even kick back some of the trust to you guys if you want."

I arched a brow. "Technically wouldn't I be eligible for that trust also?"

"It goes to the oldest girl," she replied with a tiny, unreadable shrug. "And according to the birth records? I'm older by thirteen minutes."

"How convenient," I muttered, running a hand through my hair.

"Help me out, Maddie, and I'll make sure you and *our* mother are taken care of," she said, her tone almost kind. "Having a sister might be kind of cool. And maybe we could switch lives every now and then. Then you could definitely meet Dad."

"Let's see if it even works the first time," I answered.

Madelaine stood up with a grin. "Oh, it'll work. Trust me, little sister."

CHAPTER 6

"I'll get that, miss," the flight attendant assured me as I started to reach for my carryon bag several days later.

The flight from Detroit to Los Angeles had been smooth and uneventful with the exception of my minor panic attack at takeoff. My first time on a plane had been a trip.

Pun totally intended.

I wished I had arrived earlier at the airport so I could wander through all the shops and watch people run back and forth. It was fascinating to study them as they tried to navigate the pre-boarding chaos.

"I don't mind," I assured the attendant with a smile.

"I insist," he replied quickly, eyes wide as he looked around. It was almost like he was worried that he would get in trouble for not doing his job if I kept stopping him.

With a sigh, I stepped back and allowed the man—who was a good four inches shorter than I was—to struggle with my carryon. I waited as he managed to pull it down after a few seconds of fighting with the suitcase and the bin.

Madelaine had gifted me with her wallet, which was full of credit cards, to buy whatever I wanted. She even encouraged it, saying it would help keep up the ruse that I was her since she loved to shop. Plus, there was an entire dressing suite waiting for me at her home.

A dressing *suite*.

I had needed to ask for clarification on what that even was. Apparently it was when your closet was big enough to have its own room and seating area.

Even still, I had crammed the memories of my past life into the brand-new carryon last night as I finished packing. I had even snagged a few of mom's things, because the trailer would be empty for several weeks and I didn't trust our neighbors not to take advantage.

Not that there was a lot to take. Mom had pawned, sold, or bartered most of the stuff that had any value over the years. I had kept a small stash of cash under a loose floorboard in my room, along with a few sentimental things I couldn't help but keep over the years.

Everything fit into the brand-new case Madelaine had gifted me. And I was well aware that the suitcase had more monetary value than the contents inside it combined and multiplied by a hundred.

I took the sleek rose gold handle from the attendant and flashed him a smile as I started to disembark from the plane and followed the signs to where Madelaine said a car would be waiting to drive me home.

After stopping in the bathroom, I pulled the new phone out of my purse (also new) and powered it on. A message popped up a second later.

M: Made it to the rehab center okay. She's checked in. Contact info is below. Have a fun summer. See you in two months.

The phone number and address of Mom's ridiculously overpriced rehab facility was beneath the text.

Madelaine had really delivered on the rehab center for Mom. It wasn't the usual two-week or even thirty-day program; Mom would be there for six months.

Six months where she would get clean and be taught in-depth coping skills and how to assimilate into a drug-free life while meeting with nutrition experts and therapists. Enough time for me to enjoy the summer without worrying about her ODing again and to get myself started on the first semester of my senior year.

Madelaine and I had set up everything before I got on the plane. The only thing I felt guilty about was leaving Madelaine to drop off Mom at rehab since my sister claimed she couldn't be gone for more than a week. Lainey's trip to me was on the books as a spa retreat for seven days. If she wasn't home when she was supposed to be, Mrs. Delancey—the Cabot's cook and woman in charge of the day-to-day operations of the house—would call her dad—our dad—to report a possible problem. But the rehab facility couldn't accept Mom until the day my plane departed for California.

And for the record, I felt guilty about leaving Mom, not Madelaine.

My sister could use a good reality check about the life she had narrowly avoided. Besides, Evan was helping her move Mom. Thankfully they hadn't needed his muscle as Mom had happily followed Lainey to the car for an adventure.

I quickly tapped out a text message to thank her and sent it. A second later, my phone chimed with her response.

M: BTW, she's actually kind of hysterical. Did you know she talks to plants when she's cracked out? She thanked them for their sacrifice. Fucking wild.

I rolled my eyes and didn't bother to answer as I shoved the phone back into my purse. It took all my focus to navigate through the crowded terminal and down to the baggage claim area where Madelaine had assured me a driver would be waiting.

As I descended the escalator, my eyes scanned the crowd. Relief hit me hard when I spotted a man in a suit with a digital sign that read CABOT.

I made my way to him and gave him a small smile. "Hi."

"Welcome home, miss," he told me stiffly, reaching to pull the suitcase from my grasp.

"Oh, I don't mind—"

He pulled it from my fingers and started walking away. "This way if you please, miss."

"Okay," I muttered under my breath, following behind him like a baby duck through sliding glass doors and into the bright sunshine of my life.

I shielded my eyes with a hand, taking a second to absorb the warmth soaking into my skin. Palm trees swayed in the slight breeze, the fronds reaching for the blue, cloudless sky.

By the time I glanced back, the driver was standing beside the open door of a black limousine, my bag nowhere in sight.

"Is everything all right, miss?" he asked, his brow furrowed.

I couldn't help but smile. "Just a gorgeous day, that's all."

His brows rose slowly. Surprise colored his tone as he agreed, "It is, miss."

Crap.

Madelaine likely wouldn't be standing still to take in the beauty of the sky, would she?

"Let's go," I said quickly, heading into the limo and waiting for him to close the door before exhaling hard. My hands trembled as I clicked my seatbelt into place. I folded them together as the car glided into traffic easily, racing from the airport and heading onto a busy freeway away from downtown Los Angeles

I tried to peer out the window as much as the deep tint would allow, catching glimpses of massive buildings in the distance, hugged by a haze of smog. My throat grew drier and drier the farther we got from the airport until I finally reached for the bottle of water settled beside me in a cup holder.

I took a long drink, not caring that gulping down water was a decidedly un-Madelaine thing to do. I downed half the bottle before I put it back, just in time for the car to exit the highway.

There were fewer cars as we started winding through rolling hills sparsely dotted with houses. It was a far cry from the apartments and dilapidated houses of Cliftown squeezed onto crumbling city blocks. We kept climbing higher and higher until we reached a gated entrance complete with a guard house.

The car coasted to a stop, and I strained to hear what the driver said to the men who approached the vehicle. A second later, the gates opened and we drove through. It took a minute before I saw the first house in the neighborhood, a sprawling mansion set half an acre away from the road, surrounded by the greenest grass I had ever seen. I twisted my head for a better look, but it quickly swept from my view.

It went on and on like this as we drove. Each house was more ostentatious than the next, and the road curved, winding us higher and higher until it dead ended at another set of gates.

Another guard house waited for us here, and again the driver paused to speak with the guards before we were let in.

Holy shit.

It was all I could think when we drove down the tree-lined path that opened up into a circular driveway splayed before the biggest house I had ever seen.

Madelaine had given me a rough sketch of the house so I could navigate my way around, but she had seriously downplayed its enormity. I had once gone on a field trip to a museum that was smaller than this place.

The white stone walls and slate gray roof were on point with a lot of the homes I had seen, but this was like one of those houses on steroids. I spotted no less than three fountains on the front lawn alone, and it was obvious that this was the best house in the gated community.

It sat above them all like a watchful sentry, foreboding and tempting, inspiring jealousy as it flaunted everything someone could dream up in a home. Or a castle.

Because this house totally looked fit for royalty.

A small flutter of excitement took hold in my chest. I would spend the next few weeks here, just taking the time to actually enjoy myself and relax. No worrying about Mom, or grades, or making rent. No busting my ass at the diner for minimal tips.

I couldn't stop myself from opening the door as soon as the car stopped moving. Even the confused, disapproving frown of the driver didn't sway me as I tilted my head back to gaze up at the three-story house that was now my *home*.

"I'll have your bag brought to your room, miss," he told me, pausing by the trunk to pull my suitcase from it.

My fingers itched to take the bag myself, some silly compulsion to keep a tangible piece of who I really was within touching distance. Instead, I forced my hands to my sides and started up the stone stairs.

When I reached the landing, the door swung open for me, revealing an older gentleman who gave me a solemn look. This must be Gerard, the butler.

Thankfully Madelaine had helped me memorize a cheat sheet of the household staff so I wouldn't look like an idiot. The pictures on her phone had definitely helped.

"Welcome home, Miss Cabot," he greeted, his old voice weathered from age. "May I get you anything?"

"Um, no," I stammered, trying not to be so obvious in my staring as I took in the marble foyer and massive chandelier above my head that dripped crystals. I gave myself a second to orient myself with the room, wishing I could pull out the hastily drawn map that Madelaine had made.

Two marble staircases curved up the sides of the entryway, and I started for the set on the right, remembering that the right side of the house, or the *east wing*, as Madelaine called it, was where my room would be.

"Very well," Gerard agreed easily, sounding bored with our conversation. "Mrs. Delancey says to remind you that dinner will be served at seven."

"Thanks," I said, maybe a little too brightly judging by the surprised lift of his eyebrows, but I was too absorbed in my new normal to really care.

Once I made it to the top of the stairs, I turned right and headed down the long corridor.

I glanced around to make sure I was alone before slowing to a stop and spinning in a circle to study the sheer vastness of the hallway.

"Damn," I mumbled, my fingers touching the silk of the curtains framing a window that spilled golden sunlight across the floor. "Definitely not in Michigan anymore."

I let the silk glide through my hand and kept walking, mentally reminding myself where my new room was until I was standing in front of the door.

Maybe this was why Madelaine was skinnier than me. It had nothing to do with the salads she picked at and everything to do with the mile it took to get from the front door to her bedroom.

My hand curled around the cold metal of the doorknob a second before I twisted and pushed it open.

I stepped inside the room, my jaw dropping again as I started to mentally inventory the world I had just walked into.

A world that promptly came crashing down around me when the door slammed shut and an arm wrapped around my chest, squeezing as it crushed me to the hard body at my back.

"Welcome home, sweetheart," a voice snarled in my ear.

Fuck.

CHAPTER 7

Panic fueled my fight-or-flight response. I'd taken a summer self-defense course Marge had arranged at the library last year. Another reminder of her attack and a way for her to take some control back. She wanted to make sure women knew what to do if they were ever assaulted.

I slammed my heel down on the instep of the man holding me as I twisted out of his grasp. He grunted and his hold slipped enough for me to break away.

I whirled, chest heaving as I opened my mouth to scream.

He recovered faster than the summer instructor had warned me, all but launching himself across the room at me.

A second later, a warm hand slapped over my mouth and backed me up until my legs hit the bed and I went down. He fell with me, pinning me to the mattress.

"Stop it," he snapped, his blue eyes furious as I tried to wrench away.

It was completely pointless. He outweighed me by at least fifty pounds of muscle, his knees pressed to either side of my hips as he gathered both of my small hands in one fist, the other hand still pressed to my mouth, but I still struggled with everything I had.

"Fucking chill out, Lainey," he spat, glaring at me like I was the one who had attacked him.

My heart thundered in my chest as I glared back, the terror that had gripped my system slowly being replaced by awareness as I realized I knew this face.

The sharp cut of his jaw, the cold as ice blue eyes, the messy dark blonde hair.

So much for Japan or China or building a well.

Ryan Cain was not on the other side of the world, but instead pinning me to my new bed.

Freaking awesome.

After Madelaine told me about her fiancé, I had been curious and looked him up. I'd found a ton of articles on the heir to two billion-dollar corporations. He was starting his junior year at Pacific Cross on the university side. He'd declared double majors his freshman year—business and law—and he was the star quarterback of the school's tier-one football team. Several inches over six feet of pure muscle and a face that would make a nun reconsider her vows.

Pictures truly didn't do him justice.

Ryan was fucking hot.

And also fucking crazy.

"Can you act like an adult for a second?" he demanded, arching a brow as he slowly lowered the hand smothering my face.

"You just attacked me!" I snapped as soon as I could move my lips. "So sorry for not inviting you for afternoon tea."

He rolled his eyes, and I was beginning to think eye rolling was a course they taught the upper elite kids in elementary school.

"Don't be a fucking drama queen," he retorted, a dark edge in his tone. "You're the one who stomped on my foot, *baby*."

I sucked in a sharp breath. "What the *fuck* do think you're doing? Get *off* me."

He grinned down at me and pushed a lock of my hair away, the touch almost gentle. "Doesn't sound like my sweet little fiancée is happy to see me."

"You just attacked me in my bedroom," I pointed out, trying to twist or scoot away. "Get *off* before I scream."

His eyes narrowed. "Why don't you be a good girl and shut up instead?"

"I—"

"Or," he cut me off pleasantly, but that damn maniacal glint kept me quiet, "you can keep squirming under me, and I'll give you something to scream about for real if you prefer, sweetheart."

I froze at the implication as my brain spiraled off into another dimension and he snorted a caustic laugh.

"Please. I wouldn't touch your rancid pussy if my dick was dipped in iron first."

If I wasn't so pissed off, I might've high-fived him for his snark. But I was still pinned to my bed with him *on freaking top of me*.

Swallowing, I forced my body to relax when all I wanted to do was fight.

He traced a finger down my cheek, and I considered turning my head to bite it.

"Good girl." He let my hands go but didn't let me up. If anything, he made himself more comfortable from where he towered over me, easing back to rest his weight on my thighs.

"Now," he started, his blue eyes flickering with interest, "where the hell have you been?"

I licked my lips as I tucked my hands to my chest, needing to feel like I was shielding myself somehow. My heart was threatening to pound right out of my ribcage as I struggled to breathe. "I needed a... break. I went to a spa."

It was the party line Madelaine had given me as her excuse for being gone.

He rolled his eyes once more and made a scoffing sound under his breath. "Of course you did. Next time? Make sure you give me a heads up. I don't want to have to come find you again. I told you when school ended—we're done playing by your rules."

I kept my expression carefully neutral. "Okay."

He scoffed mockingly. "Okay? What's up? Did your fall from grace cause permanent damage?"

Yeah, I had no clue how to answer that, so I stayed quiet.

My silence only seemed to ramp up his anger.

"Don't act like the fucking victim now, baby. You knew exactly what you were doing when you fucked me over," he hissed, the indifference in his eyes churning into something darker.

"I'm... sorry?" I literally had no idea what he was talking about. None. Madelaine had made it sound like she and Ryan never talked, barely co-existed.

This was decidedly *not* the relationship she had described to me.

"I might actually believe that apology if I didn't know firsthand what a conniving bitch you are, Lainey," he said. His look was pure disgust as he eyed me pinned beneath him.

"I thought you were going to be gone for the summer," I blurted out, unsure what else to say without giving away I wasn't the girl he thought I was.

He smirked down at me, looking satisfied at having caught me off-guard. "I'm leaving in a few hours. I just wanted to make sure you remember the rules from our last talk. Pull that disappearing shit again, and I'll make your senior year as miserable as you are."

I drew in a shaky breath. "Ryan—"

"I warned you what would happen," he went on, shaking his head. "I want to know where you are every single minute of every day. I'm not being blindsided by you again."

I blinked up helplessly. "I don't—"

His eyes flashed, cold and ominous. "Shut the fuck up, Madelaine. No more begging or whining or dealing. We played it your way, now we're playing it mine. I hate you just as much as you hate me, but I'll be *damned* if I let you fuck this up more than you have."

Something Madelaine told me whispered in my mind.

"You're just as trapped as I am," I reminded him, trying to imitate the cool, callous vibe my twin was able to throw off so effortlessly.

A low chuckle rumbled out of him, and the sound was anything except amused. "Were the last few weeks of school not enough for you? Do you need a reminder of how far you've fallen?"

He trailed a calloused finger across my jaw and down my throat, pausing briefly where my pulse was hammering. I was paralyzed beneath him, fear short-circuiting my fight or flight response. All it would take was his fingers tightening around my throat and my air would be *gone*.

It was mind-numbingly terrifying how utterly at his mercy I was. He was massive and immoveable atop me. Nothing short of an earthquake could knock him over.

He grinned at my fear, the cocky expression proving he knew exactly when I started to crack under his touch. "The only thing keeping you from being ripped apart right now is *me*. I'm totally happy to feed you to the wolves. In fact, it would be pretty fucking poetic to watch the people you spent years belittling tear what's left of your pride into pieces."

"I'll stick to whatever terms I agreed to," I muttered, forcing the words out for my sister's sake, not mine. In a few weeks, Ryan Cain would be a distant memory.

Madelaine could have him. They deserved each other.

"Perfect," he sneered before getting off me.

I immediately scrambled away from him.

His eyes narrowed once more as he watched me. "Where's your fucking ring?"

I glanced at my ringless left hand and swallowed. "In my suitcase."

Madelaine had given it to me, and I had tucked the giant rock into a compartment of the case. Wearing it freaked me out. I would probably lose the diamond or something.

A muscle in his jaw popped as his teeth clenched. "So much for agreeing to our terms. That ring doesn't leave your finger again, Madelaine. Got it?"

I nodded slowly. "Fine. Whatever."

His hand shot out, his thumb and forefinger pinching my chin and forcing my head up. "Watch the attitude, sweetheart. You fucked this up, not me. I'm the one saving your perky little ass."

"I got it," I ground out, meeting his gaze and refusing to cower despite the way my racing pulse made me dizzy.

"Good," he hissed, letting my face go abruptly. "Now be a good little fiancée and indulge in all the vapid, vain shit you do all summer. I'll see you in a few months. I better not come home and have to look for you again."

He crossed the room and slammed the door in his wake.

"Can't wait," I muttered at the door, rubbing my chin as I reached for my phone to text Madelaine and ask her exactly what the hell she had gotten me into.

CHAPTER 8

An hour later, I headed down to dinner. Madelaine still hadn't replied. She was probably somewhere over the Atlantic on her own plane by now.

Everything in me was still buzzing from Ryan's surprise visit. Like a soda that had been shaken up and the pressure left to build.

I sighed under my breath as I started down the back staircase that led into the kitchen.

It wasn't a visit. It was a full-on attack. An assault, even. And how the hell did he even get in here? Did this engagement come with a set of house keys Lainey forgot to mention?

The ring on my finger caught the light, and I frowned at where my hand slid along the polished gold of the railing. I had slipped it onto my finger when my suitcase had been delivered, almost nervous Ryan would make another appearance just to check to make sure I was following his orders.

Like I was a freaking dog.

Then again, the ring was on my finger, so maybe I was nothing more than a trained pet he could bring to heel.

Whatever.

This wasn't my life, and in a few weeks, he would go back to being

Madelaine's problem. The sooner I shoved all memories of Ryan Cain out of my head, the better off I would be.

I hit the last step and took a deep breath through my nose, my senses flaring to life at the decadent scents that mingled together.

"And just what do you think you're doing?" The exasperated annoyance of the voice surprised me. Mostly because everyone talked to me—talked to *Madelaine*—like she could order their head removed at any time.

But the tiny woman standing barefoot and in jeans on the other side of the kitchen didn't look afraid at all. In fact, she looked a little pissed off.

This would be the cook, also known as Mrs. Delancey. According to my sister, Mrs. Delancey had worked for the Cabots since before Madelaine was born. She was older, petite with gray hair and brown eyes that could no doubt spot bullshit from a mile away.

"Don't tell me that spa washed away your brains, too," she sniped, turning back to the pot on the stove and stirring with a wooden spoon.

It took a minute to figure out how to formulate an actual sentence. "I'm here for dinner? It's seven, right?"

Sniffing, she glanced at me over her bony shoulder. "Yes, but since when has that meant you enter my kitchen, young lady?"

"Sorry?" I frowned.

She *humph*ed and pulled the pot from the stove.

"That smells amazing," I tried, offering what I hoped was a peace-offering sort of smile.

Her face morphed into a look of absolute shock for a second before she schooled it. "Well, amazing as it may smell, it has those pesky little calories you avoid like a plague. Your salad is already on the table."

I felt my face curl in disgust. "Can I have some of that?"

Mrs. Delancey stared at me, astonished. "It has *calories*, Madelaine. Calories and carbs and sugars. All those other things you decided you hated four years ago."

"Maybe I'm trying to expand my palate," I wheedled, fighting a grin as my gaze flicked to the pot.

A laugh exploded from her mouth as she shook her head and turned back to the cabinet to reach for a plate. "Fine. But if I catch you doing one of your three a.m. workouts, I'll slap you silly."

My brows inched up. Working out at three in the morning? The only thing I did at three in the morning was sleep.

Mrs. Delancey dished out the pasta and sauce into a bowl and set it on the counter. Without thinking, I slipped onto the barstool at the island and slid the bowl in front of me.

I was met with another confused look. "What on earth are you doing now?"

"Um... eating?" I replied. "I mean, as soon as I get a fork. Do you mind?" I flashed her a pleading grin, not sure where the hell the utensils were in the massive space.

She opened a drawer full of gleaming silver and pulled out a fork and knife. "You're eating in... *here*?"

I leaned back, my gaze darting around the huge kitchen. "Is that okay?"

She sighed, brow furrowed as she looked at me, completely perplexed. "Are you sure you're all right, Madelaine?"

I scrambled to formulate a plausible, Madelaine-esque answer, but my brain was still fuzzy from traveling all day and then running into Ryan in my bedroom.

She passed the cutlery to me. "You haven't sat in here with me since you were a little girl."

I lifted the fork and gave her a small smile. "Maybe it's time for a change."

She looked less than impressed by my answer. If anything, her gaze grew more suspicious until I set my fork down.

The food was delicious, but the way she was staring at me had my stomach flipping in an unsettling way.

"Is this about last year?" she finally asked me, her voice soft and concerned.

I tried to keep my expression blank. "No. Not really."

"Oh, Lainey." Sighing, she came around to my side of the island and sat down beside me on the barstool. She took my hand. "You know, you don't have to hide it from me. I can see the pain, honey. I've known you since you were in diapers."

Doubtful, my mind whispered in response, but the genuine worry in her eyes kept me from pulling away and shrugging her off.

Besides, Ryan had also alluded to something happening at school at the end of the semester. Curiosity had me wondering exactly what Madelaine had done.

Mrs. Delancey smoothed a hand down my hair. "I know it isn't easy being in your father's shadow, and I am well aware of the expectations he's placed on you. Anyone would rebel against that kind of pressure."

I swallowed uneasily.

"I don't agree with a lot of the decisions he makes," she admitted with a wry smile. "I'm sure you've heard us fight about it more than once."

All I could do was give a noncommittal nod.

"But you've got to live your own life, my girl." She jerked her chin at the ring on my finger. "Starting with that."

I couldn't help looking down at the rock on my left hand, the weight of it a constant reminder of the guy I had encountered earlier. A shiver rippled down my spine as I recalled the way he'd easily manhandled me, pressing me into the bed with hardly any effort.

Huffing, the cook got off the barstool and practically stomped back to the stove. She snatched a towel from her hip and started rubbing furiously at the immaculate stainless appliance. "I don't know what your father was thinking, agreeing to having you marry that Cain boy."

"You don't like Ryan?" I asked innocently.

She whirled, her eyes narrowed in contempt. "Do I like seeing that boy walking around like he already owns this house? Or the way he treats you? No, I don't." She arched her brow. "I also see the way you like to poke the bear. And that's one bear you don't need to be playing with, Laine."

"Noted," I murmured, picking up my fork and starting to eat once more.

Once I was finished, I slipped off my stool and carried my dirty dishes to the sink to rinse them. I was halfway through the process when I caught the woman staring at me once more.

And I realized that I had never seen Madelaine clean up a single thing herself ever.

"Exactly what spa did you spend the last week at?" the older woman asked suspiciously. "Or did your father send you to that camp again?"

I reined in a snort. I couldn't imagine Madelaine camping. *Ever*.

"Just trying to be helpful," I said with a shrug, turning off the water. I would've loaded the dishes into the dishwasher, but I wasn't sure where it was.

A second later, a panel opened along the bottom row of cabinets and the cook loaded my dirty plate into it. The dishwasher was seamlessly integrated into the sleek lines of the counter and cabinets.

Rich people were ridiculous.

"Are you sure everything is all right, Lainey?" she asked again, her chocolate eyes worried as she watched me.

"Me? Yeah. Of course I am," I said quickly, smiling.

"I know that boy was here earlier." A frown creased her face, enhancing the weathered lines of age.

"Ryan?" Surprise colored my tone that she knew he had been in the house. Where was she when I could have used the save?

She scowled deeper. "Yes. Ryan. I still cannot believe the gall of your father. Engaging you to a boy when you were barely thirteen. No wonder you acted out last year. I would spend my last year as a free woman cavorting around town, too."

Something pricked at my neck, an uneasy awareness of a secret I didn't know. "Last free year?"

Mrs. Delancey started wiping down the counter beside the stove with more force than necessary. She misread my hesitant question as she sniped, "Marrying a girl a week after she finishes high school. He could at least let you finish college."

Yeah. I can see why anyone would need a break from that shit. I mean, I knew they were engaged, and since our birthdays were in a couple months, I knew she would be eighteen when she got married to the asshole, but still. Hearing it like this made it seem more real.

Her face fell, shoulders slumping. "I've said too much, haven't I? Lord knows I have over the years, but you should be enjoying your summer. Not worrying about that boy your father tied you to."

"Not a fan, huh?" I couldn't help but ask her.

She gave me a firm look. "I think that boy got dealt a shit hand with Beckett Cain as his father. Lord knows that man could make the devil shiver. You being his wife means you'll be tied to that family forever, and *that* I don't like."

"Well, he's gone for the summer," I said softly, shrugging a bit.

"Is that what he came here to tell you?" Mrs. Delancey practically growled. "Not sure why that couldn't be said over the phone."

I hid a smile, imagining the diminutive woman standing up to the massive wall that was Ryan. It would be like a chihuahua taking on a lion.

"Yeah," I finally answered, not really wanting to go into Ryan's cryptic "behave or else" spiel.

"Good," she said firmly, turning back to me. A smile lit her face. "Now, what are your plans for this summer? Any vacations? Trips to Europe? The beach?"

"Actually, I'm just going to hang out around here," I replied, the grin on my face genuine. I couldn't wait to lounge by that massive pool and built-in grotto I had spied out of my new bedroom window.

Mrs. Delancey nodded once more in affirmation. "It'll be good to have you home, Lainey."

I flashed her a small smile and headed back toward the staircase. I made my way back to Madelaine's room, pausing inside the doorway as my eyes took in the space.

The room was like something out of a magazine. From the four-poster bed with a gauzy canopy around it to the double French doors that led out to a private balcony overlooking the pool, it looked like a professional decorator had styled every square inch. The room was mostly white with different pastel accents.

My toes curled into the plush area rug over the gleaming, pale hardwood as I cautiously stepped in and looked around my new reality.

Exhaling when I knew the room was Ryan-free, I closed the door behind me and picked up the cell phone I had left on the desk beside a beautiful rose-colored laptop that Madelaine had said would be waiting for me to use.

I stroked the smooth metal casing, the apple icon on it giving me an idea of the hefty price tag, before I turned my attention to the cellphone. Unlocking the screen, I dialed the first of two phone numbers programmed in.

The phone started to ring as I sat down at the chair in front of the desk to wait for my twin to answer.

She never did.

CHAPTER 9

Days bled into weeks, and weeks turned into a month, then two. Time slid by faster than I had imagined. I filled my days by the pool, reading or dozing. Occasionally I indulged in a shopping trip and a spa day, but it felt weird spending money that wasn't mine.

The summer had been perfect in its simplicity. I was more relaxed than I had been in years. The only thing missing was what I had hoped to accomplish when I came to California: meeting my father.

Madelaine had said he was traveling in Asia for the summer, but I had secretly hoped that he might make a return so that I could see him in person instead of in the framed photos that hung around the house.

Then again, *not* meeting him was a relief in a way since I didn't have to try to fake being my twin to the one person who would probably know the difference. Besides, even if I hadn't connected with my dad, the leaps and bounds Mom had made in rehab made this switch alone worth it.

It had taken over six weeks before the rehab facility that Madelaine sent Mom to would let me speak to her. Their process was vastly more intensive than the state-sponsored programs the court had remanded her to, and, judging by the clarity in her voice, it was worth the price.

It had to have been close to five years since I'd had a truly coherent conversation with my mother. The four monitored, thirty-minute sessions were some of my favorite moments over the summer. I had tried calling Marge a few times, but it mostly went to voicemail. She'd answered once and seemed a little short, and I felt shitty knowing that I'd left her in the lurch as far as summer help went.

Now there was only a week left until I was supposed to switch lives back with my twin. Maybe I could beg for forgiveness when I was back in Cliftown.

Frowning, I reached for my phone on the table beside the chaise lounge I was sunning on and lowered my sunglasses to look at the screen. I glanced around to make sure the pool area was deserted before pulling up my twin's number and calling it.

Straight to a full voicemail box.

Again.

Actually, for the fifteenth straight time now.

Unease trickled into my gut as I put the phone back on the end table and stared at the surface of the pool.

I hadn't spoken to Madelaine in weeks. Hell, in almost two months. Not since she'd sent me a picture of herself in Santorini a few days after I had come to California.

I had tried texting. Then calling. I had filled up her account with voicemails, and still... nothing.

My texts weren't marked as delivered, and I had no way of getting in touch with Madelaine.

Something didn't feel right about this whole situation.

I wished we had some of that twin-intuition so I could know if she was okay or in trouble, but whatever bond we shared in the womb hadn't carried over into the outside world.

And it wasn't like I could ask anyone for help.

"Good morning, Miss Madelaine!"

I jerked up, surprised that I had missed Kenny, the head gardener, as he approached. The older man smiled at me and waved.

One change that had happened in the last few weeks was that the staff was no longer tip-toeing around me. I was a little worried what that would mean for them when the real "Miss Madelaine" came back, but I was essentially isolated here and wanted people to talk to.

"Hey, Kenny," I greeted warmly, shoving my worries of my twin's disappearing act away for the moment. "How's Alice?"

He had confided in me last week that his wife had been diagnosed with breast cancer a year earlier and just finished her final round of chemo. The sweet man had teared up talking about her. I'd made a mental note to tell my sister she needed to up his pay or something. Hell, I didn't even know if the staff here received health benefits.

"She is well, thank you," he replied, his cheeks full as he grinned. "Your asters are blooming beautifully."

Grinning, I swung my legs over the side of the chair and stood. "Thanks, but we both know that's all you."

He pointed at me. "You have a talent. Plants respond to your touch."

Pride swelled in my chest at the compliment.

Several weeks back, I had been walking around the grounds and stumbled upon Kenny as he was tending the gardens by the tennis court. After I finally got him to talk to me—*thanks a lot, Madelaine, for treating the staff like shit*—he started showing me the flowers.

The asters, which looked a lot like daisies, had become my favorite. Kenny had shown me how to take care of them, and now I looked forward to helping him several times a week. I liked shoving my fingers into the dirt and working the grounds. There was something deeply satisfying about it.

Kenny's eyes widened and he dropped his gaze before turning and walking away. I was about to call after him when a shadow fell across me a second before a hand touched my hip.

I jumped and whirled, and probably would've tumbled into the pool if two hands hadn't shot out and grabbed my biceps to reel me back in.

My pulse leapt, and immediately I assumed it was Ryan. I hadn't heard from or seen my twin's fiancé, but he was the only other person who had startled me—or *touched me*—since I had arrived here.

"Easy, Laine," the rough voice admonished, the tone amused.

My eyes jerked up and I frowned at the stranger's face.

Dark brows were slanted over even darker eyes, his thin lips pulled into a smile as his eyes raked over my body. He was only a few inches taller than I was, but easily had a couple of decades on me. Something about him was familiar, but my brain struggled to make the connection.

I shivered, glad I had kept the coverup on over my bathing suit, as I extricated myself from his grasp.

"Didn't mean to startle you, honey," he replied, the lines around his mouth and eyes deepening with unspilled laughter. "I tried calling, but it seems you've been avoiding me, naughty girl."

I swallowed roughly, trying to figure out how to play this.

He arched one of the dark eyebrows as his eyes focused on my chest. "What? No hug and kiss for me?"

What the fuck?

With a grumbling sigh, he held up his hands passively. "Sorry I've been away so long, sweetness, but it took all fucking summer to convince those microdicks at Shutterfield to cave. Don't be mad. I promise I'll make it up to you."

Something about that clicked a memory into place, and I realized I knew this guy.

Adam Kindell.

He had been featured in plenty of pictures with Gary Cabot when I was looking into the man who was my sperm donor. They worked together. More important? *This* must be the Uncle Adam my sister had mentioned.

But, holy shit, she definitely hadn't said anything about him being a creep.

His lips curled into a disgusting leer as he stepped forward and settled his meaty paws on my hips. "But the time away did you good. I can't wait to explore these new curves. We have a few hours before your daddy gets home."

The feel of his hands squeezing my flesh took a backseat to the crashing news of *my dad coming home.*

Mistaking my silence for compliance, Adam pressed his body to mine. The not-so-impressive boner poking my stomach snapped me out of the fog his news had catapulted me into.

"What the fuck are you doing?" I hissed, ripping away from him so fast he couldn't even attempt to hold on.

His eyes lit up. "Is this what we're doing? The innocent girl act? I like it better when you're in your uniform, but this works, too."

Okay, ew. No. Not freaking happening.

My left hand shot up, the ring Ryan insisted I wear glittering in the brilliant light of day. "I'm *engaged*."

Adam barely blinked. "And? Since when has that stopped us? Or is this fake moral outrage part of the role today? Am I the big, bad man forcing the naughty girl to suck his—"

I dropped my hand and shook my head as I tried not to vomit. "Just... no. Okay? No."

Not deterred, he reached out and nearly grabbed me before I moved out of range. That only seemed to entice him more.

"You know I love chasing you, Lainey," he warned, his cheeks flushed from the thrill of whatever hunt he thought this was.

"What part of *no* is confusing to you?" I snapped.

"The part where *no* isn't your safe-word," he growled, edging around the chaise I had been sitting on.

Safe-word?!

What in the fifty shades of fucked up was my sister doing with this guy?

I backed up another few steps and braced myself to just flat-out run back to the house. The guy looked fairly in shape, but I had a feeling I could outrun his geriatric ass if needed.

He licked his lips, and a shudder rolled down my body.

Yeah, I definitely needed to run.

I sucked in a sharp breath, ready to launch over the next lounge chair like an Olympic hurdler, when another voice sounded from the other side of the pool.

"Lainey?"

Adam and I both paused as Mrs. Delancey called me.

Sweet relief crashed into my system as I turned to her. "Mrs. Delancey, hey. Do you need me?"

Her eyes cut from me to Adam and then back. "I've just been informed that your father is coming home. He's requested you join him and Mr. Kindell for dinner."

"I should get ready then," I said quickly, moving forward to snatch my phone from the small table and skirt around Adam.

"This isn't over," he muttered as I hurried by.

As I ran away from yet another man, I found myself wondering what the *hell* my sister had gotten herself into.

CHAPTER 10

"Are you all right, honey?" Mrs. Delancey asked when we closed the door behind us, separating me from Adam. "Was he... bothering you?"

I paused and watched her, seeing the conflict in her eyes as she tried to make sure I was okay and not overstep. I simply nodded quickly, my neck cracking at the jerky movements. My insides were still shaking from the encounter, and my brain was trying to come up with any excuse, save the obvious and implied one, as to why Adam would act that way.

He was old enough to be my father, and daddy kink definitely wasn't my thing.

But it might be my twin's.

Ugh.

"I'm fine," I forced myself to tell the older woman, who had become the closest thing I had to a friend in this house over the summer.

Her narrowed eyes watched me, completely not buying the bullshit answer. "If something happened, Lainey..." She trailed off because, what could she do? Risk her job by calling the police?

I shook my head. "No, no. I'm good. I'm just... too much sun, you know?"

She still wasn't buying it, but she didn't push.

"When will my father be home?" The words came out more strangled than I had hoped.

Her lips thinned. "Shortly before dinner."

I glanced down at the watch on my wrist. That gave me a few hours to get myself together.

"Okay. I'll be down by seven," I assured her, turning toward the back staircase.

"A quarter til," she corrected me softly.

I paused and turned slowly.

Her blue eyes were serious as she regarded me. "You don't ever keep your father waiting, Madelaine. Remember?"

Again, I felt the forced smile crack my face. "Right." I tapped the side of my head. "Guess all the lounging around this summer bleached part of my brain."

She gave me a stiff nod, her expression unreadable, until I turned and hurried up the stairs.

I hadn't heard *Uncle* Adam follow me into the house, but I still hurried to my room and closed the door, locking it quickly behind me. Then, worried he might have a key or something, I wedged the desk chair in front of the door.

I was being stupid, right? There was no way he would come up here where the staff could possibly catch him. Finding me outside at the pool was one thing, but my bedroom?

Still, I couldn't fight off the nagging feeling of worry as I headed for the bathroom and locked that door, too, before stripping out of my coverup and bathing suit.

I took a long, scalding hot shower, lingering inside the walled area with multiple showerheads pouring down and washing away the chlorine and feel of his hands on me. I lost track of how long I stayed there.

Perks of this bathroom? It never ran out of hot water, which meant I had become partial to marathon showers.

Once I got out and dried off, I wrapped a towel around my chest and hesitated before opening the bathroom door, worried about what I would see in my room.

Thankfully, no surprises awaited me. The chair was still firmly wedged under the door, which was also locked.

Exhaling in relief, I headed to the closet area to select my outfit for the night, finally going with a simple sundress.

I'd spent a good chunk of my summer watching tutorial videos online, so I took the time to dry and curl my hair before tackling my makeup. Even still, I was left with over an hour to kill before my father was slated to arrive.

Butterflies erupted in my stomach.

I had been able to ignore the impending reunion with the man who was my dad while I was focused on getting ready, but now there was no distraction. No way to keep my thoughts from spinning out.

Will he notice I'm not his daughter?

I snorted to myself.

Unless he was as cracked out as my mother usually was, he would probably notice I wasn't the girl he had raised for almost eighteen years. Which meant this whole thing could blow up in my face.

And the first question he would ask would be, *Where is my real daughter?*

For that I had no answer.

How did I explain that his daughter was avoiding me, too?

My gaze did a quick sweep of the room that had become achingly familiar the last two months. It came to rest on a drawer I had discovered my first week there. The only contents were an older model version of the same laptop that Madelaine had left for me to use.

A laptop that was none of my business, so I never bothered looking at it. As nosy as I had been, I'd made a point never to outright search the room for more info on my twin. It seemed too invasive.

But now...

"Fuck it," I muttered, crossing the room and jerking open the drawer. I pulled the laptop out and tried to turn it on, but the battery was dead.

With a grumbling sigh, I turned to use the other laptop's charging cord, but it wasn't compatible with this older computer.

"Fabulous." I glared at the useless piece of technology before shoving it aside.

Drumming my fingers on the desk, I tried to think. There had to be some way to find her. Hell, I had stalked her before, right?

Reluctantly I went to the door and pulled the chair free to move it back to the desk so I could sit down, but I kept the door locked. No way I wanted Adam sneaking up on me again.

I opened my laptop and picked up my phone, scrolling back to Madelaine's last text and looking at the image she had sent.

M: About to make Santorini my bitch, little sister!

The picture above the caption showed her in bright sunlight, standing in a tiny dress, strappy sandals, and a wide-brimmed hat. Her hands were lifted in the air, carefree and happy.

My eyes narrowed as they caught the name of the building behind her.

Adonis Sol Hotel.

I tapped the name into the web browser and waited a second for the results to pop up.

My heart sank.

Fucking sank through my feet and puddled into the floor beneath me.

ADONIS SOL HOTEL STILL CLOSED AFTER FIRE THAT CLAIMED ELEVEN LIVES

"No," I whispered, shaking my head. There was just no way.

No *fucking* way.

I clicked another link, bringing up information on the hotel fire and scanning for the date.

June 14.

The same day that Madelaine sent me that photo.

But she could have just been standing in front of the hotel. It didn't mean she was staying there or was even in the building when the fire happened.

It didn't mean—

I jumped and let out a tiny squeak as someone knocked on my door.

"Miss Madelaine?"

I recognized the soft voice of the woman who was tasked with keeping the top floor of the house clean. Carlita was only a few years older than me with beautiful dark skin and eyes that always smiled.

"Coming," I called, the words barely audible past the lump in my throat. I slammed the computer screen shut and tucked my phone into the pocket of my dress.

Pockets in dresses should be mandatory.

I unlocked the door and yanked it open to see a nervous Carlita fidgeting. Her usual smile was absent.

"What's up?"

She lowered her voice. "It is nearly seven. Mrs. Delancey—"

"Shit!" I swore, realizing I lost track of time.

Carlita's eyes widened, but the sparkle returned to them. "Yes. You must hurry. The guests have already arrived, and your father's car is pulling into the driveway."

"Guests?" I echoed, stepping into the hallway and pulling my door shut.

"For dinner," she prompted, not getting my confusion.

Not having time to get clarification, I rushed down the hall and to the front steps, slowing down only so I wouldn't twist an ankle in these heels and end up in a bloody pile at the bottom of the marble stairs.

Now *that* would be making an entrance.

Chaos swirled inside me as I tried to sort out the barrage of emotions warring within me. Fear for my sister, anxiety over meeting my father, and disgust at seeing Adam Kindell again.

I was so in my head that when I reached the landing, I missed seeing the men standing in the foyer. My gaze landed on them and I froze, my hand still resting on the bannister.

The older of the two had dark hair, the temples slightly silver in a way that was both attractive and authoritative. And he was an older version of the man standing at his right. Both men stared at me as I paused.

"There she is," the older man said with a smile that didn't quite reach his icy eyes. He clapped the younger man's shoulder harder than necessary. "Aren't you going to say hello to your fiancée, son?"

Ryan stepped away from his father, his expression unreadable as he closed the distance between us. His gaze fell to my left hand, and I saw the smug quirk of his lips when he spotted the ring there. A second later his eyes jerked to mine, and he held my gaze until my knuckles turned white around the bannister.

He reached out and slowly pried my hand away, finger by finger, until my hand was firmly enclosed in his larger one. I bit my lower lip to stifle a gasp at how warm and rough his hand felt sliding against mine. At how delicate he made me feel.

He brought my hand to his lips and pressed a kiss on the back. His eyes were dancing as they met mine with something more sinister than amusement. "I've missed you, sweetheart."

CHAPTER 11

I couldn't breathe.
 It had been years since I'd had a panic attack, but I could feel one coming on now. Too much uncertainty was hovering like a toxic mushroom cloud after a nuclear bomb, and now I had to contend with *Ryan?*

"Lainey?" he prompted, his voice lowering slightly as his eyes narrowed.

Another wave of butterflies or pigeons or freaking eagles took flight in my chest.

That look in his eye? That growly tone? Something in my chest sparked to life that I wasn't ready to acknowledge. Something that made my breath hitch and my pulse race.

Get it together, Maddie.

"How was your trip?" I asked slowly, managing a small smile as he released my hand.

His gaze sharpened, looking for the barb my twin no doubt would have tossed into the seemingly innocent question.

"Went great," he finally replied. "Learned a few new things about the international offices, did some construction in Indonesia for a village hit by a tsunami last year."

That explained the tanned skin and why his shoulders looked even wider than the last time I'd seen him. He'd clearly added a few pounds of muscle, and the stubble on his jaw gave him an even more dangerous look.

"What did *you* do?" he asked, raising his eyebrows scathingly. "How many businesses did your credit card keep afloat this summer?"

My spine stiffened as I bristled at the implication.

He smirked. "Sorry. I meant your *dad's* credit card."

"Whatever it was, it was worth it," Ryan's dad cut in sharply, coming to his son's side and shooting him a dark look.

Ryan returned it for a second, the animosity between the men crackling like a live power line. As fast as his irritation flashed, it smoothed into something apathetic.

You're just as trapped as I am.

Ryan's words came back like the crack of a whip echoing in my skull.

"You look lovely, Madelaine," the man continued, nodding in deference to me.

"Thank you, Mr. Cain," I said softly, unable to tear my gaze from Ryan. The mask of indifference was even more troubling than when he was an outright asshole.

"Beckett," he corrected with a smile. "We're practically family, after all."

"Practically, and yet not quite," Adam droned from farther down the hall.

"Kindell," Beckett greeted with that stupid chin jerk men did. "I heard you finally managed to close the deal. Only took you, what? Four months?"

The heat of Adam's glare could be felt from where I stood. A second later, he smothered it and headed for us.

I struggled to keep from closing my hands into fists the closer he got, but I was very much aware that I was a lamb in a lion's den right now. I was out of my league and on my own.

Adam stopped short of us. "Gary will be here momentarily. He asked that we wait in the dining room for him."

Beckett smirked, an expression I had seen on Ryan's face several times now, but on Beckett... it was even more terrifying. At least I could see glimpses of an actual human in Ryan's eyes, but Beckett was a blank void.

"Very well," he agreed, walking away from us toward the formal dining room.

I watched him stalk away with a frown, missing the way Adam sidled up next to me until I caught a whiff of his aftershave, pungent and way too strong.

"Shall we, Madelaine?" His hand touched the small of my back, his fingertips brushing the top curve of my butt in a way that was completely inappropriate.

I jumped and flinched, unable to stop my body's physical reaction to get away from this man.

"She's my fiancée," Ryan ground out. "I'll escort her."

I lifted my gaze through a fringe of lashes, stunned when I saw his icy glare fixed on Adam. From where Ryan stood across from us, it would have looked like Adam's touch was innocent enough, but he had seen my reaction.

"She's still my... niece," Adam returned curtly, but his hand fell to his side as he bared his teeth. "I'm happy to take care of her for a bit longer before she's yours."

Ignoring the fact that they were discussing me like an object, I knew the last thing I wanted to be was Adam's *anything*. I shuffled back a step in Ryan's direction.

Ryan's gaze turned to me, effectively dismissing Adam. "Lainey?" He extended an arm, and I didn't even think.

I slipped my hand into the crook of his arm and tucked my body against his side, letting him guide me to the next room. I could feel Adam's gaze drilling into my back with laser-like focus as I walked away.

Ryan was anything but a white knight, but everything in me wanted to recoil from Adam Kindell. Ryan had my head spinning and my heart pounding, but not just from fear. It was like trying to choose between swimming with a shark or walking with a hyena.

My gut told me I had a better chance treading water with Ryan than running from Adam.

"Thanks." The word slipped past my lips before my brain could censor it.

He glanced down at me, surprised, and then his brow furrowed. "What the hell was that?"

I kept my eyes focused ahead. "Nothing. It's fine."

He pulled us to an abrupt stop and turned, towering over me and crowding my personal bubble. "I didn't ask if it was fine. You jumped. You *never* jump."

I lifted my eyes to meet his gaze and swallowed. "I'm probably overreacting."

He snorted and rolled his eyes. "Madelaine, Queen of the Fucking World? You? Overreact?"

I jerked my arm away. If I'd thought he was the lesser of two evils, I needed my brain checked.

"You know what? I can walk myself to the damn room."

I started to storm by, but his hand snaked out and grabbed my elbow firmly. "There you go again, thinking you're in charge."

I arched an eyebrow. "You're in *my* house."

His blue eyes glittered. "Didn't stop me last time."

My chin lifted in defiance. "By all means. Pin me to the dining room table to prove you're the boss. I'm sure no one will care."

He laughed, the sound cold and detached. "Actually? Between my dad and Kindell, they'd probably start cheering. But if you really want to explore your exhibitionist side, I'm down, baby."

"Not happening," I seethed, glaring at him. "There aren't enough diamonds in the world for that to be worth it."

His other hand shot out, pinching my chin and keeping my eyes locked with his. "Don't test me, Lainey. I'm fucking over your shit. My rules now, remember?"

"How can I forget?" I snapped. "You remind me every time I see you."

His grip tightened and I almost flinched.

"Then why did you turn your phone off?" he demanded coldly. "I've been trying to get a hold of you all week. *Sweetheart*."

"I lost my phone weeks ago," I lied smoothly. "I have a new number."

"And what? You forgot what a fucking cloud backup is for?"

I jerked out of his hold. "Maybe I wanted a clean slate."

A smile twitched on his full lips. "Do you really think a new number is going to fix your epic fuckup? Or that people will just forget? Has all that bleach sunk into your thick skull?"

I tried my best to keep my expression neutral since I was still totally lost as to what my twin had done to completely mess up her life. I was starting to think her escape this summer was less about needing a break and more about running away.

The thought of Lainey reminded me of the headline and the fire and...

Shit, I couldn't handle this right now.

I whirled, ready to stalk all the way back upstairs, when someone else entered the hall. I stopped, my knees going weak for a whole new reason as my father stepped into view for the first time and gave me a huge smile.

"Hi, honey. I've missed you," he added, closing the distance between us and wrapping his arms warmly around me.

CHAPTER 12

I had spent so many days and nights dreaming about meeting my father, but I never imagined it would be like this.

He was taller than the pictures showed, maybe an inch or two shorter than Ryan, but still several inches taller than me. He smelled like a smokey, decadent cologne, and the soft fabric of his suit was just as inviting as his embrace.

My father was hugging me.

It ended almost as fast as it started, and he looked over my shoulder to the man behind me.

"Ryan," he greeted, the warmth of his voice cooling considerably.

"Gary," Ryan replied, a mocking edge to his tone as he walked by us and into the dining room.

"Welcome home," Adam added as he came up behind us.

Gary nodded. "Good to see you, Adam. Wait for us inside. I need a moment with my daughter."

Daughter.

The word did funny things to my stomach.

Adam walked by us and closed the doors to the dining room, giving us privacy in the hallway.

Gary looked at me, his navy blue eyes sweeping up and down me as his lips pinched together. "Have you gained weight?"

My head snapped back.

Did he just say what I think he said?

I mean, I knew Lainey liked her salads, and I was a fan of all things *not* salad-like, but that was kind of a dick question.

My mouth fell open in surprise. "I..."

"You look... different," he added, his brow furrowing.

I froze and every word in the English language I had ever learned fell out of my head.

"Healthier, I suppose," he stammered, flashing me a forced smile. "New diet?

Oh.

"Mrs. Delancey's a great cook," I managed to reply.

He nodded, seemingly satisfied by the answer. "Good. And how was your summer? I know I should have called more, but work never stops."

I hid a flinch, thinking about him calling his *real* daughter and her not picking up.

"It's been nice," I chose to say instead. "I mostly just... hung out."

Sighing, his hands settled on my shoulders as he looked into my eyes. "Sweetheart, I know last year was difficult, but this is your senior year and you're turning eighteen. We can't afford any more missteps that will hurt our family."

"Of course," I replied, licking my lips nervously.

His hand slid up to touch my cheek as he smiled, the same dimple Lainey and I had creasing his right cheek. "That's my girl. Shall we?"

I nodded and let him lead me into the dining room. All three men stood in tandem as I entered, and their eyes on me were almost too much.

"Gentlemen," Gary started, his smooth voice carrying in the large space.

The formal dining room was a study in beauty, from the hand-carved table that comfortably sat twelve to the gold and crystal chandelier that illuminated the space. I loved this room. I'd found it on my first day of wandering around the house, and the opulence made me feel like I was a street urchin pretending to be rich.

But I preferred to eat in the kitchen with Mrs. Delancey.

This room was too fancy for me.

Ryan and Beckett were seated on one side and Adam on the other. The seat at the head of the table was vacant, as was the one immediately to its left. Sitting next to my father wasn't an issue, but I wasn't crazy about being within arm's distance of Adam.

The man made my skin crawl.

Gary pulled out my chair for me, and no one sat until I did. While they settled, I took the time to take a deep breath and look at the artfully arranged silverware around my place setting.

I unfolded the napkin and tucked it gently around my lap, waiting and watching.

Bracing his forearms on the table, Gary leaned forward and looked past me to the man to my left.

"Shutterfield backed out."

I wasn't entirely sure what that meant, but judging by the not-so-veiled rage of my father, the pasty paleness of Adam's face, and the smug looks across from me, the news wasn't great.

"They can't," Adam stammered. "We had a deal."

"Did you?" Beckett asked loftily, lifting his wine glass and swirling the dark liquid thoughtfully.

Adam went from pale to pink in a second. "Yes, unless you did something to fuck it up."

Beckett's brow rose comically. "How would that benefit me? Cain Global is as invested in the Shutterfield deal as you are."

"Heinrik said—"

"Fuck Heinrik and what he said!" Gary thundered, slamming a fist on the table.

Years of my mother's outbursts were the only thing that kept me from jumping a mile. Instead I shrank back into my seat and watched the drama unfold like a play I hadn't meant to buy a ticket to.

"Heinrik is a useless figurehead they let stay on the board to pacify his own narcissism," Ryan added slowly, leaning back in his chair and glaring at Adam. "Which you would know if you would get your head out of your own ass."

"What the fuck would you know?" Adam snarled. "Last I checked, playing construction worker in a third world country wasn't helping anyone."

A slow smile crept across Ryan's face, and even I knew whatever he said next would hurt Adam.

"Heinrik's granddaughter's passion project is bringing fresh drinking water to the outlying islands of Indonesia. I spent the summer building a relationship with her *and* her father, who now holds controlling shares of Shutterfield. So while you were wasting time sucking back brandy and cigars with the dinosaur, I was building a connection. Shutterfield is bankrolling the Indonesian project as part of their humanitarian efforts."

Beckett smirked across the table.

Ryan's head swung to look at Gary. "We have Shutterfield."

Gary didn't look impressed, despite the news. "I don't see a signed contract."

Ryan's lips twisted into a grimace. "We do if we want them. Heinrik's son wasn't just visiting his daughter in Indonesia. There are a few places that cater to his more... grotesque sexual desires. We have evidence."

Gary rubbed his jaw. "Enough to secure the contract?"

Beckett barked out a laugh. "I doubt the man wants to be seen going into a whorehouse full of prepubescent boys."

"What?" The horrified gasp slipped out before I could stop myself.

All eyes turned to me.

"He should be going to *prison*, not being blackmailed into a business deal," I finished, my hands curling into fists on my lap. I looked around the table, disgusted to see that none of them really seemed phased by the news.

Finally, my father sighed softly and turned to me. "While I appreciate where your heart is, we're not in the business of policing others. He'll pay when we force him into a deal that will break his company."

My eyes narrowed. "You have evidence the man is a *pedophile*. He's abusing children."

"In another country," Beckett told me dismissively. "The worst he would get here would be bad publicity. They can't try the crime in the States, and he would buy his way out of it in Indonesia."

"That doesn't make it right," I insisted.

"No, it doesn't," Ryan agreed, meeting my gaze. The glimpse of raw fury in his eyes showed he hated it as much as I did. Until, as fast as his anger had flared, his expression went neutral and controlled.

The moment of solidarity was broken when he shrugged and said, "But we can make it work for us."

"He's right, love," Gary assured me softly. "Don't worry your pretty head about it."

Only shock kept me quiet.

Did they seriously expect me to just sit here like a decoration? Is that what Madelaine did?

"It would appear my son has handled what your right-hand man couldn't, Gary," Beckett continued, still smug and obviously trying to rile up Adam.

Which was totally working.

Adam leaned forward with a growl. "Your *boy* still has a lot to learn about a lot of things, Beck."

"Not that many," Ryan cut in with a smirk. He took a drink of his water and watched the other man with open contempt.

"Oh, I beg to differ," Adam returned quietly, and then his hand touched my leg under the table, squeezing the inside of my thigh before starting to drift higher.

I cleared my throat as I tried to shift my legs away from his groping hand. "May I be excused for a moment?"

Gary frowned at me. "Of course."

I was on my feet before he finished, not giving the other men time to rise as I practically ran from the room. I managed to turn the corner and all but dove into the powder room. My heels slipped on the waxed floors and sent me crashing into the wall. I sank down against it, kicking the door shut with my foot.

"Breathe," I told myself under my breath, pulling my legs up and resting my forehead on my knees as I struggled to tame my wildly pounding heart. "Just breathe."

This was all too much. My emotional dashboard was short-circuiting, and pretty soon I was going to explode or combust or something else that wouldn't be pretty.

What world had I stumbled into?

No wonder Lainey had needed a break. But at the same time, I was starting to wonder—how much of this was she truly complaisant about? Because *this* was too much.

The way Adam kept touching me, it was clear he didn't expect to be rebuffed; he touched me the way someone intimately familiar with another person would caress the person they were *involved* with. He seemed genuinely shocked and confused that I kept turning him down.

And what kind of men let a child predator slide so they could pad their already bursting bank accounts?

My heart lurched as the doorknob twisted and the door pushed open. In my haste to get away, I hadn't locked it.

I braced myself, half expecting it to be Adam, but Ryan poked his head in. He frowned when he saw me on the floor, pushing the door open so he could step inside and then closing it once more as he leaned against it.

"What the hell is wrong with you?" he demanded bluntly.

I dropped my head back with a *thunk* against the wall. "The fact that you even have to ask is more fucked up than anything else."

"The Shutterfield thing?" His jaw dropped. "Are you serious?"

"Maybe it's a normal thing for you to let this go," I started coldly, glaring up at his perfect face, "but it's not for me."

"Since when?" he scoffed.

My mouth fell open, forgetting who I was supposed to be in this moment. "Are you kidding?"

"Are *you*?" he challenged. "Last I checked, the princess didn't give a flying fuck where her money came from as long as she got to spend it."

That sounded so disgustingly shallow... and yet held a ring of truth.

Oh, Lainey. What the hell were you thinking?

"You don't get to act all offended now, baby," he went on, his tone cold and unflinching. "Stick to what you do best—shopping and sucking dick. Leave business up to the rest of us who can think past ourselves."

I shoved myself to my feet, feeling my cheeks turn red. "You don't know *shit* about me."

He laughed, pushing off the door and looking down at me as his body practically pressed mine against the wall. "Don't I?"

I pressed my lips together, ignoring the charge of electricity between our bodies. "You really don't."

He snorted. "What's your game? Pretend you aren't the same vapid skank you've been for the last decade to make people *like* you?"

I licked my lips nervously, a forbidden thrill shooting through me when his gaze dropped to my mouth and heated.

A second later it snapped back to my eyes. "It won't work. Your little stunt last semester showed everyone what a conniving, selfish waste of space you really are. Now they all see what I've known for years."

Part of me wanted to defend myself, to defend my twin. But I was still clueless about what he kept referring to.

He braced an arm over my head, caging me in so that every breath I took, my chest brushed against his. Unlike the way Adam had cornered me before, I didn't hate this.

I should have.

But I didn't.

"What the fuck is going on with Kindell?" he asked softly, his eyes searching mine.

The change in subject caught me off guard almost as much as the sudden look in his eyes. Almost like... concern?

"I don't—"

His finger pressed against my lips. "Don't lie, Lainey. I can read you like a fucking book, and we both know it. Don't think I missed what happened in the hall."

Of course he hadn't. Ryan Cain might be a lot of things, but idiot wasn't one of them. Even I could tell that after our two encounters.

I took a deep breath, ignoring his intoxicating scent and the way my body naturally seemed to want to sway into his. "It's nothing."

His eyes narrowed slightly, the concern hardening into something more hostile. "It better be." He leaned away from me and started to turn.

"You know, maybe I took a hard look at my life this summer and realized that I need to make better choices," I said bravely, refusing to cower. "Maybe I want to be a better person."

His icy gaze studied me for a long moment before he started to laugh. My stomach dropped, and I realized I should have just left it alone. Let him leave without sticking my foot in my mouth.

"Nice try, baby." He leaned his face down until his cheek touched mine, his lips brushing the shell of my ear. "But we both know you're too fucked up to ever change. Just like I am."

CHAPTER 13

Finishing dinner amongst a group of self-righteous, narcissistic men was harder than I'd imagined.

I picked at my food, annoyed that I'd been brought a garden salad with some kind of vinegar dressing and a few tiny slivers of grilled chicken while the men around me dug into massive steaks with potatoes, veggies, and bread.

I'd caught Mrs. Delancey's grimace as she handed Gary his plate. Like she knew I didn't want rabbit food.

I spent most of the time blocking out their boastful tones as they talked about which companies they'd decimated, how much money they'd earned, and general corporate talk. I thought about my asters, wishing I could escape to the garden and do *something*.

Or, better yet, hit a burger joint for something greasy and artery-clogging.

It had been hours and this dinner was *still* happening. Dessert had been brought out for everyone except me. They had three-layers of decadent chocolate cake with mousse and I had... frozen yogurt.

I didn't even *like* yogurt. It was a pointless food that was a half-assed attempt at ice cream.

At this point, I had memorized the room. There were four paintings, seven potted plants, eight windows, and thirteen gardenias in the vase at the center of the table (five blue, eight white).

In short?

I was bored out of my damn mind.

So of course I missed the question lobbed my way as I tried to re-create the original place setting in my head.

Jerking my head up, I flashed my father a guilty look and felt my cheeks heat when displeasure in his dark eyes reflected back at me.

"Beckett was asking how the wedding plans are coming along?" he prompted.

Fuck me. I was supposed to be planning a wedding?

"G-good," I stammered, reaching for my water to wet my suddenly dry throat.

Ryan shook his head, his look easily conveying *I'm marrying an idiot.* "Picked a location yet, *honey?*"

I pressed my lips into a thin line. "I considered a church, but they don't let the devil in, do they?"

My father let out a low, aggravated sound while Adam laughed next to me.

Ryan simply smiled. "No. So we better find a venue that will actually let my bride inside."

Taking in a slow, calming breath, I rolled my shoulders back and looked at my father. "There's plenty of options, but I'm going to wait and see what the wedding planner has to say."

Madelaine totally would have hired one of those, right? Wasn't that what rich people did?

He gave me a firm nod, happy enough with the bullshit answer. "And have you selected a planner yet?"

Well, shit. Apparently my sister hadn't gotten that far.

"No, but I've narrowed it down. I'll make the final selection in the next few weeks," I assured him, the lies falling effortlessly from my lips.

I sure as hell hoped Madelaine was planning her wedding this summer, wherever she was.

Unless that fire...

Nope. Don't go there, Maddie.

"Make sure it's handled before the engagement party in October," Beckett agreed, finishing the after-dinner scotch he'd requested. "Which means you two need to publicly start acting like a real couple, since Madelaine will be eighteen in a few weeks. I know you announced your engagement at the end of the year, but it was rather dimmed by what transpired after."

All eyes jerked to me. Hiding my discomfort, I reached for my water and took a long sip.

Beckett's gaze narrowed thoughtfully as he observed me, then he transferred his intensity to his son. "We need to sell the happy couple vibe. The last thing we need is ripples of discord in our families that spread to stockholders when we're so close to closing things in Asia. There's a lot riding on the next few months, and it's time for both of you to play your part."

"We know what we have to do," Ryan said evenly, annoyance blatant in his voice.

Beckett's hand clamped on his son's shoulder in a gesture that would have been encouraging except for the force behind it and the way his knuckles turned white. "See that you do. We can't afford any missteps. Last semester—"

Ryan's gaze went lethal, and I was unable to repress a shiver.

"—was last semester," Gary interjected coldly, shooting Beckett a dark look. "Madelaine knows what she has to do. Don't you, Lainey?"

I gave a slow nod, feeling the full weight of the stares fixed on me. "Of course."

"Glad that's settled," Beckett muttered, tossing his napkin onto the table as he stood. "Gary, we'll talk later." His gaze drifted to me and he dipped his head, but the gesture seemed more mocking than genuine. "Lainey."

"Mr. Cain," I murmured, a thin smile on my mouth.

Ryan stood and followed his father without a word to any of us as they left the room.

"Gary," Adam started as soon as they were gone, leaning around me.

My father held up a hand to stop him. "Not tonight, Adam. It's been a long day and I still have calls to make."

Seething, Adam sank back into his chair, but Gary wasn't done. He stared at his business partner until he looked up.

Gary gave him a pointed look. "You can go now."

I felt Adam's gaze shoot to me for a second before he shoved away from the table and left the room. It wasn't until the doors closed behind him that I exhaled.

Gary dropped his own napkin to the table. "Don't make me a liar, Lainey."

I looked at him in surprise, freezing when I saw the way his eyes were narrowed at me.

"I understand you feel trapped by the arrangement that I've made, and I don't even blame you for acting out a few months ago," he added, almost regretfully. "But we need things to go smoothly this next year until the wedding."

My mouth was suddenly dry and filled with sand. "Okay."

Nodding, he flicked a hand in my direction. "Thank you. Why don't you get some sleep, sweetheart?"

I pushed back from the table and stood slowly. "Um... good night."

Turning, I started for the doors.

"Lainey?"

I paused and turned, surprised to see Gary on his feet and crossing the room to me. His hands came out to frame my face as he leaned in and pressed a kiss to my forehead.

"Good night, sweetheart." He smiled at me. "I've missed you."

"I missed you, too," I choked out, fully aware that it wasn't *me* that he'd missed, but the daughter he assumed I was.

The daughter who was *missing*, and I had no idea how to find her. This was too big for me to handle alone. If my sister was hurt, I needed help.

"Get some sleep," he finished, stepping away from me.

"I need..." The words tumbled from my mouth unbidden, causing him to pause and look back expectantly.

He chuckled after a second. "What do you need, honey?"

Oh, God. Was I actually going to do this?

"I'm not who you think I am," I whispered, my gaze frozen on his.

Confusion reflected in his eyes. "Oh? And who are you then?"

I took a deep breath. "My name is Madison Porter. I'm your... other daughter."

Gary's face went ashen and he stumbled back a step. "What did you just say?"

I licked my lips. "My name is Madison. And I'm—"

"You're..." He cut me off and staggered backward until he fell back into his seat from dinner. "How? How the hell—"

"Madelaine and I met a few months ago," I explained quickly, the words slipping from my lips in a rush. "I found this article when I was researching something for a school assignment. I saw Madelaine's picture and messaged her. We decided to... switch places for the summer."

"You've been here for *weeks*?" he whispered, rubbing his jaw in astonishment. "Where the hell is my daughter?"

I flinched.

I was his daughter, too.

"That's the thing," I replied softly, pushing past my own hurt at his question, "I don't know. I haven't heard from Madelaine in weeks, and before dinner, I found this article about a fire at a hotel she took a picture in front of. I don't know if she was staying there, but she was near it."

"What hotel?" he demanded, his spine stiffening.

My brow furrowed as I tried to remember. "The *Adonis Sol*? In—"

"—Santorini," he finished for me, rubbing his jaw. "She always loved Greece."

"That's... cool," I muttered, ducking my head. "But I'm worried. She was supposed to be back next week, and I have no idea if she's even okay."

Gary stood up quickly. "I need to make some calls. Find out where the hell my daughter is."

"Of course." I inched back toward the door, not entirely sure what my place was here now that I had come clean.

Gary stalked past me and out of the room, leaving me with nothing but regret and worry.

CHAPTER 14

I spent the night watching the clock start the countdown of the rest of my days in this room. Nothing could distract me from my thoughts as they swelled to dizzying new heights.

But there was some relief in the truth being out.

I had mostly reassured myself that if anyone could find Lainey, it would be her father.

No, wait.

Our father.

The guy who left me in the dust when he realized his *real* daughter was missing.

The knock on my bedroom door startled me out of my ever-darkening thoughts, and I shoved the blankets off my body and started to get up.

"Yeah?"

The door poked open and one of the maids smiled at me. "Your father asked me to see if you were awake."

My eyes narrowed. She didn't know I wasn't my twin, so whatever was happening with Gary, he hadn't outed me to the staff to be evicted. "Um, yeah. I'm up. Or getting there, I guess."

"He'd like to see you in his office," she told me, ducking back out and closing the door before I could formulate a response.

Or, more likely, a plausible excuse to avoid him.

Maybe I could uber to the airport and book a flight back to Michigan before he noticed I was gone.

Not freaking likely.

With lead in my feet and worry in my stomach, I quickly dressed and scraped my hair back into a messy bun before brushing my teeth. I stared at my pale reflection for a beat before sighing and leaving the safety of my bedroom.

I snorted as I tugged the door shut.

It wasn't even *my* bedroom.

Each step toward Gary's office on the main level felt like I was walking toward a guillotine. I half expected the massive blade to swoop down and chop off my head as soon as I crossed the threshold.

Gary looked up at me, his handsome face drawn and exhausted.

"Close the door, Made—" He swallowed and stopped himself. "Close the door, please."

I closed it and stood there, not sure exactly what to do next as the silence stretched like an endless canyon between us. Gary stared at me, his gaze probing and assessing until I felt completely exposed.

"Have a seat," he finally murmured, gesturing to the set of chairs in front of his glass desk.

The room was done in sharp, modern lines with black and white as the main colors with gold accents. It was clinical, almost sterile, inside the room. It was as welcoming as the man in front of me.

Letting out a slow breath, I moved forward and practically fell into one of the chairs before clasping my hands on my lap.

He rubbed his jaw, still watching me. "The resemblance is... uncanny."

My brows pulled together. "We're twins. Isn't that kind of the point?"

He blinked and jolted, like an electric current snaked through his body. "Of course. I mean, I was there, but I haven't seen you since you were two days old."

"Is that when you and Mom decided to split up your matching set?" I asked, unable to keep the bitterness from my tone.

"It's complicated," he replied with a grimace and a flicker of... regret?

"I'm sure," I murmured, dropping my gaze for a second. "So? Where's Madelaine?"

Gary flinched and fisted his hands on top of the desk. "Gone."

My chest contracted. "G-gone?"

He nodded, swallowing roughly. "The fire... she was there."

"You're sure?" This couldn't be happening. Madelaine had to just be hiding, or maybe she was in a hospital somewhere...

His head snapped up. "You think I didn't exhaust every option to see if my daughter was alive or dead? She's been in a box in a morgue, waiting to be claimed."

I pressed my back into the chair. "I didn't mean—"

He waved a hand, cutting me off as his shoulders slumped. "I'm sorry. I'm sorry. It's been a long night and... Yes. Madelaine is dead. I pulled some strings and spoke to the Hellenic police. Lainey was traveling under an alias, so they didn't know who to call when she passed. I'm having her remains brought back here."

Remains.

"When no one claimed her, she was cremated," he explained at the question in my eyes. "She's been sitting on a shelf for... Well, it doesn't really matter now, does it?"

My hand slapped over my mouth as I felt tears prick my eyes. "I'm so sorry."

I wasn't even entirely sure how I should feel. I'd barely known my twin for a week. We hadn't really bonded or anything, but she was still my *twin*. A piece of my soul.

Shouldn't I have sensed when she was in trouble? Wasn't that a thing that happened with twins?

But all I'd felt was silence. Just as alone as I had been for most of my life.

Gary cleared his throat and quickly wiped under one eye. "I need to know how this happened. Why did you two decide to..."

"It was Madelaine's idea," I said softly, and then winced.

Way to blame the victim, Maddie.

"I sent her a message, and she came to Michigan to find me. She wanted to switch places for the summer."

"Why?" he asked hoarsely, his eyes red-rimmed. "Was her life so awful?"

Oh, hell. How was I supposed to navigate *this* minefield?

"I think she just wanted to try something new," I hedged carefully. "She wanted to go on a trip before her senior year."

And before you married her off to an asshole.

"This is about Ryan and the wedding, isn't it?" Gary's head fell forward. "I thought she understood why we needed to do this. Why it's so important to her family."

I opted to stay quiet, because he was wrong. *So* wrong.

"I'm sorry," he muttered, rubbing a hand over his jaw. "I don't even know what to say to you... Madison."

My stupid, childish heart leapt at hearing him say my name. Acknowledging me... even if it was only because my twin sister was dead.

"I can leave," I said softly. "I know you need to plan her... funeral. I can leave to give you space. I never—I mean *we* never meant for this to happen."

"Of course you didn't," he agreed numbly. His gaze flickered to me and focused. "And you don't have to leave. Not yet."

"Okay," I whispered, fidgeting on my seat a bit.

"Actually?" he added after a beat, taking a deep breath. "I have a proposition for you."

I felt my shoulders tense. Here it was: the guillotine. I felt it in my bones.

"How much did Lainey tell you? About why she's engaged to Ryan? Our family business?"

Our family.

Now it was *our* family.

"She said there's a will," I replied slowly. "A lot of money on the line."

"There is," he confirmed, nodding brusquely. "But it's not just a lot of money... it's money we need access to, or the company will fold."

"You just got that deal with Shutter-something."

"Shutterfield," he clarified with a thin smile, "and technically, it was Ryan who closed the deal. Beckett and I inherited a mess of mistakes from our fathers, and we've been slowly untangling them, but it's not enough. The influx of cash that the wills release is enough to sustain this generation, yours, and more."

"That's a lot of money," I muttered, brushing my hair over my shoulder. "Madelaine told me that there were two of them."

"More than that," Gary explained. "Ryan's mother died in childbirth having his younger sister. *Her* parents make us all look like paupers. Old money. Oil, mostly, but they've set up a trust for Ryan and his sister, but he's set to inherit even more money when his grandfather dies, and the man was diagnosed with terminal cancer a few months ago. He won't last another year."

"Wow," I remarked bitterly. "That's really awesome to hear. Have you already started planning the party, too?"

Gary rocked back in his seat. "Madison—"

"No, no," I cut him off. "Your daughter, my *sister*, died. And you're talking about wills and sounding happy an old man is dying? What kind of world do you people live in?"

His mouth snapped shut.

I pushed myself up to my feet. "I'd like to stay for Madelaine's funeral, if that's okay. Then I'll get back home, and we can go back to forgetting each other's existence."

"There isn't going to be a funeral," Gary called to my back as I started walking away.

I spun and stared at him. "Wow. I mean, I figured you would keep it quiet since your daughter was missing for months and died before you knew about it. But you're not even going to lay her to rest?"

Gary flinched and paled.

"And clearly you aren't father-of-the-year material," I added bitingly, motioning to the space between us.

Maybe I was stepping too far over the line of too far, but this guy was seriously talking about business after finding out his child was dead. And he was too... what? Too vain to give her a proper funeral?

Whatever Mom's reasons were for keeping this guy out of my life were instantly forgiven. Clearly he was a narcissistic jerk, and I was better off without him.

"I'm not," he answered hoarsely. "I was young when your mother became pregnant, and I handled things horribly. Unforgivably. There's no excuse. The only reason I can give is that my parents had just died in an accident, and I was under an intense amount of pressure. Your mother was a distraction from my pain, and when I found out she was pregnant, I walked away. I gave her some money to handle the situation and washed my hands of it."

I was a *situation*. Another problem he could solve by throwing money at it.

Fabulous.

That stung a lot more than it should have.

"It wasn't until she showed up, seven months into the pregnancy, with an ultrasound of twin baby girls that I changed my mind. I made a deal with her." He looked away from me, shaking his head in self-disgust.

"Because you only needed *one* daughter, right?" I asked caustically.

"Yes," he admitted, finally meeting my eyes. I was surprised to see the pain in them. He cleared his throat. "I never wanted to be married or have children. It was an expectation I hated. But I knew about the codicil in the will where money was held in a trust for a daughter born into the Cabot line."

"And now she's gone," I told him flatly. "And you're back to square one."

"Am I?"

I frowned at him.

"You're a Cabot, Madison."

"Oh, *hell* no," I said sharply, backing toward the door. "No way. You can't just declare I'm your daughter so you have an option B."

"That's not what I meant," he said quickly. "Please, Madison. Please, give me a moment. I'm explaining all of this poorly."

"You have *a* minute," I shot back, ticking up one finger. "Then I'm gone."

"I hired nannies to raise your sister," he went on, blowing out a hard breath. "I was never around, until one night when Madelaine was seven. I was between trips, and the nanny had a family emergency. She left me alone with Madelaine, and Madelaine got sick."

He smiled sadly at the memory. "I had no idea what to do with a sick seven-year-old. I took her to the hospital, and the doctor said it was a nasty cold. But to watch her in case her fever spiked. I watched her all night, terrified I would lose her."

"And your money?" I asked archly.

"No," he replied honestly. "For the first time, it wasn't about the money. She was this... tiny human. Completely dependent on me. Dependent, and terrified of me. She didn't know me. I canceled my next trip and focused on her. On knowing my daughter."

I waited, silent and still judging.

"I wasn't perfect. I made mistakes, but I loved Lainey. I miss my girl. I miss her smile and her sense of humor. The way she drove me crazy, and the way she completed our family."

"That's sweet," I said after a heavy pause. "But forgive me if I can't relate."

"I was wrong, Madison. I never should have left you with your mother." He opened his laptop and spun it so I could see the screen.

A picture of my trailer was on the screen.

"I also had people looking into you last night as well," he added. "I had no idea your mom had blown through the money I gave her and the way you were living."

I took a small, involuntary step forward. "You gave her money?"

He nodded. "Of course. I wanted a clean break with her, and to also make sure that you were cared for. I gave her more than enough to raise you and for you both to live very comfortably."

He gave a junkie a massive payday? Brilliant.

I looked pointedly at the screen before meeting his gaze evenly. "That worked out great, didn't it?"

He looked down once more, flushing. "I can't apologize enough for the way you were left to fend for yourself, Madison. You have every right to hate me. To walk away and never look back."

Yeah, I did.

And yet I was still standing there.

Why was I still standing there?

"Did you know she was an addict?" I demanded.

He pressed his lips together briefly. "I knew she liked to party, but she was never out of control. Not like she was with you."

I snorted. "Nice of you to notice after the fact."

"I didn't find out until last night when I started looking into you," he replied honestly. "Madison, I was wrong. I was selfish. I tried to forget about Angie and... you."

Oh, that stung like a *bitch*.

I turned away, unable to look at him and unwilling to let him see the tears building.

"But even if you walk away now," he continued, "I'll take care of you. Whatever you need. A new house, a car... I'm not going to fail you the way I failed my Lainey. The way I failed you for your entire life."

"We wouldn't even be having this conversation if I hadn't found that damn picture on the internet," I muttered. "The only reason I'm standing here is because of a string of shit luck."

"Madison, I have no right to ask for your help, but I need it." His shoulders hunched as he aged before my eyes. Grief and worry sank into the lines of his body. "Losing Lainey is the worst sort of pain I could imagine, but now I'm also facing losing my father's legacy. My legacy, and Madelaine's. *Your* legacy."

I licked my lips. "I think I've learned my lesson, and I'm done pretending to be my sister. I also have zero desire to marry Ryan Cain."

He held up a hand. "I get it, and I would never ask you to marry him."

"Then what *are* you asking?"

"I'm asking you to give me time to figure out another way," he pleaded. "I'm asking for you to stay here. Attend Pacific Cross next semester, and play along, until I can dig us a way out of this hole."

"Play along?" I repeated, my brain not connecting the dots, but feeling like the answer was *right there*.

"Be Madelaine."

A hysterical laugh bubbled out of me. "Are you insane? No. No *way*. Pretending to be her for a summer was one thing. But I can't... I mean, I'm not... No *fucking* way."

He cringed a little but seemed determined. "Think of the chances a place like PC would offer you."

"Pacific Cross?" I spluttered, choking on a laugh. "No way. That's the most elite school ever."

"And I've seen your grades," he countered. "You're just as smart as Lainey, maybe more so, since you have more discipline than she ever did."

"Even still, how does that help me if I'm *her*?" I demanded wildly. "Do I just pretend to be Madelaine for the rest of my life?"

"If you like," he admitted with a shrug, but quickly backpedaled when he saw the look of stunned horror etched on my face. "Or not. Once you graduate *as Madelaine*, you'll be eighteen. Change your name to Madison Porter. Or whatever you like."

"No," I managed, shaking my head.

"Madelaine's grades are just as good as yours," he pointed out. "Academically it will be a lateral transfer for you. She's also captain of her cheerleading squad, as are you. The only difference is your name and location."

"Jesus, I really hope you don't think that's the only difference," I shot back, running a hand through my hair.

"Of course not," he snapped, his eyes flashing. As soon as his anger spiked, it disappeared. "Madison, I know this situation isn't ideal and I have no right to ask, but I need this."

"Why? Give me one good reason *why*."

He steepled his fingers and dragged into a slow breath. "I told you that Beckett and I are trying to work ourselves out of a quagmire our fathers left. We've been working with a pharmaceutical company on a new drug that will revolutionize health care. But we need the capital to finance the venture. The only way to keep from being outbid for the project is if we have the money, up front, for the buy-in."

"So, you're what? Broke?" I looked around incredulously at the room I was in.

"No. Not exactly," he murmured. "Our assets are more fluid than that. But this deal will set us up for life. Your life, your great-grandchildren's lives and beyond that."

"But you're asking me to step into my *sister's* life. To impersonate her to all of her friends. To her freaking fiancé!" I backed away, shaking my head. "I'm sorry that your dad left you a mess to deal with. It sucks when your dad isn't what you thought, isn't it?"

He flinched as my barb landed. "I know it's a lot to ask—"

"Try impossible," I cut him off. "Besides, I have a life back home."

"Do you?" he asked gently. "Working two jobs to make rent while your mother smokes her life away on the couch? Praying for a scholarship to a state school or community college? Madison, I can help you."

"You mean, as long as I do what you want."

"No," he answered vehemently. "I'll help you because you're my daughter. I'll transfer a million dollars into an account that only you can access for school tonight if you like. But the fact is, Madison Porter comes from a rundown town and a school with more casualties than scholarships. Pacific Cross is just what you said. An elite school that will open every door for you."

"And what about my mom? She's clean now."

He nodded. "I saw that. Madelaine paid for her treatment, didn't she?"

"Yeah. It was nice a Cabot finally stepped in to do the right thing."

"We can move her out here. I can help her get on her feet and get away from all the temptations of her old life when she's released." He gave me an imploring look.

I lifted my eyes to the ceiling and wondered if it was actually closing down on me, or if my overwhelmed mind was tricking me. "What about *my* life? My grades, my friends, my job?"

The look that crept into his eyes could only be considered as pitying. "Madison, you won't need to work one, let alone two, jobs while going to school. Your grades are fairly on par with your sister's, so academically, you'll be at the same point. But with the added benefit of a PCA diploma and the Cabot name attached to you." He took a deep breath. "And, forgive me, but it doesn't seem like you have many friends to go back to. Am I wrong?"

He wasn't. And God, putting it like that, I felt so stupid and small.

What *did* I have to go back to? A cheerleading squad that was always on the brink of not happening because getting girls to join (and stay) was a nightmare? Or my job at the diner, where my boss frequently made a pass at me and the other girls? Or maybe I would miss walking into school and wondering if my mechanical pencil would set off the metal detectors and warrant a pat-down?

Cliftown was nothing but bad memories and stale dreams.

"And what happens if this all falls apart?" I demanded, hating that I was even considering his offer. "What if you can't get out of the deals you've made? I'm not marrying a stranger for money. I'm not."

"I agree," Gary replied, giving me a smal, almost bemused, smile. "I guess if this all fails... maybe I can buy the trailer next door?"

CHAPTER 15

The only thing I refused to budge on was a burial for Madelaine. So, when her remains were delivered in a nondescript urn several days after I made my deal with Gary, I joined him in a large mausoleum that held the remains of many deceased Cabots.

It wasn't a creepy, dank room like TV and movies made mausoleums out to be. The vault was elegant and brightly lit both by wall sconces and the California sunlight that streamed in through the glass ceiling.

We were the only two mourners there, and I briefly wondered if we should have waited for Mom. Madelaine was her daughter, too.

The simple engraving next to the empty space said: **M. Cabot**

I would have snapped at Gary about being an unfeeling ass if he didn't look completely wrecked holding the urn in his hands, his knuckles white and fingers shaking a bit.

The drive here was the most father-daughter bonding we had done the last few days. He was always holed up in his office or out on business.

He cleared his throat, the sound strangled. "I, uh, don't really know what to do. All the times I've been here over the years, I never expected I would be laying Lainey in here, too."

I would have to be a total bitch not to feel moved by that.

He was still her father. Hell, he was *our* father. Maybe he was throwing himself into work so he could avoid his feelings.

Maybe that's where I got that trait from.

Staying busy to avoid unpacking an emotional suitcase was my normal plane of existence.

I hesitated for a second before placing a comforting hand on his shoulder. He glanced at me, looking stunned.

"I'm sorry," I said, not sure why I felt the constant need to apologize. Maybe because Madelaine would still be alive if I had never sent her that message. Miserable, but alive.

He gently set the urn inside the vacant cavity. "She always wanted a sibling."

The declaration rocked me to the core.

"I think the two of you would have gotten along well," he added, closing the door and securing it with a key he then pocketed.

"I used to want that, too," I admitted as I followed him out of the crypt and waited for him to lock the doors once again. "When Mom was on a bender or would go missing, I would want someone to share that loneliness with."

His eyes drifted closed, a pained expression taking over. "I failed you, Madison. I failed both of my daughters."

I couldn't really respond to that, because he was right. He had trapped Madelaine, all but forcing her to run away for a breather that led to her death. And he had completely abandoned me.

"Could we... Could we go grab something to eat? I have to leave for Paris tomorrow morning, and you're leaving for school the next day. I'd like us to spend some time together before you go." The words came out in a rush, like he was expecting me to say no.

"Sure," I agreed with a tiny shrug. "I have questions about... a lot of things."

He paused and took my hand in his. "I'll try to answer every single one of them."

I SCOOTED my chair as close to the table as I could, glancing around the upscale steakhouse and praying the white linens would fall over my legs enough to hide the fact that I was hopelessly underdressed. Leggings and a t-shirt didn't match the business suits and pencil skirts of the patrons and staff around us.

Gary didn't seem to mind, but he was also in a suit.

Our waitress paused by our table and waited as Gary perused the wine selection before making his choice. She turned to me expectantly.

"Water would be great," I said softly.

"Sparkling, still, or tap?" she rattled off.

I blinked. "Uh."

"Still would be perfect," Gary jumped in for me.

"Any infusions? We have a wonderful cucumber-lemon or our organic citrus," she added, waiting for my decision.

I pressed my lips together. "Just plain water. Please."

"Make that two," Gary added, holding up two fingers and effectively dismissing her.

"Who knew that there were so many kinds of water," I muttered, feeling self-conscious as I stroked the leather binding of the menu before opening it.

My gaze narrowed and I tried to make sense of what I was seeing. I finally glanced up at him from across the table. My gaze wandered as I took in the room. "This is nice."

"Fogo is the premier Brazilian steakhouse on the West Coast," he told me with a smile. His gaze roamed around the vast space before he winced. "And I'm realizing how ridiculous this place must look to you."

"It's definitely not McDonald's," I agreed with a grimace.

He forced a laugh. "No. I suppose it's not. But they have a wonderful chopped salad."

I tried not to make a face. "Who gets salad at a steakhouse?"

After a beat his face fell. "Madelaine only ever ate salads. I'm sorry, I just assumed..."

"You said the first night that you saw me it looked like I had gained weight," I pointed out gently. "I like my carbs."

"Of course," he said quickly. "Order whatever you like. I always worried that Lainey put too much emphasis on dieting. I'm glad you aren't the same."

I looked down at the menu. "I still don't know how to read Spanish."

He smiled softly. "It's Portuguese, actually."

I sucked in a sharp breath. "Yeah, can't read that one either."

"Of course." Shaking his head in bemusement, he rattled off several of the options and helped me decide on one.

The waitress returned to our table and set our drinks on the table before looking at Gary expectantly. "Ready to order?"

"Of course," he said smoothly, then balked and looked at me. "I never asked... Madelaine was allergic to peanuts."

I gave him a tiny smile. "I am, too."

He gave me a knowing nod before rattling off our order to the waitress. I blushed when he insisted—several times—that she note my allergy. It was oddly sweet, and I was fighting a grin as she walked away to let the kitchen know not to accidentally kill me.

I let out a shaky breath once she had gone. "So."

"Madison," he started at the same time.

With nervous laughs, we both stopped. Awkward silence lingered between us.

"Please, you first," Gary encouraged, and took a sip of his wine.

I bit my lower lip. "I'm still not entirely sure that this will work. I mean, I've done some research on the school, but won't Madison's friends know something's wrong with me?"

Sighing, Gary set his glass back on the table. "It wasn't just Ryan and the wedding that Madelaine was running from. You're a smart girl, Madison."

Frowning, I let my thoughts drift back. "At dinner, you said something about last semester? A few people have kind of alluded to it, but I don't know what happened."

He cleared his throat and lowered his voice an octave. "The truth is, Lainey and I argued before her spring break last year. We both said a lot of horrible things, and one thing you don't know is how... vindictive your sister could be. Manipulative, even."

"Okaaay... " I dragged out the word, my eyebrows raising curiously.

"She had an affair with one of her professors at Pacific Cross," he told me evenly. "And they were discovered. The entire school found out, and Madelaine was shunned by her peers for her indiscretion. He was something of a favorite teacher and was, needless to say, terminated."

"Holy shit," I whispered.

He blanched slightly at my words. "She did it to spite me. To make *me* look bad. Well, me and Ryan. She wasn't his biggest fan."

"You don't say," I deadpanned.

He chuckled and rubbed his jaw. "Once you're at school, Ryan will be busy with his studies and football. I'm sure you'll be able to entertain yourself."

"Just not with any of her friends," I murmured, reaching for my water.

He grimaced. "No. Children can be cruel, and Madelaine was... Well, she was an easy target to tear down when the scandal happened."

"And her friends dropped her? For *that*?" My nose scrunched up. "She was a kid. He was the adult."

"One thing you must know is that in this world, people will always be searching for ways to drag you down."

"That's... depressing."

His gaze sharpened. "That's reality, Madison. You're a Cabot now, and with that name comes a lot of power in our world. People will seek to destroy you simply as a stepping stone to their own power."

"You're aware of how twisted that sounds, right?" I hissed, glancing around for anyone who might be listening in. "And you're trying to convince me to live in this world full-time for the next year?"

"I'm well aware of the downside to this life, but as you said—it's just for a year," he replied sadly. "The point I was ultimately trying to make is that Madelaine's friends have all but abandoned her. Teenagers aren't known for their forgiving and understanding nature, as I'm sure you know."

I nodded mutely.

So, I was to spend the next year essentially by myself?

I could do that. I had been doing that for most of my life. Sure, I'd had a few friends and even dated a few times, but I was used to surviving on my own.

Keeping my head down and focusing on school wouldn't be a problem.

"What about cheerleading?" I found a new hole in the plan and tugged. "I don't know their cheers or routines. And Madelaine was head of the squad."

"As you were head of yours," he returned. "If I were to show you tapes of her routines, do you think you could learn them?"

"Probably. You have her cheers recorded?"

I hadn't pegged Gary Cabot as the type of dad to show up to his daughter's competitions with a handheld camera because he was so proud.

He slid a sleek-looking phone across the table to me. I gently picked it up and powered it on.

"The passcode is your birthday," he prompted.

I typed in the code, and it opened to a new screen with a generic background and dozens of apps I had heard of but never used.

"I had Lainey's phone cloned," he explained softly. "All her pictures, email, social media apps, and more are on there. I know for a fact that she recorded every cheer practice and competition. She was always looking for ways to improve her squad."

I tapped the photo button and sucked in a breath as the album loaded.

This was my twin's life. What it looked like through her eyes.

"The phone number is the same, too, so you should be able to find out any details you need about Lainey." He choked on the last word, his eyes slightly misty.

Tucking the phone into my purse, I reached out with my free hand across the table. "Thank you."

"I do have one more request," he said after squeezing my hand. "The daughter of my business associate also attends Pacific Cross. She's a bit of an outsider. She and Madelaine were good friends as children but drifted apart years ago. Her father asked if I could persuade my daughter to extend an olive branch. Malcolm Whittier is a technological genius I would love to have involved in the Shutterfield project."

"I guess." How sad would it be to have your father broker you a new friendship as a bonus to a business deal?

Said the girl pretending to be her dead twin for a chance at the college of her dreams.

Sometimes I wanted to bitch-slap my own inner voice.

"Wonderful. He's arranged for her car to take you to PC. The drive is only a couple of hours," he informed me as our food was delivered. "They'll pick you up on the way. I'll have Madelaine's car delivered by the end of next week so you can drive around as you wish."

I froze en route to picking up my fork. "I can't drive."

He gave me a funny look. "Truly?"

I nodded. "*Truly.*"

"I can arrange lessons for you." He began cutting into his steak. "And, in fact, why don't we wait on the car? You can select one of your choosing."

"You want to buy me a car?" My jaw dropped open. "What about Madelaine's?"

He waved a dismissive hand. "We'll sell it. Or, hell, maybe I'll just donate it for the write-off."

A stunned, breathless laugh escaped me. "Are you serious?"

"You're my daughter, I'm your father. Isn't it my right to purchase your first vehicle?" He flashed me an indulgent smile. "I'm aware that you're not my Lainey, and I would never try to replace her. But you are my daughter, and I intend to spoil you to make up for all the birthdays and holidays I've missed."

A tiny fissure of warmth cracked open a corner of my heart I had forgotten existed.

And damn, it felt good.

CHAPTER 16

Two days later, when I was leaving for school, a package was waiting for me. Inside was a fresh copy of Madelaine's license, her school ID, and more credit cards than I could have imagined, including a black one that I had been convinced was actually a myth.

I dressed and re-dressed, unsure what to wear on my first day of pretending to be my sister. At least the school had mandatory uniforms, so that took the guesswork out of not making some huge fashion faux pas, but I couldn't show up in my navy plaid skirt and blazer the day I moved into my dorm.

I had been doing it all summer, but the staff and the house felt like a very amateur dress rehearsal for the real stage: Pacific Cross Academy.

At least the uniforms were new and totally mine. Madelaine's hadn't fit since I was a couple sizes bigger, but she apparently got a new set of uniforms at the start of each semester. It might not have seemed like much, but at least I wasn't *literally* stepping into my sister's shoes.

"You have a wonderful semester, and I'll see you at break," Mrs. Delancey told me warmly in the foyer as a car pulled into the drive.

Of course it was a freaking limo, because God forbid rich people were driven around in anything except complete luxury.

The shiny black mammoth of a car glided to a stop in front of the house a second before the driver got out and headed to the back. He met one of the staff at the rear, and they started loading my suitcases into the back of the car.

I stepped outside when they got to the third one, wondering exactly what Mrs. Delancey had bought when I'd declined a last-minute shopping trip yesterday in favor of watching cheer practice videos on Madelaine's phone.

It was a private school with uniforms. It wasn't like I needed a lot of options. But bags four and five were added, so I was growing a little worried.

"Ms. Cabot?"

I turned and realized the driver had finished with my luggage and was now holding open the door to the limo, waiting with an expectant look on his dour face.

"Thank you," I murmured as I slid into the backseat.

The driver closed the door as soon as I was tucked inside.

The interior was roomy, with two leather benches, tinted windows, and a mini bar. And a girl curled up with a tablet on the far side, her big hazel eyes looking warily at me.

"Hey," I greeted, forcing a smile.

Her jaw dropped, those doll-like eyes getting even rounder on her face. "Um, hey."

"Rebecca, right?" Maybe I could rekindle a bit of that childhood friendship vibe. It couldn't hurt having *someone* to consider a friend.

Or something close to it.

"Uh, yeah," she stammered. Her gaze roved around the ceiling for a brief second. Her jaw clenched like she was irritated. "Like you didn't know. How was your summer, *Madelaine*?"

A complete train wreck.

"Uneventful," I answered quickly. Silence stretched between us, and I grappled for words to fill it. "I like your hat."

Actually, I liked everything about her outfit. From the army green cloche hat to the fishnet stockings and ripped denim jeans, she looked like a petite rocker chick. A few chunks of her brown hair looked purple or blue, but it was hard to tell in the lighting.

It looked insanely more comfortable than the pencil skirt, blouse and kitten heels I had on. I felt like I should be going to a board meeting instead of my senior year of high school.

Her brows lifted comically at my compliment, though. "Excuse me?"

"Your hat," I repeated, waving a hand at it. "It's cool."

Her eyes narrowed. "My hat is *cool*?"

Was there an echo in here? Was *cool* not a word these people said when something looks good?

I nodded slowly.

She dropped the tablet to the bench beside her before leaning back and glowering at me. "Fine. Let's hear it."

"Hear what?" I frowned at her, confused as hell.

"Whatever bitchy comment comes next," she snapped. "Or is this like seventh grade when you convinced me that Birkenstocks were coming back into fashion so I wore them for a damn year."

Truth be told, I was not entirely sure what a Birkenstock was, but judging by the way she practically spat the words at me, it couldn't be a good thing.

Also? Yet another clue that my twin was a serious bitch.

"I didn't mean anything other than I like it," I replied quietly.

Rebecca only blinked at me. I'm not sure which one of us was the most confused now.

"Did you have a lobotomy or something?"

I glanced down at my hands and realized I was picking at my nails. I chipped a fleck of pale pink polish from my pinky.

"Or something," I muttered as the car started and began its descent down the long driveway.

Rebecca sighed, and I was stunned to see tears in her eyes when I looked up.

"Can we just not, Madelaine?" she whispered, looking out the window. "It's our last year of school. I'm pretty over all the deception and lies and manipulations. I get it. You *hate* me. Making my life hell is your number one form of entertainment. But I kind of thought after what happened to you last year, you'd have learned your lesson."

Last year.

When my sister got busted for sleeping with a teacher and the student body turned on her like a school of piranhas.

Unease prickled up my spine. "Rebecca, I really didn't mean anything. I like your hat. That's it. I'm not trying to be a bitch or anything."

"Bullshit!" she exploded.

The switch from quiet mouse to roaring lion made me jump.

Her small fist thumped on the empty seat beside her as she glared at me. "You've spent the last *decade* making my life a living hell, Madelaine."

Oh, shit.

I knew the look of a bullied girl when I saw one. I'd seen it on too many people in my old life to count, including me in middle school when I went through a seriously awkward phase.

Whatever my sister had done to Rebecca was bad...

... and Rebeccca thought I was Madelaine.

"You expect me to believe that you're suddenly a new person? That all this sweetness is legit?" Rebecca blinked away furious tears. "What's the endgame? You think if you remind everyone at Pacific Cross that I'm still a loser that they'll welcome back their queen?"

"No—"

"Because you're wrong," she raged on, not caring that I was trying to speak. "Everyone remembers. It's all anyone has talked about for months. Even a *loser* like me knows about it. Your reign is over. Thank fucking God, the queen is *dead*."

I flinched and sucked in a sharp breath as her words hit a little too close to home.

Madelaine *was* dead.

But I highly doubted she knew that. The symbolic social death she was talking about was something my dearly departed sister hadn't mentioned and I was only starting to grasp the depth of.

Then again, there was a *lot* Madelaine hadn't mentioned about her life that I was starting to wonder if I would ever get answers to.

I glanced down at my hands once more, unsure what else to say or do. The only thing I had left to offer was the one thing my twin probably never gave.

"I'm sorry," I apologized softly, genuinely. I prayed that she heard the sincerity in my voice, because it was there. This girl deserved an apology for whatever shit Madelaine had pulled.

I met her eyes as I repeated the sentiment. "I'm really sorry, Rebecca."

Rebecca frowned, her hazel eyes flaring wide. I'd caught her off guard, but she was quick to rally her defenses.

"It doesn't really matter now, does it, *Maddie?*" She hurled the name at me like an insult, but it was the first time in weeks that I had heard my name on someone's lips.

The tears that pricked my eyes hit too fast for me to cover them up, and Rebecca was watching me too sharply to miss them. I braced for the onslaught of her rage to rise up again, but instead she softened. It was a small hesitation, but I latched on to it like a boon.

"I'm really sorry, Rebecca," I whispered again, not looking away and letting her see the single tear that fell.

Her lips mashed together in a mulish line. She was trying to figure out if she could trust me or not, and I couldn't blame her.

"I haven't seen you cry in years," Rebecca admitted quietly. "Not since that night in the hospital before... Before you decided to cut me off."

"I made a mistake," I said, knowing in my heart it was true. Something about this girl was genuine and true, and I wasn't willing to cast her aside the way my sister had for some reason.

Rebecca scoffed under her breath. "I wanted to help you. That's why I went to the hospital. You were my *best friend*. You told me about what your dad was making you do. And then you went away... "

I bit the inside of my lip, her words making me curious. "I don't remember much about what happened."

Rebecca's gaze sharpened. "It's no wonder, considering all the meds they had you on." Dark clouds filled her expression as she recalled a memory I was oblivious to. "And then you came back and acted like I was insane. Told everyone I was an obsessed stalker who wouldn't leave you alone. Remember *that*?"

The bitterness was back in her biting tone, and I rapidly tried to think of a way to pull her back from the edge of anger.

"You tried to be my friend," I said slowly, cautiously, "and I was... I was a mess, Rebecca. I was a bitch. I know that now."

"Now that the school has turned against you?" she added frostily. "Pretty convenient."

"I don't deserve your forgiveness," I continued, scrambling for words to make the apology meaningful without showing I was hopelessly confused by a lot of backstory I wasn't privy to. "But I am sorry."

"Why did you do it?" Rebecca asked after a long pause of silence.

"I don't know." It was the truth. The complete truth. "I really don't know what I was thinking back then. But taking it out on you was wrong."

"Then *why* do it?"

I considered the question and thought about what possible reason Madelaine could have had for screwing this girl over. Perfect Madelaine was nothing more than a pretty painting for the world to see.

Somehow Rebecca had seen the messy, fraying canvas underneath.

"You were too close," I murmured, looking away. "Cutting you out of my life meant I didn't have to think about... what had happened."

Rebecca stared at me for another beat before shutting off whatever emotional pull she was feeling toward me. "Yeah, well, it's ancient history now, right, Maddie?"

Again she tossed my name out like I should have been offended.

"Rebecca—"

"Bex," she cut me off coldly. "Only my family calls me Rebecca. You're *not* my family. You aren't my friend. You're... You're *nothing*."

I closed my mouth and leaned back in the seat.

So much for making a friend.

CHAPTER 17

Pacific Cross was even more impressive than I had thought from pictures on the website. I was left standing on a beautiful cobblestone path in amazement after the driver unloaded our bags and passed them off to a staff member to deliver to our rooms.

The academy dorms were located on the far eastern side of campus. There were five total: two for the boys, two for the girls, and one for staff. The staff one was notably smaller and not nearly as pristine as the students' dormitories, which boasted white walls, sharp lines, and lots of glass windows.

Bex disappeared within seconds of the first bag being unloaded, pulling her hat down and hunching her shoulders as she made a beeline for the upperclassmen girls' building without saying a word to me.

Clearly *that* relationship was a dead end.

Which meant I was truly on my own.

But, standing in front of the main building on the Pacific Cross campus, I couldn't help the tendril of excitement that threaded through the fog of doubt.

This next year could set up my entire future. I could go to the college of my dreams, wherever that might be. Maybe even land the job of my dreams. I didn't have to be Cabot-rich, but it would be nice to not worry about rent payments being late or choosing between groceries and electricity. I could survive a year as Madelaine Cabot before I changed my name to Madison Porter. Or Cabot.

Honestly, I wasn't sure what I should do once this year was over. But I knew I couldn't keep my sister's name forever. I didn't want to take over her life, but I did want to honor it.

I couldn't change what had happened, but maybe living my life to the absolute fullest would somehow balance the scales for my sister's death.

I let myself wonder for a second what it would have been like to step into this world with her at my side. The daydream lingered long enough for tears to start misting my eyes.

Unfortunately I was snapped out of my musing when a hard body collided with mine and nearly knocked me down.

"Sorry! So sorry!"

I glanced at the guy who had run into me, smiling a bit at his decidedly British accent. Between the accent, the green eyes, and the windswept chestnut hair, he was easily one of the hottest guys I'd ever seen.

He squinted at me. "Are you all right?"

"It's fine," I assured him after a second. "I probably shouldn't be standing in the middle of the path."

"You *are* much too pretty to be a statue," he agreed with a grin that showcased matching dimples.

I felt a blush creep across my cheeks and I dipped my head. "Thanks."

"My mum would have my arse for being so rude," he muttered, rolling his eyes and holding out a hand. "Charles Winthrope the Fourth."

I blinked several times before accepting the handshake. Seriously? *That* was his name?

Charles Winthrope *the Fourth.*

A million *Star Wars* jokes ran through my head before I realized I still hadn't told him my name, and now a weird amount of time had passed, making me look totally spastic.

"Madi—" I coughed to cover my almost slip. "Madelaine Cabot. My friends call me Maddie."

"Pleasure to meet you," he replied. "I just transferred in from Oxford, and I'm a bit lost."

"It's a big campus."

"Would you perhaps have time for a tour?" he asked, innocently enough, but I was as much in need of a tour as he was.

"Oh. Um..."

The answer was still formulating in my brain when a lithe body inserted herself between us, her heels stepping on my toes too hard to be accidental.

"I'd be happy to show you around, Charles," the girl between us purred, flicking a mane of dark hair back to slap me in the face. "Or do you prefer *Your Grace*?"

Charles glanced over her shoulder at me, just as confused as I was, until the girl turned and I placed her from Madelaine's cheer videos and a few of the social media posts from when I first started trying to find my twin.

Brylee Sallinger.

Looked like she wasn't just a raging bitch at practice. It extended to everyday life, too.

When replaying Lainey's cheer videos, I'd watched her ream out girls on the squad when they made the smallest of mistakes, but there was a shrewd cattiness to her gaze that the camera hadn't quite captured. And judging by the way Brylee was glaring at me, she absolutely hated Lainey.

"Oh, sorry, Madelaine. Didn't even see you there," she chirped, her dark eyes gloating as she tossed a glossy wave of mahogany hair over one shoulder.

"Charles is fine," he confirmed, pulling her attention back. "But Maddie and I were just talking."

Her laughter was as sharp as her angular body. "*Maddie*? I believe *Maddie* has to meet her fiancé."

"Fiancé?" Surprise colored his voice.

Brylee turned, slipping her arm inside the crook of Charles' with practiced ease. "Yes." She glanced up at him through a fringe of false lashes. "But I would love to show you around. My father is part of the board and was so excited to have a duke attending Pacific Cross this year. We're all thrilled."

Charles looked between us, just as uncomfortable as I was.

He gingerly extracted himself from her claws. "Yes, well, it's been a taxing day, and I would love a rest before dinner."

"I'll save you a seat," Brylee told him, her smile turning brittle at the edges and then vanishing completely as he walked away.

I started moving around her, but froze when her hand shot out and grabbed my arm, her nails digging in.

"*Maddie?*" she scoffed, eyeing me up and down. "You think switching your name will make people forget what a slut you are?"

I grit my teeth. "I was just being polite."

"Is that hooker slang for easy?" She smirked.

I tilted my head to the side. "So, am I a slut? Or a hooker?"

"Same difference," she spat.

I *tsk*ed at her and shook my head before yanking my arm away hard enough to send her teetering on her heels. "It's not. See a hooker gets *paid*. A slut does it for free. It's a subtle difference, but it's there."

Her lip curled up in disgust. "Whatever. Keep your skanky gash away from Charles."

"It's a free country." I sighed with feigned regret. "And I'll flash my *skanky gash* anywhere I please, thanks."

She stepped closer to me, her eyes flashing. "Not for you, it isn't. I'm done playing backup to you. Things are different this year, and if you need a reminder, I'll happily give it to you."

I pressed my lips into a thin line. "Noted. Are we done here?"

"For now," she said mockingly.

"Great," I muttered, walking around her since she sure as hell wasn't getting out of my way.

I had secretly been hoping for some solidarity from the cheer squad, but apparently Madelaine had burned those bridges to the ground and scattered the ashes.

Honestly I wasn't surprised. The videos had been hard to watch.

My twin had been merciless with her squad, berating and belittling in her quest for perfection. I had even stumbled on a document on the phone where she tracked the girls' weights and made notes.

In a lot of the videos, Brylee had been her wingwoman, happy to tear down any girl Madelaine deemed lacking.

Gary had been right; people were happy to see Madelaine fall.

I focused my attention on hurrying to my dorm, threading through the pathways until I came upon the ten-story white-stone building named Harrison Hall for one of the school's founding fathers.

The dorms were set up on a bit of a hill and when I turned, I could see the rest of the campus sprawled below me across several miles. There were separate buildings for the university and academy students for academics, but they shared a few communal buildings, like the dining hall and theater. Farther away was the university housing, including a few dormitories but then an almost out of place row of houses for the fraternities and sororities on campus. If you took a snapshot of only the Greek row, it would look like your typical millionaire mansion-lined street, complete with grassy lawns, pools, and lush trees.

Black asphalt paths snaked around the campus for drivers, and cobblestone paths wound between buildings for pedestrians. There was a large, grassy quad area in the center and a small lake tucked along the back of the property where I could just make out a rowing team gliding across the glassy surface.

Hopefully all this open space meant Ryan would stay on his side of the campus and I could ghost my way through mine.

Nine months. Barely one hundred and eighty days.

That was all I had to survive for my senior year.

I headed inside Harrison Hall, ignoring the squeals and shouts of friends reuniting, the slamming doors and the girls running back and forth. Several ran into me, as oblivious to my presence as they were a wall.

Others glared at me. Some whispered.

I kept my head down as I stepped into the elevator and used my keycard to activate the button for the top floor, then positioned myself at the back of the car while others crowded in.

No one spoke to me, but all of them looked at me. Most with derision, one with shock.

I was the only person left when the elevator reached my level. It was quiet on the top floor. No one was milling around in the halls and suddenly I could see why.

Instead of a hallway of door after door after door, there were barely twelve doors on this floor, six on either side of the hall. From the ground I had seen that this level boasted balconies and decks, so it didn't take a genius to infer this was the highest-dollar district of the school. I didn't want to know how much Gary had shelled out for this.

Pacific Cross was a school for the richest of the rich, but even it had a hierarchy and it started with where you slept.

My room was at the end of the hall to the right, and I sighed in relief when I saw no one was around as I hurried toward it.

Toward my own personal sanctuary.

I slipped the key in the lock and twisted, then shoved the door open and stepped inside before slamming it and flipping the locks. I leaned against it and sucked in a ragged breath, my eyes closing as I sagged.

"Rough morning, baby?"

My eyes snapped open and my jaw dropped.

How in the actual hell...

Ryan stood up slowly from the desk chair, his cold smile anything but welcoming as he looked at me.

So much for my sanctuary.

CHAPTER 18

"What the hell are you doing here?" I blurted out, my back stiffening as I straightened and stared at him.

The door was situated in a small alcove, and he prowled to the opening, effectively caging me in the tiny space. I could try to turn and unlock the deadbolt, throw open the door, and make a break for it.

But that would have been utterly pointless.

He would grab me before my fingers grazed the metal of the bolt.

"I just came to make sure you got settled in," he said innocently enough, leaning a massive shoulder against the wall like we were old friends and this was a normal social visit.

It was almost painful trying to keep the tremors from my voice. I couldn't let him see how off-kilter his presence threw me. "Thanks for that. I'm good."

"And already making friends," he went on, his tone sharpening enough to send warning bells trilling in my head.

"Not exactly," I answered.

His gaze turned thunderous, and I knew I'd said the wrong thing.

"The duke isn't someone you want to be friends with?" His brows lifted, mocking and challenging. "I hear he's quite the catch."

"Well, you officially have my blessing to make a play for him," I snapped, annoyed and tired all of the sudden. "I can probably snag his number if you need it."

He was in my face a second later and all my snark disappeared instantly.

"Stay away from him," Ryan hissed, his chest brushing mine as it heaved. His icy blue eyes lit with fury. "I'm not fucking kidding, Madelaine."

I pressed myself as hard against the door as possible, but the wood might as well have been made from steel for as much as it gave. "He bumped into me. We said hi."

"And we all know how *friendly* you can be," he growled.

I flinched. If he only knew the truth.

I was definitely not as *friendly* as my sister.

The closest I had come to being considered friendly was when I went on a date with Kevin Lewis last year. Instead of the movie we'd agreed on, he drove us to an abandoned parking lot to "talk."

He kissed me. I said no. He tried shoving his hand down my pants, and I damn near Mike Tyson'd his ear.

"It really wasn't like that," I muttered, shaking my hair out of my face.

"It better not be," he warned, still using that growly tone that made my stomach flutter.

Truthfully, though? I wasn't sure if it was from fear or some other emotion I wasn't willing to label.

He leaned in closer, the scent of his cologne—clean but masculine—filled my senses. "You're *mine* as far as this school goes, and everyone knows I don't share. So if you think I'm going to stand for you to flirt with some other guy—"

I snorted. "I wasn't flirting. Jesus."

His hand shot out, holding my throat with enough pressure that I could feel the strength behind his grip. My heart slammed against my ribs as I gasped.

"You better not be," he murmured darkly. "If I need to fuck you in the middle of the quad to show everyone that you're mine, I will."

My eyes narrowed even as my pulse raced. "You wouldn't dare."

"Wouldn't I?" he refuted archly. "Baby, I would strip you, tie you to one of the benches and show the entire fucking school *exactly* what belongs to me."

"I thought you wouldn't touch me with a cast-iron dick," I shot back, reminding him of our last encounter.

He snorted, his eyes flashing dangerously. "I might make an exception to prove a point. Don't underestimate me."

I swallowed loud enough for him to hear it. "Let me go."

His thumb swept the pulse point on my throat, and I knew he could feel my erratic heartbeat. "Or maybe you'd like that. Maybe that video last year wasn't an accident. Who knew you were a little exhibitionist?"

"Let. Go." I jerked back in an effort to get his hand off me and cracked my head against the door.

His lips thinned and, after a second, he let his hand fall from my neck. "I mean it, Lainey."

Then his head tilted to the side, part of his mouth kicking up in a half smile that was way hotter than it should be for such an asshole.

"Or is it *Maddie*?" The words danced across his lips mockingly.

My jaw dropped. "What—"

"Do you think you can say a single fucking word that I won't hear?" he taunted. "I even know what color panties you're wearing."

My eyes narrowed, and I stupidly said the first thing that came to mind: "Maybe I'm not wearing any."

His eyes widened for a fraction of a second, and a thrill shot through me knowing that I'd surprised him. The hand that had been on my neck now rested on the outside of my thigh. I could feel his touch burning through the fabric of my skirt.

"Is that an invitation to test that theory?"

"N-no," I stammered, shaking my head, realizing my snark had, not for the first time in my life, propelled me into a situation I really didn't want to be in. "I was just... I didn't mean..."

He snorted and ripped away from me so fast, I was left stunned by the abrupt absence of his touch.

"Don't worry, *Maddie*, I wouldn't actually touch you with a ten-

MAD WORLD

foot-pole covered in five condoms." His gaze dropped to my skirt with a sneer. "I'm not into STDs, and fuck knows, your cunt has had more traffic than LAX."

My spine snapped to attention. "How about if you fuck all the way off?"

He dropped back into the chair he'd been in early. "We still have shit to work out. Sit."

"I'm not a damn dog," I snapped.

His smirk turned even crueler. "But you *are* my bitch, so sit the fuck down before I make you."

I folded my arms across my chest in defiance.

"Actually? I like you standing better," he said after a pause. He waved a hand down his body. "I sit, you stand. Like a king presiding over a... peasant."

"You're an asshole," I hissed, moving forward and taking a seat on the couch. I tossed my purse on the other side and glared at him.

"Let's start with the attitude first," he started, leaning back in the chair. "You want to act like the bitch you really are in private, go for it. I couldn't care less if you're happy about this shit or not, but in public? You're my doting fiancée."

"And what makes you think I'll agree to that?" I scoffed, shaking my head.

"Baby, I can make your life miserable really fast. Do you actually want to test me?" The coldness of his tone was like freaking Elsa came down and built an ice castle in the room.

Instead of verbally agreeing, I just nodded.

"You'll be at all my games with the squad anyway," he went on, "but you'll wait for me outside the locker room like a good little girlfriend."

I wrinkled my nose. "But why—"

He clicked his tongue against his teeth and a vein throbbed at his temple. I was quickly coming to realize that was a sign he was getting annoyed.

Hell, he was *always* annoyed.

"Team parties, fraternity parties, and anything else I decide you'll attend, you will. And you'll look the fucking part even if I have to pick out your outfits myself."

"You have some serious control issues, don't you?" I sighed, rolling my eyes.

"You mean since it came out that my fiancée was fucking my—" He cut himself off, hate twisting his beautiful face into something to be feared. Raking a hand through his hair, he pinned me with a glare. "Yeah. If we want to sell this relationship, you're going to show the world that you can go from dirty skank to actual fucking lady."

I literally bit down on the insides of my mouth to keep from replying.

Or screaming.

Honestly? It could've gone either way.

"If I'm such a disappointment, why not break this off and save us both a lot of trouble?" I demanded hotly.

His gaze went from scary intense to scarier. "You fucking know why."

I didn't, but I had a feeling now wasn't the time to play twenty questions with him.

"Yeah, right," I mumbled. "Are we done?"

Please say we're done.

Ryan stood up slowly. "I'll be back to pick you up at eight."

"Why?" I asked flatly, having zero interest in spending any time with him.

He flashed me a grim smile. "Welcome back party at my fraternity house. And it'll be our first public appearance together on campus. Make sure you look hot."

"So you can show off your *skank*?" Disgust flooded my tone as I sent him a sharp glare.

He leaned over me, eyes bright as he used his index finger to tip my chin up. "You might be an evil bitch, and we might be stuck together, but you're gorgeous. And I'm happy to show off what's *mine*."

I should've been offended by that "mine" comment, but I was still (stupidly) hung up on the "gorgeous" part. It warmed up places in me that should have stayed dormant and frigid. At least where Ryan was involved.

"Okay," I agreed, capitulating easily enough.

"Good girl, *Maddie*," he whispered. He pulled back and cocked his head. "You know, when I heard you were going by that name, I thought it was yet another bullshit attempt to distance yourself from last year. But it suits you."

"Does it?" I asked hoarsely.

"Yeah," he agreed with a grin. "It sounds just as common as you really are."

I flinched at the barb, which only made him chuckle as he left me alone. The door slammed shut with a bang that shook the walls.

I really needed to have new locks installed.

CHAPTER 19

P art of me was secretly glad that Ryan had decided to come and pick me up for the party. Pulling up to the massive, three-story brick house with people spilled all over the front lawn and the doors thrown open to show even more people crushed inside, I knew I would've chickened out and turned around.

Ryan pulled effortlessly into the open driveway and into a reserved parking spot in the frat's private lot.

I glanced at the sign marking the spot and blinked.

VICE PRESIDENT CAIN

Being a junior, it wasn't really surprising that he would be in some sort of leadership role at the biggest (and probably douchey-est) frat at PC.

"Let's go," he muttered, opening the door of some fancy Italian sports car that was a gorgeous shade of blue so deep it looked black. He didn't come to help me when he slammed the door, which meant I needed to figure out how to get out of this bucket seat without flashing everyone my underwear.

I wouldn't have had that issue if Ryan hadn't made me change.

Apparently the sundress and flip-flops I had selected looked like I was going to a church picnic.

Ryan stormed into my closet and yanked out a tiny eggplant-colored dress and strappy black heels, throwing them on the bed and telling me that I had five minutes to change or he'd strip me himself.

Admittedly, the short skirt and the heels made my legs look amazing. And the purple was a stunning color.

But the dress had hardly any give, and I wobbled like a baby deer in the heels.

I pushed open the door and struggled to my feet as Ryan watched. Finally on my feet, I shot him a glare across the hood of the car. "Thanks for the help."

He gave me an innocent look. "Did you need help, sweetheart?"

My eyes narrowed, but I walked around the front of the car and reluctantly took his arm so he could escort me up the walkway and into the house.

I would have held on to the Grim Reaper's arm to navigate the stone path in these death shoes.

The music from the stereo pulsed in my blood before we even made it to the front steps, and the journey seemed to take forever as people stopped to talk to Ryan... and completely ignore me.

Okay, that was a lie. Only a few ignored me. Most looked like they wanted to pour their alcohol over my head and flick a lit cigarette in my direction.

A few girls even hugged Ryan, pressing their barely constrained tits against him as their arms wrapped around his neck. All while I was literally hooked to him with my arm. Shouldn't girl code have kicked in here? Who threw themselves at a guy who was *clearly* with someone else?

If this was a normal date, I probably would've been offended, but as it was, I could only hope one drew enough of his attention so I could hide out in a corner and pray he forgot I existed.

I entertained myself by looking around, watching people who hadn't noticed, or didn't care, that Ryan and I had arrived. A lot of them looked... normal. Ripped jeans and faded t-shirts with dirty shoes.

"Do all of these people go to Pacific Cross?" I wondered out loud.

Ryan glanced down at me before looking around. "No. A lot are townies from Pac City."

I nodded. Pacific City was the small town that surrounded the base of the school. I wondered if the school had been built on top of the town to show the townspeople who was really in charge... or if the town was created to hire workers to help maintain the pristine grounds.

I turned my head to keep looking around, but I froze when I saw Brylee and two more girls from the squad, Kayleigh and Hayley.

Add in *Lainey* and they were a perfectly horrendous quad of rhyming mayhem. The four of them were always together in Madelaine's photos, each girl more gorgeous than the next.

And now they hated me.

Mean girls made the world go round. Or, at least, the high school.

"Oh, my God," Brylee squealed, breaking from her friends to run up to Ryan. "You look amazing, Ry. That summer away totally must have helped you... recoup."

I narrowed my eyes but smirked inwardly when Ryan stiffened beside me.

He wasn't a Brylee fan.

Look at that. We finally had something in common.

"Yeah," he muttered, managing to shake her off.

Her gaze sharpened and then turned to me. "Lainey, you look..." Her nose wrinkled. "I mean, I've heard of eating your feelings, but I assumed you'd show a *little* self-control."

Hayley, a petite blonde, who was skinnier than a twig, snorted. "Please. We all know Lainey can't control a damn thing. Her appetite, her mouth... the way her legs fall open."

A wave of giggles and gasps rose up from the small crowd we'd amassed as people kept trying to talk to Ryan.

"Don't take your hangry out on me," I replied with a shrug. "Eat a burger. It does wonders for the soul."

"And nothing for your ass," Kayleigh sniped.

"Oh, I disagree," Ryan cut in warmly, looping an arm around my chest and anchoring my back to his front. His hips rocked against mine suggestively. "Her ass is spectacular."

Oh, hell.

The last thing I needed was for my hormones to react to the biggest douche in existence pressing himself against me.

And yet... my traitorous body was really enjoying the feel of him.

Brylee flushed and leaned back a bit. "Well, just remember that when you're trying to do a layout and can't get off the ground."

I tossed her the sweetest smile I could manage. "Guess I'll have plenty of padding to break my fall."

Rolling her eyes, she huffed and stalked away with her entourage and more than a few hungry male stares.

Ryan's breath slid across the exposed column of my throat as he whispered, "Nicely played."

I shot him a surprised look. "I'm actually a little surprised you took up for me."

Something in his gaze shifted. "It's the truth. No guy wants to fuck someone they're worried they'll break when things get rough."

My mouth went dry as my brain suddenly conjured up a million sinfully delicious scenarios. "*When* things get rough?"

His eyes sparkled in a way that caught my breath. "If you're doing it right."

"Oh," I mumbled.

He blinked, and the glimpse of a human I had seen was replaced by a sneering jerk once more.

"Guess those moans in the video were as fake as you," he told me in a low tone, his full mouth curving into a smirk.

I jerked back from him but didn't get far because his arms were wrapped around me. "Let me go."

The flash of teeth in his smile was nearly feral. "No. I told you— we're doing this my way, Maddie."

I tilted my head and grinned at him. "Unless you want me to piss on your leg like I'm marking my territory in front of all these pretty people, I suggest you let me go so I can use the bathroom."

His fingers dug into my hip, a bite of pain that woke up nerve endings I hadn't known existed.

That wasn't supposed to happen.

He reached into his pocket and handed me a key.

I frowned. "What's this for?"

"The key to my room so you can use the bathroom, unless you plan to wait in line for an hour," he replied, looking at me like *duh, you should know this*. "I switched rooms—top floor, last door on the right. You have five minutes to return my key."

I closed my hand over the metal, feeling the grooves bite into the flesh of my palms.

"Hurry back, sweetheart," he ordered, pressing a firm kiss to my temple. His voice dropped to an even lower level. "Don't make me come looking for you."

"Wouldn't dream of it, *honey*," I shot back, taking advantage of his position to plant my own kiss on his jaw, pleased when I saw the cherry red lipstick smeared on the hard line with a light dusting of stubble.

His head snapped back and his hold loosened enough for me to step away.

I would've loved to make an exit full of sashaying hips and seductive grace... but I was on a cobblestone path in *heels*. I was freaking lucky I made it to the stairs and inside the house without face planting.

Inside, the temperature had risen an extra ten degrees from the bodies packed wall to wall. Furniture had been shoved against walls in one room to let people writhe and grind against each other to the beat of the music pouring from a stereo in the corner. The other room had several pool tables, but only one was being used for an actual game. The other was full of coeds doing body shots.

Exhaling hard, I pushed my way through the bodies between me and the stairs. Thankfully, the staircase was blissfully empty, and I realized why when I was stopped by a guy before I could step foot on it.

"Upstairs is off limits," he told me, folding his muscular arms over a neon green tank top. There was a nametag that simply identified him as Pledge 7.

"I just need the bathroom," I told him.

He jerked his chin to the side of the house. "Use the downstairs."

"You don't understand," I started, getting ready to show him Ryan's key.

"Hold up," a sharp voice ordered, pushing through a pair of girls making out.

I looked up at a massively tall, ridiculously muscled guy. His vibrant green eyes stood out starkly against his dark skin in a contrast that could only be described as beautiful.

"She's Cain's girl," he told the guardian of the stairs. "She can go up."

I glanced at the man by the stairs. "See? I have permission."

Pledge 7 shrugged and shuffled aside. "Whatever you say, bro."

"Uh, thanks," I told the new guy with a smile, grateful I didn't have to wait in the line I could see snaked through two rooms.

"Five minutes, and then one of us will come after you, princess," he told me flatly, his eyes burning as he stared at me with obvious distrust.

"Got it," I answered and wondered if the five-minute thing was a frat-wide rule or if Ryan and his buddies had set up this system in preparation for me.

I hurried up the stairs before he could decide to join me and watch to make sure all I did was use the bathroom.

The pulse of the music throbbed through the floorboards as I made it to the top level, but the noise level was quieter up here. Enough so I could hear myself think, anyway.

I turned down the right hall, my eyes on the door at the end. It unlocked it with ease, and I closed it behind me. I gave myself a second to stare at the large room that doubled as a bedroom with a separate living area.

It was amazingly neat and clean. The king-size bed was made with a black comforter that matched the black headboard and furniture. There was minimal clutter, and the only picture I spotted was on a bookshelf filled with actual books. Textbooks *and* fiction.

The bathroom door was open on the other wall, but I hesitated a second and went to the bookcase to pick up the photo.

Ryan and a young girl smiled at each other in it, their foreheads pressed together as they laughed, the photographer clearly catching a candid moment between them.

This must be his younger sister. The one his mother died having.

I set the framed photo back reluctantly and headed for the bathroom.

Washing my hands when I was finished, I looked in the mirror. I looked like... Lainey. But the anxiety and frustration in my eyes? That was all Maddie.

Sighing, I dried my hands and started back out of the room.

I pulled the door open and stopped short, frowning at the now-open door next to Ryan's room. I eased Ryan's door closed before locking it again.

"Jesus," a muffled voice said, laughing, "how much did you use?"

"Enough for her to finally loosen the fuck up," another voice replied.

I tiptoed forward and peeked around the open door. Two men stood with their backs to me. My stomach sank when I saw the bare legs of a girl dangling from the edge of the bed. She was wearing only one shoe.

Goddammit.

"What the hell are you doing?" I demanded, straightening my spine and bracing for the confrontation.

Both guys turned, their expressions surprised, and then smiling.

"Welcome back, Lainey," the guy on the left, and the owner of the first voice, greeted. His gaze lingered on my legs before turning to his friend. "You good?"

"Yeah. Thanks for the assist, Josh," he replied, watching his friend push by me before looking at me and grinning. "You wanna help?"

"Help?" I echoed. "What are—"

He stepped back and gestured to the body on the bed. "I know how much you hate the bitch."

My heart sank to my feet as I got a good look at her.

Bex.

It was *Bex* on the bed, barely conscious as she blinked up at the ceiling, her gaze unfocused and glassy.

"What the fuck?" I shouted, walking around him and leaning over her. "Bex? Can you hear me?"

A strong hand grabbed my arm and yanked me up.

"Let go!" I snapped, trying to pull free.

He held on harder. "What the fuck are *you* doing?" He manhandled me out the door. "Shut the fuck up."

I stumbled as he literally shoved me into the hall. I caught myself on the wall before I could fall.

"What is your problem?" he demanded, blocking the door. He shoved his black hair out of his muddy brown eyes, his lips pinched. "You hate this cunt as much as I do."

"And that gives you the right to drug her?" I gasped.

His brows shot up. "That accusation might have a little more weight if I hadn't seen you do the same fucking thing more times than I can count. Shit, I got this pill from *you*."

My jaw dropped.

"Are you joining us?" His skeevy gaze raked over me and he licked his lips.

I shoved down a wave of vomit.

"Fine." He stepped back and slammed the door. My heart sank as I heard the lock click into place.

"Holy shit," I whispered, my mind trying to make sense of what I had just seen.

I tried the doorknob just to make sure it was truly locked, and it was. I slapped my open palm against the wood, hissing at the sting.

I needed help.

And there was only one person I could ask for it.

CHAPTER 20

"Where's Ryan?" I demanded as I reached the bottom of the stairs.

Pledge 7 gave me a blank stare.

"Ryan!" I repeated, snapping my fingers in his face.

"Probably out back," he grunted before turning to shoo a handsy couple away from the stairs.

Because God forbid they walk in on a date rape in progress.

I started down the long hall that led toward the rear of the house, and my ankle twisted in the heels.

"Fuck!" I hissed.

A couple making out against the wall glanced at me.

I did the only sensible thing I could think of; I removed my heels and kicked them away before hurrying down the hall and through the kitchen. A collapsible glass wall had been pulled aside to open the space between the kitchen and the patio and pool area.

I paused, my eyes scanning the crowd until I found Ryan.

It wasn't hard. He was holding court on the patio, sitting in a chair by a firepit with about a dozen people around him. I spotted the green-eyed guy, too, as he handed Ryan one of the beers in his hands.

Taking a deep breath, I broke into a jog, ignoring people's stares until I was in front of Ryan.

If I hadn't been so panicked, I might have laughed at how confused he suddenly looked when I appeared.

"Where the hell are your shoes?" he asked, his brow wrinkling.

"I need you," I said breathlessly, waving a hand.

His brows rose in amusement as his eyes scanned up and down my body. "You *need* me?"

"Is there a fucking echo?" I hissed. "Yes. I need you to come with me."

A male snorted. "She *needs* you, Ry."

The girl next to him giggled. "We all know how... *needy* Madelaine is. Better go with her, Ryan, before she asks someone else for *help*."

Ryan turned his head, effectively dismissing me. "You're making a scene. Sit down."

I wanted to scream in frustration. Clearly I wasn't getting through, so I tried another tactic.

I stepped closer to him, positioning myself between his spread legs. "Ryan. *Please.*"

His eyes narrowed slightly, probably annoyed because when *wasn't* he annoyed with me, and then he pushed himself up. "What?"

My gaze darted around. "Alone?"

"Ooooh," a couple voices hooted, thinking this was definitely something it was *not*.

Huffing, Ryan pulled me around to a patch of grass a few feet away. "What, Madelaine? Where the fuck is my key?"

I slapped it into his open palm and held back a scream of frustration. "The guy in the room next to yours. He has a girl in there."

He snorted and took a drink. "Seriously? You came out here to tell me people were hooking up?"

"No," I hissed, "I came to tell you that the girl he's hooking up with is *barely* conscious. He and another guy dragged her in there—"

And Ryan was gone.

One second he was in front of me, the next he was whirling away.

"Ash!" he barked, jerking his head at the house.

The green-eyed guy's head snapped up, and then he was abandoning his beer and following Ryan into the house.

I trailed after them, catching up as they reached the stairs and we all ran up them. Two more guys followed, peeling away from the party and flanking us as we turned down the hallway.

Ryan stopped in front of the door and looked back at me, his expression terrifying. "Are you sure of what you saw?"

I nodded. "She didn't even know I was in the room, Ryan. That girl is not capable of knowing what the hell's going on."

"Aw, shit," one of the guys behind me muttered, scrubbing a hand across his jaw. His dark eyes flashed.

"And you saw Dean?" Ryan insisted.

I threw my hands up. "What does it matter if I saw Tom Cruise on a purple elephant? That girl is completely unable to make any kind of decision."

"Madelaine!" Ryan snapped. "Was it Dean?"

"Dark hair? Looks like a constipated rodent?" I returned.

"That's an accurate description," the other guy behind me said with a dark chuckle, his blue eyes brimming with mirth.

Ryan looked at him. "Get the brothers and start clearing the party, Linc."

Linc's jaw dropped. "Dude. Seriously?"

"The last thing I need is to be cleaning up a dead body tonight," Ryan answered, and fear shot through me as I realized he was serious.

Linc glared and scrubbed a hand over his face. "Fine. But I still want a piece of that asshole."

"Noted," Ryan gritted out.

With a sigh, Linc turned. When he got to the stairs, he shouted, "Party's over, assholes! Everybody *out*!"

My hands clenched and unclenched as I realized Bex had been alone with this Dean guy for way too long.

"Ryan—"

I yelped as Ryan lifted a leg and kicked in Dean's door. The lock buckled under the force of his kick and the door exploded inward.

Ash and the other guy behind me surged forward with Ryan into the room.

"What the *fuck*?" Dean bellowed as he was lifted off Bex.

"What the fuck indeed," Ryan said darkly, his cold eyes sweeping the room and quickly assessing the situation. When his eyes landed on Bex, a muscle ticked in his jaw.

"What? Are you three the fucking cock police?" he snarled.

I slowly entered the room to see the guys had Dean held up between them. His shirt was gone and his jeans were undone. Ryan was between him and—

"Bex!" I gasped, hurrying to the bed and sitting on the edge. My hands fluttered across Bex's body, tugging her skirt back down and pulling her shirt back into place. Her eyes were closed, but she was breathing and her underwear was still in place.

I pushed her hair off her face before turning to glare at Dean. "What exactly did you give her?"

Dean sneered at me. "Shut up, bitch."

Ryan's fist shot out, smashing into Dean's jaw.

I'd seen enough beatings in Cliftown to know a solid right hook when I saw one. Ryan was no stranger to throwing punches.

"Easy, Ry," Ash admonished, his pale green eyes narrowed. "We need him conscious and able to speak for the meeting."

The other guy scoffed, shaking his dark hair out of his even darker eyes. "Do we? I think this scene pretty much speaks for itself." He shoved Dean hard enough that his head cracked against the wall. "Motherfucker."

"Enough, Court," Ryan murmured to the guy who looked ready to rip Dean's head clean off his shoulders.

"Yeah, Court, listen to your master," Dean commented with a sneer.

I winced as Court *and* Ash slammed Dean against the wall hard enough to dent it. Dean let out a wheezing moan.

"You're done, O'Shea," Ryan growled, his hands still curled into fists.

Dean spat a mouthful of blood onto the floor. "I'm the fucking president, Cain. You know who my father is."

"I do," Ryan agreed, smiling like this was a normal conversation, "and I'm sure he'll love seeing the footage of you attempting to rape an unconscious girl. And I'm sure this won't affect his reelection chances."

Ryan pointed to the corner of the room where a small camera was embedded into the crown molding, a red light on and blinking.

"Forget we knew you had those damn cameras in here to record all your shit? Ash, think you can pull that footage?"

Ash chuckled darkly. "Not a problem. The question is, are we just sending it to daddy, or should I include the local police department?"

Dean paled, looking unsteady for the first time. "Oh, come on. That chick is a nobody. Hell, your *girl* has done worse to her."

I flinched and looked away, back at Bex as her eyes fluttered open.

"Hey," I said softly, "you're okay, Bex."

Her brow furrowed. "Maddie?"

I nodded and shifted positions so I could cradle her head in my lap. "We're going to get you out of here." I looked up at Ryan. "We should call for an ambulance."

"No," Bex protested weakly. "I can't... my dad..." She broke off with a pitiful whimper.

"What did you give her?" I asked Dean again.

He shot Ryan a glance.

Ryan simply folded his arms over his chest, waiting for the answer. "Tell her."

Dean rolled his eyes and coughed. "You should know. It's only GHB. The shit I got from you last year, and it wasn't even that much."

"Was she drinking?" I asked, my mind running through the times my mom had ingested the same thing.

"Maybe a beer?" he muttered.

I looked at Ryan. "Can you help me get her back to my room? I'll watch her. She should be able to sleep it off."

Ryan looked back at the guy I didn't know, his expression unreadable. The guy's gaze swept over Bex, pinching in anger, but he gave a short nod, answering whatever unspoken question Ryan had posed.

Satisfied with his friend's agreement, Ryan looked at me. "Okay. Court will help you get back to the dorms. Rebecca will stay with you tonight."

Court, the guy with the dark hair and menacing expression, stared at Ryan for a beat and then gave another jerky nod. He released his hold on Dean and came over to help me with Bex.

He started to lift her, and she groaned... and I recognized that sound, and what came after it, from years of being around my mom.

"Wait!" I ordered, pushing him back and helping Bex roll over enough to vomit over the edge of the bed. I held her hair back, waiting for the heaving to stop.

"Oh, that's *sick*," Dean griped. "Someone better clean that up."

My head whipped around to glare at him. "This is your fault, you disgusting fuckwad."

"Bitch—" he started.

Ryan shoved him against the wall, the force hard enough to send a few pictures crashing to the floor and deepen the dent. "Don't fucking talk to her. To either of them."

With a moan, Bex rolled back over. "I don't feel good, Maddie."

"I know," I whispered, stroking her hair. "Let's get you out of here."

I sighed and nodded to Court, who lifted her up with surprising gentleness. His fierce expression softened a little as she curled against his chest with a hiccuping sob. He quickly exited the room.

Ryan let Dean go as I got off the bed. He grabbed my arm to stop me. "I'll come by and check on you after I handle things here."

"You don't have to," I murmured, watching Court carry Bex out of the room.

"Yeah, I do," he replied softly. He jerked his chin at Ash. "We'll get everything handled here, but it might take a while."

"I'll be up," I answered with a small shrug.

Ryan's gaze darkened with concern. "Is she going to be okay?"

I nodded. "Yeah. The drugs should work their way out of her

system in the next few hours. She'll probably feel like crap, but we got here before he could do anything." My gaze slid to Dean.

He flipped me off. "Not sure when you became such a self-righteous hypocrite, Lainey."

At some point I was going to have to unpack all of his innuendos and accusations about Madeleine. About how she treated people, especially ones she didn't like.

But right now Bex was my focus.

I looked back at Ryan, and something shifted between us. A weird sort of camaraderie or understanding.

I pointed at the door. "I'm gonna go."

He nodded, his gaze following me out the door.

CHAPTER 21

Court stayed only long enough to get Bex tucked into my bed. He stepped back with a tight expression. "Dean's an asshole."

"You won't get any arguments from me," I muttered. "Can you watch her for a second? I'm going to get some towels from the bathroom."

He gave me a curt nod and I hurried into the en suite to grab some linens. I brought them with me to the bed, surprised at the soft look on his face while he watched Bex sleep. "I have bottled water in the fridge. Can you grab her one?"

"Uh, yeah." He turned and left, and I could hear him rummaging around in the outer rooms. A minute later he came back and handed me the bottle. "I need to head back."

"Right." I stood up and walked him to the door.

"Don't leave," he warned me as he opened my door and gave it a meaningful tap. "And lock this."

"Yes, Dad," I chirped, rolling my eyes.

Court stared at me, and having those coffee-colored eyes focused on me was almost too much. He saw too much. My smile slipped as I shifted restlessly.

He licked his lips, the movement dragging attention to the scar above his top lip, as he shook dark hair out of his eyes. "You're... not what I expected."

All I could do was raise my eyebrows.

Court grunted and jerked his chin at my bedroom. "I thought you hated that girl. Shit you've done to her over the years... Maybe as fucked up as what Dean tried to do."

I ducked my head in shame... and anger.

What the *hell* had Lainey done?

"Maybe I've changed," I muttered, tucking a piece of hair behind my ear. I had to amend whatever legacy Madelaine had left behind.

Court pointedly looked at my bare, dirty feet. "Clearly."

I peeked up at him through a fringe of lashes, my toes curling into the soft fibers of the rug.

He was still staring thoughtfully. "The question is, is it too little too late?"

I didn't have an answer for that. It was hard cleaning up a mess blindfolded.

"Call us if she gets worse or if you need anything. Goodnight, Madelaine," he told me, leaving my dorm room and pulling the door closed.

Taking his advice, I flipped the locks before leaning my back against the door and exhaling.

Talk about a crazy night.

I pushed away from the door and started pulling off my dress as I went back to my room, nearly ripping the fabric as I tripped on air like the graceful person I was. I tossed the dress into a corner, not caring that I had essentially thrown a pile of cash on the floor, as I went into the bathroom and then scrubbed all the makeup from my face.

I exited into my room minutes later and pulled on a pair of cotton shorts and an oversized t-shirt, before going to check on Bex.

Her breathing was steady as she slept, and I was contemplating whether or not to try changing her into something more comfortable than the dress she had on, when she cracked open an eye.

"Maddie?"

"Hey, yeah. I'm here," I said quickly. "Do you need anything?"

She licked her lips, her gaze still unfocused. "W-water?"

I grabbed the bottle of water Court had brought to the bedside table and unscrewed the cap.

I helped her sit up before bringing the bottle to her lips. I cut her off after a few sips and tucked her back in.

"How are you feeling?" I asked softly.

Her brow wrinkled. "Fuzzy. I feel... weird."

"Yeah," I whispered, pushing her hair off her face gently. "Just try to sleep, okay?"

"Where did it go?" she asked, as her eyes started to close again.

I looked around, wondering if we'd forgotten to grab her purse or something. "Where did what go, Bex?"

She yawned and turned her face into the pillow. "Your scar. It's gone."

"My scar?" I echoed, my pulse stuttering.

She was silent for a long moment. So much so that I thought she'd fallen asleep. But then her sleepy voice mumbled, "Your wrist. From... before you hated me."

Bex slipped back into sleep, leaving me wondering what she was talking about. I didn't remember Lainey having any scars. And I *did* have a scar, but it was on my back from jumping off a makeshift treehouse when I was eight and catching my back on a nail sticking out.

I wouldn't get an explanation from her tonight. I pulled the fluffy blanket at the foot of my bed up around her shoulders and tucked it around her body, then slid the trash can near the bed in case she got sick again and replaced the bottle of water with a fresh one.

I left the bedroom door open in case she needed me, and started doing what I always did to chill: stress clean.

Not that there was much to clean in the room. It had been prepared for my arrival with fresh sheets, clean counters and floors, and my schedule and books left out on the desk for when classes began in a week. I had unpacked the suitcases of clothes and shoes and toiletries, more than I could ever imagine needing, but otherwise, I was left to wander aimlessly around the dorm room that was more like an upscale apartment.

It was a corner room, with large windows in the living area and bedroom. There was a private en suite bathroom with a large soaker tub and separate glass-walled shower. A half bath was situated off the living room. The top floor meant I also had skylights to provide more natural light and a balcony area off the bedroom. I loved the neutral color scheme with pops of mint and blush.

There was a small kitchenette with a fridge already fully stocked with drinks and fruit, a dining table, and a microwave.

The dorm room was bigger than the trailer mom and I had shared my whole life.

I wandered to the couch and sank down on the soft cushions before turning on the TV. I kept the volume low but was unable to settle on a channel. Eventually I turned it off and grabbed the binder that contained my schedule and generic information about the school.

I scanned the schedule, a little annoyed that I would be taking Algebra II. I had taken that last year and was supposed to be moving on to Pre-Calc my senior year. Madelaine's grades and mine stacked up comparably in almost every subject except math.

A small smile twisted my lips as I realized maybe I had an academic edge on my twin, even if my school was lightyears behind Pacific Cross.

I got up and checked on Bex again before getting a glass of water for myself. I leaned a hip on the counter by the sink and took a sip as someone knocked on the door.

Pushing off the counter, I crossed the room and checked the peephole.

My heart rate kicked up when I saw Ryan.

I slowly unlocked the door and pulled it open. "Hey."

He held up my shoes. "Forget something, Cinderella?"

"Thanks," I murmured, taking them from him. I stepped aside to let him in. "Do you want something to drink?"

He turned, surprise on his face. "Uh, no. I'm good." After a second he added a hasty, "Thanks."

"Sure." I went back to the couch and closed the binder, tossing it on the coffee table.

Ryan slowly approached and perched on the arm of the sofa. He looked around the space. "How's Rebecca?"

"Sleeping," I answered softly, my gaze darting to the door on instinct. I shrugged and felt the collar of my shirt slip off the shoulder.

Ryan's gaze dropped to my bare skin for a second. He let out a long breath. "I'm trying to figure out the angle here, Madelaine. But I'm tired, and I don't feel like playing mental gymnastics with you. So what's the game?"

I blinked up. "There's no game. No angle."

He snorted. "Bullshit. I know you."

My instinct was to tell him he was wrong, but that didn't seem to have any effect. Instead, I sighed and leaned back. "Believe what you want, Ryan. I don't care."

"Doesn't sound like the Lainey I know," he said harshly.

I shrugged again, not willing to debate the Lainey he knew.

"Still can't believe that you, of all people, helped her out," he added, shaking his head.

I glared at him. "Sorry. Next time I'll just let a girl get raped so I'm a little more normal for you."

"Don't be a bitch," he shot back, but with less heat than he normally used with me. He sounded tired, more than anything else.

"You're in *my* room," I snapped, shooting him a scowl. "Jesus, what do you want from me?"

"I want you to remember your place," he ground out, blue eyes flashing with ice and hate. "And I don't want you to think that acting like a decent human a couple of times will make shit all better."

I clenched my teeth, a headache starting to pound behind my eyes. "It's late. Are we done?"

"No," he replied. "Bex can't testify or file a complaint against Dean. You need to make sure that happens."

"Excuse me?" I stared at him like he'd grown another head, which maybe he had. Why the hell would I protect a would-be-rapist?

"Dean's been handled," he told me coldly. "But Rebecca can't cause waves or the deal we made with his dad won't stand. And we can't afford to rock the boat with Dean's father right now. Fucker actually loves his kid, if you can believe that."

"Like you needed that fucking deal in Asia? The one where you let a child predator keep his balls attached to his body?" I snarled, shooting to my feet.

Ryan stood up as well and folded his arms over his chest. "You don't know what you're talking about."

"You know, you keep saying how I'm not acting like myself," I started, ice freezing my words as I glared with unconcealed hatred at him, "but the only one with a fucked-up personality in this room is *you*."

"Wow," he muttered, running a hand through his dark blonde hair. "You need to stop talking about shit you're clueless about."

"Then fucking clue me in!" I hissed, trying to keep my voice down so I wouldn't disturb Bex. "Because all I see is a guy I'm supposed to marry who is doing his damndest to protect people who violate women and children."

His gaze shuttered as he brushed by me. "We're done here."

"Oh, *now* we're done?" I challenged, following him as he headed for the door. "Did I strike a nerve, *baby*?"

He yanked the door open. "You don't know shit."

"Neither do you," I retorted.

His eyes searched my face. "Believe it or not, I didn't come here to fight with you."

"Then why did you come here?"

He looked away. "I don't know. Maybe I just..."

"Just what?" I asked, sighing as I leaned against the door jam. All of the fight melted out of my body, replaced by a bone-deep exhaustion.

A muscle ticked in his jaw. "I don't know."

"Right," I whispered, hating the note of vulnerability that crept in. "Well, when you figure it out, let me know. Or don't. I really don't care."

He frowned. "Madelaine."

"Good night, Ryan," I told him and closed the door.

CHAPTER 22

"Maddie?"

I gasped into consciousness, my eyes snapping open.

Bex jumped back. "I'm sorry. I didn't... What's going on?"

I glanced around the room. I must have fallen asleep on the couch, because sunlight was now streaming inside and giving the space a warm glow.

"How do you feel?" I asked, pulling my legs up to give her space to sit down.

She gnawed on her lower lip and lowered herself to the couch. "I don't remember a whole lot about last night. How did I get here?"

"We were at a frat party," I answered.

"Together?" Her brows shot up.

"No," I assured her, shaking my head. "I went upstairs to use the bathroom, and I... kind of found you. You were pretty wasted."

Her face paled. "Was I... alone?"

I shook my head.

Bex swallowed audibly, a tremor rippling through her body. "Oh, God. I don't even remember drinking."

"He drugged your drink," I told her.

"H-he?" she stammered, eyes wide.

"Dean? The frat president?"

"Dean *O'Shea*?" She looked even more terrified than before.

I nodded. "Yeah."

"My dad is going to *kill* me," she whispered, pressing her trembling fingers to her lips. "He hates the O'Sheas."

"You didn't do anything wrong," I said firmly. "He *drugged* you. He tried to... Well, he tried to, you know."

"But he didn't?" Her eyes found mine.

"No. I tried to stop him, but he locked me out of the room, so I got Ryan."

She stared at me for a heavy moment. "You tried to help me?"

"Of course," I replied, squirming a little at the look she was giving me.

"Why?"

I gave her a blank look.

"Why did you *help me*?" she elaborated, her expression going chilly.

"Because it was the right thing to do," I answered slowly. "You were barely conscious."

"Like in tenth grade when you spiked my drink at a party? Because it was *so funny* when I fell into the pool and almost drowned."

Oh, shit.

"But I guess that was better than when you took all my clothes when I was in the shower and you pulled the fire alarm. That little hand towel you left me was *really* helpful."

My eyes slid closed.

"I think my favorite memory, though, was when my grandmother died last year, and you said you could understand why, since being related to me would kill anyone."

Fucking fuck.

My sister was a bitch.

What was worse than a bitch? Because Madelaine was just that. And at that moment, I hated my sister. Hated who she was and the hell she had inflicted on people.

And then I realized that maybe the world was a little better off without her.

As soon as the thought slithered through my brain, I felt like shit. Who thought that about their sister? About their *twin*?

"But hey," Bex went on, sniffling back tears, "you helped me last night, so bygones, right?"

"I... God, I am *so sorry*," I told her, choking on my words.

The look of absolute betrayal on her face was gutting me.

"Why help me? What's the game this time?"

Ryan had asked me the same thing. More than once. And so had Bex in the car yesterday. Everyone assumed I was playing them... and I had no idea how to show them I wasn't. I *couldn't* even if I wanted to.

I had been thrown into this game the same way they had, and I didn't know the rules either.

"You've said that before, too," she replied tearfully, wiping her eyes with the back of her hand. "Usually right before you set me up. And stupid me, I always believed you. I always wanted to believe that I could have my best friend back."

My heart cracked open. "I wish I could take it all back. You don't know how much."

"I always kept your secrets, you know?" she went on, ignoring my words. "I could've told people about what happened. About what I knew. I always protected you, and I don't even know why."

I didn't have an answer. If I had been in her shoes? I would have burned Madelaine's world to the ground with whatever info I had. The shit Bex had been through was wrong on so many levels. Madelaine didn't deserve her loyalty.

"You probably should have," I agreed in a low voice.

Bex exploded off the couch. "No! I'm not *you*. I wouldn't exploit your darkest secrets because I would never want someone to feel as shitty as you constantly made me feel."

"Then you're a much better person than I will ever be," I admitted hoarsely. I spread my hands in front of me, palms up in surrender. "Rebecca, I am so, so sorry. I know you won't believe me, and you shouldn't. Hell, you should stay far away from me."

"I hate that there's still this stupid part of me that wants to forgive you," she whispered. "That part of me still believes you."

"I swear I'm not that girl anymore," I assured her. "That's why I helped you last night. And if you want to walk out of here and forget it ever happened, we can do that. If you want to hide out here for the rest of the day, you can do that, too. Or I can go with you to file a police report."

Fuck Ryan and his needs.

Maybe I couldn't do anything about those kids in Indonesia, but I could protect Bex and make Dean pay.

Bex looked hesitantly around the space. "I can't go to the police. I can't handle that kind of pressure. Or the whispers and the looks..." She shuddered. "That makes me sound pathetic, doesn't it?"

"There's no manual for surviving an assault. Whatever course you decide is the right one for *you*, and that's all that matters," I answered. "I'll support you no matter what."

She licked her lips. "Can I take a shower? My floor has the community bathrooms, and I'd rather not look at people right now."

"Towels are in the closet," I said. "Feel free to use whatever stuff I have. There's an extra toothbrush in the top drawer of the vanity, and I'll set out some clothes for you."

I glanced at my body and then her more petite one. "You'll probably be swimming in my clothes, though."

"That's... I don't mind." She blinked innocently at me. "Um, thank you."

"Are you hungry? I can order food for us. Or maybe run down to the dining hall and bring something back?"

She shook her head. "No. Just the shower, and then I'll get out of your way."

I wanted to tell her she wasn't in my way, but she scurried back into my room, and the bathroom door closed a second later. I waited until the shower turned on before I went into my room and pulled out a t-shirt and yoga pants for her. I left them in a neatly folded pile on the bed and went back into the living room.

I tried watching TV again as Bex showered, no doubt taking the time to scrub and scour every inch of her skin.

I turned off the TV as she came back into the living room thirty minutes later, swimming in my clothes and towel drying her damp hair. She gave me a strange look.

"Feel any better?" I asked softly. "I have Tylenol or whatever if you need it."

"Actually? I was hoping you could answer a question."

"Okay." If I had the answer, I would give it to her.

She balled the towel in her hands and crept closer. "What's my birthday?"

I stiffened in surprise. Of all the things she could have asked, that hadn't been one I expected.

And I definitely didn't have the answer.

Worry started to coil low in my stomach.

"Um... May?" Total shot in the dark.

"Close," she replied in a completely even tone, giving nothing away. "January."

I winced. "Sorry."

"Don't be," she said, sitting on the other end of the couch. "Can I see your arms?"

"My... arms?" My brows shot up.

She nodded.

I slowly extended them.

"Huh."

My arms fell and I wrapped them around myself, suddenly cold. "Why?"

"Last question," she said, holding up a finger. "Where were we when you decided we weren't best friends anymore?"

Full-blown panic exploded in my chest. She was fishing for something, and I wasn't sure if I was completely missing the bait... or had already latched on and was about to be reeled in.

"My house?" Another guess.

She glanced away with a sad smile. "I only remember pieces of last night. Like fragments of memories. I remember going to the party because I promised my mom I would try making friends my senior year."

I twisted my fingers together nervously and waited.

"I remember Dean coming up to me. Something about our dads burying the hatchet? He handed me a drink, and I remember checking to make sure the bottle was still sealed. It was." She frowned, her brow furrowing. "I remember his room smelling like... cigar smoke. I don't remember you seeing me, or Ryan. But I remember waking up here and not seeing it."

"Not seeing what?"

Her eyes snapped to mine. "Your scar."

"My... scar?" I echoed.

Her gaze dropped to my hands. "It's not there."

I looked down at my pale, scar-free hands. "They have plastic surgeons who deal with those things."

She grimaced. "I'm well aware. My mom is the best plastic surgeon in the state... and she said there was no undoing the damage you did. Your dad insisted she do *something*. She helped minimize it, but it was always there. It's why you always wore a chunky bracelet or a watch. To hide your one imperfection."

There was no answer for that. All I could do was hold my breath as the feeling of coming untethered rapidly swelled around me.

"I found you in the bathroom that night," Rebecca went on sadly. "I called for help. There was so much blood. It took forever for the ambulance to show up, but I stayed with you. Even when Mrs. Delancey tried to make me leave. I couldn't because you were my best friend."

Madelaine had tried to commit suicide.

The realization slammed into me like a blizzard, leaving nothing but icy cold in my chest and frost in my veins.

I bit my lower lip and tried to keep my hands from shaking. I couldn't imagine my twin doing what Bex was saying. It didn't match up with the Madelaine I knew.

But, then again, maybe I never really knew her.

And now I never will.

It was a bitter pill to swallow.

And it came with a lot more ramifications that I had to deal with now. I looked helplessly at Bex. "I don't..."

Bex smiled at me. "You're her, aren't you?"

Her?

The unasked question must have haunted my eyes. But her answer rocked me to the fucking core.

"Madelaine's twin. The one she told me about when we were younger."

CHAPTER 23

My world stopped. Full stop. It happened so quickly, I wondered if I would fall off and drift away into space.

Or maybe that was wishful thinking.

But Bex was still in front of me, a soft and knowing smile on her mouth, waiting for me to reply.

Deny or admit?

What was the right answer?

"She told you about me?" I finally asked, going with admittance. Bex had been through enough; she didn't need me lying when we both knew the truth.

"Holy shit," she said with a giggle. "It's so crazy. I mean, you look just like her. Well, duh, you're *twins*. I mean, part of me always thought it was something she made up or whatever. Wait. If you're here, where's Madelaine?"

My heart sank like a stone. "There was an accident. A fire."

Bex's eyes rounded. "No way."

"Madelaine convinced me to switch places with her at the beginning of summer," I explained. "I didn't even know she existed until I found a random picture of her on the internet months ago. I messaged her, and she showed up where I lived. Out of the blue."

MAD WORLD

Bex snorted. "Sounds like Lainey, all right."

"But she told me that she didn't know about me until I messaged her." I frowned, thinking back to that first night we'd talked.

"Well, that's bullshit," Bex said frankly. "I was there the day after she found your birth certificates. She went looking for hers when we were thirteen so she could file for emancipation."

"Emancipation?" I repeated, stunned.

Bex nodded. "Oh, yeah. She hated her dad. Well, your dad, too, I guess."

"She *hated* him?" I blinked, trying to digest that. It definitely wasn't the happy family picture Gary had painted for me.

She shrugged. "I mean, I guess things could've changed in the last few years. It's not like Madelaine kept me in the loop."

I dropped my head into my hands and tried to think. Tried to *breathe*. Everything was spiraling out of control.

"Shit," Bex muttered, and I felt her shift closer to me on the couch. A second later, a soft hand settled on my shoulder.

"He made it sound like they had a good relationship," I mumbled through my hands. "And Madelaine never said anything..."

Bex gently pulled my hands down. "Okay, let's rewind and take it from the top, shall we? Tell me what you know, and I'll try to fill in any details I can."

I stared at her. "You're being nice to me."

Her nose wrinkled. "Yeah, well, you were nice to me. And I can't exactly hate you for shit your evil twin did."

"Was she really that bad?"

Bex tilted her head to the side. "Imagine the love child of Charles Manson and Cruella de Ville on the first day of her period, but every single day. *That* was Madelaine on a good day." She bit her lip as I blanched. "Or, that's the Madelaine I knew for the last few years. Before she cut me off."

"I wish I knew why she did that," I admitted.

"That makes two of us," she agreed. "I guess I'm never going to know, am I?"

I shook my head slowly.

"You said it was a fire?" Pain flashed across Bex's face.

"Yeah. She put me on a plane for California then went to Santorini. It was just supposed to be for the summer. She told me she needed a break. That her life was suffocating her."

Bex snorted. "I'm guessing she left out the part where she was the architect of her own demise?"

"She left out a lot of details," I replied grimly.

Taking a deep breath, Bex squared her shoulders. "Okay, let's start at the beginning. Tell me everything."

MAYBE TELLING Bex *everything* wasn't the best decision, but once I started telling her about finding Madelaine and meeting her, I couldn't stop. She listened patiently, her face reacting in varying degrees of shock as I kept talking. I started by telling her about growing up in Cliftown and my mom's addictions. The assignment that led to me finding I had a twin sister. Meeting Madelaine and agreeing to her crazy ass plan.

Then I told her about the first time I met Ryan (her jaw dropped open), my deal with Gary (her eyes narrowed into suspicious slits), and being completely overwhelmed and confused at stepping into my sister's life (she held my hands).

"I feel like I've made a huge mistake," I finished, blinking back a sudden wave of tears.

Bex looked down at her hands. "If you hadn't decided to come here? Last night would have ended very differently for me."

"Maybe not," I said, but the words rang false. "Someone might have come."

"No one would have," she replied bluntly. "I'm not someone that... matters. I'm not a Cabot."

"You matter," I insisted.

"Not in this place," she replied. "It's just how it is. And I was stupid. I never should've accepted a damn thing from that weasel."

"He really does look like a rodent," I added with a smirk, making her giggle. "But don't blame yourself. And I really do have your back if you want to go and report his ass."

She sobered instantly. "No. Things just don't work like that here, Ma—" She broke off and shot me a strange look. "I don't even know your name."

"Maddie," I answered.

"No, your *real* name."

"Madison," I replied with a small smile. "But everyone called me Maddie, so..."

"Holy shit." Bex clapped a hand over her mouth and laughed. "Seriously? Madelaine and Madison?"

I shrugged and smiled. "I know, right?"

"Maddie," she said, grinning, "I like it. It suits you."

"It's what you used to call my sister," I pointed out.

She rolled her eyes. "Yeah, when she had a soul. Thankfully, you seem to be the less sadistic of the Cabot twins. Plus, I kind of like having a friend named Maddie back in my corner."

The corner of my mouth lifted. "So, we're friends now?"

"God, I hope so," Bex sighed. "Although I've been known to seriously misjudge friends before."

"I won't be one of them," I assured her, reaching for her hand and squeezing it. "It's such a relief for someone to finally know."

She squeezed me back for a fraction of a second. "It's still trippy as hell seeing you. I mean, you look like her, and you don't."

I cocked my head to the side. "How so?"

"I mean, it's all there," she told me, waving a hand in my general direction. "Eyes, hair, bone structure. But your face is softer."

I rolled my eyes. "Yeah. People like to remind me how much weight *Madelaine* has gained."

Bex snorted. "Really? Like who?"

"Brylee and her friends," I muttered.

"Brylee and her sycophants are jealous because you're gorgeous. Madelaine was, too, but she was super skinny. You have curves, and in the right way. Trust me."

I flushed as she winked knowingly. "Uh, thanks."

"Don't worry," she smirked, "I know you're taken."

My heart sank as I looked at the ring on my left finger. "Don't remind me."

She winced. "I'm guessing Ryan hasn't made things easy on you?"

"He *hates* me. Or, he hates who he thinks I am," I muttered, picking at the hem of my shirt. "I mean, I guess I get it? I know Madelaine cheated on him with a teacher or whatever, but it's not like he was in love with her."

"Wait, wait," she cut me off with wide eyes. "You think he hates you because your twin cheated with a *teacher*?"

I frowned and nodded. "That's what my dad said. I mean, he kind of glossed over it, but a favorite teacher got fired or something?"

"Wow. That's like saying the *Titanic* hit an ice cube." Bex got off the couch and headed for the kitchenette. "Can I grab a drink?"

"Help yourself." I waited for her to come back with two diet sodas and took the one she offered me with a grimace. I set it down on the coffee table, unopened.

She popped the top of hers and took a sip. "Want something else?"

"I'm good. Just not a fan of diet," I replied with a shrug.

"You really aren't Lainey *at all*. She counted carbs like a gambler counts cards."

I exhaled hard, changing topics so I could maybe get some actual answers. "So, what did you mean about the affair she had with a teacher?"

Shaking her head, Bex settled deeper into the cushions. "Not a teacher. A coach. The football coach, to be exact."

I frowned, still not getting it.

"Pac Cross is a small school," she explained, smirking when my brows lifted. "I mean, yeah, there's a couple thousand of us between the academy and the university, but we all grew up in the same circles, for the most part. The foretold marriage of Ryan Cain and Madelaine Cabot was, like, just a known fact that was made official last year. Beckett Cain and Gary Cabot were best friends, and they ruled Pac Cross in their day."

Which was probably why they were so deep into business together.

"And everyone knows about the Cabot will," she added pointedly. "There's a lot of rich kids here, but the Cabot clause is infamous."

I rolled my eyes. Rich people and their... riches. Whatever.

"So, Lainey and Ryan were never super public about their engagement, but everyone knows. Last year she started wearing that ring around school after winter break, but then the whole cheating thing came out in the spring."

I winced.

"If you get down to the details, Lainey slept with him in the fall before they were *officially* engaged, but she obviously knew in the fall what their families had planned. Hell, it might be why she slept with his coach, but what happened with Coach King was... damn. There was a sex tape that got released, but it wasn't just them having sex." Bex clicked her tongue against her teeth.

She leaned forward, lowering her voice like someone might hear. "She got close to the coach so she could look at the playbook. She leaked several things to other teams. They were in bed and even joked how easily Ryan could get hurt if someone happened to miss a block. They were totally setting him up, and it worked. Ryan got knocked out in the championship game last year. Massive concussion, and it cost the team the game and our school the title."

And *that* explained the school-wide hate.

Pacific Cross, both at the academy and collegiate levels, was known for its dominating football teams. The fan base at the school was rabid. And my sister had screwed over their star player.

"And, if that wasn't enough, Brylee was also sleeping with the coach."

My eyes flew to Bex. "Seriously?"

"Oh, yeah. It was how the whole thing was found out," Bex confirmed grimly. "She went over and found the tape of him and Lainey. She went public, but it was after Ryan's concussion. The whole school turned against Madelaine, and Coach King was fired for sleeping with a student. I think Brylee actually had feelings for the coach, to be honest, and in the video, the coach mentioned that he was only entertaining Brylee because he was trying to get her father's support to invest in his new line of sportswear or some shit."

My head dropped, my chin touching my chest.

"Yeah. So, Brylee hates Madelaine more than ever, and is quickly taking over as the new queen bee." Bex shot me an apologetic look.

"And Ryan hates me because he thinks I tried to hurt him," I murmured. "Why would my sister do that?"

She looked at me a little helplessly. "I wish I knew. Madelaine did a lot of stuff that never made sense after she tried to, you know."

Grimacing, I leaned back and sighed.

"She wasn't always like that," she added, almost regretfully. "And she didn't always hate Ryan and his friends, either. We used to vacation together."

My brows shot up in surprise. "Seriously? I didn't think Gary or Beckett would be big into family vacations."

"They weren't," she agreed with a smirk, "but she always came with *my* family, and Ryan often went with Court's. My family and Court's had houses next door to each other. Our families used to be really close."

"Used to be?" I asked.

She looked away, her expression going hollow. "Yeah. That was... that was a long time ago."

"Court was the one who brought you back here," I offered, hoping to maybe soothe some of the raw edges of whatever was haunting her.

If anything, that made her look even more sad. "He's always been a good guy. Ryan, too. I mean, he's never been one of the bullies around school. In fact, he usually keeps them in check."

I scoffed. "Yeah, that doesn't apply to me. He's made it abundantly clear that I'm supposed to obey his every command."

She made a face. "Shit. Sorry, girl. After what she did last year, I'm not surprised he's keeping a close eye on you. But maybe he'll relax when he realizes you're nothing like her?"

"That actually seems to make it worse. He thinks I'm playing a game," I replied.

"I wish I could say this year is going to be easy for you, but Madelaine fucked you over. You've got everything stacked against you, *and* a wedding hanging over your head. Isn't it supposed to happen next summer?"

I shook my head. "No. I talked to Gary. He asked me to play along for now until he can figure out how to end the engagement. I just have to fake it for the rest of the year, I guess."

Bex looked even more concerned than before. "Maddie, that sounds... Absolutely nothing like Gary Cabot. There's a reason Madelaine wanted to file for emancipation. A reason she tried to kill herself, and I hate to say it, but there's something seriously wrong with Gary Cabot."

CHAPTER 24

I could have stayed and talked to Bex all day. I had more questions, but I'd run out of time to ask them.

It was the first Saturday at PC, and cheer practice began today. A practice that I would be expected to lead with a squad I was expected to know for the first game later in the week.

I knew the routines. I'd spent hours analyzing the choreography, including a few new moves that Madelaine had recorded of herself but hadn't quite worked out some of the details of.

The squad was already waiting as I crossed the grassy area to where tumbling mats had been arranged. As I approached, Brylee and her friends turned as one. The rest of the girls suddenly were fixated on the ground.

Coach Rixon hadn't arrived yet, so I wasn't late, but something in their eyes made me realize I was missing more than my sister's memories.

"I can't believe you actually showed your face," Hayley sniped, planting a hand on her hip.

Kayleigh's lip curled in disgust as she brushed a dark curl off her forehead. "Oh, my God. Did you even attempt to work out? Your cankles are showing."

"She prefers to work out on her back," Hayley reminded her friend, the two trading catty remarks as Brylee simply watched.

A tiny wave of giggles swept over the other girls, but Brylee waited for them to settle before addressing me herself.

"We took a vote," she informed me. "You're out as captain. This squad has an image to maintain, and we're trying to look more professional than pornstar. I'm sure you understand."

I resisted the urge to smirk. These girls were barely athletes. They used the tiny uniforms to prance around and get attention. Only a handful of them actually seemed to care about the athleticism that went into the sport. Lainey's frustration routinely came through in her videos as she barked out orders to the girls who were watching the football team practice instead of stretching.

I smiled back at Brylee, baring my teeth. "Of course I do."

Mild shock lit her brown eyes when she realized I wasn't fighting back. With an airy sniff of superiority, she started to turn back to the squad.

"But you already voted for me last year, so unless Coach decides to change it up *this* season, it's not your call, is it?" I added, with just the right amount of steel in my voice.

Brylee turned slowly, her eyes narrowed.

I jerked my head in the direction of where our coach was coming out the side door of the gymnasium and approaching fast.

Brylee took a step forward, her pretty features twisted in an ugly scowl. "Quit now before we make your life hell, *Laine*."

Instead of cowering or waiting for adult intervention, I stepped up so our white shoes were toe-to-toe. "I'm not going anywhere, *Bry*."

She smirked. "Your funeral."

As she retreated in time for the coach to start barking orders, I wondered if I had made a massive mistake or if I had finally shown these girls I wouldn't be bullied.

∼

Mistake.

Fucking hell, I had made a mistake.

I blinked up at the blue sky and tried to catch my breath by counting clouds. Tears welled in my eyes unbidden because that had freaking *hurt*.

"Are you okay?" A pale face with pinched lips appeared above me, her strawberry blonde ponytail hanging over one shoulder as she gave me a sugary smile.

I tried to remember her name—Brandi or Candi or something that belonged on a pole. But my face was on fire, so thinking was hard.

"Fucking fabulous," I grunted, pushing myself up and feeling my face start to throb and swell from where her foot had caught me in the cheek.

She stepped back to let me get up without offering a hand. "I could've sworn it was a *left* high-kick."

"What the hell was that, Sandi?" the coach barked, glaring at the girl.

"Sorry, Coach," she called in a clear voice. "It won't happen again."

The snickering behind me said otherwise.

"Jesus," Coach Raines said, running a hand through her short, brunette bob. "Did *any* of you practice? What happened to camp? You look like a bunch of uncoordinated idiots."

Brylee lifted a hand in the air. "I think we're just having trouble coming together as a team, Coach. Camp is such a bonding experience, and not all of us attended."

I resisted the urge to roll my eyes.

Coach Raines arched a brow. "I might agree, Brylee, if Madelaine wasn't the only one capable of completing an entire routine today."

Flushing, Brylee stepped back, and I grinned inwardly.

It was true.

Half of the squad was so intent on sabotaging me that they looked like bumbling fools. Still, I knew my cheek would be swollen for a while, and I was going to have knee-shaped bruises up and down my spine.

Glancing at her watch, Coach Raines blew the whistle around her neck. "Okay, that's it for today. But we're picking it up again tomorrow. Six a.m."

A chorus of groans rose.

"Too early?" Coach smiled, but there was nothing sweet about it. "Make sure you're warmed up before then. Including a two-mile run for conditioning."

Wisely, no one else complained.

"Showers," the coach ordered, turning away and effectively dismissing us.

I gathered my poms and started toward the side door, taking my time so I was one of the last ones into the locker room. I dropped the poms off in my locker before closing it and snagging a towel and my change of clothes.

I showered quickly, ignoring the loud chatter of girls talking about whatever party was happening tonight.

A party I would *not* be attending.

Ryan hadn't said a word about it, and I was seriously set to curl up with a bowl of popcorn and find a new show to binge watch on Netflix. Especially now that there was a mandatory six a.m. practice.

My sore body ached at the idea of another strenuous practice, but there was no avoiding it unless I quit the squad.

And that wasn't an option.

I liked cheering. I liked the tumbling, the choreography, and adrenaline rush of a screaming, fired up crowd.

Brylee and her bitches didn't get to take that from me.

I turned off the shower and reached for my towel to dry off.

My towel that wasn't on the hook where I left it.

Shit.

I guess juvenile pranks weren't above Brylee.

Sticking my head out of the stall, it was obvious all my clothes—both used from cheer and fresh—were gone.

I glanced down at my body.

It's not like I hated my body. Objectively it was good. For all the comments about my weight, it was mostly muscle. It's not like I had anything to be ashamed of. I didn't have a third nipple or hairy moles.

Brylee expected me to cower in this stall until someone came to help me.

I wasn't going to give that girl a fucking thing she wanted.

Shoving the curtain back, I stepped out onto the tiles and walked through the shower area and toward my locker.

"Oh, my God!"

"Holy shit!"

The cackles and whispers started as soon as they saw me. I kept my head up and went for my locker, thankful I had a back up pair of shorts and a t-shirt in there.

As I rounded the corner to my locker, I was met with a piercing, sharp flash of light.

Brylee grinned from behind her phone as she lowered it. "You're looking a little saggy, Lainey."

I forced myself to smile at her. "It's called a D-cup, honey. Your little Bs probably don't understand gravity."

She glared at me. "Let's just see what everyone else on campus has to say, shall we?"

I shrugged. "Just make sure you call your lawyer first." I rolled my eyes at her confused look. "I'm seventeen. Disseminating child pornography is a felony."

I mentally high-fived myself for that extra credit paper I had written in current events about a guy whose girlfriend sent him nude photos of herself. After they broke up, he sent them to his friends. Problem was, she was only sixteen and technically a minor.

"This isn't child porn, you freak," Brylee snarled, but I noticed her hesitating.

I brushed by her and opened my locker quickly, thankful I'd had the foresight to bring extra clothes. I yanked on my shorts and top, regretting not having a backup set of underwear and shoes.

"Legally it is," I told her, slamming the locker door shut. I smirked at her. "So you do whatever you want with that picture. But you and I both know my dad will have your ass in court by the end of the week."

Her eyes narrowed.

I turned at the entrance to our bank of lockers. I motioned to

Hayley and Kayleigh behind her. "Oh, and if you even think about having Tweedle Dumb and Dumber do it for you? Everything can be traced back to that phone you took the picture on."

"You *bitch*," Kayleigh seethed, her dark eyes flashing.

Hayley flipped her auburn hair over her shoulder. "You know we're going to make your life hell, right?"

I spread my arms wide as I walked backward. "Bring it on. But before you focus on me too much? You might want to work on your back tuck. It's sloppy as hell."

I shoved through the double doors of the locker room and into the hallway before they could reply, and barreled head first into someone else. It was like hitting a wall, and I almost went down except for the hands that caught me.

"Whoa. You good?"

I looked up, recognizing the guy as one of Ryan's friends from last night.

Linc. The guy who had helped Court hold Dean while Ryan smashed a fist into his face. He was the shortest of Ryan's three friends by a couple inches, putting him a little taller than me, but he was built like a football player. Wide shoulders, narrow waist, and hard lines. The dark hair and stormy blue eyes were what elevated him from athlete to GQ model, though.

"Cheer practice over?" he asked with an easy smile.

A *smile*.

I didn't think any of Ryan's friends were capable of smiling at me.

"Yeah."

He glanced down. "You forgot your shoes again, Cinderella. Is this a new thing? Like you embraced your inner zen while in isolation this summer?"

I faked a bright, toothy grin. "I do love the feel of dirty tiles under my toes."

He snorted and grinned back. "Right." He squinted at me. "What happened to your face?"

I touched the swollen part of my face with a grimace. "Cheer accident."

"And they say it isn't a sport," he muttered good-naturedly.

I couldn't help but smile at the compliment. Cheering often was thought of as less than a sport, but my aching muscles begged to disagree.

"I'm actually on my way back to the dorm," I told him, hitching a thumb in the general direction of my room, even as my stomach growled.

"Hungry?" His smirk deepened and he folded his arms across his chest. "I was just about to meet the guys in the dining hall."

"Pretty sure shoes are a requirement for dining," I commented, suddenly glad for my missing shoes and the out it gave me. Eating with Ryan and his friends?

No. Just... no.

The less I saw of my fiancé, the better.

"Okay," he agreed easily, "we'll stop by your place for shoes first." He reached out and touched the tangled wet strands of my hair, which I hadn't stopped to fix while facing off with Brylee. "And maybe a hairbrush?"

I sighed heavily. "And here I thought I might be starting a new hair trend."

"Bird Nest Couture?" he chimed in, falling into step with me.

"I hear it's all the rage," I agreed with a decisive nod.

He pushed open the front door and led us into the sunlight. "After you."

It felt weird walking across the campus with Linc at my side. We got more than a few looks, but I wasn't sure if they were looking at him or the mess that I was.

"How's Rebecca?" he asked suddenly. "Last night... That shit was fucked up."

I nodded, my spine stiffening. "Yeah. She's okay."

"Gotta admit, I was surprised you came to her rescue," he muttered, rubbing the back of his neck. "I thought you hated her."

"People change," I replied evenly. "And Bex is cool. She didn't deserve that. No one deserves that."

"I mean, agreed," he said quickly, "but you've gotta see the hypocrisy. All the shit you've pulled over the years? Damn."

I jerked to a stop and glared at him. "So, I should have done nothing? Let Dean rape her?"

Linc flushed, anger flaring in his eyes. "Of course not."

"Not that it would matter if he had, right?" I added scathingly. "Ryan ordered me not to let Bex go to the police, so I guess you guys protect fellow scumbags."

His hand shot out and grabbed my wrist as I started to turn away. "Hold the fuck up. Ryan? Me? Our friends? We're *nothing* like Dean. Which you should know, since Ryan usually intervened when *you* got out of control with the shit you pulled."

He did?

I filed that away under "things to investigate later." Admittedly, that file was getting pretty full.

"I don't know what this sudden personality transplant is," he went on, "but it's about time."

"Well, Ryan seems to think I'm playing a game."

"Are you?" he challenged.

I looked him square in the eye. "No. I'm not the same girl you knew last year."

He let my wrist go and stepped back. "Okay."

"Okay?"

"Yeah. If people can't change, then we're all pretty fucked, aren't we?"

I nodded slowly. "I agree."

"Perfect." He clapped his hands together. "Now, can we hurry up and get you shoes? I'm starving and we still have another practice this afternoon. Fucking two-a-days are brutal, and I need some food before I waste away to nothing." He patted his stomach, and I could see the outline of well-defined abs through his thin shirt.

"I don't think you'll waste away," I replied, but started walking toward my dorm again. "But I guess I can hurry up just to be on the safe side."

He slung an arm around my shoulder. "See? I knew we could be friends."

My brows shot up. "Is that what we are?"

He glanced down at me. "Would you rather we be enemies?"

I had enough of those.

"Okay," I said slowly, smiling slightly. "Friends."

CHAPTER 25

I took as much time as I could finding my shoes, brushing my hair, and making myself somewhat presentable, knowing the whole time that Linc was waiting outside for me. As nice as our agreement to be friends sounded, I wasn't exactly looking forward to lunch with *his* friends, which inevitably would include Ryan.

My only saving grace was when the elevator doors opened on the way down and Bex appeared.

"Hey," she greeted, flashing me a genuine smile.

"Please tell me you're going to get food," I begged, not bothering with saying hi back.

Her brows shot up. "Uh, I am. It's lunchtime, so..."

"Sit with us?" I was just this side of dropping to my knees and pleading. I needed as many buffers as possible between Ryan and me.

Her look turned skeptical. "Who is *us*?"

"Linc and his friends," I mumbled.

She sighed. "I don't know. I mean, people will think it's weird if we're together."

"I don't give a shit about other people," I replied firmly. "You're my friend. And I could use the backup."

"I mean, okay," she agreed reluctantly as the doors opened again on the ground floor. "But you're not going to be helping yourself re-climb the social ladder."

"The ladder can suck my dick," I announced as we pushed through the front doors.

Linc blinked in surprise from where he was lounging against the stone stairs. "I always knew there was something different about you, Lainey. Didn't think having a dick was it, though."

I rolled my eyes. "Linc, this is Bex. Bex, meet Linc."

"We've met," Bex mumbled, huddling a little closer to my side. She gave me a sharp look and I flinched inwardly. If Ryan had vacationed with Court's family then Linc likely had as well.

And Madelaine would've known that.

Linc flashed her a grin, ignoring my misstep. "Nice to see you conscious, Bex. It's a good look."

Bex's cheeks turned pink, and I resisted the urge to slap the back of Linc's head as we started toward the dining hall.

"But seriously," he added, looking down at her, "are you okay?"

Bex barely lifted her head but gave a quick nod. "Yeah. Um... thanks, I guess? Maddie told me that you guys helped get me out of there."

The smile vanished from Linc's face, replaced by a darker, menacing look that almost made me shiver.

"Dean's been dealt with," he informed Bex coolly, his wide shoulders bunching up with tension, "but if he gives you any shit or even looks at you funny, you come tell me. We'll handle it."

Bex's gaze darted to mine. I could only shrug in reply.

"Thanks," she murmured.

A second later, Linc was grinning again as he pulled open the door to the dining hall for us. "No worries."

I followed him inside, my eyes immediately going wide at the spacious room and array of food and drink. The room was only about half full, and my gaze slid instantly to the group in the back corner.

Multiple tables and chairs had been pulled up to accommodate all the extra bodies—the large bodies—of the football players. Ryan sat close to the middle, his dark blonde hair messy from practice. Ash and Court were with him, looking just as disheveled.

I gave myself a second to really study Ryan as he laughed at something Court said. The way his blue eyes sparkled, the way his broad shoulders shook. He looked almost normal. Almost human.

Bex's fingers cut into my wrist like talons. "I don't know if I can do this," she hissed, panic rolling off her body in palpable waves.

I looked at her to see her eyes round and wide with fear, her gaze darting around like she was looking for an escape.

"Hey," I said, forgetting Linc and turning so I was in front of her and blocking her view of the room. "We can go back. No worries."

Linc came back after realizing we had stopped following him. "Ladies? Is there a problem?"

Bex swallowed, uncomfortable being put on the spot. "N-no. No problem."

"Okay," he drawled. "Let's get our food and sit down."

We joined him in the line, and I flashed the first attendant the card that showed my food allergy before I happily selected a slice of sausage pizza and a basket of garlic knots. Bex picked a spinach salad with some fruity vinaigrette dressing that looked wholly unappealing. Linc, on the other hand, almost needed two trays to contain the amount of food he grabbed.

I glanced back at Bex as Linc asked for extra meatballs in his spaghetti.

"Where do we pay?" I murmured, looking around for the cashier.

Bex frowned. "Pay? For the food?"

I nodded.

Understanding blossomed on her face. "Oh, no. It's all included in the tuition."

"This way," Linc beckoned, jerking his head toward the table.

"Actually? The table looks pretty full," I said suddenly, grasping for an out as Ryan's eyes found me and narrowed. "Bex and I can sit on our own."

"What? No way," Linc replied, shaking his head. "Come on."

Sighing, I followed him with Bex trailing after me.

As soon as the guys realized Linc was there, a seat was instantly freed up for him. He set his tray down and looked back at us, and then at Ryan.

Everyone's eyes turned to Ryan. Waiting for an order or a decree.

I was about to walk away, feeling uneasy under the weight of the dozens of eyes boring into me, when Ryan simply jerked his chin at the guys to his left.

Two seats opened up like they had been waiting for us.

I carefully picked my way around the cluster of guys until I could set my tray down next to Ryan. As I sank into the seat, Bex doing the same to my right, I caught Ryan's brow lift at my tray.

I grabbed the pizza and took a big bite before he could correct my choice of food.

Interestingly enough, a smile twitched at the corner of his mouth. He looked past me to Bex.

"How are you, Rebecca?" he asked in a low voice as conversations resumed around us.

Bex responded by choking on the mouthful of spinach she had just taken a bite of.

"She's good," I answered for her, watching as she reached for her bottle of water and took a massive swallow.

"I'm good," she croaked, the blush on her cheeks extending to the tips of her ears.

Ryan nodded, satisfied with the answer. He leaned into me and whispered, "Not sitting with your *friends*?"

The cheer squad had taken up tables in the center of the room. Most were taking advantage of the few days we had left before uniforms were mandatory, providing as much eye candy and temptation as they could in tight tops and short skirts.

"I'd rather eat in a pit of vipers," I replied grimly, then paused. "Although, I guess it's the same thing."

The corner of his mouth lifted again.

I fake gasped, dropping my garlic knot onto my tray and pressing a hand to my chest. "Oh, my God. Is that an actual smile from something I said?"

His lips flattened to a thin line almost instantly, and I sort of regretted my sarcasm.

After what Bex had told me, Ryan had a good reason to hate who he thought I was.

"What happened to your face?" His critical gaze assessed the mark on my face.

I focused my attention on my food and gave a little shrug. "Just an accident at practice."

I could feel his eyes on me for another second before he turned his head away from me and started talking to Ash, who was still glaring at me just as hard as the night before from where he sat on Ryan's other side.

Actually, as I looked around, I realized most of the team was outright shooting me death stares or pointedly ignoring me.

I dropped my gaze back to my plate and started tearing my garlic knots into little pieces and popping them into my mouth as anxiety churned in my gut, trying not to give them another reason to hate me.

When I glanced to my right, Bex didn't seem any more comfortable than I was. She was studying her salad like it held the answers to all her questions in life.

I was trying to figure out the best way to extract us from the situation when a shadow fell across us. Across from me, I saw Linc's eyes harden into glaciers.

A hand settled on the back on my chair and Bex's, bracing someone over us. Bex's fork clattered to her plate.

"You left early today," Dean informed Ryan, who barely spared him a glance. "We're scheduling a house meeting for tonight."

"We had practice," Ryan replied, his tone clipped and annoyed.

Dean huffed. "You wanted this meeting, Cain. I set it up."

"Tomorrow," Ryan ground out, still not bothering to acknowledge his presence. Most of the football team went silent, watching as their leader interacted with the frat president.

"You said—"

"I fucking said *tomorrow*," Ryan cut him off, finally turning in his seat with a glare that sent shivers down *my* spine.

I felt his hand curl around the back of my chair, his knuckles brushing my back, as he and Ryan continued their stare-off.

Snorting, I twisted around. "Get off my chair."

His surprised gaze snapped to me and then narrowed. Slowly he removed his hand but left the other on Bex's chair. In fact, he extended a finger out to drag along her spine. Bex started to shift away, but I shoved my chair back into him. Dean rocked back a few steps, his head tilting enough that I got a clear view of the bruising around his jaw from where Ryan had punched him.

A sick sense of satisfaction almost made me smirk.

"Don't touch her," I hissed, fury for my friend and what he had tried to do—and gotten away with—lighting a fire in me. "Don't even *look* at her."

It took him a second to respond, but when the shock wore off, he pushed the chair away and was in my face. "Bitch—"

More chairs scraped as people stood up, and I felt Ryan start to get up beside me, but before he could intervene, my anger snapped. Maybe no one else wanted to do something about this cockroach, but I was going to.

My fist swung, landing solidly against his nose with a satisfying *crack* that my self-defense teacher would have been proud of.

"Fuck!" he shouted, staggering back several steps and covering his face.

I smirked when blood seeped from between his fingers, but I'd barely had time to enjoy the sight before Ryan's massive form blocked my view. I could make out the dusky outline of a large tattoo on his back through the thin white shirt he wore, but then he was stalking forward, fisting Dean's shirt in his clenched hands and propelling the other man backward.

"I warned you before," he snarled, finally shoving Dean into an empty table. He leaned over Dean's sprawled body and whispered something too low for me to hear, but enough to make the still-bleeding douchebag flinch and pale.

A hand brushed my still clenched fist, and I looked up to see Ash at my side, a perplexed look on his face as he watched me.

I glanced around to see that everyone was staring. All conversations had stopped, and a few people had phones out. I wasn't an expert in this world, but I doubted what Ryan was doing would go over all that well.

Even if the asshole deserved it.

I shook off Ash and closed the distance, placing a soft hand on Ryan's back and feeling the power of the muscles under my touch as they rolled and contracted.

"We have an audience," I murmured, tugging gently at his shirt.

Ryan hesitated a second and then moved back, anger still rolling off him in palpable waves.

Dean pushed himself up, swiping under his nose with the back of his hand. A sluggish stream of blood still dribbled to his lip. He glared at us both for a beat before masking his hate.

"Sorry for the confusion," he finally uttered. "I meant no offense."

I snorted in derision. "Your entire existence is an offense."

Laughter rippled around us, but Ryan reached back to grab my wrist and give it a warning squeeze, the *be quiet* message loud and clear.

I pressed my lips together and rolled my eyes, but stayed quiet.

"This is done," Ryan informed Dean. "Go."

Dean's hand started to make a fist before he seemed to realize who he would be threatening. And the wall of Pacific Cross football players ready to back up their star player. He hunched his shoulders and stalked out of the dining hall, nearly knocking over a couple of freshmen who weren't fast enough to scurry out of the way.

Ryan turned back to his team, still holding my wrist. With a subtle nod of his head, they all sat down.

My eyes found Bex, and I winced at the stark fear in her eyes.

"Court." Ryan's warm voice was more soothing than I had anticipated. "Can you make sure Rebecca gets back to her dorm?"

Court nodded, his face still tight with anger.

"Let's go," Ryan told me, already starting to pull me away.

"Wait," I insisted, tugging back until he had to stop or literally drag me outside.

He paused, waiting for me, but not looking happy about it. Probably wondering if he could actually get away with dragging my body through the room and getting pissed when he realized it would *definitely* attract attention.

I would deal with his irritation in a minute. Right now I was worried about my friend.

"Are you okay with this?" I asked Bex. If she needed me, Ryan could go fuck himself. I wouldn't leave her.

With a gulp, Bex looked around and slowly nodded. "I'll catch up with you in the dorms?"

"You're sure?"

She flashed me a weak smile. "I'm good, Maddie."

I nodded and trudged behind Ryan, brushing off the curious stares from classmates as we made our way outside.

Ryan tugged me around the corner of the building, and I yanked my arm back, having had enough of being treated like a little kid who wandered off in the mall.

"Would you stop?" I demanded, glaring at the spot where his hand was still clamped around me.

He whirled so fast that I jumped back a step. "What the fuck was that?"

My eyes narrowed, anger rising again like a tidal wave. This time when I pulled my arm, it came free of his hold. "I could ask you the same thing, buddy."

His brows shot up incredulously. "What did you just call me?"

"I should be calling you Captain Liar after last night," I snarked. "What happened to Dean staying away?"

"He won't bother you again," he replied coldly, his voice tight. "I promise."

"I don't give a shit about him bothering me. I can handle myself," I fired back, holding up my hand. My knuckles were red from where they'd connected with Dean's face. "He needs to stay away from Bex."

He caught my fist in his larger hand, his touch gentle despite the rough calluses. He studied my hand, turning it slowly. "This is going to bruise."

"I'll be fine," I muttered, embarrassed by his attention.

He let me go. "I can't believe you punched him."

I arched a brow. "Well, someone had to do something, and clearly whatever you told me you did to him last night didn't work."

"You let me worry about that."

"I would if I thought you actually had a handle on your psycho *brother*," I retorted.

"Goddammit, Madelaine," he swore, shaking his head. I got the vague impression he was barely resisting the urge to grab me by the shoulders and shake me. "I told you—"

"That I only do and say what you want," I interrupted sarcastically. "Yeah, I got it. I'm your little puppet. You pull all the strings."

"Then act like it," he snapped. "Unless you need a reminder?"

I shrugged and spread my arms wide, welcoming whatever he wanted to dish out. "Going to lace my drink and throw me in Dean's bed next? Help him cover *that* up, too?"

Ryan's face flushed with rage. "I swear to God, you need to shut up about shit you don't understand."

"I understand that my *fiancé* is comfortable assisting men who like to assault women and children." Ice settled in my blood as I glared at him.

He shook his head, raking a hand through his hair. "You really don't know what you're talking about."

"Then enlighten me."

He watched me for a long moment, almost like he was weighing letting me in on whatever secrets he was currently holding. Then the soft consideration was replaced with a stone-cold facade. "Just stick to the plan. Play the part of the dutiful fiancée, and we won't have a problem."

"And if I say no?" I asked archly.

His blue eyes turned to ice. "Then me leaving you unconscious in Dean's bed will look like a fucking day at the beach compared to what I do next."

CHAPTER 26

"Are you out of your mind?" Bex demanded as I walked up the front steps of our dorm. She stood up from where she was sitting on the top step, stomping down to meet me midway.

I shrugged my shoulders. "I've been called that before."

"You punched Dean. You physically attacked him!"

"He physically attacked *you*!" I practically shouted, then glanced around as I realized we were outside and I needed to stay quiet. "Why is it so surprising that I would punch that douchenozzle?"

Bex shook her head. "We can't talk about this here."

"I'd invite you to my room, but Ryan apparently likes to let himself in whenever he wants."

She snorted. "My roommate is at swim practice. We can talk in my room."

I followed her inside and up to the fourth floor where her room was. She unlocked and pushed open the door, giving me my first view of her room.

The space was about half the size of just my living area alone. There were two double beds, each pushed to the opposite side of the room with a window between them. A desk was at the foot of each bed and flanked by two small closets.

I felt like an asshole by comparison for how much space I had all to myself.

"Because Madelaine never would have," Bex replied, exasperated as she closed the door behind us.

"I'm not Madelaine!"

"Yes, you *are*," she shot back, going to the neatly made bed and sitting down. "For all intents and purposes, *you* are Madelaine Cabot. And she definitely doesn't *punch* people."

"Maybe she should have," I replied, dropping into the desk chair closest to her and making a face.

Bex gave a small laugh. "She might've broken a nail."

I held up a hand, inspecting my manicure and wincing when I realized almost every finger had chipped polish. With a groan, my head fell back. "I seriously can't do this. What the hell was I thinking? I can't be *her*."

"Maddie," Bex's voice softened.

"No, really," I said, lifting my head and looking at her. "I'm really starting to wonder if all of this is even worth it."

"You want to go back?" Bex asked quietly.

I shrugged. "Maybe? All I know is, at my old high school, I knew where things stood. Avoid the gangs, don't walk alone at night, and make minimal eye contact with people on the streets. All I had to do was keep my head down and graduate, and pray Mom didn't kill herself while I was at school or working." My lips quirked into a twisted sort of smile. "Those were the good times."

Her mouth hung open a second before she snapped it shut. "I don't even know what to say to that."

I laughed, feeling the smile stretch my lips.

"Is that really what it's like?" she whispered, leaning forward.

"I mean, mostly?" I lifted my shoulders helplessly. "We lived in a crappy town outside of Detroit. My mom has been high or drunk or both for most of my life."

"Who took care of you?"

"Mostly I did," I answered. "When I was little, a few neighbors would check on us. Make sure I had food."

"And now your mom's in rehab?"

I nodded.

Bex snorted. "Well, most people here have a parent who checks into some kind of rehab at least once a decade."

"I'm just hoping it takes this time," I murmured, realizing I hadn't checked in with Mom for several days. We were overdue for a chat, and I missed hearing her voice.

"You said Madelaine set up the facility?"

"Yeah. And Gary said he would keep covering the cost," I added. "He's planning to bring her to California so she'll be closer to me when she's finished her program."

Her eyes narrowed, and she looked less than impressed.

"What?"

"All I know is, Gary Cabot doesn't do a thing unless it benefits Gary Cabot," Bex replied. "He's not what you'd call the generous type."

The conversation at dinner flashed through my mind, and the way he was so easily accepting of a child molester if it meant he got the upper hand in business.

"He said he owed me," I said in a small voice, not sure if I was trying to convince myself or Bex that his heart was in the right place. He was my *dad*. There was a piece of my heart that naturally wanted to believe he wanted to help me.

"He absolutely does," she agreed, "but just be careful, Maddie."

I frowned. "Why did my sister want to file for emancipation?"

Now Bex's mouth pulled down, her brow furrowed. "She was kind of weird about the whole thing. All I know is something must have happened around her thirteenth birthday, because that's when shit started going south."

"How so?" I toed off my shoes and pulled my legs up onto the chair before resting my chin on my knees.

She glanced away, thinking back. "She had this big party. I mean, *duh*. She's Madelaine Cabot, and I remember her being excited because her dad actually came home for it. The party was great, and I was supposed to spend the night, but I got sick and went home."

"Okay," I said, trying to figure out what might've triggered a thirteen-year-old girl to file for emancipation and then try to kill herself.

"Then my family went away for Thanksgiving," Bex went on. "When I came home, Madelaine was pissed as hell at something. She wouldn't tell me what, but that's when she mentioned emancipation and... you."

I sighed unhappily. It still irritated me that Madelaine had known about me for *years* and done nothing. And now I would never know why.

Bex flashed me a thin smile. "Honestly, I thought you were something she made up. Madelaine wasn't the most honest person, so I figured she wasn't really serious. I mean, who has a long-lost twin sister outside of a soap opera?"

The fact that my sister had lied and known about me for *years* stung like hell. I had reached out to her almost as soon as I had found her. And then she took *weeks* to actually respond to me. Weeks, when she'd known I existed all along.

"When did she try to..." I swallowed, unable to say the words.

Bex's head dropped, and she picked at a thread on her peach comforter. "The day after Christmas. I went over to give her this necklace I'd gotten her. One of those best friend ones? I found her in her bathroom. She'd cut her wrist. She'd been pulling away from me for months, since her birthday, but I never expected she was suicidal."

Her eyes fell to my left wrist, and I touched the smooth skin that she saw.

She took a deep breath. "After that, it was chaos. Her dad came home—"

"He wasn't home for Christmas?" I interrupted her.

She shook her head. "No. I asked her if she wanted to spend the holidays with my family, but her Uncle Adam was visiting. Her dad traveled a lot, and he stood in a lot as a parental figure."

A creepy sort of awareness tingled up my spine and into my scalp. I resisted the urge to shudder. "Adam Kindell. I've met him."

"I always got the feeling that Lainey hated him," Bex said. "He was weird, but I didn't see him much when we were little. Then again, we spent most of the time at my house."

I bit my lower lip. "I think he and Madelaine were... involved."

"Involved?" she repeated blankly.

"Like," I lowered my voice for some reason, "intimately."

Her mouth gaped open. "Oh, God. Ew. *Ew*. Are you serious?"

I nodded morosely, remembering when Adam had found me by the pool and then the way he touched me at dinner.

With a disgusted noise, Bex scooted away to lean her back against the wall. "I always knew he was pervy, but I didn't think he would actually, like, do anything."

"I mean, I don't have proof, but he said and did some things that make me think he was more than just a pseudo uncle to my sister," I admitted.

She waved her hands in front of her, looking more than a little horrified. "I can't even think about that."

I felt the exact same way. Adam was old enough to be, well, my uncle. Or father.

"If she was involved with him," Bex added after a second, "it would probably be on her phone."

"Gary cloned her phone and gave it to me," I said.

"Were there any weird emails or stuff?"

I slowly shook my head. "No. All her apps are on the phone, but I don't know any of her logins. Social media, email... I can't access it."

"Can I see your phone?"

I pulled it from my pocket and handed it over.

"You don't have it locked?" She glanced up at me in surprise even as she thumbed through the screen.

I shrugged. "What do I have to hide? It's not like there's anyone I can call or whatever except my mom and Gary."

After a beat, Bex flashed the screen at me. "Now you have my number."

I smiled at her, relaxing as she kept going.

Suddenly her brows slammed down. "Whoa."

"Whoa, what?" I asked, leaning forward to see the screen.

"You have a CryptDuo app," she replied, looking up at me.

I stared blankly back.

Sighing, she ran a hand through her hair. "It's like a military grade cyber security system for phones and laptops. It's not actually available in an app store. It can encrypt all sorts of data. Basically makes your device unhackable without the right password."

I must have still looked confused, because she laughed and added, "My dad is a contractor for the Department of Defense. He designed the program. It's on his phone and computers. We even have it integrated into our house's security system. But it's not available to the public."

"I have no idea how it got on there," I told her honestly.

Bex's frown deepened. "I mean, someone could have given her the details to the program to download it, but why? What the hell could she have on her phone that required that type of security?"

"Maybe there's nothing on it?"

"No, most of the memory in this phone has been used up. The media files alone are taking up two-thirds of the memory."

"There's a lot of videos of cheer practice and random stuff." I leaned forward to look at the phone in her hand.

"How many?"

"Videos?" I shrugged. "Maybe fifty?"

"That wouldn't be enough to use this much data," she murmured, handing the phone back. "And why did she save it as a hard copy when she could've backed it up to the cloud?"

I looked down at the now-blank screen. "Is there any way to find out what's on it?"

"I can ask my dad," she replied. A strange look crossed her face. "Or you could ask Ash."

"Ash? Ryan's friend, Ash? The guy who looks at me like I'm the scum on the bottom of his shoe?"

The whole three times I had seen the tall, green-eyed guy, he'd glared at me like I was the one who shot his puppy.

Or hurt his best friend.

"Yeah, but he's also stupid smart and a genius with computers.

Rumor has it he even hacked the CIA when he was thirteen," she whispered loudly with a grin.

"Doesn't change the fact that he still hates me. A lot," I added pointedly.

Bex sighed heavily. "I'll ask my dad, but I think Ash is your best bet."

I groaned and closed my eyes, dropping my forehead to my knees.

Freaking fantastic.

CHAPTER 27

The idea of approaching Ash for anything was about as appealing as playing tag with a rabid pitbull.

Except that the pitbull might be a little more approachable.

After I left Bex's room, I went up to mine and tried to figure out a way to plead my case, but every scenario I envisioned ended with him telling me to fuck off before slamming a door in my face.

I could have asked Ryan, but the last thing I wanted was to be indebted to Ryan in *any* way. Besides, he might agree and then use whatever he found on the phone against me.

I stared down where the phone sat lifeless on the coffee table. Some TV show played on behind me. I'd turned it on when the silence in my room became deafening. Honestly, that run coach was forcing on us tomorrow sounded fun, but I wasn't too sure about venturing out on my own at night.

Anxious energy was fizzing in my blood like a shaken-up soda bottle.

Wiping my palms on my thighs, I rolled my neck and shoulders, trying to relieve the tension.

"This is stupid," I muttered to myself before swiping the phone and tucking it into the convenient pocket of my leggings.

It took me seconds to throw on my running shoes and pull my hair into a messy ponytail. I grabbed an old baseball cap from my backpack. One of the few things I hadn't let go of throughout the years.

During a sober moment when I was little, Mom had taken me to a baseball game in Detroit. Well, more like the guy she was seeing took us. His name was Hank, and he had kind green eyes and a little bit of a beer gut. He laughed loud enough to make me want to join in, and he made Mom smile.

Until he died in a car wreck four months into their relationship.

Mom went on a bender that brought child protective services to our door, but I still kept the beaten-up black hat as a reminder of Hank. It wasn't even a hat that supported the Detroit Tigers, but the visiting East Coast team with an orange and black bird smiling from the brim.

I threaded my hair through the opening at the back and pulled it low on my forehead, hoping the cap and my dark clothes would keep people from noticing me going for a run.

I'd had my fill of hateful stares over the last twenty-four hours.

I yanked the door to my room open and froze when I realized there was a body on the other side, hand poised like he was going to knock.

"Ryan," I said, jerking to a surprised stop.

His eyes narrowed and swept the length of my body before the cool blue irises hardened suspiciously. "Where are you going?"

"For a run," I replied.

"Like that?" He waved a hand at my outfit.

"Well, I thought going naked might be a little much," I answered, sarcasm thick in my tone.

He reached up and rubbed a hand through his hair. Judging by the mess, he had been doing it frequently. "Christ. Can I come in?"

My eyebrows rose slowly. "You're asking permission? Isn't breaking and entering more your style?"

"I haven't broken shit," he grumbled, shifting on his feet. Exhaustion lined his eyes, and I remembered the team bitching about the strenuous two-a-day practices the coaches were demanding.

Some stupid, traitorous part of me softened at seeing him worn down, and I found myself relenting.

I stepped backward, leaving him an opening. "Come on in."

He moved inside the room, and I closed the door and leaned against it as he walked into my living room like he owned the place.

"So, what did I forget to do this time?" I asked with a heavy sigh, ready to hear whatever he needed to bitch about so I could go for a run.

He glanced back at me over a massively muscled shoulder. "I'm sure I'll think of something."

I rolled my eyes. "It's getting late, and I have an early practice."

"So do I," he replied, still looking around the room like he was expecting to find me hiding someone in the space.

"Then can we get this over with? I'm really not in the mood for a fight. I'm tired."

"You were going out for a run," he pointed out, turning and giving me his full attention. He folded his arms across his chest, the black t-shirt pulling taut around his biceps.

I shrugged and pushed away from the door, then walked around him to the kitchen. "My brain is tired. My body... not so much. I thought I could burn off the excess energy before bed."

He cocked his head curiously, a wicked glint in his eyes. "You could burn it off *in* bed."

I opened the refrigerator door and paused, looking up at him in astonishment. "Pass."

He moved closer, and I suddenly realized that he was moving to block the only exit in this little galley-style kitchenette.

"Huh. And here I thought you might be into it," he added quietly, his low tone hinting at something.

I snatched a bottle of water off the top shelf and slammed the door, mentally bitch-slapping myself for feeling an ounce of pity for this guy. "Right. Because that's what I do." I unscrewed the cap and took a drink before setting the bottle on the counter. "Think your new coach is up for visitors?"

I knew I was poking the lion with a cattle prod, but somehow that didn't stop the words from tumbling out.

I sucked in a breath when he stalked into the kitchen, backing me against the wall with minimal effort. The stark fury in his eyes made my stomach dip.

"Do you think this is a fucking game?" His eyes searched mine, anger radiating off his body in palpable waves.

I swallowed and put a coaxing hand on his chest and felt the steady thump of his heart. "I'm sorry. That was a low blow."

It was. And I could admit it.

Even if the asshat deserved it.

He looked down at where I was touching him, his forehead creased with uncertainty. A second later, he backed away from me. "This isn't what I came here for."

I stayed where I was, my back pressed to the wall. Distance between us was a good thing.

Clearing my throat, I asked, "What *did* you come here for?"

The lines in his face deepened. "Shit. Can you sit down?"

"It's never a good sign when a guy asks you to *sit down*," I murmured, but did as he asked and moved to the couch. I dropped down and waited as he sat in the armchair across from me.

"Are we breaking up?" I deadpanned.

His head jerked in surprise, a muscle ticking in his jaw. "What? Why would you think that?"

I smirked. "You showed up to *talk*. A talk I needed to sit down for. I'm just waiting for the *it's not you, it's me* part."

His head tilted. "Oh, it would definitely be you, and not me."

"Fine," I agreed. "It's all me. Want your ring back?" I held up my left hand, the diamond catching the light.

"Do you always have to be such a fucking smart-ass?" he griped, glaring at me.

I bristled at his tone. "Hey, you showed up on *my* doorstep. I didn't come looking for you."

He leaned back in the chair, his long legs sprawled wide open as he rubbed his jaw thoughtfully. "I really thought after last year that you couldn't surprise me, but here we are."

I held back a snort. Great. This was another *Madelaine is a heinous bitch* speech.

"I even set up a few contingencies to make sure you couldn't fuck things up," he added softly.

My eyebrows rose curiously. "Oh?"

He stood up quickly, moving with the grace of a panther stalking its prey, and slowly walked to the bookshelf. "Leave it to you to prove me wrong."

"I aim to please," I chirped brightly, folding my hands in my lap and watching as he paused, running his finger along the spines of a couple of books and then pausing on the framed photo of Madelaine last year with her squad.

All smiles, she was firmly in the center of the group. Their leader.

Ryan picked up the picture and turned the frame over in his hands.

"I don't trust you," he murmured quietly, tossing me the frame.

I caught it on reflex, the corner digging into my palm. I started to flip it over and froze when a small black square on the back caught my attention. I squinted, trying to figure out what I was seeing.

"Court bugged this place when he dropped Rebecca off the other night."

The frame slipped out of my fingers as my heartbeat started to thunder.

"I wanted to make sure that whatever you were going to pull, I knew about first. I planned to put it here the day you got to school, but you showed up right after I did. Court was planning to break in while I had you at the party, and then you literally opened the door for him." He went back to the chair and sat down, his gaze piercing me. "Imagine my surprise at what I heard today when I finally got around to listening to the recordings."

I swallowed, my mouth going dry. My breaths came in fast, shallow pants, and I wondered if this was how an animal felt when it was trapped.

He leaned forward, his forearms braced on his knees as he stared at me. "Care to guess, *Maddie*?"

The blood drained from my head fast enough to make me dizzy. "Ryan."

"I'd ask who the fuck you are, but your conversation gave me a lot of what I needed to know. Especially the one the morning after the party. The rest Ash found when I asked him to dig into your background," he went on conversationally, like he hadn't just dropped a bomb in the middle of the room.

"Truth be told, I'm not sure if your dad is an idiot or a genius for keeping you hidden, Madison."

My eyes slowly closed, like I could block this moment out. Maybe if I didn't see him, this wasn't really happening.

"Huh."

I opened my eyes to see him watching me curiously.

He smiled grimly. "I guess I kind of expected you to lie or flip out. That's what *she* would have done."

My tongue darted out to lick my lips. "I'm not Madelaine."

"Clearly," he retorted. "So, why don't you tell me why you're *really* here, Madison?"

CHAPTER 28

The silence gaped between us for several beats. My brain struggled to catch up with the realization that Ryan *knew*. He knew my secret.

"I can..." I trailed off, not sure how to finish.

I could do what? Explain?

His brows lifted, daring me to try and lie my way out.

I was so sick of this shit. I desperately missed my trailer and my old, less complicated life.

I exhaled hard, shaking my head in defeat. "We were just supposed to switch places for the summer. She said she wanted a break and... and I wanted one, too, I guess."

Ryan continued to stare at me. "You're sure she's dead?"

My head snapped up. "What? Of course she is."

"I wouldn't put it past her to fake her death or some shit," he explained nonchalantly. "In case you missed it, your sister was a manipulative bitch. She fucked up last year, and I can see her running away."

"She died in a fire," I choked out. "I was there when our dad put her ashes in the family crypt. He was destroyed that she's gone."

He scoffed. "More like destroyed he might lose a fortune."

I shot to my feet, anger surging forward to wash away the numbing shock. "Seriously? My sister is *dead*. Can you at least act like there's some humanity in you?"

He gave me a blank look. "And I'm supposed to, what? Feel bad? Cry? Mourn the bitch?"

My jaw dropped open. "Jesus, could you be more of an asshole?"

"I thought about throwing a party, but it feels like that might be a *little* crass," he added with a smirk.

"Get out," I snapped. "Get the fuck out."

"No."

"Get out or—"

"Or *what*?" he demanded, his eyes glittering. "What the hell are you going to do?"

"Walk away?" I suggested coolly.

Again with the damn smirk.

"Walk away?" he repeated the words with disdain, like me doing just that was incomprehensible. "The broke daughter of a junkie is going to throw away millions?"

"This broke daughter of a junkie is used to living with nothing," I hissed while my hands balled into fists. My fingernails dug into my palms, the bite of pain grounding amidst the emotional tsunami raging in me. "You all need me more than I need you. I told Gary as much."

He laughed, the caustic sound echoing in my ears. "Right."

"Believe it or not, Ryan, it's the truth. I'll walk away from all of this tonight."

"And Gary will just let you go? Maybe you tried too many of the drugs your mom was shooting up." He shook his head. "You're not walking away from this."

"I think it's time for you to leave," I ground out, my teeth clenched so hard I was worried they might crack.

Ryan's head tilted to the side, and he smiled. "But we're not done talking."

"Yes, we are," I shot back. I lifted a shaking hand and yanked the baseball cap off my head.

"Sit down."

My spine welded into steel. "No."

"Sit. Down." His cold eyes bore into me. "Listen to what I have to say."

I folded my arms across my chest.

"Please," he added, gritting out the foreign word.

Scoffing, I shook my head.

"Don't leave," he implored, holding up a hand when I started to interrupt. "Just... wait a fucking second and let me talk, okay?"

I clamped my mouth shut and glared at him, but reluctantly sat down.

"I get why you're here, and I'm sure Gary promised to give you all the things you didn't have growing up. Money, a car, whatever."

"I can't drive," I muttered, toying with the ends of my hair. "I don't need a car."

"Okay," he agreed, almost amused. "No car for Madison. I'm not going to stand in the way of your happily ever after, but I could use you."

"Use me?" I repeated skeptically. That didn't sound good at all.

"Madelaine wasn't the only one stuck in this engagement," he admitted bitterly. "But you leaving will complicate a lot of shit for me that I'd rather not deal with."

"Oh, well, if I'm doing *you* a favor, then of course I'll stay," I told him sarcastically. "You've been such a great guy to me."

"I thought you were someone else," he replied, shrugging unapologetically. "And your sister honestly deserved all the shit that's landed at your feet."

"Maybe," I agreed, "but the stuff with that deal in Asia? Or, hell, with your frat brother? The people in your world may be okay with letting pedophiles and rapists roam free, but I'm not. I don't want any part of this."

"It's more complicated than you know," he said, frustration evident in his voice.

"No, it isn't," I countered. "Bad guys get reported to the police. End of story."

"Police won't touch guys like Dean. He'll buy his way out of whatever charges get thrown his way. Same with the prick from Shutterfield. Indonesia doesn't give a shit what village brothels he's visiting so long as the checks keep clearing to the public officials in his pocket."

"That doesn't work for me," I said woodenly.

He watched me for a second, and then sighed. "It doesn't work for me either."

Confusion muddled my thoughts. "But you said..."

"I said it was complicated, and it is. But I never said they were going to walk away," Ryan informed me.

"How?" I demanded. "If the police can't touch them, then *how*?"

He smiled softly at me. "You're new to this world, Madison, but we have ways of making people pay that are more damning and much more severe than a prison sentence. I'm handling it."

"Handling it *how*?" I pressed.

"Look, we're getting off topic," he said, dismissing my question. "I can help you out here. What's the real reason you took Gary's deal?"

I hesitated, but finally opted for admitting the truth. "College. I knew that with Pacific Cross on my resume, I could get into any college I wanted... and Gary would pay for it. He's also agreed to help get my mom back on her feet."

The corner of his mouth hooked up. "Fuck me. Could you be any more idealistic?"

I glared at him.

"Sorry," he apologized, sounding anything but. "You're right, though. This school will open all the doors for you, and Madelaine was smart. Her GPA alone should carry you through if you tank this year."

I glowered at him. "I can hold my own, thanks."

"Then you should definitely stay. If you can hack it." His gaze flitted over me. "Your sister left some messy shoes to fill."

I gestured to my dark clothes and the hat. "I wasn't dressed like the cat burglar for fun. People *hate* me here."

"They hate your sister," he corrected.

"Who I now *am*," I concluded. "I had a feeling things would be hard, but this? This is crazy. I don't belong in this world."

"No, you don't," he agreed flatly. "But I can make things easier for you if you agree to stay and keep being my fiancée."

My shock must have been obvious because he added, "I told you. Madelaine and I each had our reasons for being engaged."

"Hers involves a lot of money. What's your reason?"

A dark look shuttered his eyes. "My reasons are mine. Let's leave it at that."

I lifted my chin. "How about if I just leave it, period?"

"None of my reasons affect you," he said in a clipped tone. "But I'm offering to make your life exponentially better here."

"And how can you do that?" I laughed. "Because you're Ryan Cain?"

"Exactly," he answered smoothly. "I say the word, and you're back at the top of the social ladder, Maddie."

I snorted. "Really? It's that easy?"

"Yeah. It's that fucking easy," he replied. "Your problems with the cheerleaders and students will be done. Madelaine Cabot can once again rule the school."

I bit the inside of my cheek. "I don't want to *rule the school*. I just want to get good grades and graduate."

"Even better." Ryan smiled at me. "I can make your life easy as hell. All you have to do is keep playing my fiancée in public."

"Meaning what?"

"Parties, games, social events... Any function, you're on my arm, all smiles. I mean, Gary asked you to keep pretending to be my fiancée, too, didn't he?"

I shifted uneasily, glowering at him. "You know he did."

"Us being a thing will keep both our fathers off our backs," he said. "It's win-win."

"And if I say no?" I held my breath waiting for the answer.

His smile never slipped. "Then enjoy your double wide."

After a beat, I chuckled humorlessly. "Don't knock it till you've tried it, Cain."

He laughed, the sound a warm rumble that did funny things to my stomach.

"Let me make your life easier," he coaxed with that grin that probably routinely melted panties.

But those words rankled something in me. I'd heard them before, grunted through a door when my mom had a *friend* over and I was supposed to stay in my room.

"I'm not sleeping with you," I told him sharply.

His brows shot up. "I'm pretty sure I didn't ask you to."

"I'm just making sure that we're clear that isn't part of the deal," I forced myself to say even as my cheeks flamed.

Understanding dawned on his face. "Got it. But while we're on sex? I would appreciate it if you didn't repeat what your sister did and make a sex tape. It doesn't exactly sell the happy couple vibe we need to show."

"Are you planning on riding the celibacy train, too?" I asked.

"No," he answered honestly. "But I'll be discreet."

This wasn't a real relationship, and I had zero interest in dating guys. If he wanted to screw girls who weren't me? That was fine.

Even if I felt like I was only trying to convince myself with those thoughts.

"Deal," I said stiffly.

"Last question." He ticked up a finger. "Who else knows who you are?"

"Besides Gary and Bex? You... and I guess Ash."

He nodded. "Linc and Court also know."

"You're not very good at keeping secrets, are you?"

His gaze hardened. "Those guys are my brothers. I've known them since I was little. They won't say shit, but they can also help you out if you need it. Pretending to be your sister will take some work. If I'm not around, call one of them."

He tapped a few keys on his phone, and a minute later I had their contact information on mine. I saved each one, lingering on Ash's.

Maybe he'd be inclined to help me with Madelaine's phone now that he knew I wasn't her?

Still, something kept me from asking Ryan.

Every layer I peeled back revealed something new—and unlikeable

—about my twin. I wasn't sure I was ready to process anything else quite yet.

"So, we're good?" Ryan asked, standing up and looking down at me.

I nodded slowly, tilting my head back to peer up at him. Then my spine stiffened. "Hold up. Are there any other bugs around here?"

"Maybe," he hedged with a smirk. "Why? Got any more secrets you're keeping in that pretty head?"

Okay, ignoring the way parts of me melted a little at being called *pretty*, I glared in response.

He grinned at me again, and the butterflies swooped back in. "Court only had time to plant that one, so you're good. I'll see you later, Maddie. Call me if you need me."

He let himself out, and I didn't release the breath I was holding until he was gone.

Minutes ago I had been so full of anxious tension I'd felt like running for five miles. Now I was so drained all I wanted to do was sleep.

I had a feeling this wouldn't be the last time Ryan flipped a switch on my emotional state.

In fact, this was probably just the beginning.

CHAPTER 29

The next day dawned way too soon. I preferred to spend my Sundays sleeping in, especially when I was starting school the following day, but Coach's early morning run killed that dream.

I prepared myself for another practice of cattiness and bruises, but at some point during the night, I had walked my way into the *Twilight Zone*. That was the only explanation for what happened after our two-mile punishment run.

"Did you *see* how short Sophia cut her hair? I mean, it makes her face look rounder than a donut," Brylee informed me as she stretched beside me. She shook her dark ponytail over her shoulder and shot me a knowing look.

Stretched. Beside. Me.

As in, she had willingly come to join me where I was sitting on the grass after our run and started chatting me up like we were best friends. For that matter, the whole team had greeted me as soon as they'd regained their breath.

But Brylee and her friends had surrounded me with chipper smiles as they started gossiping like we were long-lost friends. I'd been too stunned to ask them what the hell they were doing.

I glanced over at the petite Sophia, the victim of Brylee's newest criticism. Her short hair made her look like a pixie. Honestly, she was stunning and adorable; a tricky combination to pull off, but her bone structure was out of this world and the haircut only enhanced it.

I shrugged and reached for my toes. "Actually, I like it."

Hayley's head quickly bobbed across from me. "Oh, I know, right? Totes adorbs."

Brylee tilted her head. "Yeah, I think you're right, Lainey. It suits her face. She looks like a doll."

What the *hell* was happening?

Kayleigh touched her own dark locks, like she was considering sheering them off. "Think I could pull it off, Laine?"

"Um, sure," I answered, glancing around at the girls surrounding me. I straightened my back, wondering if this was a ruse before someone stabbed a knife between my shoulder blades.

It was like everyone had had a personality transplant in the past twelve hours.

Coach Rixon blew her whistle and everyone stood to gather around her. I hung back and had just joined the fringe of the group when Brylee's hand clamped around my wrist and she dragged me forward with a giggle.

"You're the captain, silly," she whispered, "get your skinny ass up here, front and center."

My brows shot up.

So *now* my ass was skinny?

As the coach started laying out the drills and routines she wanted to cover, Brylee leaned into me.

"Oh, my God," she started in a low, excited tone, "are you going to the mixer tonight at Kappa?"

My gaze jerked to hers in surprise. "Uh, I don't think so."

Her hazel eyes went wide with confusion. "But we never miss a party, Laine. And you know I need my wing-woman. Since you and Ryan are so tight now, maybe you can arrange a little chit chat for me with Linc." She winked conspiratorially and shrugged a shoulder. "I hear he's a total animal in bed, and I could use some tequila and orgasms."

I damn near choked on my spit. She wanted me to hook her up with one of Ryan's friends?

Ryan.

Son of a bitch.

Let me make your life easier.

This had to be Ryan. There was no other explanation as to why everyone would suddenly start treating me like a human being out of the blue.

I was still mulling over that realization when I realized everyone was watching me expectantly.

Shit. What had I missed?

Coach Rixon's eyebrows slowly lifted. "What do you say, Captain? Think you can handle it?"

Brylee's arm linked with mine. "Of course we're in, Coach. We're only too happy to support the team, and Lainey's our best choreographer. She'll come up with a kickass routine that shows the PCU squad who has the real talent."

"Perfect," Coach said, looking out at the smiling faces of the squad. "Let's get started."

The squad split into groups, and I started to pull my arm away from Brylee.

"What the hell did I miss?" I asked softly.

She giggled and nudged me with her hip. "Jesus, how late did Ryan keep you up last night?"

And there was my confirmation.

This was all Ryan's doing.

"Late," I replied vaguely, flashing her a weak smile.

"She asked if you could come up with a routine for the PCU homecoming pep rally next month," she informed me. "I told her you'd be happy to, so get to work on it. Good luck sharing the spotlight with Molly. You know how my sister can be."

I watched her bounce off toward a few girls as I digested that. I couldn't help but wonder if this was Ryan or because Molly actually wanted to collaborate.

"Hey, Lainey?"

I jerked when I realized Sandi was standing beside me. Shit, I really needed to pay attention.

"Think you can show me that high kick of yours?" she asked in a sugary sweet voice that made my teeth ache. "I can't seem to get my leg as high."

I pressed my lips together. She certainly hadn't had a problem getting her leg high enough to kick my *face* yesterday.

"Sure," I muttered, and stalked off without waiting to see if she followed. But of course she did.

Because Ryan had thrust me to the top of the social ladder just like he promised.

But I didn't remember asking for that, and I never had been a fan of heights.

I HAD three shadows attached to my ass that never stopped talking for the rest of the day, and I was about to tell them all to get away from me before I slapped them.

Seriously, these girls put the *itch* in *bitch*. The longer I was around them, the more my skin felt like it was crawling.

They'd followed me to my dorm after practice—apparently it was where we all usually hung out to tear apart the other girls on the squad. I felt like an asshole for just sitting there listening to their vitriol, and I found myself stupidly annoyed that they immediately agreed with anything I said. Even if it contradicted exactly what they had just said.

When I finally announced I was heading to lunch when it was barely eleven in the morning, they all got up and followed me like a honking gaggle of goslings I couldn't shake.

I shoved through the doors to the dining hall harder than necessary, as Kayleigh's high-pitched giggle yet again assailed my ears.

This was a sound I would hear in my nightmares, and I wondered (not for the first time) what the hell my twin had been thinking by being *friends* with these people.

I ground my teeth together as I moved through the lunch line, grabbing whatever looked good. The protein bar before practice had worn off long ago and my stomach needed real food.

"Um," Hayley murmured, confusion heavy in her reedy tone, "that's a lot of carbs, Lainey."

I glanced down at my plate of pesto pasta with a side of wheat bread before making the impulsive decision to grab the biggest slice of chocolate cake on the dessert tray and flashing her a smile. "I'm not worried."

The uneasy expression she shared with the other two was all the proof I needed that their newfound personalities were coerced and not genuine.

Like I'd actually had any doubts about it.

Smoothing her expression, Brylee smiled at me. The tightness around her eyes gave away how hard she was working not to say something rude. "So, about the party? I was thinking about wearing my emerald—"

A heavy arm dropped around my shoulders, turning me toward Linc's grinning face.

"Maddie!" His words were almost too vibrant, too loud, but I saw the imploring look flash in his eyes a second before his voice lowered and he added, "Don't bitch-slap the bitches."

I stiffened and gave him a long-suffering look. "No promises."

Linc flashed the three girls staring at us a charming grin. "Ladies. I hope you don't mind if I steal Madelaine away. Ryan wants her to sit with us. They have engagement shit to discuss for the party next month."

Glee lit up Kayleigh's eyes. "I cannot *wait*. Lainey, have you been keeping secrets from us on the party plans?"

"Yeah, you know we'd love to help," Hayley chimed in.

"Anything for you, *Maddie*," Brylee purred, but I saw the hate in her eyes for the second she forgot to school it and in the way her gaze narrowed on Linc's arm on my shoulders.

Hayley wrinkled her nose. "Maddie? Your name is *Lainey*."

"Family nickname," Linc cut in for me, still smiling. "You know my parents and Madelaine's family go way back."

Brylee was still glaring at the way Linc was touching me, and (totally unable to resist) I balanced my tray with one hand and looped my arm around his waist. "Way, way back."

Brylee's cheeks flushed, and I thought she might say something before she swallowed back whatever hateful thoughts were zipping through her pretty skull.

"Don't let us keep you from your fiancé, Lainey," she said brightly. "We'll catch up with you tonight."

"Can't wait," I muttered as they flounced away to a table full of other cheerleaders.

"Tell me the truth," Linc whispered, "on a scale of one to Hiroshima, how nuclear were you about to go on their asses?"

I dropped my arm and angled myself to give him a slow blink. "Chernobyl."

Chuckling, he guided me toward the football table. "Yeah. I figured I should run interference before you smashed all the good will we threw out there for you."

"We?" I echoed in surprise.

He grinned. "Well, yeah. I gotta admit. I didn't see this plot twist coming. Did you really live in a trailer?"

I jerked to a stop, irritation rolling up my back. "Did you really just say that?"

He looked confused at my reaction to his genuinely curious question. "Are you always this defensive?"

"Are you always this dense?" I fired back.

His serious expression cracked a second later and he chuckled. "Yeah. Ash bitches I've had too many concussions on the field."

"Seriously?"

He nodded.

"Isn't that dangerous?"

"I guess so," he replied. "But it's not like I plan to be a wide receiver the rest of my life. I can only do it until college ends, and then it's board rooms and suits instead of jockstraps and sweaty cleats. Might as well make the most of it."

"That's... oddly poetic. And ridiculously stupid," I offered as we approached the table.

"Thanks," he replied, sitting into the open seat between Court and another football player. Which left one open seat at the table between Ryan and Ash.

Ryan's electric blue gaze pierced me as I rounded the table. He pushed the chair out for me. "Hey, babe."

I hesitated halfway into sitting down before gravity took over and my butt landed. "Hey. *Babe*," I added.

He hooked the leg of my chair with his foot and pulled it flush to his before laying his arm along the backrest. His fingers absently lifted the ends of my ponytail and twirled it as he started talking about some new offensive play.

"Hi."

I jolted in shock to see Ash was looking at me with something other than contempt.

"Hi," I returned back, the wobble in my voice giving away my nerves.

He smiled softly, and the transformation was breathtaking. His green eyes went from cold to warm, a dimple appearing deep in his left cheek. "How's it going?"

"You mean being the darling of PC? Fab," I drawled, shaking my head.

A low chuckle rumbled out of him. "Not liking your sister's designer shoes?"

I arched a brow. "The shoes are great, don't knock 'em. It's the people I'm struggling with. Is everyone she knew so..."

"Annoying?"

"I was going to say vapid, but sure." I laughed a little when he did the same.

His mossy green gaze cut across the room to the cheerleaders' table. "I never cared much for your sister or her friends."

I almost bristled on Madelaine's behalf, but... was he wrong?

"I figured by the death glares you liked shooting my way that you weren't a fan of hers," I replied, tearing off a piece of my bread and popping it into my mouth.

"She messed with my best friend," he said flatly. "Even before that, there was no love lost between us. She's been an annoying bitch since I met her in grade school."

I fixed my gaze on my plate and focused on chewing as Ryan's fingertips dusted across the nape of my neck. He never stopped talking to his teammate, but I had a feeling he had heard every word Ash and I had spoken.

I forked a bite of pasta into my mouth and chewed slowly, letting my gaze rove around the dining hall as it filled up.

"There's Bex," I said, not sure who I was announcing that to, as she exited the food line and hesitated, looking for a seat.

Before I could stop myself, I waved her over. Her face got more and more skeptical as she drew closer, and I noticed Brylee and the other cheerleaders take note of her approaching the table.

"Hey," I greeted, ignoring their questioning stares. "Grab a chair."

Bex looked around the full table, which was actually *two* tables pulled together with over a dozen chairs squeezed around them. And it wasn't like these were tiny guys sitting shoulder-to-shoulder.

"It looks full," Bex said quietly, starting to step back.

"Hammonds," Ryan barked beside me. "Move down. Rebecca, have a seat."

I shot Ryan a surprised look. He gave me a short nod, the only concession he seemed willing to offer, as the guy he'd told got up and grabbed a chair from another table. Bodies shifted enough for them to jam another chair in.

Cheeks flaming red, Bex dropped into the chair across from me, next to Court. She ducked her chin to her chest and tried to make herself as small as possible until Linc leaned around Court and started talking to her.

Ryan's fingers snagged on a tangle in my hair and gently worked through it.

I wasn't an idiot. I knew what Ryan was doing—the touches,

letting Bex join us. He was showing to the world that we were a couple.

But there was an entirely too giddy part of me that was happy to let him keep stroking my hair like I was a cat, lapping up attention like the rays of sunlight after a long winter.

After several minutes, he gave me his attention. "I'll pick you up at eight for the Kappa party."

Not a request. A statement.

It rankled a little, but then Bex burst out laughing at something Linc told her.

I settled a hand on his thigh, feeling the hard muscles bunch under my touch as I leaned into his side. "Thank you," I said softly.

The corner of his mouth hitched up, and he looked down at me with an unreadable expression that made my tummy swoop dangerously.

Shit.

The last thing I needed was a crush on my fiancé.

CHAPTER 30

With the nearest town small and lacking in entertainment aside from a single nightclub, the thing to do at Pacific Cross was to go to whatever party was being hosted wherever that night. Greek parties were supposed to be off limits for the academy students, but I was quickly learning that no one here really seemed to care or enforce that rule.

I pushed open the door of Ryan's sports car after he parked it and killed the ignition. The school grounds were just sprawled out enough that it would have made the one-and-a-half-mile trek in heels a bitch if he hadn't offered to get me.

I swung my legs out the door and looked up in surprise when Ryan materialized in front of me with his hand extended to help. After a small hesitation, I slipped my hand into his and allowed him to pull me out of the car.

"Thanks," I said softly.

He smiled at me, making my heart do a little flip flop in my chest, before he closed my door and started leading us up the drive of the sorority co-hosting tonight's party. He kept my hand in his, keeping me close to his side as we joined the already swarmed party.

Students were everywhere; spilled onto the lawn, the wraparound porch, and inside the brightly lit, three-story brick structure that housed the upper echelon of PCU's female students.

Kappa Delta was the top sorority at the school, and I wondered if Madelaine had planned to pledge when she graduated. But it sucked they needed a frat to co-sponsor a party. What kind of archaic shit forbade women from throwing a party on their own?

I glanced at Ryan. "Was my sister planning on being a Kappa?"

He slowed to a stop, looking back at me. "Yeah. Her—I mean, *your* father is a legacy at the school. He was in my fraternity, so she would be expected to rush Kappa."

I looked around at the marble fountain spraying colored water in time to the beat of the music inside. At the beautiful women in designer clothes with flawless skin and gleaming teeth.

"She would have fit right in," I murmured, feeling out of place even in a tight emerald dress that cost more than I made at the diner in a month.

Ryan turned his back to the party, his focus entirely on me. "Maddie, you have as much right to this world as she did. You just have to take it."

I was on the taller side for a girl, but I still needed to tip my head back to meet his gaze. I felt a sardonic smile twist my lips. "You're kidding, right? I don't know my Gucci from the Gap. These girls spent their summers in Europe and on private islands. I spent mine in a diner with bulletproof glass."

Something flashed in his eyes. He looked almost... unhappy.

"This isn't my world," I reminded him.

His fingers squeezed around mine. "It is now."

I wrinkled my nose. "It still feels like a dream."

"A dream come true?" he teased.

I giggled, surprised to hear the sound bubble past my lips from something he said. "I didn't take you for the Disney type."

He scoffed, his blue eyes lighting up. "Are you kidding? Those princesses are hot as fuck."

"They're cartoons," I corrected, still laughing. "They're fake."

He shrugged. "Almost everything in my world is fake. Why not my childhood crushes?"

I tilted my head curiously. "That's a really depressing way of looking at things."

His gaze roved around the party goers. "There's a reason most of the people here are on antidepressants or self-medicating, Maddie."

"I'm sorry," I told him softly.

His eyes snapped to my face. The shock wore off quickly, leaving him looking rather uncomfortable. "It is what it is," he muttered. He shook his head. "But we have an appearance to make, so let's go inside, okay?"

I nodded, letting him pull me forward.

As we approached, people started calling Ryan's name, clamoring for the attention of the PCU prince. I was amused watching him navigate his subjects until people started calling *my* name.

Well, the name they thought was mine.

Unsure how to greet them, I waved and smiled as I tucked myself closer to Ryan. He was more than big enough to be my human shield, and I was a coward enough to use him as one.

When he realized what I was doing, Ryan dropped my hand and wrapped an arm around my shoulders.

I ducked my head, grateful for the extra protection he was offering.

"You know," he started quietly, "this isn't how *she* would be acting."

"In case you forgot," I countered, "I'm not *her*."

He paused and met my eyes. "I haven't forgotten."

A slow shiver rolled down my spine, my tongue darting out to wet my suddenly parched lips. His eyes followed the movement, but his expression gave nothing away.

I cleared my throat. "So, you and my father are frat brothers."

He blinked slowly. "We are."

"Does this mean I'm engaged to my uncle?"

He laughed loudly, shaking his head and pulling me forward. "Never a dull moment with you."

We walked through the front door, and I was immediately overwhelmed by the smell of expensive perfume and too many citrus candles burning. It was enough to give me a headache.

People were crushed together as far as I could see. Even the stairs were full of people clustered in groups.

"I wonder if Bex is here yet," I said absently, looking around for the only girl I would willingly call a friend.

"You really like her, don't you?" Ryan looked down at me, amused.

I shrugged. "She's pretty great, and she's been really cool about my... situation."

"It's got to be difficult for her," he replied with a grimace. "Madelaine tortured that girl for years. Some of the shit she did was fucked up."

I frowned at him. "So I've heard. But maybe I can make up for some of the shit my sister was slinging."

He chuckled warmly. "You're really nothing like her, are you?"

I met his gaze evenly. "I'm really not."

He sighed. "I was a dick to you before. I'm surprised you don't hate me."

"Oh, I do," I shot back with a grin, "I'm just practicing my acting skills now that I'm on the West Coast."

He laughed again, the sound warm and hypnotizing at the same time. "Got it. You're just using me to win your first Oscar."

"I'll totally mention you in my acceptance speech," I answered in a haughty tone, flipping my hair over one shoulder for a little extra dramatic flare.

Having the full weight of his smile land on me was dazzling. His blue eyes glittered with mischief that made me wonder what he'd been like as a kid. Probably forever playing pranks and laughing.

It felt nice to not be at odds with Ryan, but that in no way made me feel calm around him. If anything I was even more nervous, my nerves forever fritzing and sparking to life when he was near.

His gaze slid past me, and the smile on his lips turned into a grimace that he punctuated with a sigh. "Incoming."

I started to turn curiously, watching as a slender redhead threaded her way through the crowd, her dark eyes fixed on us.

Well, on *Ryan*.

"That's Molly," Ryan whispered in my ear, ducking his head while wrapping an arm around my waist to anchor me against his front. "She's Kappa's president, PCU's head cheerleader, and Brylee's sister."

That explained why she had the same pinched, almost constipated, expression Brylee always wore. It was genetic, not learned.

"And apparently my new partner in crime," I murmured back.

Ryan gave me a confused look. Guess that meant the cheering collab hadn't been his idea. Before I could explain, Molly was in front of us.

"Oh, my God, Lainey!" She practically shrieked the words when she was close enough to wrap a twiggy arm around my neck. The red colored drink in her hand sloshed against the glass and nearly spilled over. "How *are* you? I was so happy to hear that you and Bry-Bry squashed your little spat. Kappa wouldn't be the same without you two next year. And I can't wait to start seeing what cute little routine you're working on for homecoming."

"Right," I mumbled, trying to pull away.

Molly let me go, her gaze narrowing on Ryan with open interest. "And Ryan. We *have* to talk about the fall mixer. Kappa and Alpha always throw the best combined parties. I was thinking we could tie it into the homecoming game?"

I could feel Ryan's hand tighten around my hip.

"You'll have to talk to Dean," he told her flatly, all humor gone. He looked completely uninterested in anything she had to say as he looked around the party. "He handles the fraternity's schedule."

Molly pouted, jutting her lip out in a way that made me embarrassed for her.

Seriously—did girls think that shit worked?

She sucked in a big breath that pushed her impressive tits even farther up. "But Ryan—"

"There's Linc," I said sharply, cutting her off before she could launch into a nasally whine about why Ryan should be the one to help her plan her next party.

"Excuse us, Molly," he said smoothly, grabbing my hand and taking the out I'd given us.

Molly scoffed as we dismissed her and headed toward the back of the house where I had spotted Linc.

"Nicely done," he murmured. "I can't stand that bitch."

I smirked at him, admittedly a little proud of myself until I realized Linc was currently in the kitchen, surrounded by my three new best friends.

Sarcasm.

So much sarcasm.

Hayley spotted me first, her red lips curving into the fakest smile I'd seen yet. "Lainey!"

I winced as her shrill voice broke some kind of sound barrier.

"Hey," I muttered, giving a halfhearted wave.

Linc looked at us with annoyance, his gaze dropping to where Brylee's nails were curled into his bicep.

"Laine, you look *divine*," Brylee told me, laying her free hand across Linc's chest. "I was just telling Lincoln that we just have to double date sometime soon."

"Yeah," Linc drawled, his eyes flaring as his voice lifted into a mocking falsetto. "We just *have* to."

The skin around Brylee's eyes tightened as his insult landed, but she didn't let him go. Her gaze focused on me, and I had the feeling she wanted me to back her up.

"With our schedules, Ryan and I don't get much alone time together, so we're pretty selfish about sharing." The lie slipped out of my mouth before I could censor myself.

It was a dick move, and definitely not going to win me any favors with Brylee and her friends, but it was worth it to see the way her face twisted with anger.

I felt Ryan's chest shake as he held back a laugh that Linc didn't bother hiding. His loud laugh echoed in the kitchen, drawing the attention of other people near us.

Brylee glared at him, finally letting his arm go before turning her scathing eyes to me. Kayleigh and Hayley looked utterly fascinated by the sudden tension.

"I'm getting a drink," Linc announced and headed to the island where an assortment of bottles was available. "Court and Ash are out back with some of the team."

Kayleigh's dark eyes lit up. "The football team?"

Linc paused, his lips thinning as he gave her a blank look "No, the chess team."

She frowned, her pretty head angling to one side. "I didn't know you hung out with the chess team."

Ryan laughed. Linc snorted and muttered something under his breath as he walked away.

"Jesus, Kayleigh," Brylee hissed, grabbing her friend's arm. "Are you for real?"

"What?" Kayleigh asked innocently, blinking owlishly at all of us.

With a huff, Brylee shook her head and looked away, jaw clenched.

Linc rejoined us, passing Ryan a beer and me a bottle of water. I twisted the cap off and smiled at him in gratitude. "Thanks. Have you seen Bex?"

He shook his head and twisted the cap off his beer.

Brylee's head snapped back around. "What did you say?"

I stared back at her, taking the time to take a drink and swallow before answering. "I invited Bex."

Hayley's nose wrinkled. "Why?"

I shrugged at her, getting more annoyed by the second. "Why is anyone invited to a party? So she can have a drink and hang out."

Hayley started to say something else, but Brylee cut her off.

"She's right, Hay," she said sweetly. "We're seniors. We can all hang out."

Hayley looked ready to argue, but I was over it. I turned to Linc. "You said everyone else is outside?"

He nodded slowly, his gaze darting to Ryan before coming back to rest on me. "Yeah. Let's go."

I followed him out the back door, Ryan's hand pressed against the small of my back as he guided me down the steps and across the lawn to the firepit area with a stone ledge and a handful of Adirondack chairs where a lot of football players and twice as many girls were gathered. Two seats in the center opened up immediately for Linc and Ryan.

I hesitated for a second before Ryan snagged me by the waist and pulled me onto his lap without warning.

I landed with a small squeak, my soft curves yielding to the hard lines of his body as I fell against him, the deep bucket seat of the chair making it impossible for me to really do anything but recline against Ryan's chest. Still, I struggled to sit up until he wrapped an arm around me to keep me in place.

Squirming a bit, I glanced over my shoulder at him. "Um..."

He lifted an eyebrow curiously, taking a drink from his beer.

"Maybe I should find my own seat," I whispered as quietly as possible.

He took another drink, his gaze shuttered. "Do you see another chair?"

A quick glance around showed there wasn't one. Sighing, I shifted my weight again and suddenly froze when I felt the semi-hard ridge of him pressed against my ass. Stunned, I whipped my head around to stare at him.

He smirked and turned his head to talk to Court.

Okay, then.

I let out a shaky breath and tried to force myself to relax against him. Maybe this wasn't so bad.

As he talked his hand slipped from my hip, down my thigh and to my knee before he dragged the back of his knuckles against my bare skin on the way back up. My traitorous skin pebbled and came alive under his touch. The shiver that rolled down my body, from my neck to my toes, pressed us closer still, and now there was nothing *semi* about the hardness pressing insistently against me.

I downed the rest of my water with a couple of long gulps and glanced around, trying to take my mind off the way it felt to have Ryan touching me, breathing under my body.

The night was fairly mild as the sun finished sinking behind the horizon, but even the soft breeze wasn't enough to soothe my over-heated body. Everything felt raw and exposed, and I seemed to be the only one who was struggling.

His hand smoothed up and down my leg, finally coming to a gradual stop on the inside of my thigh.

God help me, but I wondered what would happen if we were alone and I opened my legs a little...

The plastic bottle crinkled loudly in my hand as I squeezed it. Ryan's body moved under mine as he chuckled.

"I need another drink," I announced, scrambling off his lap before he could stop me.

His head rolled back curiously. "You okay, babe?"

I glared down at him and had to clear my throat before speaking. "Perfect."

He held up his drink. "Grab me another?"

I nodded and turned away, marching across the lawn as fast as I could until I made it back inside the house.

It was somehow easier to breathe in the crowded kitchen than it had been outside on Ryan's lap.

I managed to get over to the cooler that was full of bottled water and grabbed one. I straightened in time to see Bex ducking between two guys as she made her way to me in a white blouse and pink plaid leggings. She looked adorable.

"Hey!" I greeted, genuinely happy for the first time that night. I impulsively hugged her quickly.

"Hi," she breathed when I let go, her big eyes darting around the room.

"Water?" I asked, pointing to the cooler.

She nodded quickly, and I passed her a bottle. She clutched it between her fingers and edged closer to me. "This place is crazy."

"You've never been to a sorority party?"

"No," she answered, taking a drink of her water. "You?"

"All the time," I deadpanned. "You know how I was living it up in Cliftown."

She giggled.

I waved a lofty hand. "Honestly, I'm less than impressed right now. It's truly degrading to be in such a... decrepit shack."

The Kappa house was, outside of my dad's house, the most ostentatious place I had ever been in. Everything from the gilded crown molding to the gleaming crystal chandeliers screamed wealth and opulence.

"Got it," Bex nodded solemnly. "We'll do a couple of circuits to appease the peasants and then head back to your place for caviar and champagne."

"Exactly," I confirmed with a sharp nod. Unable to keep up the ruse any longer, I grinned at her. "Seriously, thanks for coming. I don't think I could've handled this on my own."

"Ryan being an ass?" she questioned curiously.

More like he had been grinding on *my* ass.

"No," I replied honestly. "I don't know. I just feel like you're the only person here who is a halfway normal human."

"That's probably an accurate assessment," she laughed.

"We're sitting outside," I told her. "Please, please say you'll join us so I can stop staring into space, pretending to have fun."

"Well, we can't have that, can we?" She inclined her head to the door. "Take me to your people."

I sighed. "Let's go."

We made it halfway when Bex gasped sharply, loudly, and the entire room went silent except for the thumping bass from the stereo. It echoed around us like a stuttering heartbeat. Something splashed on the back of my legs.

I turned slowly, my shoes slipping in pooling liquid.

Brylee, Kayleigh, and Hayley all stood behind Bex, empty cups in their hands.

Empty because the red liquid was currently dripping off a now drenched Bex.

CHAPTER 31

"What the fuck?" I demanded, looking beyond Bex to where Brylee was standing with a smug grin on her red lips.

"Oh, my God," she gasped mockingly, lifting a hand to her chest in feigned horror. "I totally slipped. So sorry, Becky. I just didn't even see you there."

Laughter echoed in the room, and a couple people pulled out their phones to take a picture.

Bex ducked her head, screwing her eyes shut like she could blink herself out of this moment of humiliation.

"Are you kidding me?" I snapped, my temper flaring.

Brylee's eyes found mine and hardened. "It was an accident, Lainey."

"Bullshit," I spat, and this time the gasps from the crowd around us were accompanied by a few low "oohs" as people gave us their full attention. More than a few cell phones were whipped out to capture this moment as it went down. The music in the other room died a second later as more people came to see what was happening.

I glared at Brylee. "You did that on purpose. Why?"

Brylee's brow lifted slowly. "Do I need a reason? She wasn't invited."

"*I* invited her," I reminded her coldly.

Her head cocked, a cruel smile on her cherry lips. "Listen, we may have to play nice with you because Ryan said so, but we're not a fucking charity. And we're not lowering our standards for this trash. We gave you a pass. Not this gutter dweller."

Hayley giggled behind her. "So true."

I slammed my bottle of water on the counter and rounded Bex to get between her and Brylee. "I don't give a flying fuck what Ryan said," I hissed, my eyes narrowing.

"Do you think anyone here would be giving you a second chance without him basically *ordering* it?" she asked scathingly. "Please."

"I never asked for a second chance," I pointed out. "And I sure as shit don't need it *or* you."

"Burn," someone stage-whispered. A wave of giggles swelled around us.

Her face flushed. "Careful, *Lainey*. You're close to losing my good graces."

"You mean you're close to losing me as the connection to Linc's dick in your mouth," I returned frostily.

"Oh, shit!" A guy laughed, slapping his friend's shoulder as they watched the train wreck of the night barreling into the station.

I wasn't nearly done with Brylee, though. "But the truth is, he wouldn't touch you with someone else's dick covered in ten condoms."

"Watch it, bitch," she snarled, inching forward and stepping on my toes.

I shoved her back a step. "No, *you* watch it. Stay the hell away from my friends, and stay the hell away from me. I don't need you. I don't *want* you."

"You're finished," Brylee told me, hate in her eyes. "I'll ruin you at this school."

I spread my arms wide, embracing her threat. "Go for it, honey. Do whatever you need to do to feel better about your pathetic existence."

"We're finished," she hissed, shaking her head. "I'm done playing nice for you. I don't give a shit who you're spreading your legs for."

"Thank *fucking* God," I announced for everyone to hear. "If I had to listen to you and Tweedle Dumb and Dumber much longer, I was going to drive nails through my eardrums."

I felt the breeze of the door opening behind me, but there was no way I was turning around to see who it was. Rule number one when fighting a bitch: Don't turn your back.

A pair of large hands settled on my shoulders, pulling me back into a strong chest.

"What the hell is going on?" Ryan demanded as his friends gathered around us. I noticed that Court and Linc stepped in front of Bex, tucking her away from the prying eyes of our peers and their cameras.

"What's going on is Brylee and her bitch squad thought they could go all Carrie on Bex, and I'm over their shit," I replied evenly.

Brylee lifted a haughty chin. "Look, we tried, Ryan, but Madelaine is a lost fucking cause. I'm done pretending to accept this whore back into our circle. You know she isn't worth it. She's a fucking cancer, and you should cut her off before she spreads on to you, too."

"And we all know how easily she *spreads*," Kayleigh giggled.

Ash's cool gaze leveled at her. "Not as easily as the football team says you do, Kay."

Her jaw dropped open like a gaping fish.

"Just so we're clear," Ryan said in a soft voice, the weight of his tone enough to silence the room and hold everyone's attention, "you're choosing yourself over my fiancée."

Brylee bristled. "No, I'm—"

"Saying you're better than her?" Linc cut her off smoothly, his navy eyes glimmering with mirth as he watched her try to talk her way out of the mess she'd created.

She fidgeted, starting to realize the tide was shifting, and not in her favor. Her cheeks flushed as her gaze jumped around.

"The only cancer I see around here is you," Ryan added, his arctic tone sending shivers down my body. "Thankfully, we can cut that shit out now."

A shocked whisper rippled around us as people watched.

Her chest rose and fell rapidly, her eyes darting around for an ally. "Ryan."

"Get out," he ordered. "Consider yourself officially uninvited from any party for the rest of the year."

"You can't do that!"

Ryan's gaze moved around the room. "Anyone think I can't do that?"

No one spoke up. In fact, people near Brylee and her friends edged away, giving her a wide berth.

Brylee looked around, her eyes snagging on her sister. "Molly!"

Molly pressed her lips together and lowered her eyes.

Jesus, that was cold. Her own sister was icing her out.

Ryan's fingers slid down my arms and wound around my waist. He dipped his head to rest his chin on my shoulder, watching Brylee freak out with complete indifference.

"Hayley? Kayleigh? Do you feel the same way?" he asked her friends in an almost sweet tone.

"No," Hayley answered quickly, stepping away from her so-called best friend. Kayleigh scrambled away as well, leaving Brylee completely alone in the middle of the room.

Part of me almost felt bad for Brylee, but then I turned and saw where Bex was still huddled behind Court, sticky red liquid drying on her pale skin.

I cleared my throat and stared at the brunette. "This is the part where you get out."

Her spine went stiff, her small hands balling into fists. "You're going to pay for this."

"Are you threatening her?" Ryan's already frigid voice went colder still, icy and deadly. The air in the room seemed to shimmer with his fury.

Brylee kept her mouth shut and pivoted on her foot. She stalked out of the room.

"That was fucking intense," Linc finally cracked with a laugh. He raised his beer bottle over his head and announced, "Ding-dong, the bitch is dead!"

A cheer went up in the room and people toasted with him as the music started back up. People turned away from us, going back to their own conversations as things returned to normal.

But I was still rocked to the core by what had happened. Not just that Ryan had taken up for me, but at the power he wielded so effortlessly. In a matter of seconds, Brylee had gone from HBIC to persona non grata.

All because the man at my back declared it so.

"Holy shit," Hayley breathed, coming to stand in front of me with Kayleigh. "That was so intense. It's about time someone knocked her down a peg."

"For real," Kayleigh agreed, nodding like a damn bobblehead.

I snorted. "Just... get away from me."

They exchanged hurt, confused looks.

"But, Lainey," Hayley started to whine.

"Get. *Away*," I snapped.

They scurried out of the kitchen without another comment.

"Fucking bitches," I muttered, before turning in Ryan's arms to get a good look at Bex.

"Are you okay?" I asked her softly.

Her wide eyes found mine. "I need to go. I can't..."

"I'll walk you back," I told her, trying to pull away, but Ryan refused to let me go. I twisted my neck around to look at him, but he was staring at his friends.

Court set his drink on the counter. "I've got her."

Apparently he was the bodyguard of the group, and at six-and-a-half feet of solid muscle, there was no wondering why he'd fallen into the role. He had carried Bex to my room the other night like she weighed less than a box of tissues. But for all the raw power he exuded, as he turned to my friend, there was a kindness in his eyes that made me feel marginally better.

Bex stepped backwards. "Oh, um..."

"I can do it," I insisted.

Ryan's lips turned to whisper against my ear. "You need to stay here and not go slinking off into the night with your friend. Stand your ground."

I turned my head, my nose brushing his. "I guess reminding you it's a school night is pointless?"

"Completely," he deadpanned, his warm, minty breath fanning across my cheeks. His blue eyes turned serious. "Besides, I need to talk to you."

Unease coiled in my stomach, and I wondered what I had done wrong now.

CHAPTER 32

Ryan led me back outside and toward the area where we'd been sitting with the football team. I watched as Court led Bex away, craning my neck to see her until they disappeared around the side of the house.

"She's fine," Ryan groused, his fingers still twisted around mine as he pulled me past the ring of chairs by the firepit our group had taken over. He tugged me to the far side of the pool, where people were shrieking and splashing.

He stopped in front of a set of wicker outdoor furniture that was unoccupied and dropped his large frame into a chair. I moved to sit across from him, but he jerked me forward until he had arranged me straddling his lap.

I squeaked in alarm as my dress bunched indecently high on my legs. A second later his hands came to rest on the exposed skin of my thighs.

"Ryan!" I whisper-hissed, trying to scoot back so that my crotch wasn't pressed to his, but all that did was grind us together with enough friction that lights flashed behind my eyes and I had to bite back a moan.

He smirked. "Relax. No one can see you."

I looked around, mildly satisfied to see that he had pulled me to the rear of the property where no one seemed inclined to gather. The hanging lanterns and twinkle lights barely cast shadows this far away from the house. The party was still in full swing, but no one could see me in the darkness here.

No one except for *Ryan*. If he glanced down, he'd have a clear shot at the pink lace panties I had picked out.

I was rapidly developing an addiction to matching underwear and all the frilly ways they came. My days of WalMart sports bras and cotton underwear were quickly becoming things of the past. I loved this pale pink set, but I hadn't planned on sharing it with anyone, let alone my fiancé.

To his credit, his blue eyes held mine and didn't wander below my chin.

I swallowed uneasily and resisted the urge to play with the ends of my hair. "What did you want to talk about?"

"I'd like to know why you just derailed all the ground-work I laid for your re-entrance into a social circle that wasn't subterranean, for starters," he told me.

I lifted my chin a notch. "Brylee was a bitch to Bex."

"Brylee's a bitch to everyone," he countered.

"Yeah, well, Bex is my friend," I shot back. "That bullying shit doesn't fly with me."

His fingers flexed on my skin. "Your sister spent years making Bex the human equivalent of a kickball at this school. You can't expect them to forget that overnight."

"*You* can," I returned archly.

He paused. "What did you say?"

"You made everyone forget that I was the campus pariah," I added pointedly. "You could do the same for Bex."

His eyes narrowed. "I helped you because it helped *me*. Having my fiancée be the joke of the school doesn't benefit me at all."

"Bullshit," I fired back without heat. My eyes searched his. "You did it because you now know I didn't deserve the shit they were slinging. You did it to help me."

"Because you agreed to help *me*," he countered. "I'm not in the business of handing out freebies. I helped you so you would agree to keep playing this role."

"And now I'm asking you to help Bex," I said, frustration lining my tone.

"What's in it for me?" he asked plainly. "Give me one good reason to pluck that girl from social Siberia."

"For me?" I asked, unsure of what else I could offer.

His gaze raked down me, this time there was no mistaking the heat in his eyes as he studied the exposed space between my legs. "For *you*?"

Heat flared in my cheeks, and I prayed he thought it was from anger.

But anger was only part of the reason my skin was flushing and my heartbeat ratcheted up.

"I'm not sleeping with you," I told him, my tone a little too breathless to be absolute.

He scoffed. "And I'm not in the habit of paying for sex in any form. No pussy is that good."

"I meant as a favor for me," I gritted out.

He chuckled darkly. "And what could you possibly offer me? A coupon to some heart attack in a drive thru? Maybe a bus pass?"

I leaned back from him as far as I could while still perched on his lap. "You don't have to be a dick."

"And you don't have to be stupid," he spat. "Helping you is one thing. I'm not a fucking charity for all the poor and pathetic souls you decide to surround yourself with."

"My dad asked me to play nice with Bex," I remembered, grasping at straws. "Wouldn't that mean you need to play nice with her, too? For business or whatever?"

His gaze sharpened. "The only reason Gary would play nice with her father is because he needs something."

"Isn't that what they do?" I huffed. "So, helping Bex means more money for whatever shit our dads are up to."

"Maybe," he agreed, "if my dad knew anything about it. But it's good to know Gary's making his own plans with someone who deals in Department of Defense security."

Ryan's gaze leveled me, and I realized I might have just fucked up and overplayed a hand that Gary was playing close to the vest.

"Ryan—"

"I'll help her," he cut me off suddenly, a dark glint in his eyes. "But I'll need something from you."

I eyed him warily. "Okay. What?"

"A favor at a time of my choosing," he said with a flippant shrug.

My brow furrowed. "I'm not giving you some carte blanche check to hold over my head."

He smirked. "That's the deal, baby."

I sighed and bit my lower lip, watching how his eyes lingered on my mouth. "No sex."

A laugh burst out of him. "What?"

"The favor," I said, feeling myself blushing again. "I'm not sleeping with you."

He leaned back in the chair, his fingertips grazing up the tops of my legs and leaving a trail of gooseflesh in their wake. Unable to stop myself, I shivered and pressed my center against him.

Shit.

There wasn't a single piece of his body that wasn't carved steel designed to exude strength, and that included the hard on he was sporting between his legs.

He toyed with the hem of my dress. "I'm not in the habit of forcing the unwilling," he informed me coolly. "So, sure. I'll take sex off the table until you ask for it."

"Never going to happen," I ground out.

"Never say never," he murmured, lifting a hand and sweeping my hair off my shoulder. His fingers grazed my jaw and slipped down the side of my throat before he traced the curve of my collarbone.

My heartbeat slammed in my chest so hard I wondered if he could hear it.

"Do we have a deal?" he asked softly.

A deal? What deal?

My head was swimming and fuzzy, and I struggled to remember what he had been talking about.

"I'll help Bex in exchange for a favor of my choosing when I decide," he clarified with a smirk. He knew exactly what he was doing to me, and the smile in his eyes showed it. "Except for sex."

Asshole.

"Fine," I muttered. "Help Bex, and I'll help you out."

"See?" Ryan grinned at me. "That wasn't so bad, was it?"

"I feel like I just made a deal with the devil," I mumbled, shaking my head.

He laughed loudly, his other hand smoothing across my leg. "Oh, Maddie. I wouldn't say that."

I lifted an eyebrow. "You wouldn't?"

He winked. "The devil doesn't have shit on me."

CHAPTER 33

"Is this where the party is now?" Linc asked, materializing out of the darkness and dropping into the wicker chair across from us. He lifted his beer to his lips and took a long pull as Ash joined us and sat on the loveseat, sprawling his long legs out.

Ryan snorted at his friends and shook his head. I twisted in his lap, trying to get up, but his hands tightened on my waist to keep me still.

"Can I get up now?" I asked drolly, not sure why we needed to keep up the PDA if his friends knew who I really was.

His blue eyes narrowed as he looked at me. "I'm kind of cold."

It was still in the eighties. The California sun had dipped below the horizon, but the late summer air was still warm.

I stared back at him. "I'll get you a blanket."

"Nah," he disagreed, reaching around me to take the beer Ash offered.

I pressed my lips together to keep from growling. Instead, I glowered like a petulant little kid who found herself stuck in an awkward situation with no way out.

Freaking awesome.

Ryan smirked, as if sensing my displeasure. With a huff, I turned away from him.

MAD WORLD

Linc grinned at me and winked. "So, Maddie, tell us all about... where did you grow up? Bumfuck... Somewhere?"

Ash's arm swung out, punching Linc. His green eyes flashed with warning. "Shut up, dude."

Linc rolled his eyes and rubbed his arm. "No one's around. For once."

"Michigan," I muttered quietly, my gaze darting around nervously.

"Great state. Home of Eminem and American muscle," he agreed with a nod.

Ryan snorted behind me. "Shut up, Linc."

"I'm just curious as to what Maddie thinks about our world," he went on, leaning back in his chair and giving me a curious look. "Are you sufficiently awed by the glamor and shit?"

I snagged Ryan's beer and took a long drink before handing it back to him, smiling a little at the surprise that lit his eyes a second before his lips closed over where mine had just been.

I turned back to Linc. "I'm sufficiently awed by the amount of shit that goes on. Does that count?"

Ryan barked out a laugh, and even Ash's lips twitched.

"I like her so much better than her sister," Linc announced with a chuckle.

I stiffened and mashed my lips together.

Linc raised his hands in surrender. "Sorry. I didn't mean to speak ill of the dead."

Ryan's hand traced up the line of my spine and I felt myself relax unexpectedly.

"It's fine," I murmured. "I'm getting that my sister had a lot of... issues."

"Well, she definitely wouldn't have thrown down for Rebecca the way you did," he replied. "Gotta admit, I almost expected you to punch Brylee like you did Dean. That was kind of hot."

Ryan growled behind me, annoyed. He probably didn't like the fact that I'd stepped out of line *again*. But I really didn't care.

"I should have," I admitted with a grin, stealing his bottle again and finishing it before handing it back. I smiled sweetly at him. "You're out."

His white teeth flashed in the dark, feral and unsettling. "Then I guess you better go get me a refill."

My eyes narrowed. "I'm not your servant."

"No, worse," he agreed, eyes glittering. "You're my fiancée." His palm slapped my ass suddenly.

I jumped up and yelped at the sharp jolt. A flash of heat suffused my skin in a way that wasn't entirely unpleasant, but I still shot him a glare.

"Seriously?" I demanded, glad for the dark so he couldn't see the flush I felt creeping up my neck.

He lolled his head back with a lazy smile as he held the bottle out for me to take. "Thanks, babe."

I swiped it from his hands and grumbled, "Asshole."

"Love you," he called into the dark, his voice carrying so that at least a couple people looked at me with a knowing smile.

Sighing, I ducked my head and hurried back into the kitchen to grab a bunch of drinks for everyone, because I wasn't making this trek again. I tucked several bottles into the crook of my arm and turned to go back outside.

"Jesus," I gasped as Hayley appeared in my path.

She smiled widely at me. "Can I help?"

I gave her a long look before saying, "No. I'm good."

She let out a breathy giggle. "Come on, Lainey. You can't keep all the hot guys for yourself. And Linc is looking seriously hot."

I frowned. "Isn't Brylee into him?"

Her head tilted in genuine confusion. "Huh?"

"Brylee," I repeated emphatically. "Your best friend?"

She giggled. "Please. She's a total person non gracias."

"Persona non grata," I corrected with a grumble.

"Huh?"

"Nevermind," I said quickly. "She said she was interested in Linc, remember?"

Not that I wanted her claws anywhere near Linc or any other halfway decent guy.

Hayley rolled her eyes. "Yeah, and Ryan just dismissed her. She's on her own. Besides, we both know she's a bitch who really just wants your man in her bed."

My disgust must have shown on my face, because she leaned in with another annoying giggle and wrapped herself around my arm. "I know, right? Total *biotch*."

A total biotch that she would've been following around like a baby duck had Ryan not kicked Brylee out of the party and drastically changed her social standing.

But also, how the hell did he have the power to just command her to the bottom rung of the social ladder?

That was absolutely ridiculous.

I tried pulling away, but Hayley clung like a baby panda.

"I need to get the drinks back," I told her, a little desperately.

"Oh, right!" She let me go and promptly grabbed half the bottles. "I'll help."

She was prancing out the door before I could stop her.

With a sigh, I followed her out, catching up to see her pass out bottles to Linc and Ash before turning to sit in the open space beside Linc.

"That's Lainey's spot," Ryan informed her coolly.

Hayley hesitated and let out a nervous laugh. "But she was sitting on your lap earlier. I'm sure you want her back, right?"

He simply stared back at her, not speaking.

Hayley's uneasy gaze cut to me, and I could see her eyes begging me to step in.

"Here's your drink." I passed Ryan's beer to him and crossed over to sit beside Linc.

A small, frustrated furrow popped up between Hayley's eyes as she looked at me and then awkwardly around the circle. She forced a smile. "I'll go grab another chair."

"We're good," Ryan said coldly.

"Thanks for the beer," Linc said, smiling easily at her.

She flushed. "Any time. In fact, maybe we could—"

"Why are you still here?" Ryan cut in flatly.

"See you tomorrow, Lainey," she muttered and all but ran away.

I turned my attention to him. "Think I could get a recording of you saying that so I can play it whenever she latches on to me?"

He smirked around his beer before settling his lips around the rim and taking a long drink. "Welcome to the top of the pack, baby."

"Is that where I am?"

"It's where *I* am," he corrected smugly. "And you're attached to me, so..."

Linc turned his smile to me. "It's fun to be one of us, Maddie."

"You guys are ridiculous," I sighed, shaking my head. I twisted the top off my beer and took a drink.

Ryan stared at me, a slight frown pulling on his full lips. "Why are you sitting over there?"

I lowered the beer. "You told me to?"

Snorting, Linc patted my shoulder. "Oh, Maddie."

"Consider me your chair," Ryan informed me nonchalantly, beckoning me with his index finger.

My brows shot up. "But you said to Hayley—"

"Fuck her," Ryan grumbled coldly, but still gave me an expectant look. After a second, his eyes narrowed. "Do you need me to come and get you?"

I found myself pushing up to my feet and stalking back over to him while Linc and Ash laughed. I paused in front of him, watching as his gaze traveled from my heels up my legs, lingering on my hips and chest, before meeting my eyes.

"You done?" I asked archly.

"With you? Not even close." His hand shot out and he tugged me back onto his lap.

I landed on him with a huff of annoyance. "Happy?"

His lips curved wickedly as he rocked his hips into me.

My breath caught.

I had serious doubts that it was a banana he was pressing against my ass.

I could feel my cheeks heating and needed to change the subject. I needed to throw him off kilter the way he was wreaking havoc on my system.

My traitorous system that apparently wasn't getting the message that our fiancé was off-limits.

"I guess I'll humor the second-best quarterback in college ball right now," I said flippantly over my shoulder.

Ryan stiffened under me while his friends burst into laughter.

"And who the fuck is number one?" he demanded.

I glanced over my shoulder at him. "That guy from Huntington University. Have you seen his arm?"

"How the hell have *you* seen his arm?" Ash asked, still smiling. It was a good look on him, breaking up the broody, sullen stare into an expression that made him seem approachable.

"Even Michigan has TV," I answered.

"You watch college ball?" Linc leaned forward, his aqua eyes glittering with interest.

"Duh," I replied. I fell in love with the sport while cheering, and now I watched it when I could. Although, truthfully, college football hadn't been my thing until I started looking closer into Ryan.

He was a hell of a football player, and his instincts were almost always perfect when he launched the ball into the air. He could easily go pro, but I doubted his dad would ever let that happen.

Which made me wonder why Ryan didn't just tell his dad to screw off and take a multi-million-dollar contract with an NFL team.

I looked back at the guy in question. "You need to work on your short pass."

"Excuse me?"

"You can launch a ball thirty yards no problem, but your short pass game is barely seventy percent." I shrugged a shoulder. "Huntington's QB threw a seventy-yard pass last year and his pass completion was almost seventy-eight percent, *and* he's a year younger than you."

"Hold the fuck up," Ryan sputtered, leaning his face closer to mine. "My stats are well above the national average."

I patted his wide chest. "It's okay, baby. You can't be great at everything. I'm sure you'll be able to close business deals easier than passes when you graduate."

Ash grinned and took another drink of his beer.

"Yeah, baby," Linc chimed in.

Ryan pointed a finger at him. "You can shut the fuck up."

I leaned around him to give Linc a pitying smile. "Sorry, Linc. He gets pissy when his flaws are brought to light."

Linc threw his head back and laughed louder. "God, I love this girl."

I flashed Linc a smile.

"Statistically speaking, she's right," Ash chimed in.

Ryan stood up and nearly upended me. His hands settled on my waist until I was steady, but still giggling.

"We're leaving," he announced, shaking his head and grabbing my hand. "Fuck you both."

"But I'm having fun," I protested.

"And now you're done," he told me with a grimace. "I'll see you two back at the house."

"Night, Maddie!" Linc called as Ryan pulled me back to the center of the party.

"Was that a good time for you?" he asked.

"Immensely," I replied, still grinning.

He paused and looked down at me. Surprisingly, his gaze softened. "Good."

"Good?" I echoed.

"Yeah," he said softly. "I know your life before wasn't the easiest. You can trust my friends. They're good guys."

"And you?" I asked quietly, hating the note of vulnerability that crept into my tone. "Are you a good guy?"

A small crease appeared between his eyes. "I guess we'll see."

Not the ringing endorsement I was hoping for, but something that felt suspiciously like hope fluttered low in my stomach.

He squeezed my hand and pulled me around the backyard and to the front.

"Yo! Cain!"

Ryan's head snapped up to where a guy was wildly gesturing him over.

"Can you give me a sec?" he asked.

I nodded and let him step away while I melted into the background of the party against the side of the house.

More of the party had spilled into the pool, and several people were swimming naked. The hot tub area looked like one big orgy.

Yeah, I was ready to go.

A shoulder brushed mine as Molly came to a stop next to me. She lifted a cup to her lips and took a sip.

"Watch your back, Lainey," she murmured lowly.

"I'm sorry?" I turned and gave her my full attention.

"Not yet," she said, looking at me coolly. "But you will be if my sister has any say in it."

"That wasn't on me," I said evenly.

"No, but you're a lot more accessible than Ryan," she replied. Her eyes flicked up and down my body. "If you think Brylee is going to sit back and take it, you clearly don't know my sister."

She was right; I didn't know her.

And I didn't want to.

"I can handle myself," I assured her with a tight smile.

"I sure as hell hope so."

I tilted my head curiously. "Why warn me? Isn't Brylee your sister?"

"She is," Molly answered before taking another sip. The scent of the fruity drink permeated the air. "But she should've known better than to insult Ryan or his friends, and clearly that blanket of protection now covers you. I know where the power is in this school. I love my sister, sure, but she's on her own."

I blinked once. "Wow. That's a really bitchy thing to say."

She smiled at me. "Don't be naive, Lainey. We all have our roles to play. Brylee clearly forgot the rules."

"And what are the rules?"

"That Ryan Cain makes them, and we all simply must follow."

CHAPTER 34

The first week of school passed in a haze of chaos and surrealism. My classes were even more challenging than I had anticipated, but it was clear why Pacific Cross had such a stellar academic reputation. The teachers were at the top of their game, and they expected the same, if not more, of their students.

Unfortunately it was pretty obvious from the glares a lot of them gave me that they weren't my biggest fan. Probably since Lainey had gotten one of them *fired* last year for sleeping with a student.

If that wasn't enough, cheer practice went into overdrive preparing for the first game of the season on Thursday, and I had begun choreographing the routine for homecoming. But the strangest part was what happened the morning after practice when Brylee showed up and was iced out by everyone.

Brylee was out, and apparently I was in.

The whole week I'd had to deal with girls talking at me nonstop about the stupidest shit. Did I like their new shirt? Who should they consider hooking up with? Most of those questions included not-so-veiled hints at me setting them up with Ryan's friends.

The worst offenders were my two new shadows.

I was ready to go off on Hayley and Kayleigh. They had followed me around all freaking week. The only break I seemed to get was when I went to class or hid in Bex's room.

Yes, *Bex's* room, because they had taken to staking mine out and knocking incessantly when I was inside. They were like damn bloodhounds when it came to finding me.

I was relieved we had a night off from practice to attend the first official game for the university team on Friday night. Or, I was until I realized that the academy cheer squad and football team were expected to all sit together and support the team.

Which was how I found myself sitting in the stands, surrounded by a sea of blue-and-white-clad people supporting the Pac Cross Knights as they took on the Huntington Archers to a sold-out crowd.

My eyes scanned the players in blue until they landed on the white block letters of Ryan's jersey. He was on the sidelines with Linc, our team having lost the coin toss and the defense taking the field first.

Court and Ash took their positions on the defensive line. Ryan and Linc huddled, watching closely, as they talked to a coach and a couple other guys.

Hayley's blue nails latched on to my forearm. "Oh, my God. I freaking love those tight pants."

Kayleigh giggled. "Right?"

I looked at them out of the corner of my eye, wishing I was sitting a couple sections over with Bex. A row behind her was Charles. He caught me glancing over and gave me a wave that I reluctantly returned. I had seen him a few times in the hallways at school and with his own friends during meals, but I hadn't spoken with him since move-in day.

The guys behind us stood up and roared when Ash recovered a fumble. I grinned, watching Ash and Court high-five and run back to the sidelines as Ryan led the offense onto the field.

It was hard not to be impressed at the way Ryan commanded his team. He was more than good. He was downright gifted as a quarterback. His instincts were sharp and honed, his entire being focused on the game.

I watched as he launched ball after ball, sending his team marching down the field until they scored yet another touchdown.

"Girl, you look ready to eat your man," Kayleigh crowed, tossing her head back with an obnoxiously shrill laugh.

My lips twisted into a grimace as I looked at her. My attention snagged on Brylee, sitting alone at the end of the row. She glared at me before turning her attention to her phone.

I rolled my eyes, not giving a damn about her being pissed at her newfound social position.

"What are we doing tonight?" Hayley asked me.

I grit my teeth. "I'm meeting Ryan after the game."

He had sent me a text message reminding—okay, ordering—to show up at the locker room. Apparently it was where the girlfriends waited after the game.

Hayley rolled her eyes. "Yeah, but what about after that? You know the guys have their stupid first-game ritual shit."

I didn't know that. I figured there would be another party, like the academy team had done last night. The team had lost, though, so I'd felt justified in leaving the party after making an obligatory ten-minute appearance with the rest of my squad.

"I'm not sure," I answered, brushing her off as I watched Ryan return to the sidelines and yank his helmet off his head. His blond hair stuck up in different directions and his throat worked as he quickly downed a cup of water someone had passed him. He crumpled the cup and tossed it into a trashcan before glancing up.

His electric blue gaze landed on me, the corner of his mouth hooking up in a smirk.

Stupidly, I found myself smiling back until he turned away.

Kayleigh groaned loudly and fanned herself. "You are so lucky, bitch."

I barely paid her any attention as the game continued, finally ending in the smallest of victories when the Knights edged out the Archers with a last-minute field goal.

The crowd in the stands went nuts, people shouting and hollering. The football team behind us acted like *they* had won the game.

MAD WORLD

I shot to my feet. "I have to go."

My shadows frowned at me. "But what about tonight?"

"I'll text you later," I said, starting my way down the stands.

I wouldn't be texting them later. If anything, I would throw my phone in the ocean so *they* couldn't text *me*.

I slowly maneuvered through the crush of the crowd, gritting my teeth when a screaming guy bumped my shoulder. Finally I made it to the hallway that led to the locker room.

A massively large guy with a perpetual scowl glared down at me. "No fans."

I huffed a laugh. "Yeah, I'm here for Ryan Cain."

His lips thinned and he jerked his head to the side where a group of girls were standing. "So are they. Wait with them."

My nose wrinkled and I heaved a sigh before holding up my left hand. "I'm his fiancée. He asked me to wait for him."

His eyes narrowed. "Name?"

"Madelaine Cabot."

He shuffled back. "Second door on the left."

I skirted around him, half expecting him to grab my arm and stop me as I walked down the brightly lit hall. I pushed the door open and was surprised when I saw several other girls waiting inside.

A few were gathered by a table with finger foods, and several were seated on the couches thrown around the room. They all looked up as I entered, and more than a few looked less than happy to see me.

Odds were these were other girlfriends of players, and I could see where they would be less than psyched to see the girl who'd tried to take out the team's QB last year while literally fucking him over.

I quietly made my way to an empty corner chair and sat down, pulling out my phone. I thumbed through a few apps absentmindedly until my thumb hovered over one of the locked areas on Madelaine's phone.

With a grimace, I turned the screen dark.

"Pretty ballsy showing up."

I looked up to see a girl with gorgeous dark skin and vibrant golden eyes sit across from me. She swept a curtain of black and gold braids over one shoulder.

I licked my lips, unsure. "Ryan asked me to come."

"Ryan's a fucking idiot if he thinks a viper like you can be trusted," she said bluntly.

I sat up straighter, hating that I instantly liked this girl. She wasn't cowed because Ryan had commanded everyone to accept me, and she had no problem telling me as much.

She arched her brow. "Nothing to say?"

"I'm sorry," I apologized quietly. It was all I had to offer.

She scoffed and pushed herself to her feet as the door opened again and a few players, including Ryan, entered the room.

Ryan shot her a glance before looking curiously at me.

"Another member of Madelaine's fan club," I murmured for his ears only as I got up.

His lips pressed together, and he gave a short nod. "Sorry about that. I've known Imani since we were kids, and she's been dating one of the guys on my team since they were fifteen. She's not Madelaine's biggest fan. Never has been, but after last year..."

I made a face. "Got it." I glanced back at her, noticing that she lit up when a tall guy ambled into the room. A moment later, she launched herself at him, wrapping her long legs around his torso and giving him a kiss so hot that I felt embarrassed witnessing it.

Turning my attention back to Ryan, I noticed him smile faintly at the couple before dropping his gaze to me. His hair was wet from his shower, and he smelled like soap. Damp spots on his white t-shirt made the cotton fabric cling to his muscles.

It was a damn good look on him.

"I'm going out with the guys tonight," he informed me. "It's a team thing we always do after the first game of the season. Usually it doesn't take long, but it's mandatory."

I frowned. "So, you had me come here to tell me that you're going out with the team?"

He tapped the tip of my nose. "No, smart-ass, I had you come here because it's what the other girlfriends on the team do. It's all about optics."

"Well *optically*? All the girls in here hate me."

"Not you," he corrected with a smirk. "Just who they think you are."

"Same difference," I shot back.

He shrugged indifferently. "I guess."

I exhaled hard. "Okay. Bex actually asked me to go somewhere with her. I think there's a band playing nearby that she wants to see?"

"Not hanging out with the squad?"

I glared at him. "That better be a joke."

The smile that crept across his face was breathtaking. "It was."

"Good," I muttered, running a hand through my long hair. "I'm *this close* to punching them in their fake noses."

He barked out a laugh, drawing the attention of the other people in the room. "Try to avoid punching people if you can."

"Zero promises."

"Oh, there's one other thing," he said softly.

My attention snagged on his tone. Curiosity and wariness warred for dominance in my brain.

"We won tonight."

"Yeah, congrats," I told him genuinely. "It was a great game."

He grinned. "It was. But that means the team is celebrating. We're all expected to celebrate the night of our first win, especially against a team like Huntington."

I smirked. "You got lucky their QB is out or he might've shown you up."

"Please." Ryan snorted, as if amused by the mere thought of someone besting him in anything. "Even if Locksley had shown, I still would've kicked his ass."

"I'm sure you believe that." I flashed him a winning grin.

His eyes narrowed. "Whatever. We're still celebrating, and you're my fiancée."

I gave him a blank look.

"It means you're spending the night, Maddie." His blue eyes glittered.

I started to step back, but he wrapped an arm around my waist to pull me closer.

"I am *not*—"

He pressed his index finger to my lips. "Optics, Maddie."

My teeth clenched.

His long finger traced the curve of my lips. "What kind of guy doesn't celebrate with his fiancée after a win?"

"You won by a point. *One* point. And I thought you had plans with the team."

"Winning's winning, baby." His fingertip ghosted down the line of my jaw. "And we're celebrating tonight *after* I get back with the guys."

I swallowed hard, wanting to rip my gaze away from his, but it was like I was caught in some hypnotic snare. "I'm not sleeping with you," I breathed.

The corner of his mouth hooked up, his finger now trailing along the slope of my throat. "And I want my girls willing. Sex isn't on the agenda tonight, unless you're asking."

"I'm not," I shot back quickly, feeling my pulse flutter as I became acutely aware of all the places our bodies were touching. My words came out breathier than I would've liked.

He smiled down at me, his touch finding the delicate arch of my collarbone as his other hand splayed low on my back. "But I still need you to spend the night."

Ugh, part of me knew he was right. My blood heated at the idea of spending the night with him, even if we both only meant *sleeping* in the literal way.

And then immediately my brain went straight into porno-mode wondering what spending the night with a guy like Ryan Cain would really entail if this arrangement was the real deal.

I cleared my throat and ducked my head to hide the blush creeping up my cheeks. "Fine. Do your thing with the guys, but I'm going out with Bex."

"Just be at my place by midnight," he told me. "Oh, and Maddie? One more thing."

I waited, my head tilted to one side as his hand slipped around my neck and tangled in my hair. He tugged my head back possessively.

And then his lips found mine in a blistering kiss.

I gasped into his mouth, my hands grabbing his shoulders for balance as his lips coaxed mine open and his tongue slid against mine.

Recovering from my initial surprise, I rolled to my toes and kissed him back, almost whimpering when his hand slid from my hip to my ass, pressing me against him with a low growly noise that made my toes curl and my head spin.

Abruptly, Ryan pulled back, smiling down into my dazed eyes.

When I licked my lips, I could still taste him. "Wh-what was that?"

I glanced around furtively to see almost every set of eyes riveted to us. I felt my cheeks heat and knew they were probably turning crimson.

His grin turned my insides into liquid. "Optics, baby."

Then he kissed the tip of my nose and released me so fast that I stumbled as he walked away.

CHAPTER 35

"Earth to Maddie," Bex teased with a laugh, snapping her fingers in front of my face.

I blinked and jolted in my seat, turning my head to face her.

Bex laughed and drummed her fingers on the steering wheel to the beat of the song on the radio. "Where the hell is your head? You've been distracted since the game, girl. Are you worried we won't be back by Ryan's midnight curfew?"

Yeah, his curfew chafed a bit, but it wasn't a big deal. The game had ended with enough time that Bex and I had three hours to ourselves. But that wasn't what was distracting me.

Biting my lower lip, I glanced at her. "Ryan kissed me."

Her head swung toward me, her mouth agape, and the car swerved toward the shoulder.

"Bex!" I shouted, bracing my hands on the dash as she jerked us back into traffic. The annoyed car behind us honked.

"Shit, sorry," she apologized, "but you can't just drop that on me."

"How do you think I felt?" I grumbled, glad the interior of the car was dark as we drove into the city limits for a much needed girls' night away from PC. I could still feel the heat of my blush as I remembered the way Ryan had kissed me like he owned my mouth. The way his hands had molded around my curves.

A shudder rippled down my spine before I could suppress it.

"I thought you hated Ryan," Bex said slowly, looking at me as she stopped at a red light.

"I did. I mean, I do."

Obviously.

The guy was an alpha asshole who had done nothing but order me around like a future Stepford wife.

So what if that was the best kiss of my life?

Crap.

I caught myself absently licking my lips again.

Bex lifted her brows with a low chuckle. "Yeah. Sounds like it."

"I don't know," I muttered, toying with the ends of my hair. I had pulled it into a high ponytail when I had changed after the game to meet Bex. She hadn't told me where we were going, just to look hot.

Whatever that meant.

"Maddie," she began, a smile creeping over her face, "do you *like* him?"

I bit my lower lip, considering. I went with the only answer I had to give. "I don't *not* like him."

Her head dropped back as she laughed. "Oh, God. Seriously?"

"I'm an idiot, right?" I closed my eyes as the light turned green and Bex started driving again.

"Not an idiot," she conceded, turning down a side street. "But be careful. I know Ryan and Madelaine hated each other."

I frowned and glanced at her. "You think he holds me responsible for what she did?"

Her mouth flattened in thought. "Honestly? No. I grew up in the same circles as Ryan and his friends, even though they're older than us. Truthfully, they're decent guys as long as you're on their good side."

"And if I'm not?"

She sucked in a breath through her teeth before shooting me a guilty look. "There are still planes that fly to Michigan daily."

I groaned and rolled my eyes as she parked the car. "Great."

Killing the engine, Bex unhooked her seatbelt and gave me her full attention. "From what I've seen, Ryan isn't looking to hurt you. If anything, he's been protecting you. Why would he go through the trouble of putting the entire campus on notice that you're off limits?"

"To build me up and dump pig's blood on me at homecoming?" I deadpanned.

She giggled and covered her mouth. "You've seen *Carrie* too many times. Besides," she said, pushing open her door, "the university students don't even go to the homecoming dance. It's an academy-only event."

I stared at the door she slammed shut and muttered, "That's not comforting," before opening my door and getting out.

I looked down the street to where the tail end of a long line had formed around an industrial-looking brick building. "Where are we?"

"Fallout," she answered, locking her car and joining me on the sidewalk.

"You say that like I should know what it is."

Linking her arm with mine, Bex propelled us down the concrete. "It's the only decent club in town, and one of my favorite bands is playing tonight. My cousin is their manager. She got us backstage tickets."

"What band?" I asked.

"By the Edge."

I grabbed her arm and jerked her to a stop. "Are you for freaking serious?"

Her hazel eyes glittered. "I take it you're a fan?"

I barely resisted the urge to squeal and jump around. "Are you *kidding*? I love them. I have all their albums and the box set of their TV show."

"Then we need to get our asses inside so we can *meet them*," she told me, urging me forward.

We rounded the corner and I saw the brightly lit sign for the club. My eyes widened as I took in the crowd waiting to get in.

Bex snagged my hand and pulled us to the front of the line, flashing a smile at the guy manning the door. "Hey, Colt."

"Bex, you look good," he told her, his eyes warming as they swept up and down her body. "Jayme told me you'd be stopping by." He lifted the papers on his clipboard and handed her two laminated passes, one of which she passed to me.

"You two have fun," he said with a wink before pulling open the massive door behind him for us.

I followed Bex inside, taking in the open space with wide eyes after pulling the lanyard and badge over my head. Fallout, true to its name, had a very industrial feel, with concrete floors and a lot of exposed steel beams. It had an artfully aged grunge look that made it look like a fallout shelter that someone decided to make into a club.

A club that was clearly the place everyone in town headed to, judging by the packed dance floor of writhing bodies and the crush of people around the bar. No less than seven bartenders moved quickly back and forth to fill orders from a crowd that was four people deep.

A DJ was set up to the left of the stage, setting the tone of the club with a heavy remix of a top-40 single.

"This way!" Bex called loudly, taking my hand in hers and pulling me deeper into the club. We threaded our way toward the back of the stage, where Bex simply walked past a group of girls who shot us death stares.

When we flashed our passes, the massive bodyguard opened the door. It closed behind us a second later, muffling the noise on the other side abruptly.

"Rebecca!"

"Jayme, hey!" Bex released my hand and hurried down the hall to hug a petite woman with neon green hair scraped into a messy knot atop her head.

I followed slowly, assuming this was Bex's cousin.

"Jay, this is my friend, Maddie," Bex introduced when she let her go. "This is my cousin."

I offered her a smile and sidestepped as a man ran down the hall pushing a clothing rack on wheels. "Thank you so much for the passes. This is... Wow."

Jayme grinned back, the diamond in her Medusa piercing catching the light. "It's crazy, right? The guys are getting ready to go on soon, but I can take you back if you want to meet them before the show."

"Seriously?" Bex jumped up and down a little. "Yes, please."

Nervous butterflies rioted in my stomach at the idea of meeting the guys. By the Edge was one of my favorite bands ever, and no one was happier than I was that they had reunited earlier this year and were kicking off their reunion tour.

Bex shot me a wide grin as we trailed after Jayme until she pushed open a door marked Private.

An apple sailed through the air, landing with a *thunk* against a wide male chest.

Roman Edge bent and picked up the apple that had struck him, buffed the skin on the sleeve of his black shirt, then took a large bite and grinned at the man on the other side of the room. "Thanks, asshole."

I watched in utter amazement as all my teenage fantasies came together in this one beautiful moment.

This was it. I'd peaked a few weeks before my eighteenth birthday.

The man who had hurled the fruit was none other than Theo Edge, fellow band member and Roman's older brother. His full mouth twisted into a smirk. "Fuck off, dipshit."

Still grinning, Roman took another bite and turned to see us in the doorway.

"Do I even want to know?" Jayme rubbed her forehead, looking utterly exhausted and annoyed at the same time.

"He started it," Roman said quickly, pointing at his older brother.

Jayme snorted. "I'm sure." Her gaze swept the room. "Where the hell are Leo and Cash?"

"Cash had to take a shit," Roman informed us unapologetically. "You know how he gets before we go on stage."

Theo sighed from where he sat on the sofa across the room. "Leo's talking to his wife."

"Right," Jayme muttered. "This is my cousin, Rebecca, and her friend..."

"Maddie," I supplied quickly when she cast me a questioning look.

"Right, Maddie," she confirmed with an apologetic shrug. "Sorry. My brain is pretty fried right now."

"You work too hard," Roman told her, tossing the apple core into the trash and grabbing a handful of gummy bears from the table full of snacks and bottled drinks.

"Someone has to," Jayme told him saucily. "It's not like you do."

Roman clutched a hand to his chest. "You wound me. And in front of company?"

Jayme glared at him, but I could see the sparkle in her eye. "Yeah, I'm sure you'll survive. I'll be back in a minute, okay?" She shot Roman and then Theo a stern look. "My underage cousin and her friend better be in one piece when I get back."

Theo held up his hands innocently.

"No faith in us, Jay." Roman sighed heavily, hanging his head. "But fine. We'll keep the coke and vodka locked up until you get back."

"He's kidding," Theo interjected as Jayme left the room. "We don't do that shit."

"In front of new people," Roman added seriously, his turquoise eyes sparkling. "Not unless you ask really nicely."

"Jesus fuck," Theo groused, running a hand through his dark hair. "The last thing we need is an Edge brothers doing drugs scandal, douche."

"I was *kidding*," Roman snapped, shaking his head. "Lighten up, dude."

Theo stood and walked over to us, extending a hand. "Sorry. I'm Theo. This dumbass is Rome."

We shook his hand and laughed.

"No worries," I assured him.

"Want a drink?" Theo offered. "And by drink I mean something like water or soda."

"Or tequila," Roman added with a wolfish grin.

"Rome!"

Roman rolled his eyes, meeting mine. "You knew I was joking, right?"

"Uh, sure," I stammered, still a little starstruck. My gaze volleyed back and forth between the brothers, amazed at how completely normal they seemed.

Well, as normal as two international rock stars who looked like they'd been carved from whatever material made Greek gods.

These guys were easily as hot as...

Ryan.

Dammit. Why was my brain going there?

"So, you're PC girls?" Roman was saying, leaning against the food table and folding his arms over his chest with an easy smile. "Damn, I'm not sure we're supposed to be talking to you since we're technically townies."

"You're from Pacific City?" I asked, surprised. I thought I'd read that they were from an East Coast city.

"We grew up outside of Baltimore," Theo confirmed, "but our mom and her family are from Pac City. Our uncle owns this club. It's one of the first places we played when we signed with a label. We thought it would be fitting to work it into the tour."

Roman nodded to his brother. "Exactly. It's where we started, so it's nice coming full circle."

The door on the other side of the room opened and Cash stepped into the room. His eyes widened when he saw his brothers weren't alone.

"Uh, hey," he greeted with a smile that flashed dimples. "I didn't know we had guests."

"Bex and Maddie," Theo said. "Bex is Jayme's cousin."

Cash snapped his fingers and walked to the end of the table, grabbing a sports drink and twisting off the cap. "Right. She mentioned you'd be coming. Sorry I wasn't here when you showed up."

"It's seriously *no* problem," Bex assured him.

"We told them you were in the bathroom," Roman informed him with a wicked look in his eyes. "You know. Unloading all your problems before we hit the stage."

Cash scowled at his older brother. "Fuckface."

Roman burst into laughter while Theo chuckled.

Grumbling under his breath, Cash turned to Bex and me. "I was in the back room doing a breathing treatment. I'm asthmatic and sometimes the fog irritates my lungs."

"Cool," Bex stammered and then flushed. "I mean, it's not cool that you have asthma and can't breathe. Cool that you're taking preventative measures."

"I've been a fan of you guys since your TV show," I admitted, trying to shift some of Bex's embarrassment onto myself.

"Thanks," Cash said with an easy smile.

A knock on the door had everyone turning a second before the door pushed open and a man with a headset stuck his head in. "Time to go, guys. Leo's already waiting."

"Nice meeting you," Theo told us as he and his brothers left to join their drummer, the only non-related member of the band.

"Same," I agreed quickly, watching all the Edge brothers leave.

The man who called them to the stage looked at us. "Jayme said she'll be back in a minute if you want to hang out here, or I can take you back out front to see the show. She grabbed you a VIP table upstairs."

Bex and I exchanged a look.

"We'll watch the show," Bex chirped with a wide grin.

He smiled back at us, waving us into the hallway and leading us to the door we'd entered that led to the side of the stage. As soon as the door opened, we could hear the thunder of the audience on the other side.

Security guards kept people back from the stage as the guys started setting up.

"Jayme said to come back after the show if you want to hang out! The VIP staff has your name for the table!" The guy yelled at us before pulling the door shut once more.

Bex turned to me, her eyes bright. "That was insane!"

"I know!" I practically squealed, hugging her. "Thank you!"

"Upstairs or down here?" she asked me.

I looked around at the dance floor. It had several raised platforms to give the space different levels. After Cash stepped up to the microphone to introduce the band, the drummer, Leo, dropped a heavy beat that launched into one of my favorite songs.

"Stay here and dance?" I proposed, hoping Bex would be cool with that.

She grinned and nodded. "Sounds *awesome*."

We pushed our way into the dance floor, joining the people who were already moving to the music. One song bled into the next, and I gave myself over to the beat.

Bex and I mostly danced together. A few guys approached us, but we kept our attention on one another until they got the hint and found more willing partners. At some point, one of the staff invited us onto one of the platforms with a few other girls.

As the sixth song ended and faded into a soulful ballad, I fanned my face with my hand. "I need water," I told Bex.

She nodded, her cheeks flushed. "Same!"

I turned to go to the stairs on the platform, keeping to the side as new people came up to take our places. It took almost half the song to make our way from the dancers to the edge of the bar, and when I did, I stopped short.

"Is that..." Bex trailed off behind me, surprise coloring her voice.

I swallowed, my throat suddenly drier than I'd ever thought possible when my gaze connected with Ryan's.

CHAPTER 36

"Maddie!" Linc shouted, coming around Ryan to grab me up in a bone-crushing hug. When he pulled back, his eyes scanned my body and he gave a low whistle. "Damn, girl. No wonder Ryan looks like he's ready to punch someone."

A smile twitched on my lips, but I had eyes only for Ryan as I stepped around Linc, who quickly turned his hugging to Bex.

Dragging in a nervous breath, I closed the distance separating us. "I thought you had plans with the team."

"I did," he replied, his tone giving nothing away as his gaze searched mine. "We're done. Linc wanted to see the band. I figured I'd tag along since I had time to kill before seeing you." He smiled, the dimples in his cheeks flashing. "I also figured this was the concert Bex might be bringing you to."

"Oh." I wasn't sure what else to say.

His eyes flicked behind me. "You looked good out there."

I surrendered to the small grin fighting to break free. "I love dancing."

The corner of his mouth hitched up. "I can tell."

"Where are the other two horsemen of the apocalypse?" I asked, looking for Court and Ash.

"Busy," he answered, giving me no further explanation.

I shifted my weight, growing uncomfortable under his heavy stare. And, judging by the way his mouth was moving, he was enjoying the fact that I was unnerved. "Right, well, I'm dying. I need a drink."

"Water? Or something else?" he asked.

"Water," I answered, my brow furrowing.

"Watch them," Ryan ordered Linc before turning and maneuvering his way to the front of the crowd around the bar. He flagged down a bartender, flashing a grin that had her ignoring the other waiting patrons to fill his order.

Less than a minute later, Ryan appeared with two waters. He passed one to me and the other to Bex.

"Thanks," I said, surprised, as I twisted the cap off and drank greedily. "I could've gotten it myself, though."

"No worries."

"I don't need a babysitter," I added.

His gaze snapped to mine and his eyes narrowed. "Clearly you didn't see all the guys checking you out when you were dancing."

I smirked. "I grew up in a pretty shitty area, Ryan. I've been taking care of myself for a long time."

His frown deepened into something darker. "I protect what's mine."

I paused in the middle of lifting the bottle to my lips. "Is that what I am?"

The sharp glint in his eyes made my breath catch.

"Yes," he replied finitely. His eyes dared me to challenge him.

I wanted to, on principle. The idea of being owned by someone, especially a guy, was offensive and archaic.

But it was also kind of hot when the guy was looking at you the way Ryan was looking at me. Like I was something equal parts precious and edible.

"I didn't know you were coming here," he said suddenly, tilting his head as he watched me.

"Bex's cousin is the manager of the band," I supplied. "She surprised me with this." I held up the backstage pass.

He reached out and took the laminated pass between two fingers while the back of his hand brushed my chest.

"Am I losing you to a rock star so soon?"

I forced myself not to pull away as he inspected the badge. Pull away, or worse, lean into his touch. "I mean, it's By the Edge. They're my favorite band."

"One of mine, too," he admitted, dropping the pass and shoving his hands into the pockets of his jeans. It pulled them low on his washboard abs, giving me a tantalizing view of a strip of tanned skin and a blond trail of hair that disappeared beneath the denim.

His teeth flashed as he grinned, not missing the way I was blatantly checking him out.

Feeling my cheeks heat, this time not from dancing, I turned away and finished my water. Bex looked up from where she was laughing with Linc as the band's next song started up.

"Want to go back?" she asked.

I nodded. "Yeah."

Large hands settled on my bare waist, and I caught the warm scent of Ryan's cologne as he pulled my back to his chest. Bex's eyes widened, and Linc smirked at us. Every nerve ending in my body came alive, suddenly electrified by his touch.

"Are you trying to make me jealous?" he practically growled in my ear. The rumble of his words vibrated through my back and settled around my racing heart. His fingers toyed with the edge of my jeans.

My stomach flipped. I turned my head to address him, sucking in a sharp breath when I realized his face was right next to mine. My gaze instantly dropped to his lips, watching them curve into a smirk as my mind replayed our kiss from hours earlier.

"My eyes are up here, baby," he whispered.

If I'd thought looking into his eyes would be easier than staring at his lips, I was wrong. This close, the color around his pupils looked gray before bleeding into an almost navy color. The ice I was so used to seeing had thawed, and I felt my heart rate spike.

"Better?" I asked archly, going for flippant and praying he didn't notice how much he was affecting me.

"Not really," he drawled, his minty breath warm as it fanned across my face.

"Can I go now?" I pressed.

Sighing softly, he squeezed my hips. "Fine. A couple more songs and then I'm taking you home."

"That's not the plan," I replied, shaking my head. "Bex and I—"

"Linc will take Rebecca home," he cut me off, looking at his friend.

Linc grinned at us, throwing an arm around Bex's shoulders. "Absolutely. Becky and I are already getting along."

"Bex," she hissed, elbowing his side and trying to get out from under his arm.

His face crumpled into a feigned look of hurt. "But I like Becky. It could be our thing."

"Or not," she fired back, still trying to squirm free, but I could see a small smile playing on her lips.

Linc tightened his hold on her shoulders and turned to face me. "See? We're already bonding."

"No way," I told Ryan, twisting to face him as his hands settled on my hips. God, he was really freaking tall. This close together, I had to crane my neck back to look him in the eye.

"Yes way," he countered coolly.

"We have backstage passes." I shook my head. "No way am I missing that."

A dark glint entered his eyes. "If you think I'm going to stand here while you go throw yourself at Cash Edge, you're out of your fucking mind."

"Who says I like Cash?" I demanded.

He rolled his eyes. "Please. *Everyone* likes Cash."

Dammit, he was right. The youngest Edge brother was by far the most popular with women, and a lot of men. I'd totally had several pictures of Cash on my walls when I was growing up. Cash also had the bluest eyes. Eyes eerily like the guy in front of me. Except Ryan's were more of a vibrant blue and—

Stop it, Maddie.

"I like Roman," I lied, swallowing the dishonestly with a gulp.

"Sure," he scoffed.

"We totally hit it off backstage before the show," I went on. "I think there might be something there."

"Well, shit," Ryan murmured, pressing his lips together. "That's too bad."

I patted his chest. "There, there, honey. I'm sure you'll find some girl whose standards are lower."

I started to step away, but his hands gripped me tighter and pulled me closer than before. My chest pressed against his, and I wondered if he could feel the thumping of my heart through our shirts.

"I mean, it's too bad I'm going to have to end Roman's career for stealing my fiancée," he murmured, dropping his lips to whisper against my ear.

I shivered, my fingers curling into the sides of his shirt and feeling the hard muscles flexing and moving. "What?"

"By the Edge is contracted under Starfire Records. My family owns fifty-one percent of the controlling stock. One call, and the whole tour goes away," he explained softly. "The tour, their record deal... Hell, I'll have the rest of their stock in a WalMart bargain bin by the end of the week."

My jaw dropped open in shock.

With a low chuckle, Ryan lifted a finger and traced my bottom lip. "Careful, baby. Where I'm from, an open mouth is an invitation I don't think you're ready for me to accept."

I snapped it shut as fast as it had fallen open. All I could do was blink as my brain short circuited at the visual that immediately branded into my mind. The scary thing was, it didn't repulse me at all.

Oh, hell.

He tapped his finger against my mouth. "Go have fun with Bex. I'll wait here for you."

I stumbled back a step, wishing I could blame my heels and not the fact that Ryan had completely thrown me for a loop. I turned to Bex and took her extended hand, frowning when Linc followed us onto the dance floor.

"What?" He shrugged indifferently. "I like dancing. And bonus? I'm with two of the hottest girls in this place."

I narrowed my eyes but caught the blush dusting Bex's cheeks as she ducked her head. I started dancing, then noticed Bex was hesitating.

"What's up?" I asked, leaning in so she could be heard.

Her gaze shifted furtively to Linc.

I waved a dismissive hand. "Ignore him."

"Don't ignore me!" Linc demanded, pushing between us and settling his hands on Bex's hips as he started to dance with her.

I couldn't help but giggle at the shock on Bex's face as Linc leaned in and whispered something in her ear. A second later, Bex's eyes narrowed and she wrapped her arms around Linc's neck to dance with him.

Twisting my arms above my head, I closed my eyes and let the music sweep me away. The energy of the dancers combined with the sultry beat of the song thrummed in my veins. Occasionally I would open my eyes to see Linc and Bex together, but usually my gaze zeroed in on the guy standing by the bar, casually sipping a beer as his gaze drilled into me.

One song melted into the next, and Linc let go of Bex to twirl me around. A laugh burst from my lips as he repeated the move with Bex, spinning us in a riot of directions until I was dizzy and laughing more than dancing.

I staggered back, bumping into a body.

"Shit, sorry," I apologized with a laugh as I turned to look at an older man with dark eyes. He was good looking in a generic sort of way, with an athletic build and sharp jaw. He grabbed my shoulders to steady me.

"I'm not," he returned with a grin. His gaze traveled the length of my body, lingering on my chest for longer than I was comfortable with. "I'm Devin."

I held up my left hand. "I'm engaged."

"But not married? I can work with that." His thumb rubbed the bare skin of my arm.

"No, thanks," I told him and started to turn away.

His grip tightened. "You don't have to be a bitch."

"Excuse me?" I demanded, knocking his hands away.

"What the fuck?" Linc shouldered his way between us, glaring at the guy across from me.

"You might want to keep your girl on a tighter leash," the guy warned Linc, gesturing at me with a hand. "She's pretty much advertising for anyone to come and get it."

Rage flashed through my body, and I was a heartbeat away from decking this asshole. Before I could step forward and tell him what I really thought, a broad back stepped into my line of sight.

Assuming it was a security guard, I backed up into Bex until I realized it was Ryan.

"Pretty sure my fiancée has the right to dance without being accosted by a misogynistic douche," Ryan informed him coldly. "Now why don't you walk away while your legs still work the way they're supposed to?"

Bex's fingers gripped my arm and I realized we were starting to draw the attention of the people around us.

I reached out for Ryan, smoothing my hand down the length of his rigid spine. "It's fine. Let's go, okay?"

"He owes you an apology," Ryan ground out, still glaring at the guy in front of us.

The guy stared back until finally lifting his hands in surrender. "Shit, man. Yeah. I'm sorry."

Ryan gave him a curt nod and started to turn away.

"I mean, I'm sorry your girl is such a slut," the guy added, scorn heavy in his voice. "Sucks for you."

I sucked in a sharp breath. "Ryan—"

Ryan whirled, his fist connecting with the guy's jaw so hard I heard something crack even amidst the music. The guy went down hard and didn't get back up.

CHAPTER 37

I stormed into the frat house ahead of Ryan, ignoring the curious looks we got from a few of his brothers. It was a miracle that we hadn't all been thrown out of the club after Ryan threw a punch that knocked that asshole out.

The band had even stopped playing as the security guards came to see what had happened. I'd apologized to Bex, who'd stayed behind with Linc—who now had *my* backstage pass—and left with Ryan before he could get in another fight.

The drive to his place was made in silence, him giving me sideways looks and me fuming silently that he had ruined my night with my friend, and more than a little conflicted about why I was so mad at him.

But even in the dark of the car, I could see that Ryan's knuckles were swelling. The knuckles on the hand he used to launch footballs down the field.

I shifted my attention to the one thing I could control; cleaning up what was left of this mess. That was my sole focus as I walked through the front door and cut a path toward the back of the house.

Ash and Court peeled themselves away from a group playing pool and followed us to the kitchen. I yanked open the freezer door and reached in for a handful of ice.

"Sit," I ordered Ryan, jerking my chin at the barstool around the island.

Ryan rolled his eyes and did as I demanded. "You're overreacting, Maddie."

I dropped the ice into the lone towel hanging limply from the oven door and shoved it at him. "I cannot believe you did that."

"Did what?" Ash asked, jumping up and sitting on the counter. His green eyes flickered back and forth between us.

Ryan put the ice on his bruised hand while Court leaned over and gave a low whistle. "The fuck did you do, bro?"

"He punched someone," I shot back before he could answer. "Twice, actually. First Dean and then the asshole tonight. Why can you punch someone and it's okay, but if *I* do it, you flip out?"

Ash nodded sagely. "That's a valid question."

"Double standard much, Ry?" Court added, shaking his head.

"First? Fuck you both," Ryan said without heat before settling his eyes on me. "Second, I was defending you."

"Defense of your woman is a solid reason," Court agreed.

A prickle of awareness tingled along my neck at being called *his*.

Ash turned to me. "Maddie? Care to counter-argue?"

I glared at Ryan across the massive island in the kitchen. "I didn't need defending."

"The guy was a dick," Ryan snapped. "He's lucky he walked away with just a chipped tooth." He lifted the ice pack from his hand, flexing his long fingers with a wince.

"Put the ice back," I told him crossly.

"Why the fuck are you being so pissy about this?" he snarled, glaring at me.

I planted my hands on the top of the counter and leaned in. "Because you may have just fucked up your hand over some stupid comment from an asshole who meant *nothing*."

"She has a point," Court conceded. He reached over and lifted the ice to inspect Ryan's hand himself. "Probably just bruised, not broken. Keep icing it."

I stared at Court until he chuckled and explained, "I'm pre-med, Maddie."

"Oh." I frowned slightly, realizing that I didn't know a lot about Ryan's friends.

"Finance," Ash told me when I turned my attention to him.

That answer made Ryan and Court laugh and exchange knowing looks. Ash cracked a rare smile and ducked his head.

"What's so funny?" I asked.

Ryan sobered and looked at me. "It's funny because Ash always gives that answer. It's a lot easier to explain away than saying what he really does is more like a version of forensic accounting."

"I still don't get it," I admitted with a shrug.

"People hire me to find out where a company is weak." Ash grinned at me unabashedly.

I cocked my head to the side curiously. "Is that legal?"

All three cracked up, but it was Ash who shook his head and told me, "Not exactly."

"What if you get caught?"

"I don't," he replied smoothly. "I'm good at what I do. Computers are my playground."

My mind instantly flitted back to the phone and my twin's mystery encrypted file. Bex had said that Ash might be one of the only people who could help me, but looking at these three, it felt like trusting them would be the equivalent of playing pin-the-tail-on-the-lion.

Ryan tossed the towel and ice into the sink. "Okay, I'm good."

A glance at his bruised, red knuckles proved that was a lie. "Bullshit," I said.

He sighed loudly. "I'm fucking fine, Maddie. Okay?"

"Then imagine how much better you'd be if you hadn't punched that guy," I retorted with a bright, fake smile.

"It either was me who punched him or Linc was going to," Ryan told me darkly. "I figured the guy would be happier with a busted mouth than a week in the hospital."

I paused uneasily. "What?"

"Shit, Linc was there?" Ash muttered, raking a hand through his dark hair.

"Relax," Ryan replied. "I handled it, the guy was thrown out of the club, and Linc stayed behind with Bex. He was calm when I left."

"Hold up," I cut in. "Why does it matter if Linc was *calm*? And should I be worried that he's alone with my best friend?"

"It's cute that you made a friend." Ryan smirked, and I flipped him off.

Court glared at Ryan before addressing me. "Linc wouldn't hurt her. Ever. But he does have a bit of an anger issue with guys who get out of line."

"His older sister was in an abusive relationship when she was in high school," Ash explained softly. "Linc was eight when her boyfriend put her in a coma."

"Jesus," I whispered, horrified as I pressed a hand to my chest. "Is she okay?"

Ryan's jaw clenched as he looked down. "No. She never woke up. They took her off life support last year."

"Please tell me the dickhead she was dating is in prison," I hissed, furious for Linc and his sister.

"He was never convicted," Ash said calmly, "but he did die in a car accident last year."

"Good," I said vehemently.

Ryan smirked at me. "Easy, killer. But now do you see why I jumped in? If I hadn't, Linc would've, and shit probably would have gone even worse. That guy was being an obnoxious prick, and you, or any other woman, shouldn't have to deal with being harassed."

I slowly blinked at him. "You're aware that you legit terrorized me when we first met, right?"

His eyes narrowed and gave me an intense look. "Let me amend that statement: no *innocent* woman should deal with being harassed. Things are different now."

Because I wasn't my psycho twin.

Right.

I closed my eyes and leaned against the counter, suddenly exhausted. "Can we just go to bed?"

Of course I would ask that question just as one of Ryan's frat brothers walked into the kitchen.

"Don't keep her waiting for that D, Ry," he chortled, eyeing me with interest.

"Shut up, Morrison," Ryan ordered coldly, but he got off the stool and exchanged looks with Ash and Court before motioning for me to follow him.

I traipsed after him slowly but stopped when we got to the stairs. "Can we run by my place? I need to grab some stuff for tonight."

He shot me an impatient look. "What stuff?"

"Pajamas? Shampoo? Toothpaste?" I rubbed my forehead. "I packed a bag, but I forgot it in Bex's car."

You know, because Ryan was knocking people out.

"All stuff I already have here," he countered, a calculating glint in his eye. "You can sleep in one of my shirts."

I glanced down at my jeans and halter top. "And what? Walk of shame it in front of your brothers tomorrow?"

The corner of his full mouth hitched up. "Basically? Yeah."

I narrowed my eyes. "You're being an ass. Again."

Huffing in annoyance, Ryan leaned against the bannister. "Most of us won't even be here in the morning. We have a team meeting, and since almost all of the guys are on the team..."

"Fine," I muttered, stomping up the stairs behind him.

Ryan unlocked his door when we got to it then made a point of closing and locking it behind us. I gave the lock a dubious look before glancing at him.

He tossed his wallet and keys on his dresser.

"You always keep that locked?"

"When I'm not here? Absolutely." Ryan dropped into his desk chair and faced me.

"Trust your brothers that much, huh?" I couldn't help goading him.

"I don't trust anyone except for Linc, Ash, and Court," he told me, his eyes going flat and emotionless.

I blinked in surprise. "Wow. That's... awful."

"The people who live in this house are awful," he replied. "The brotherhood shit is just that. This is a place where you're expected to sharpen your blade to perfect the art of being cutthroat."

"Then why join, and why stay here?" I lowered myself onto the corner of his bed and sat down.

"For the same reason you're wearing that ring on your finger. It's what's expected," he answered. "We all have our roles to play, Maddie."

"That's a horrible way to view the world," I murmured.

"It's reality," he countered evenly. He waved a dismissive hand. "All this shit is what's expected of me. Of us. It's the world you live in now. Though why the fuck you agreed to come into it, I'll never know."

"You're kidding, right?" I leaned forward. "I needed an out. My mom needed help. Gary is giving us that. I can handle being surrounded by rich kids all day long. Trust me, it's easier than dodging bullets or avoiding alleys because you don't want to be gang raped."

His eyes flashed dangerously.

"You want to know why I was so pissed tonight? It's because I don't need you charging into my life like some white knight to fix my problems." My hands balled into fists on my lap. "I've been taking care of myself for years, Ryan. *Years*. I didn't have a driver to call when I stayed late at the library and had to walk home in the dark. I didn't need you then, and I don't need you now."

"I never said you needed me, Madison," he said icily, using my full name like a curse. "I'm well fucking aware of your life before your twin intervened. You think I didn't have Ash dig up every piece of shit about you from your elementary school teacher's name to the name of your mom's favorite dealer?"

I stared back at him.

"Mrs. Benton and Kenneth 'K-Dog' Smith," he added caustically. "Though 'K-Dog' is a little ironic considering all his teeth have rotted out of his mouth."

I held up a hand. "Fine. You had your friend investigate me or whatever. We've already established I came from a world that is completely opposite yours."

"I also found out how smart you are," he admitted quietly. "You started taking college courses your sophomore year. You worked your ass off at some shithole diner and then doubled down on a second job to save more money in the summers."

I shifted uneasily under his penetrating gaze.

His tone softened. "I know you're the reason your mom isn't dead."

My head snapped back.

Something like compassion shimmered in his eyes. "You called 911 when she overdosed last year, and you gave her CPR until the paramedics arrived."

I swallowed roughly around the sudden clog of tears in my throat. I hated the note of vulnerability that crept into my tone and my heart. "What's your point?"

"I know you can take care of yourself," he finished almost gently, "but maybe you shouldn't always have to."

It wasn't until I blinked that a tear slipped down my cheek, a fissure cracking open in my heart. My whole life, all I had wanted was someone to take care of me. For someone to *care* enough to want to take care of me.

I quickly swiped the tear away and ducked my head, but I knew Ryan had seen it. Sniffling, I blinked back more tears. "Thank you."

He frowned slightly.

"For standing up for me," I clarified with a watery smile. "It's... I'm not used to that. And you didn't have to."

"You're mine, Maddie," he said quietly, solemnly. "And I told you —I protect what's mine."

A strangled laugh loosed from my chest. "How very caveman of you."

His gaze met mine, piercing through my defenses and peeling back layers I had spent a lifetime erecting around my heart. It was terrifying to realize how easily he scaled the walls I'd meticulously built.

"Tell me you hate it and I won't say it," he offered.

I chewed on the inside of my mouth, my fingers twisting together helplessly in my lap. "I don't hate it," I breathed.

He smiled slowly, and somehow, that was the most terrifying and beautiful thing I had seen him do all night.

I cleared my throat. "Is that why you exiled Brylee?"

He snorted. "She had it coming. She's always been an annoying little clinger. That was more because I thought it was fun than to help you."

"Right. Of course." I rolled my eyes.

"But seriously? If she gives you shit, I want to know, okay? I'll handle it."

All I could find myself doing was agreeing. "Okay."

Nodding slowly, Ryan walked to his dresser. He pulled it open and yanked out a t-shirt and a pair of athletic shorts. "You want the bathroom first?"

I nodded and got up, my fingers brushing his as I took the clothes he offered.

He held on to them for an extra beat, his gaze searching mine before he lifted a free hand and tucked a loose piece of hair behind my ear. My breath caught at the subtle but intimate gesture.

A second later, he turned away from me. "There's an extra toothbrush in the top right drawer."

"Do you have a lot of girls sleep over?" That sounded a lot more bitter than it probably should have. This engagement wasn't a real thing, and I had no grounds to get jealous.

"I've never had a girl sleep in here," he told me seriously.

I glanced at the king-size bed and then back at him. "Sure. So I'm the first girl who's been in your bed?"

"I didn't say that," he replied. "I've fucked plenty of girls in this house. But none of them have ever stayed the night. If I don't trust my fraternity brothers, I sure as shit don't trust those women."

"Wow. So romantic," I deadpanned.

"Romance is for poor people and movies," he answered with a nonchalant shrug.

I arched my brow. "And yet you're trusting *me* to sleep in here."

His brows knit together.

I held up a hand. "I get it. It's all for optics and appearances. You probably already stashed all your valuables in a safe or whatever shit you rich people do."

"You being here is for optics," he agreed, "but as for me trusting you?"

I stupidly held my breath, waiting for him to continue.

"I guess we'll see," he finished cryptically.

"Right," I whispered and then scurried into the bathroom. I leaned against the door for a moment, exhaling hard before catching my breath.

I found the brush where he said it was and used his soap to wash the makeup off my face. I left my hair in the ponytail and quickly changed. His shirt was practically a dress on me, and I pulled the shorts on and cinched the drawstring as tight as I could.

I looked in the mirror and giggled. I looked like a kid playing dress-up.

When I stepped back into Ryan's room , I damn near swallowed my tongue.

He had changed into a pair of shorts and... that was it. Which left a lot of tan skin and muscle on display. My brain fritzed out as I tried to figure out a place to look that wasn't his chest. Or abs. Or Adonis belt. Or... lower.

Shit.

Chuckling, Ryan walked toward me, pausing to lift an index finger and tap the bottom of my chin.

"Remember what I said about open mouths, Mads," he murmured before going into the bathroom and closing the door.

"Fuck," I whispered, mentally slapping myself.

Dragging in a few uneven breaths, I looked around the room, trying to focus on something else. Anything else.

I wandered to his bookshelf and read the titles until my pulse settled a bit. He definitely had a thing for the classics.

My attention lingered once again on the picture of Ryan and his sister. I picked up the frame and was studying it when he came back out.

"What are you doing?" he demanded.

I turned. "Is this your sister?"

His expression darkened. "What the fuck do you know about my sister?"

"Not much aside from what I found online," I admitted, not thinking that was a bad answer until his entire body stiffened.

"What?"

"Chill," I said quickly, putting the picture back. "You have Ash, but all I have is the internet. I saw an article that said you had a sister. Your... mom died having her, right?"

Jaw tight, he gave a curt nod.

"I'm sorry," I said, genuinely meaning it. "Losing your mom as a kid must have been tough."

He blinked slowly and then scrubbed a hand across his jaw. "Sorry. I get a little defensive where Cori is concerned."

"Cori?" I echoed with a small smile.

"Corinne," he corrected, flashing a dimple as he grinned a little. "She's a sweet kid."

"You're close?" I edged closer to the bed.

He nodded again. "Yeah. Well, as much as we can be with me being here and her being home."

I glanced at the bed, wondering how this would work. I mean, the bed was huge but so was Ryan, and I was terrified I would wind up wrapped around him by morning like a baby koala.

"So, is this going to be a thing? Me sleeping here?" I asked, trying to stall a little as my nerves twisted into a ball of anxiety that settled in the pit of my stomach.

"Maybe. Is that a problem?"

No.

Stupid, traitorous brain.

"That's what I thought," Ryan murmured with a smirk.

"I didn't say a word," I protested weakly.

"You didn't have to," he replied smugly. "I was going to give you next weekend off for your birthday, but now..."

I glared at him. "Asshole."

Ryan looked down at the bed and sighed. "I guess a gentleman would take the floor and give you the bed."

I smiled, grateful, as my shoulders sagged in relief. The knot of tension in my gut loosened. "Thanks."

"No problem," he replied as he peeled the sheets back and slid between them, giving me a flash of the tattoo that graced the majority of his back. He moved too fast for me to clearly make it out. Something with wings that wrapped around his ribs.

But right now I was too focused on the guy in the bed to wonder about the ink. "What the hell are you doing?"

He bunched up the pillow under his head and gave me a long look. "Going to bed."

"But you said—"

He grinned wolfishly at me. "That a gentleman would take the floor. But I'm definitely not a gentleman."

I stared at him, flabbergasted.

"Get in bed, Maddie," he ordered.

I didn't move. I *couldn't* move.

Sleep with Ryan?

I mean, yeah, it was only sleeping with him in the literal sense, but whoa.

"Or sleep on the floor," he finally replied, reaching over to grab a remote from the nightstand. A second later, the room was plunged into darkness.

"Dammit, Ryan," I hissed, the sudden loss of sight propelling me in the general direction of the bed. I swore violently when I stubbed my toe on the corner of the frame.

He chuckled. "You okay over there?"

I dropped onto the bed and crawled toward the top, then managed to work myself under the sheets with a huff. "You're such a douche canoe."

He sighed dreamily. "You say the sweetest things in bed, baby."

I glared at him even though he couldn't see me. "I hate you."

"No you don't," he returned with another chuckle before rolling onto his side.

The worrisome thought was that he was right; I really didn't.

CHAPTER 38

I woke up to the soft sounds of birds chirping as sunlight slanted into the room and warmed my body. Sighing, I snuggled deeper into my pillow, not ready to get up yet.

And then I froze.

Because my pillow was *moving*. And hard as hell.

I popped my eyes open and realized my head was firmly on Ryan's chest.

Oh no.

I quickly inventoried where my limbs were. One arm was thrown around his waist while a leg had tangled itself between his. The others were pinned under my body as I lay on my side, my breasts smashed against his ribs.

And Ryan? One arm was curled around my back, anchoring me to his side, while the other was tucked up behind his head.

Narrowing my eyes, I zeroed in on the tattoo on the inside of his bicep. It was nothing but a few seemingly random numbers.

10.01

7.18

2.05

I lifted my head up to get a better angle, but Ryan's arm tightened around me so suddenly that I face planted onto his chest, my lips a centimeter from his nipple.

"Umph," I muttered, trying to push myself free.

Miraculously, his hold on me slacked.

But I was pushing so hard that my momentum rolled me right off the edge of the bed in a tangle of legs and sheets.

"Shit!" I yelped, my ass hitting the hardwood.

Laughing, Ryan's head popped over the side of the bed and into my vision. His sleep mussed hair and bright blue eyes made him look almost boyish.

"What the hell are you doing down there?" he asked me.

I scrambled to my feet. "I... I fell."

"Clearly." His eyes were brimming with amusement. "I had no idea you were a cuddler."

My eyes narrowed. "Uh, you were clearly on *my* side of the bed."

"You have a side now?" His head tilted quizzically. "Damn. You spend one night and—"

"You know what I meant!" I interrupted, slashing a hand through the air as embarrassment blasted through me.

Still chuckling, he rolled off the other side of the bed and stood up, stretching his arms over his head with a wide yawn.

I bit my lower lip as I watched the muscles in his chest and stomach contract deliciously, my eyes skirting lower until—

"Oh, my *God*," I hissed, spinning around.

Ryan snorted. "Seriously?"

"Put *that* away!" I ordered, gesturing wildly behind me. My cheeks were on fire.

"Chill out," he said easily. "It's morning, okay? It happens. You'll get used to it."

"I don't *want* to get used to it," I ground out, knowing the image of his morning hard-on pressed against his thin boxer-briefs would be forever seared into my brain.

Jesus, that thing was *huge*.

A deep throb between my legs was the last thing I needed to feel.

I needed to get out of here.

"I'm going to take a shower," he told me.

"Good, that's good," I said in a rush. "I'll grab my stuff and just... leave. See you later?"

"Do what you want, but if you leave before I do, expect to run into several guys on your way out," he advised.

Shit. I definitely wanted to avoid that.

"Why don't you hang out until the team leaves? You can use my shower, if you want," he offered.

I dared a peek over my shoulder, vowing to keep my eyes above the line of his shoulders. Thankfully he had pulled on a pair of sweatpants that contained some of his... situation. I turned fully to face him and managed, "Uh, sure."

Still smirking, he shook his head. "I had no idea you were so..."

"So what?" I challenged archly. "Prudish?"

"Innocent," he answered. Surprisingly there was zero judgement in his tone. If anything, he sounded kind of sweet.

I scoffed, my defenses still up. I'd been called uptight by a lot of the guys in my class back at Cliftown when I wouldn't date or hook up. "I guess that's one way to put it."

"How else would you put it?"

"Self-preservation?" I gave a small shrug.

He frowned, not getting it.

"Where I come from, teen pregnancy is a very real, very normal thing. I never wanted that to be me, so I made sure it wouldn't be."

His eyes widened, almost comically, in surprise. "Shut the fuck up. You're a virgin?"

I almost cringed but forced my back to remain straight. "Yes. Is that so bad?"

"No," he said quickly, emphatically. "That's just... wow. I didn't expect that."

"Why? Because you're used to girls whose panties melt when you walk into a room?" I rolled my eyes.

"Yes," he said bluntly. "But also because you're beautiful."

I paused and then felt my lips starting to curve up.

"I guess the guys where you come from are, what? Blind?"

"I wasn't interested in dating," I admitted softly. "I tried a few times and it just wasn't what I wanted. And honestly, I didn't have time for it. Between school and working and my mom... " I trailed off with a helpless shrug.

A guilty pang hit me. I'd been so busy with school and cheering and Ryan that I hadn't taken the time to call her this week.

"What's that look for?" he asked me.

I toyed with the end of my hair. "Are you psychic or something?"

"No," he answered, "you just have a shit poker face."

"I was thinking about my mom. I haven't talked to her in a while. Guess I'm a pretty shitty daughter, huh?" I flashed him a weak smile.

"Are you kidding me?" Ryan stared at me like I was crazy. "Maddie, the only reason your mom is alive is because of you. You twisted your life around to work to pay *her* bills when she should've been taking care of you. Hell, you sold your fucking soul to all of us to give her a shot at getting better."

Tears burned the backs of my eyes, and I started blinking quickly to stave them off.

His expression softened. "Whatever you want to think, being a shitty daughter is the last thing that should be going through your head. You're amazing, Mads."

My tongue darted out to wet my lips. "Thank you," I whispered, my voice cracking.

"Okay," he said with a heavy sigh and a soft smile. "I'm going to take a shower. You good?"

"Yeah," I said quickly, forcing a bright smile. "I'll leave after you do, if that's all right."

"Absolutely," he assured me. He grabbed a few things from his dresser, giving me a chance to look at the tattoo on his back.

"A phoenix?" The question escaped before I could cut the line between my brain and my mouth.

He glanced back at me. "Yeah."

"Why?"

He shoved the top drawer shut and turned to look at me. "It's a long story."

"Oh." I glanced down at the floor. "And the numbers on your arm?"

"Important dates," he answered vaguely.

"Like?" I couldn't help myself. I felt like I was the only one in this room completely exposed. I needed *something* from him to balance the scales a little.

His mouth flattened. "Like dates that are important to me."

Nodding, I let it go, and he went into the bathroom. But the rejection stung. A minute later the shower turned on.

With nothing else to do, I wandered back to the bed and flopped down, inhaling deeply. This bed smelled like Ryan in all the best ways.

Rolling onto my side, I grabbed my phone and checked my text messages. There were a couple from Bex.

The first was a selfie of her and Linc backstage, sticking their tongues out at the camera.

The second said: **Hope everything is ok! Call me in the a.m.!**

I would call her, but there was a call I needed to make first.

I pulled up the number to the Golden Grove Treatment Center and waited as the phone rang.

"Thank you for calling Golden Grove, this is Betty," a warm voice greeted a moment later. "How may I assist you today?"

"Hi, Betty," I started. "My name is Madison Porter. I'm calling to talk to my mother? Angie Porter?"

"Of course. Just a moment," she requested before putting me on hold.

I rolled onto my back and stared at the ceiling as I listened to the neutral muzak.

"Hello?" a voice asked as the line clicked over.

I frowned. "Mom?"

"No, this is Dr. Shelton," the woman said. "Is this Madison?"

"Uh, yes. Sorry. Is my mom okay?" Worry gnawed in my gut. The last few times I had called, they had just connected me to her room directly.

"Of course," Dr. Shelton assured me in a monotone voice. "However she's in group right now. Unless this is an emergency, we don't want to disrupt her."

"Of course not," I agreed quickly. "Can you just tell her that her daughter called?"

"I will. Have a nice day." She hung up before I could reply.

"Okay," I muttered, dropping the phone as the door to the bathroom opened.

Ryan emerged in a fresh pair of sweatpants and wet hair. A few drops of water rolled down his chest, and I caught myself watching with interest.

"You keep looking at me like that," he said, his tone rough as he turned and yanked a shirt out of his dresser, "and I might decide to skip the meeting and hang out with you instead."

I gulped and smoothed my face into what I prayed was a look of innocence by the time he turned around.

"The first one is Cori's birthday," he said suddenly, putting on his watch. The muscles of his forearm rolled as he deftly did the clasp.

"What?"

"The dates," he said, loosing a breath as he looked at me. "The first one is Cori's birthday. The second is the day my Nana died. The third is when Linc, Ash, Court, and I got the phoenix tattoos."

A smile twitched on my mouth. "You got a tattoo to commemorate the day you got a tattoo?"

He smirked and shook his head. "Yeah."

"And you all have them? The phoenix tat?"

He nodded as he walked to the edge of the bed. "Mine's the biggest."

I smirked playfully up at him. "I'm sure you think so."

"Smart-ass," he chided with a chuckle. "Ash isn't into needles. His is the smallest. It's on his shoulder. Court's is on his ribs."

"And Linc?"

He tipped his head back and laughed at a distant memory. "*His* is right above his dick."

My brows shot up as a laugh burst from me. "Seriously?"

Ryan grinned. "Yeah. He lost a bet, and Court got to pick the place he got the tat."

"Oh, God." I covered my mouth with my hands, feeling my cheeks ache a little from smiling so hard. "Look at you, being sentimental," I told him softly.

He shrugged a massively large shoulder. "Guess I'm full of surprises."

"I guess you are," I agreed.

Ryan grabbed his keys off the dresser and twisted one off the ring. "Here."

I sat up and frowned, taking the key from him.

"Lock up when you leave, okay?" he asked.

"You're trusting me with your key?" Surprise colored my words as I stared up at him.

"Yeah," he said slowly.

"I'll give it back when I see you..." I wasn't sure when that would be. Ryan usually set the terms of our meetings and outings.

"Lunch," he informed me, but it didn't feel like the type of order he usually issued. It was more like we were making plans. Like we were friends or something.

"Lunch," I echoed. "Got it."

He sat on the edge of the bed and pulled on his shoes. "Keep the key. I have another."

"You're giving me a key to your room?" My breath caught at the implication.

First the tattoos and now a key?

He nodded and looked back at me. "Yeah."

"You trust me?" I asked in a small, hushed voice.

Sighing, he reached out and tugged the end of my ponytail before touching my jaw. "Your skin is insanely soft, you know that?"

I smiled, unsure what else to say. The compliment warmed my insides in an addictive way.

"Yeah, Mads, I trust you," he answered, but I could see the conflict in his eyes. He was at war within himself. "I probably shouldn't, but I think I do."

I leaned into his touch and his eyes widened in surprise. We stayed like that, suspended in time in a moment that felt too intimate and pure to shatter.

"I think I trust you, too," I admitted quietly.

He gave me a soft look as he stood up and drew his hand back to his side. "I'll see you at lunch, okay?"

"Okay," I agreed, watching as he left.

The scales weren't balanced, but they were a lot closer to being equal than they'd been when I woke up.

And I was definitely catching feelings for my fiancé.

I dropped back onto the bed and closed my eyes.

CHAPTER 39

"Nice high kick, Claudia!" I called as I gathered up my bag at the end of practice almost a week later.

"Thanks, Maddie," my squad-mate replied with a broad smile before waving and heading toward the locker room with two other cheerleaders. Both waved at me, and I returned the gesture.

Sighing, I bent and zipped up my bag and grabbed my bottle of water. It was kind of a relief that more people were starting to call me Maddie now that Ryan and his friends did. I hardly saw them during the day, but we almost always had dinner together. Bex was finally relaxing around the guys. She and Linc had bonded at the concert and were constantly bantering and bickering like an old married couple.

I liked hanging out with them. And I especially liked it when Ryan walked me back to my dorm each night. The more I talked to him and he opened up, the more I liked. It was getting harder and harder to reconcile him with the guy who'd pinned me to a bed at our first meeting.

I was actually a little bummed that I wouldn't see him tonight, but I needed a night with my first ever best friend.

"You were, like, so nice to her," Hayley gushed, coming up behind me.

I gritted my teeth for a second before swallowing a mouthful of water. "She's doing a good job."

"Yeah, because her daddy paid to have a private coach help her over the summer," Kayleigh groused.

Hayley giggled. "He really *stretched* her out."

Kayleigh cackled back. "Totally."

"You realize how jealous you both sound, right?" I asked archly, glaring at them each in turn. "If she looks good, the squad looks good. Which means we *all* look good. Don't get pissy at Claudia because she gets more height on her kicks than you do, Kayleigh."

Kayleigh's mouth dropped open a little. Hayley looked flustered.

I'd been doing this for the past week. Throwing jabs back at them when they got catty. I was over their bitchiness, especially when I was making genuine headway with this squad. *My* squad.

I loved cheering, and Kayleigh and Hayley weren't messing that up for me. But anytime I fired back with a snide comment aimed at either of them, they both looked like I had dumped water on their internal circuit boards. Like they were trying to do a system reboot and put their world back to rights.

I didn't give a shit how confused they got.

"Well, what are we doing tonight?" Kayleigh asked, changing the subject.

"Yes!" Hayley clapped her hands. "It's your birthday tomorrow, so we totes need to celebrate tonight. Kappa is throwing another party, but we can always—"

"I have plans," I cut her off.

My plans were a movie night with Bex, because it was a rare Friday night when PCA and PCU didn't have a game. I had already told Ryan I was hanging out with Bex, but I was expected to be on his arm for the party tomorrow night after his game.

I could barely control my absolute joy and excitement at the thought of spending a night with people I truly detested.

It was about as enticing as a pap smear.

I would have rather spent this birthday the way I did most of my others: with a carton of ice cream while I watched a movie,

But Ryan and the guys would be there, and Bex had also agreed to come. Hopefully it wouldn't suck too bad if I stuck with them.

"Boo," Hayley muttered, jutting out her lower lip. "You're no fun now that you're engaged."

"And we're not even getting any fringe bennies," Kayleigh whined. "I mean, it's totally selfish to keep all that man meat to yourself, Laine."

I coughed. "Man meat?"

"Ryan's *friends*," she trilled with a shrill giggle. "I mean, so much sexy. I would love to spend a night mapping Court with my tongue."

"Okay, ew." I made a face and turned away. "I have to get ready to show Coach what I've come up with for the homecoming routine, okay?"

It was a lie, but I needed something to get them to leave me alone before my brain liquefied and dribbled out of my ears.

"Whatevs," Hayley replied flippantly. "See ya, beotch!"

"Later, hussy," Kayleigh added, slapping my ass on the way by.

I closed my eyes and silently counted to ten.

"They're so annoying, right?"

I peeked over to see Brylee standing behind me. She looked decidedly nervous and small. She'd all but faded into the background on the squad and around school since Ryan kicked her out of the party.

"Yeah," I agreed reluctantly. "They're a bit much."

Brylee's nose scrunched up. "I know. I mean, this summer was awful. I, like, never got a break since you... Since you weren't around."

I pressed my lips together and shrugged.

Her gaze darted away as she bit her lower lip. "Lainey, I'm sorry, okay? Like, really sorry. Not just for the shit with Rebecca, but also for this summer and not having your back. I should have called or texted or something."

"Okay," I said slowly, not sure what I could say to that.

She exhaled hard. "I've always been jealous of you, and when Richard picked you over me..."

Was that the coach's name that Madelaine had slept with? I hadn't bothered to learn it.

"Anyway, we've been friends for, like, ever." She gave me a small, hopeful smile. "I miss you, bitch."

Such a beautiful term of endearment.

"And your birthday's tomorrow," she pointed out. "We always spend the night before doing something fun. What do you say? We could do something, just us."

"I have plans with Bex," I said coolly, crossing my arms.

Her eyes widened. "So, that's really a thing? You being actual friends with her? I figured it was some long con, with how much you hated her."

"Things change," I replied curtly. "And, yes, Bex is my friend. It's not some twisted game."

She held up her hands in surrender. "Okay, cool. I mean, I can be okay with that."

"Okay." I watched her the way someone would watch a scorpion crawling up their leg; with a healthy dose of apprehension and fear.

"Isn't that your dad?" Brylee pointed behind me.

I spun around and my jaw dropped as I saw Gary headed down the path toward me in a business suit

"It is," I remarked, stunned as hell.

"Looking good, Mr. C!" Brylee called.

"Dude!" I turned and gave her a grossed-out look. "That's my dad."

Her green eyes glittered. "Well, your dad can be my *daddy* any day."

"Ew!" I cried as she laughed and danced away with a giggle.

"See you later, *Maddie*," she chirped over her shoulder with a wave.

I turned and waited for Gary to close the distance between us. He stopped a foot from me, giving me an awkward smile.

"Hi, sweetheart," he greeted.

"Uh, hi," I stammered, looking around. "What are you doing here?"

He rubbed the back of his neck sheepishly. "I should have called, I know. But it's your birthday tomorrow. I wanted to see you before I leave for Berlin."

"You're going to Germany?" I didn't know why I was surprised; aside from a random text or two, I hadn't heard from him since I'd gotten to school. I hadn't even known he'd returned from his last trip.

"Beckett and I both are, but we thought we'd take you and Ryan to dinner tonight to celebrate," he informed me with a wide smile.

I winced. "I actually have plans tonight."

He frowned slightly. "Plans?"

"With Bex," I explained. "Rebecca."

He smiled broadly. "Ah, Malcolm Whittier's daughter. Well done, Maddie."

"Excuse me?"

"Befriending Whittier's daughter explains why he accepted our proposal so fast last week. You move fast, my girl." He tossed me a knowing wink.

I gave him a strange look. "I'm friends with Bex because I *like* her. Not because of who her dad is or what deal he accepted."

"Of course you are," he assured me. "I would expect nothing less. But certainly Rebecca can survive without you for the night?"

I nibbled softly at my lower lip. "I guess so."

"Wonderful! Why don't you get changed and we'll pick you up outside your dorm in, say, an hour? I have a meeting with the headmaster."

"Sure," I agreed with a shrug.

He watched me for a beat, and then suddenly hugged me. His arms came around me stiffly, like he was performing an obligatory action and not a genuine one. As soon as my hand patted his back, he pulled away.

I WAS SLIPPING a silver hoop through my ear when someone knocked on my door. Securing the clasp, I went to answer it.

Ryan waited on the other side in a black button-down shirt, the sleeves rolled up past his forearms, and dark pants.

"You look... wow," I managed, feeling a surge of butterflies take flight in my stomach.

"You look pretty *wow* yourself," he returned with a grin, letting himself inside and closing the door.

I glanced down at my simple sapphire colored dress and matching heels. The full skirt landed just above my knees and the halter ties at the base of my neck left my back bare. My boobs were held up by some wonky tape that Bex had assured me would handle all the weight my bra usually carried, but I had my doubts.

Thank God she had been okay with canceling our plans and came over to help me pick out an outfit for tonight.

"I thought I was meeting you all downstairs," I called over my shoulder as I turned and went back into my bedroom. I gathered my purse and turned to see Ryan in the doorway.

He walked to my bed and picked up the stuffed elephant that had seen much better days.

"Stop fondling Sir Trunks-a-lot," I told him with a smile. That elephant was one of the few things I had saved from my childhood.

Grinning, he set the animal back down. "I wouldn't want him to get the wrong idea."

"He's a very proper elephant," I informed him primly.

"I'm sure." His face sobered. "Our dads are waiting in the car downstairs."

"Okay. Let's go."

He caught my arm gently as I tried to walk by. "And your Uncle Adam."

I jolted, remembering Adam's clammy hands pawing at me. I jerked my arm away from Ryan and tried to swallow my grimace.

But of course, Ryan missed nothing.

His eyes narrowed and he closed the distance between us. "Maddie, look at me."

Sighing, I slowly lifted my eyes.

"Did he do something?" Fury lit his blue eyes as they searched mine. "Fuck, that dinner at the house, I thought something might've been going on. I was so mad at your sister that I didn't really make sure you were okay."

My eyes slid shut and I shook my head before I opened them once more. "I think Madelaine was sleeping with him."

His eyebrows shot up. "What the fuck?"

"The day he came home? He... said some shit to me when he found me by the pool."

"What shit?" he growled, gaze narrowing.

Without thinking, I tossed my purse aside and rested my hands on his chest. The thump of his heart under my palm was steadying. "He thought I was her, Ryan. I managed to get away—"

His jaw clenched and he looked away, but I turned his face back to mine with one hand.

"—and nothing happened. But what he said made it obvious he and my sister had something going on. And then at dinner that night, he touched my leg. That's why I jumped up and went to the bathroom. I haven't seen him since then."

He exhaled hard through his nose, clearly pissed.

"I'm sorry," I apologized softly.

His focus snapped to me. "For what?"

"For Madelaine cheating on you. *Again*," I whispered.

"Mads, I don't give a fuck about your sister," he replied roughly, his hand finding my hip and pulling me a little closer. "I care about him making *you* uncomfortable. About him being a fucking predator."

"I'm fine," I assured him gently.

Jaw tight, he gave me a pained look before looking away with a hiss.

"What?" I pressed.

He swallowed hard. "I was just thinking that... that I wanted to kiss you."

I sucked in a sharp breath, my eyes flaring wide.

He chuckled humorlessly. "Shit. I'm sorry. I shouldn't have—"

"Okay," I cut in, my pulse throbbing in my veins.

The corner of his mouth hooked up. "Okay?"

I nodded slowly. "Yeah. If you want."

His gaze sharpened, turning almost predatory as his gaze dropped to my mouth. His smile twisted into a feral thing that made my stomach flip in anticipation. "Oh, I want."

I barely had time to breathe before his lips crashed into mine. The hand on my hip tightened as his other came up to cradle my jaw so he could angle my head exactly where he wanted.

My fingers grabbed the front of his shirt as I gasped, and he took the literally open invitation to stroke his tongue into my mouth. I whimpered as he deepened the kiss, taking control and dragging me along for one hell of a ride.

With a rough groan that curled my toes, he pressed his hips to my stomach. My world tilted on its axis as he ground the growing length of his cock against me.

"Shit," he whispered, tearing his mouth from mine and lowering his lips to nip and kiss at the column of my throat.

I tilted my head back to grant him all the access he needed.

"We need to leave," he muttered against my flesh, rocking his hips into me.

"Uh huh," I agreed mindlessly, breathlessly. One of my hands slid up his chest and around his neck.

He laughed warmly. "I'm serious."

"Then stop kissing me," I muttered as his lips moved across my collarbone.

His hand lingered at the knot in my dress behind my neck. "If we had more time, I would peel this dress off and eat *you* for dinner."

I shivered in his arms.

"You like that idea?" His voice went gravelly and dark. "The idea of me pinning you to that bed and fucking you with my tongue while you scream my name?"

Another shuddering whimper rolled out of me.

"Dammit," he hissed, placing one last, almost chaste, kiss on the side of my throat where my pulse thundered.

I leaned back and sucked in a ragged breath as I struggled to get my body to calm down.

Using his thumb, he wiped under my lip where my gloss had

smeared. He kissed the tip of my nose next. "We need to get downstairs before they come up here looking for us."

I cleared my throat and took a wobbly step back that made him smirk.

"Shut up," I muttered, turning back to the mirror and fixing the lip gloss streaks and reapplying.

Ryan came up behind me and wrapped his arms around my waist, his erection digging insistently into my backside. He peppered kisses along my bare shoulder as I finished getting myself together.

"We should go," I said quietly, meeting his eyes in the mirror. The flush on my cheeks had nothing to do with the blush I'd applied earlier.

"Stay near me tonight, okay?" he requested as he straightened.

I gave him a confused look through the glass.

His hands tightened briefly on my hips. "I'd rather not have to break Adam's hands if he tries touching you."

I settled my hands atop his and smirked up at him. "Because I'm yours?"

I meant to say it lightly, teasingly, but his expression turned fierce. A wave of desire rolled through me unexpectedly.

"Because you're mine," he swore.

CHAPTER 40

My lips were still tingling as Ryan escorted me to the car, where our fathers and Adam were waiting inside. He opened the back and let me slide in first before joining me.

Gary and Beckett sat across from us while Adam sat on the side bench by himself. His gaze dropped to my bare legs, and I felt Ryan tense beside me.

I waited for him to sit down then slid against him and put a comforting hand on his leg. He relaxed slightly, his arm winding around my shoulders and tucking me to his side as he closed the door.

Beckett started laughing as he watched us. "Has hell frozen over? You two are actually getting along?"

"You could say that," Ryan answered, glancing down at me with a secret smile that I easily returned.

"It's about time," Gary commented with his own grin. "Does this mean you've been discussing the wedding?"

"Of course," Ryan lied smoothly, dropping his hand onto my leg and stroking the skin on my thigh. "Plans are coming along nicely."

"Wonderful," Gary said, his eyes gleaming in the dark interior. "Your engagement party in a few weeks will be a splendid event. Almost everyone invited is coming."

"Fabulous," I chirped, hating the fake smile I plastered on my face. I glanced down at the ring on my finger and wondered what it would feel like if the meaning behind this ring was real. If Ryan and I were *really* together.

"Congratulations," Adam drawled, his gaze boring into me. "I'm sure you're very happy together."

"We are," Ryan replied sharply, glaring at Adam until he looked away.

I zoned out as they started discussing business. My mind rolled back to our kiss, replaying the desperate way Ryan's hands had held me as he kissed me.

Then I looked back down at the ring.

This ring probably cost enough to buy my old trailer park. The giant diamond gleamed from the platinum setting where it was nestled against a bed of smaller diamonds.

It isn't real.

I had to remember that. No matter how good the kisses were or how much I was starting to fall for Ryan, this could all vanish in a second. I wasn't planning on living Madelaine's life forever; this year was a means to an end.

So why did my heart ache sharply at the idea of taking his ring off and handing it back?

A soft sigh escaped my mouth.

"Are you okay?" Ryan asked quietly so only I heard him.

I gave a small nod. "Yeah. Just thinking."

His forehead creased with concern, but he let it go. Instead, his fingers on my leg absently traced circles as he turned his attention back to whatever deal they were discussing. It was all foreign to me, the names and countries they tossed around just more pieces of a jigsaw puzzle I didn't have the picture to.

I glanced around the spacious interior of the limo, blatantly ignoring the jealousy blazing in Adam's eyes as he watched Ryan and me.

For a little extra *screw you, asshole,* I leaned my head against Ryan's shoulder and forced my brain to think about something else.

I was mentally choreographing the end of the homecoming routine when the limo pulled to a stop in front of the Italian restaurant with gas lamp posts along the front.

Ryan opened the door and helped me out before waiting for the others. I hid a smile when I noticed Ryan made sure he was between Adam and me as we walked inside.

The restaurant was packed with patrons in dimly lit chairs and tables. Even in the middle of the week, there was barely an open table available. A string quartet played soft music in the corner.

We bypassed them all on our way toward the rear of the establishment and into a separate room with a private table. Once the hostess escorted us to our seats, Ryan gently pushed me to sit on one side of the table and started to take the seat beside me.

"I can sit there," Adam offered nonchalantly. "Why don't you sit across from your beautiful fiancée so you can see her pretty face?"

Ryan gave him a look that could've frozen the fires of hell. "Because she's more than a pretty face, and I like touching her whenever I want."

I ducked my head at the implication of his words.

Beckett and Gary exchanged amused looks with one another as they found their own seat; Gary sat at one end of the rectangular table beside me while Beckett took the opposite seat beside Ryan.

Adam slunk into the seat across from me with a scowl.

I bit my lip to suppress a smile when Ryan scooted his chair flush to mine and wrapped an arm around me.

I turned and gave him a wry look. "Are you planning to piss on me next?"

"Nah. Golden showers aren't my thing," he whispered back, his eyes glinting. "But I love fucking with Kindell."

My eyes narrowed playfully. "Behave."

"Or what?" His mouth curved into a devilish grin. "You going to spank me?"

I lifted a shoulder and turned to my menu. "Maybe I'll let *you* spank *me*."

His sharp intake of breath was all the satisfaction I needed.

"Tease," he muttered, shaking his head.

I giggled softly.

"I never thought I'd see the day when you two actually smiled at each other," Gary remarked.

"Things change," Ryan replied offhandedly.

"So, you two are *really* together?" Adam scoffed.

"We really are," Ryan answered smugly, his fingers twirling a lock of my hair between them.

Adam leaned forward, his eyes only on me.

"You once told me that you couldn't stand him," he reminded me.

I met his gaze unflinchingly. "Like Ryan said—things change."

He snorted at me. "So it's love then?"

"Is there a reason you're so concerned with *our* relationship?" Ryan demanded. "Almost sounds like you're jealous."

Adam reared back. "Of course not. I'm simply concerned for my niece."

"She's my concern now, so maybe you should back off," Ryan gritted out, his eyes flashing dangerously.

I dug my fingers into his thigh, begging him silently to let it go. I could see Gary and Beckett watching us with confused interest.

Ryan shot me a look, but I saw his eyes soften around the edges as he loosed a breath and let it go. For me.

"I'm glad to know my little girl is in such good hands with me being on the other side of the world," Gary remarked with a wink.

"Leaving again?" Ryan asked scornfully, looking at him.

"Germany. Now that Shutterfield is a done deal—well done on that, son—we're moving into the next phase of development," he explained.

"What phase?" I inquired.

Beckett gave me a bland smile. "Nothing you need to worry about, honey. I'm sure you're busy making plans for the wedding and shopping for whatever it is you'll need."

I bristled at the implication. This time Ryan's fingers tightened on my thigh, silently asking me to let it go.

I would. For now.

For *him*.

"How are the wedding plans, sweetheart?" Gary turned to me as the waiter appeared at his side. "I'll have a cognac."

"Bourbon, neat," Beckett stated.

"Single malt," Adam chimed in.

"Water," Ryan said.

"Same," I agreed, flashing the waiter a smile. "Thank you."

He looked surprised at that but left to fill our orders.

"Can't hold your liquor, boy?" Adam smirked.

"He has a game tomorrow," I cut in sharply. "The last thing he needs is alcohol the night before."

Adam glowered at me but shut up.

Beckett cleared his throat. "You were saying about the wedding, Lainey?"

I winced a little at the name. "Uh, right. The wedding." I gritted my teeth and tried not to glare at Gary for bringing up wedding plans he knew damn well I wasn't making.

"We're thinking early summer," Ryan cut in smoothly. "Maybe mid-June?"

I desperately tried to school the look of incredulity on my face as I joined him in the outright lie. "Outdoors will be best for photography. We're thinking of something coastal at sunset."

"The Karrington Club would work," Gary mused, rubbing his jaw as our drinks were delivered. "We could take the venue for the weekend. Did you have a specific date in mind?"

"No," I answered honestly. "We just thought June would work best, then we'd have the summer before I start college."

Beckett chuckled. "You realize no one expects you to actually attend college, Lainey. Hell, you can spend your days in a spa or shopping. Whatever tickles your fancy. I'm sure Ryan won't mind footing the bill to keep his wife looking gorgeous."

My muscles locked up as I tried not to grind my teeth.

"Maddie's smart as hell," Ryan said sharply. "I think it's a good idea for her to get a degree."

"*Maddie?*" Adam scoffed.

I noticed that Gary's gaze had zeroed in on me, an unreadable expression blanking his emotions. But I had the feeling it wasn't a "honey, I'm so proud of you" look.

Ryan didn't bother responding to Adam. Instead, he looked at his father. "How are things going in Indonesia?"

Beckett grinned. "Perfect. You laid some excellent groundwork for us this summer."

Ryan nodded, but I noticed the way his jaw tightened and the slight tremble that rippled from his hand to my leg.

The waiter reappeared to take our orders, and it was then that I realized we hadn't even seen a menu. And I highly doubted this was a place where a hamburger would be on it.

Gary finished requesting a beef dish and then added, "My daughter will have the Waldorf salad. Dressing on the side."

I'm sure my surprise showed on my face, but the waiter disappeared before I could correct him.

Gary gave me a smile and covered the hand I had rested on the table with his. "I know how picky you get about your food when you're in the middle of cheer season, and I advised the staff about your allergy when I booked the room."

Sighing, I bit the inside of my lip and resisted the urge to say something back. Yes, it was the middle of cheer season but I had burned a ton of calories today. I wanted *food*. Not some fancy ass salad that I'd never heard of.

I could feel Ryan watching me, but I let the whole thing roll off my shoulders. This dinner wouldn't last forever, and I could grab something when we got back.

But it still irritated the hell out of me.

As if sensing my sour mood, Ryan leaned closer and changed the angle of his hand so he was stroking my hair instead of my shoulder.

Admittedly, it worked. I'd always had a thing for people playing with my hair. It was like my personal Xanax or something. It totally zenned me out.

The conversation wound back around to business, and I mostly didn't pay attention. I was mentally rehearsing the homecoming routine and trying to remember the timeline of the first world war for my history test next week as I waited for dinner to arrive.

Despite the full house at the restaurant, our food was delivered quickly. I picked at my lettuce, chicken, and apples, grimacing as my stomach gave a low rumble from the scents coming from the others' plates.

"You've got to try this," Ryan told me, holding up a forkful of his steak.

I took the bite gratefully, nearly moaning as the meat melted in my mouth in a burst of flavor.

With a grin, Ryan pushed half his steak onto my plate and took a bite of my salad. By the time the meal was done, I had eaten half his meat, most of his mashed potatoes, and a little bit of salad. I'd graciously left him the mixed veggies on his own plate, and he'd finished the bulk of my salad.

As the plates were cleared away, Gary touched my hand. "I have something for you."

"For me?" My brows lifted in surprise.

He smiled and handed me a small box wrapped in red with a white bow. "Happy birthday, honey."

A pang of sadness hit me as I realized that this was supposed to have been Madelaine's birthday, too. The first we could have celebrated together.

My hands shook as I took the box and slowly opened it. Inside the box was a key.

I frowned and looked up at him. "You got me a key?"

He laughed loudly. "It's the key to your new car."

"You bought me a *car*?" I whisper-hissed. "I told you that I can't—"

"Accept it?" He cut me off with a razor-sharp smile that pretty much said *shut up before you fuck up*. "Of course you can. You're my baby girl, and you deserve a new car."

"Thank you," I said softly, overwhelmed but also touched by the gesture. He had mentioned wanting to buy me my first car, but I hadn't put much stock in what he'd said, to be honest.

I'd learned a long time ago that promises were just like eggs; easily broken and frequently spoiled.

Maybe Gary was different. Maybe this time was different.

"I figured you and Ryan could drive yourselves back tonight," he added with a wide grin. He handed me a slip of paper. "Here's the valet ticket."

Adam chuckled. "Remember when I taught you to drive, Madelaine?" His suggestive smile was hard to miss. He licked his lips, salivating at whatever disgusting memory he was conjuring about my sister.

"Not really," I replied with an indifferent shrug.

Ryan snorted beside me and drank the rest of his water.

"Maybe you need a refresher lesson," Adam ground out, his lips thinning as he pressed them together in anger.

I nodded slowly, considering his offer. "Maybe I do." I turned and grinned at Ryan. "You up for being my teacher?"

Smirking, Ryan leaned in so his nose bumped mine. "Anytime, baby."

Adam grunted in annoyance and shoved back from his chair. "I need to make a call. I'll be back." He stormed away, nearly knocking down our waiter as he came back in bearing a carafe of coffee.

"He seems more tense than usual," Beckett remarked, leaning back in his seat.

Gary waved a dismissive hand. "He's practically been Madelaine's second father. I think he's having a hard time realizing she's not our little girl anymore."

My phone vibrated on my lap through my purse with an incoming text. As discreetly as I could, I pulled the phone out. I half expected the message to be from Bex. She had offered to call in an emergency to get me out of dinner if I needed her.

I smiled, thinking of her as I unlocked the home screen and tapped the message.

UNKNOWN: I am not amused. Get out here now I can remind you who you belong to, slut.

A hollow pit opened in my stomach, and I swallowed roughly. Sucking in a shaky breath, I put the phone back into sleep mode.

On principle I had deleted Adam's contact info from my phone as soon as I'd gotten it, but this couldn't be anyone except him.

"What's wrong?" Ryan asked me quietly.

I shook my head as my phone vibrated again.

Ryan took the phone from me and turned it on. He scrolled through the messages, his face darkening with each thing he read.

I glimpsed the newest message over his shoulder.

Oh, gross.

A stubby dick in a nest of dark pubes filled the screen with the caption: **I want you on your knees.**

Ryan's fingers tightened around the screen so much I worried he would shatter the screen. And then one more message rolled in.

UNKNOWN: I'll carve my name into your tits and cunt so that impotent asshole knows who you really belong to. You are mine.

"Ryan—" I started, but he jumped out of his seat. I grabbed for him but only touched air.

"What's wrong, son?" Beckett demanded, getting up as well.

"It's a friend of ours," I lied quickly, sliding my chair back and getting up. I shoved the key into my purse. "It's an emergency. We have to go."

Ryan was already storming out of the room with little regard to our fathers.

"Of course," Gary said slowly. He stood up and hugged me.

I returned the hug. "Thank you for my gift."

"Happy birthday, Maddie," he whispered in my ear. "We'll talk soon."

"Definitely," I agreed with a thin smile, my stomach a mess of knots.

Beckett grabbed my arm on the way by. "Is my son all right?"

I nodded quickly. "Of course. Just worried about our friend."

His eyes narrowed, cold and calculating. "I hope that's all it is. Remind him to call me later. We still have things to discuss."

"I will." I pulled free.

"And Madelaine?"

I turned at the door, frustrated and ready to scream at the interruption.

"Happy birthday." Beckett raised his glass to me.

"Thanks," I muttered before hurrying from the room. I looked around the full dining room, but I didn't see Ryan kicking Adam's ass across it, so I had to assume they were outside.

Pushing open the door, I looked around, but the street was mostly empty except for the valet.

"Shit," I muttered. I didn't even have my phone because Ryan had taken it with him.

I was still looking when the door opened behind me and Ryan came out, his expression cold and lethal.

I took a step back on instinct. "What did you do?"

Ryan glared at me and handed the phone back. "Nothing. Fucker was in the bathroom, but there were other people inside. He ran out like a little bitch when he saw me coming." His hands balled into massive fists. "I'm going to kill him, Maddie."

I grabbed his hand and gently unfisted it, then twined my fingers with his. "It doesn't matter."

"The fuck it doesn't," he hissed, his blue eyes flashing in the low lighting.

"He's a pathetic scumbag," I said, keeping my tone soothing. I inched my way closer to him until he wrapped his free arm around me and crushed me to his chest.

"Do you know how much I want to rip him apart?" Ryan muttered against my hair. "I swear to God, Maddie. If he would have been alone in that room, I would have killed him."

I smiled against the hard planes of his chest. "Then I'm glad you didn't."

He snorted. "Oh, yeah?"

"Yeah." I tipped my head back to look at him. "It would be hard for me to kiss you again if you were in prison for murder."

A low laugh rumbled through his chest. "We could always get married before I get locked up. Conjugal visits might work."

My eyes narrowed. "I don't think so."

He sighed heavily. "Yeah, I guess you're right. The first time I bury myself inside your body, I don't want an armed guard on the other side."

I felt my cheeks blush. "Oh. I mean, sure. That would be awkward."

His grin devastated me, twisting my insides and bringing that insistent throb back between my legs. "What would *really* be awkward is them running into the room while I'm making you scream."

Oh, hell.

All coherent thoughts left me in a fuzzy haze of confusion and lust.

I was in trouble. So much trouble.

CHAPTER 41

I stepped out of the dressing room the next afternoon, wrinkling my nose as Bex watched. Her eyes lit with excitement.

"That. You have to buy that dress," she practically ordered me. "It's *perfection*."

I glanced down at the mint green dress. The fabric was so soft that it poured like liquid over my skin, landing *just* this side of decent on my thighs.

"Oh, maybe with a pair of strappy heels? I'm thinking Jimmy Choo," Bex mused as she tapped her chin. Her eyes glazed over as she mentally dressed me.

Chuckling, I glanced at myself in the mirrors.

"It's pretty," I admitted, but then I looked at the price tag and winced. *That* was less pretty.

Bex sighed. "What's wrong, Maddie?"

"This dress costs almost a thousand dollars," I hissed, looking around furtively for the saleswoman, whose eyes had turned into dollar signs when Bex and I walked through the doors.

Bex had insisted we go to Pacific City to do some "much needed retail therapy." Her words, not mine.

As we'd driven down the mountain away from Pacific Cross, I'd been amazed to see how the town of Pacific City had essentially been divided into two unequal parts, divided by Fallout. There was a small, upscale section that held a handful of restaurants and boutique shops. That was where we had gone to dinner the night before. The rest looked like a normal town with a pizza joint, a diner, and an old bookstore I was hoping I could convince Bex to stop at on the way back to school.

It was clear that the high-priced part of the town had been added for the benefit of the students, though. The only people in the shop besides Bex and I were two girls I recognized from campus.

There was more luxury shopping an hour north of school, but Bex said she liked finding things in town that weren't totally mainstream. I was beginning to realize that my friend had a major fashion obsession.

Bex's face scrunched up with confusion and then gave way to understanding. She got to her feet. Even in her heels, she was still several inches shorter than my five-nine height.

"Maddie, part of being *her* is looking the part," she told me softly. "And Madelaine wasn't a jeans and t-shirt kind of girl."

I gave her a long look. "Was she a leggings kind of girl?"

She giggled and shook her head. "Definitely not. Look, you have a freaking black card, okay? Gary can afford for you to buy everything in this store and the one next door."

"That doesn't mean I have to," I insisted, my resolve wavering as I looked back in the mirror. I really did love this dress.

Bex rose to her tiptoes. Her large hazel eyes peered over my shoulder in the mirror. "Think of all the birthdays he missed. Consider this one of your many missed presents."

I rolled my eyes. "He bought me a freaking car, Bex. I think that made up for all of my birthdays until I'm forty-five."

With a sigh of frustration, she went back to the couch she had been sitting on while I gave her a mini-fashion show. "Maddie, you've got to stop thinking like, well, *you*."

I frowned. "And how do I go about not thinking like me?"

She leaned forward. "Think like *her*."

"You're the last person I expected that advice from," I said wryly.

"I don't mean bring back the evil queen," she huffed. "It's pretty obvious that you've done wonders in turning around her reputation."

I gave her a droll look. "Ryan did that. He waved a magic arm and commanded everyone to accept me again."

"Maybe," she hedged. "But Ryan didn't make people come up and talk to you. You said the squad has been asking you to hang out with them, and not just Satan's sycophants."

I smothered a laugh. "They really are awful."

Tipping her head back, Bex groaned. "The *worst*."

I came over and sat beside her. "I'm still sorry for the way they've treated you."

"Part of me wishes they would go back to hating me," she muttered. "Kayleigh actually sat next to me at dinner yesterday. She asked me where I got my skirt, and I think she actually *meant* it."

I burst out laughing.

"I can't *stand* her. I want nothing to do with her," she argued, slapping my shoulder. "I think I enjoyed being invisible."

"I mean, you do have an impeccable sense of fashion," I offered, still grinning widely.

"That's a given," she scoffed. "But I'm not used to a world where..."

"Where what?"

She ducked her head a little. "Where people *like* me?"

"You said you grew up with the guys," I pointed out.

She rolled her eyes a little and huffed a laugh. "Yeah, but they're three years older. Our families vacationed together, but once they got to middle school, they stopped letting me tag along. They were too busy staring at girls with boobs."

I snickered a little, imagining the guys doing just that.

"Then my family and Court's had a falling out, and that was it." She shrugged sadly.

"What happened?"

She frowned, the pain obvious in her eyes. "I don't know. I was too young to really understand. All I know is my parents almost got divorced over it. My dad moved out for almost six months."

"Damn," I muttered.

She blew out a long breath. "But I had Madelaine, so I didn't really care. And then she dropped me..."

My heart softened, breaking a little for her. Madelaine had royally fucked up her chances at having a social life. Everyone had spent years avoiding Bex to avoid Lainey's wrath. She had put Bex in social Siberia and quickly cut down anyone who made an attempt to befriend her.

Thankfully things seemed to be thawing now. I'd seen Bex around school talking to a few people, and I knew she'd eaten a few meals with her roommate.

I reached over and covered one of her hands with mine. "I know how much that must have sucked. I really do."

She gave me an incredulous look. "You're telling me you were bullied and treated like shit at your last school, Miss Head Cheerleader?"

"No," I admitted, letting the barb roll off my back. "But I never let people get close. It was too hard because I was always worried about what they would think of my mom. I spent all my time working and studying and busting my ass to be the best I could. It didn't leave a lot of time to be social."

"Okay, but that's not the same as having people who spent their lives making you feel like shit suddenly want to be your friend," she pointed out, bitterness in her tone.

I sucked in a sharp breath between my teeth. "I guess I didn't think about that."

And now I was wondering how she felt about being friends with the girl who shared the same face as her biggest tormenter.

"Don't go there," she told me sharply. "This isn't about you, Maddie. I know you aren't *her*. I've never confused you with her or held anything she did against you. Not since I found out the truth."

"I know," I said quickly, brightly. "But it can't be easy."

"Maybe it's easier because I know you're nothing like her. Now, unless the terrifying triplets have long-lost twin sisters, too..."

I smiled. "What are the odds?"

With a laugh, she shook her head. "I don't even want to consider it. What I really want to think about is how hot you'll look in this dress at the beach tonight."

One of Ryan's teammates had a beach house a little ways up the coast from school. He was throwing a party there after the game tonight. Ryan had texted me to ask—yes, actually *ask*—me to come. And he told me I should bring Bex. Hence the shopping trip.

I stood up and bit my lower lip. I loved the dress.

"Okay, fine," I said with a breathy laugh. "I'll get the dress."

"Now we need shoes," Bex sing-songed as I went back into the dressing room to change.

"I have shoes," I told her as I exited the fitting room once more, the dress gently draped over my arm.

She gave me a confused look. "I've seen your closet, Maddie. While you have a few adequate options, it's your birthday. We're going for the *wow* factor."

"Oh, are *we*?" I teased as I took my dress to the counter.

"Lovely choice," the saleswoman remarked as she rang up the dress.

I tried to ignore the way the price jumped when sales tax was added on. Holy hell. That was so expensive. I hesitated, holding the card in my purse.

"No waffling!" Bex cried, forcing my hand out of my bag with the card between my fingers. She slid it across the counter for me.

The woman snapped up the card and charged me before I could overthink. She carefully wrapped the dress in gold tissue paper and placed it inside a stiff shopping bag as gently as a mother would put her newborn in a car seat.

"Thanks," I murmured, taking the bag and letting Bex lead me out of the store and into the sunlight.

"Okay, the shoe store down here has all the best stuff. They have a few Italian indie designers that are to *die* for," Bex gushed as she linked her arm with mine and led me down the street.

Nearly an hour later, my feet ached from trying on so many pairs of heels before Bex finally decided on the perfect ones to match the dress.

I still couldn't pronounce the designer's name, and as I was trying to figure it out, Bex paid for my shoes.

"Happy birthday," she told me sincerely, handing me the box.

My jaw dropped. "Bex! No. You can't do that."

"Funny, because I totally just *did*," she pointed out with a giggle as she pulled me from the store and back toward the car.

"It's a shame we don't have time to hit a few more stores," she bemoaned. "There's this adorable boutique that always has the cutest accessories."

I was carrying nearly fifteen hundred dollars worth of new items. "I think I'm good."

Her mouth turned down. "Are you *sure* you have to be back at school? Can't we skip the game?"

"I wish," I said dryly. "At least you can sit with your roommate. I have to sit next to—what did you call them?"

"Satan's sycophants," she reminded me seriously.

I snapped my fingers. "That's it."

"Yeah, you win. But tell my new bestie Kayleigh that I said hi," she told me with a healthy dose of sarcasm.

I narrowed my eyes playfully at her. "Maybe I'll suggest you join the squad."

Bex looked legitimately horrified. "God, no."

I tipped my head back and laughed. It felt good; the sun was warm on my face and laughter bubbled from my chest as I walked with an actual friend.

"Hey, Maddie! Bex! Wait up!" a voice called out.

We paused on the sidewalk and turned to see Linc and Court striding toward us.

"What are you two doing here?" I asked as they approached.

Linc grinned, his eyes lighting up. "Looking for a couple of hot honeys."

Court groaned. "Seriously, dude?"

Linc ignored him and waggled his eyebrows at us. "So? Whatcha say, ladies?"

"I'll ask my fiancé," I smirked.

Linc made a face. "Yeah, don't tell him I was doing anything remotely close to hitting on you. Whatever happened last night has him all raged out."

My eyes widened.

"Wait, what happened last night?" Bex demanded. "Did something happen at dinner?"

Sighing, I gave them all the abbreviated version of events.

"That guy's lucky Ryan didn't fucking kill him," Court muttered, scrubbing a hand across his scruffy jaw. The dark shadow gave him an almost dangerous look, but it was the quiet fury coming off Linc in waves that worried me.

"Nothing happened," I told Linc quietly.

His stormy eyes met mine. "It's fucking bullshit, Mads."

"I agree," Bex chimed in. "I vote we fuck up uncle fuck-face."

That broke through Linc's mood. He smiled at Bex. "How did I miss the little firecracker you turned into?"

"Probably because you've been too busy screwing whatever girl is throwing herself at you since you realized what an erection was to actually notice that women have more to offer than a few convenient holes to stick your dick in," Bex deadpanned.

Linc blinked once, thunderstruck. "Marry me."

Court rolled his eyes, shouldering past his friend and nudging us to start walking again. "Ignore this idiot."

"I usually do," Bex said smugly, but I noticed she blushed a little as she smiled at Court and fell into step beside him.

"Ryan and Maddie are getting married. We can make it double," Linc suggested as he caught up.

I couldn't help but glance down at the ring on my left hand. Every morning I put it on my finger, it felt like the lines of why were getting more and more blurred.

"Don't," Linc said in a low voice. He grabbed my elbow gently and pulled me to a stop as Bex and Court walked on. "Look, obviously I don't know everything that's going on, but whatever is happening with you and Ry? Just... let it happen."

Unsure, I shifted my weight on my feet. "It's hard, Linc."

It was a testament to how much Linc loved Ryan that he didn't jump on that opening.

"I'm serious, Maddie. I've seen him with girls, but not like this. It totally unhinged him last night, what happened with your uncle."

"That's because he's a good guy," I argued weakly.

"He isn't," Linc said flatly. "Ryan Cain is one of my best friends, but he's also selfish as fuck and can be as ruthless as they come. But he's different with you. He's different *about* you."

"It's only been a couple of weeks," I pointed out. "And yeah, things are going good now, but I don't belong in this world, Linc. We both know this will never go anywhere."

"Says who?" he challenged me. "Fuck what other people say. What matters is what you and Ryan feel. And if you ask me? You both deserve a win. You both got dealt shitty hands."

My eyes narrowed. "What do you mean?"

He exhaled hard. "That's Ry's story to tell when he's ready."

I twisted the engagement ring on my finger. "But it feels like everything is moving so fast."

"So what if it is?" He shrugged. "There are people who are together for years before they get married, and they divorce within a year. Other people get married after a month and are together forever. Fuck what society says. Life's too short not to follow your heart."

"Maybe you're right," I allowed softly.

He snorted and wrapped an arm around my shoulders, guiding me down the sidewalk. "Of course I am."

I smacked his stomach, almost wincing when my hand landed on solid muscle.

"Do you guys just work out all day?" I groused.

"Obviously," he replied. "How else am I going to land my dream girl? We can't all have a ready-made fiancée or our own fucked-up version of *Sleeping Beauty* with the girl-next-door."

"What?" I laughed.

He inclined his head to where Court and Bex had paused in front of her car ahead of us. "I think Court's crushing on her. Has been since the night he took her back to her dorm when Dean drugged her."

"I think it might be mutual," I stage-whispered, watching as Bex giggled and ducked her head at something he said.

An odd look passed his face. "They lost a lot of time."

I tilted my head curiously at him.

Flashing me a quick, but obviously forced, smile, Link shrugged. "Their families used to be close. Court... He and Bex were close."

"Yeah, she made it sound like he was kind of like a big brother or something," I said.

He snorted. "I can assure you that the *last* thing Court thought about Bex was as a sibling."

Surprised, I glanced ahead at them and watched to see Court brush a lock of Bex's hair from her eyes.

"Ah, young love," Linc sighed dramatically.

"And what about you?" I asked, teasing. "Don't you want love?"

All playfulness left his expression. It turned dark and brooding. Almost haunted. "Sometimes," he finally answered.

"Sometimes?" I repeated doubtfully.

"Yeah. Sometimes it would be nice to have someone who I could share everything with. Someone who wouldn't freak out at all the broken, twisted up parts of me. But I also realize that would be kind of shitty of me, you know? To expect someone to walk in the dark with me."

I grasped his wrist, stunned. "Linc."

"We should catch up." He gave me a tight smile and dropped his arm from my shoulders. He walked ahead of me, leaving me to wonder what darkness he was carrying around.

CHAPTER 42

"Sit still before I burn you," Bex ordered, brandishing the flat iron dangerously close to my forehead.

I froze out of self-preservation from where I had been fidgeting as she painstakingly straightened every single strand of hair on my head.

"I'm *hot*," I whined, knowing I sounded like an annoying little kid, but honestly? After the game (which Ryan *crushed*, leading the team to a massive 43-10 victory), I'd come back to my room to shower and get ready for the beach house party. Between the hot shower and Bex blow drying my hair and now flat ironing it, I was burning up.

And okay, maybe I was also a little excited to see Ryan.

"You're not hot yet," Bex snarked back, running the iron over the same section of hair. "But you will be when I'm done."

Huffing, I sat back and let her finish. As soon as she was done, I quickly applied some makeup and pulled my dress on, then finished the look with the heels Bex had bought me for my birthday.

"You look stunning," she gushed.

I grinned at her, taking in the way she'd loosely curled her dark hair and showed off the multicolored streaks in it, and she had smoked out her hazel eyes. In a merlot-colored dress and sky-high heels, she looked ready for a party herself.

"Back at ya, babe," I said with a wink as someone knocked.

Butterflies erupted in my stomach.

Bex rolled her eyes and went for the door. "Chill, girl. It's a party, not your wedding."

That really didn't help settle my nerves.

She pulled the door open and sighed dramatically at me. "Maddie, it's for you."

"Hey," Ryan greeted as he came in the door in jeans and a black t-shirt that did amazing things for his chest and abs. "Happy birthday, Mads."

I pointed at him and glared at Bex. "Why does he get to wear jeans? You told me no jeans tonight."

"Because you're a girl," Bex replied with an indifferent shrug as she grabbed her purse. "It's our job to look pretty while being as uncomfortable as fuck."

"I want a new job," I announced.

"I think you look hot," Ryan told me, his eyes heating as they swept over me.

Okay, maybe this whole dressing up thing didn't suck as much when I got *that* kind of reaction.

I bit my lower lip. "Thanks."

"The guys are downstairs with the car. Are you two ready?" Ryan's gaze flicked to Bex before settling back on me.

Nodding, I grabbed my bag and let Ryan lead us down to Linc's massive SUV. Ash was in the front passenger seat while Court waited in one of the middle row seats.

Ryan linked his fingers with mine. "We'll take the back," he announced, getting in first before letting me climb in back with him. I sat down and started to buckle my seatbelt when Ryan slid me toward him on the leather bench so I was in the middle.

Bex closed the door and flashed Court a smile ahead of me.

I glanced up at Ryan.

"You were too far away," he said softly, his blue eyes searching mine as he tucked me against his hard body.

I melted a little at that as Linc drove the car away from our dorm and toward the main road off campus.

Ryan's fingertips grazed the bare skin of my leg almost curiously. I shivered in response as he grinned.

"You two behave back there," Linc called, looking at us in the rearview mirror.

"Watch the fucking road," Ryan replied with a smirk, flipping him off.

Ash turned around from the front, his green eyes narrowed in amusement. "I'll keep an eye on them."

"You're both hilarious," Ryan deadpanned as I stifled a giggle.

He looked down at me. "Don't encourage them."

I shrugged helplessly. "Sorry?"

Bex turned in her seat so her back was to the door. "You guys played great tonight."

"We *always* play great," Linc informed her from the front.

I snorted. "Not always."

"You dare question our worth, woman?" Linc demanded indignantly.

"I question that pass you nearly fumbled in the third quarter," I said dryly.

"Damn," Court hooted, turning around to high-five me.

"I didn't fumble a pass," Linc argued.

"She said *almost*," Ash pointed out. "And she's right. You did."

"I got hit by *three* guys!"

"You should've zagged left. You had an open lane," I countered flippantly as Ryan started to laugh.

"Maybe if I had someone decent throwing the ball," Linc said pointedly, looking at the guy next to me.

Ryan bristled. "Don't even. That pass was perfect."

"Well..." I hedged.

"Excuse me?" Ryan looked at me, his brows lowered.

"See? Tell him, Maddie!" Linc yelled.

I peered up at Ryan. "I'm just saying, you wobbled the pass a little."

His head snapped back in shock. "There was no wobble. I don't *wobble*."

"There was a little wobble," Court added, smirking back at his friend. Clearly they loved riling him up.

I patted his chest patronizingly. "Maybe you should practice more."

He snagged my hand, his eyes piercing me "Oh, it's not practice I need."

My blood heated at the intensity in his gaze. I swallowed uneasily and watched his lips curve into a knowing smirk as he realized how I was affected by his implication.

"There's a blanket in the back," Linc sighed, shaking his head. "If you two are going to fuck each other, use that on the seats."

I ducked my head as I felt my cheeks flush.

"Ass," Court muttered, kicking Linc's seat.

"What?" he cried. "It's Maddie's birthday. Let her have a birthday orgasm."

"You really have zero filter," Bex huffed. "Stop embarrassing her."

"Can't. Won't," he clarified. "After years of being subjected to Madelaine the Ice Princess, it's nice having a girl who actually reacts to shit around here with a smile."

The mention of my sister was like having ice water dumped over my head.

Between shopping with Bex, the game, and having fun, I had sort of pushed away the fact that today should have been Madelaine's eighteenth birthday, too.

We could have celebrated together.

Instead, I was living her life, and now she was just gone.

"Fucking idiot," Ryan muttered. He gently turned my face to his with one hand. "Ignore him, okay?"

"I didn't even think about her," I confessed.

"Because you're living your own life," he said gently, thumbing my bottom lip. "There's nothing wrong with that."

"I'm living *her* life," I countered. I held my hand up. "This is *her* ring. You're *her* fiancé. It's *her* squad. That car Gary gave me? It should have been Madelaine's."

He looked ready to argue with me.

"I'm not hers," Bex cut in innocently. "I'm here for *you*."

"Same," Court agreed, and Linc nodded.

Ash turned to look at me. "We all hated Madelaine. The reason we're not all driving separately is because we like hanging out with *you*, Madison."

"And people like *you*," Bex added with a small smile. "People were always afraid of her. She was mean. You know that."

"I do," I admitted. "But she was still my sister. My twin. And she's dead. This was the first time we could have celebrated together."

"No," Bex argued, shaking her head, "that's a lie. I told you—Madelaine knew you existed *years* ago."

"Wait—what?" Court turned to me.

"Yeah," Bex went on. "When we were still friends, Madelaine told me she had found another birth certificate with hers. She knew she had a twin for years. She didn't reach out until Madison contacted her."

A sour feeling curdled in my stomach. Bex had told me that, but I hadn't really unpacked that truth. With Madelaine dead, it seemed kind of pointless. I couldn't ask her why.

"When did she find out?" Court demanded.

Bex frowned. "We were almost thirteen? She wrote me off a few weeks later, and we never talked about it again."

"And it was her idea for you to switch places, right?" Ryan added quietly.

I nodded.

He exchanged a look with Ash.

"Are you two keeping secrets again?" Linc sighed. "Ash and Ryan frequently forget it's supposed to be the *four* of us."

"You didn't play the tape for them?" I asked. I had assumed that when Ryan admitted to bugging my room that he had shared everything he'd overheard with his friends. Apparently only Ash knew that my sister had known about me.

"It didn't seem important," Ryan admitted. "I told them who you were. The fact that Madelaine knew about you years ago could have meant a lot of things."

"Like?" I asked, almost afraid of the answer.

He exhaled, his cheeks puffing out. "She was selfish, Maddie. Maybe she didn't want to share the spotlight? Maybe she thought you would be competition."

"Which you totally would have been," Linc supplied.

"Not helping," Bex growled at him when my face fell a little.

I didn't want to be her competition. I wanted to be her *sister*. I wanted to not be alone.

Ryan touched my hand. "We'll probably never know, and I'm sorry for that."

"You are?"

"Don't act surprised," he murmured with another one of those smiles that made my knees turn to Jell-O. "In case you haven't noticed, I kind of like you, Madison Porter."

"It's been a long time since I heard my full name," I whispered. I gave him a small smile as his thumb smoothed over the back of my hand.

Ash cleared his throat. "And it really isn't important anyway, Maddie. You're here now. Whatever your sister's reasons were don't matter."

I frowned and looked at Bex before glancing up at Ash. "Actually? I could use a little help."

"Name it," he said, his green eyes sincere.

"Gary cloned my sister's phone so I would have access to her stuff. I guess to make the transition a little smoother? Anyway, there's this encrypted file I can't get into."

"It's a CryptDuo," Bex added.

Ash's brow furrowed. "How the fuck did she get a CryptDuo app on her phone?"

"What's CryptDuo?" Linc asked with a frown.

"A super secure app that encrypts whatever files you want it to," Ash replied, looking a little concerned.

I shrugged and pulled it from my purse. I handed it to Bex, who passed it to Ash.

"What's your password?" he asked.

"My birthday," I replied.

Every head swung in my direction. My shoulders hunched. "What?"

"Your birthday?" Ryan shook his head. "Maddie, that's one of the easiest passwords to guess."

I narrowed my eyes at him. "Well, we can't all have special numbers tattooed on our arms. Besides, I needed something easy to remember."

Sighing, Ash shook his head at me. "I don't know if I can access all the data on this, but I can try. I might need your phone for a few days."

"That's fine." I had lived most of my life without a cell phone. I wasn't attached to it the way some of the kids at school were.

"I'll get you a new phone tomorrow," Ryan said.

"I don't need a new phone." I snorted. "I can live without it for a little while."

He pressed his lips together. "Actually? I'm more concerned that Gary might've downloaded something to keep tabs on you."

Unease trickled through my chest and settled in my stomach. "He wouldn't do that."

"He *would* do that," Bex insisted. "I told you, Madelaine *hated* him."

"He told me they had a great relationship," I countered softly.

"Baby, he was trying to get you to go along with whatever the fuck he was selling," Ryan murmured. He sucked in a deep breath through his teeth. "You can't trust him."

Ash put my phone in the glove compartment. "I'll start working on it tonight."

"Thanks," I called up to him as Linc parked the car.

I peered into the darkness, seeing a fully lit house with more glass than walls and people already packed inside.

Ryan held me back as everyone got out of the car.

"Why didn't you tell me about the app?" he asked.

I tilted my head to the side to watch him. "Honestly? I didn't think about it. And when Bex mentioned it, she said I should ask Ash, but that was before..."

"Before what?" He challenged me with narrowed eyes.

I met his gaze steadily. "Before I started actually trusting you."

He stayed quiet beside me.

"It's just an app," I said slowly, not getting why this was such an issue. "There's probably a bunch of random cheer videos or something on there."

"You can't really be that naive, Maddie," he scoffed.

My spine stiffened.

"Look at the world you're in," he continued, his eyes flashing. "Madelaine might have been a lot of things, but she wasn't an idiot. Whatever she saved to that file was important enough that she hid it in one of the most secure ways on the planet."

I glanced down at my hands. "Madelaine hid that file, Ryan."

"Exactly."

I held up a hand. "Let me finish. *She* did that. I didn't mention it because I honestly didn't think it was important. And that maybe I would learn even more ways that my sister was an awful person. Either way? It didn't matter to me. Maybe that makes me naive, but it's bullshit if you're going to use that as a reason to get pissy."

His expression remained stony.

"Whatever," I muttered, getting up and out of the car.

"Everything okay?" Bex asked suspiciously as Ryan got out and walked over to Ash without a word.

I glared at his back. "Just peachy."

Bex took my purse from my hands and put it next to hers in the car before closing the door. A second later, Linc locked it.

"Ignore him," Bex encouraged me, linking our arms as we walked up the drive to the house.

"It's what we do when he gets like this," Linc agreed as he fell into step beside me.

"I can hear you, asshole," Ryan snarled behind us.

Linc glanced back. "You were meant to, *asshole*."

"Prick," Ryan muttered.

Linc grinned at me. "I swear, I'm less drama if you want to give it a go, Maddie."

"Don't tempt me," I muttered, knowing in my heart that while Ryan was infuriating, he was the one I was attracted to.

Ryan grumbled something back and a second later, his hand latched on to my arm and pulled me to a stop.

"Keep walking," he ordered the others when they slowed. "We'll catch up."

I waited for them to walk away before jerking my arm back. "What the hell is your problem? Are you really this pissed about a fucking app on a phone that isn't even mine?"

He rubbed a hand through his hair and hissed out a breath. "I don't fucking know, Maddie." He wrapped his hands around the back of his neck, his biceps flexing. "You drive me crazy."

"No," I said sharply, shaking my head. "Don't put this on me. Your inability to handle your emotions is on *you*. I might put up with a lot of shit, Ryan, but I thought we were done with me being your verbal punching bag."

"Fuck," he snapped. "That's not what I want."

"But it's what you're doing." I crossed my arms. "When you thought I was Madelaine, I could accept it or at least understand it. But you know *me* now, Ryan."

"I do know you," he replied tersely, his hands falling heavily to his sides. "What I don't know is why I can't control how I feel about *you*, and it's driving me fucking crazy."

I threw my hands up in the air. "What does that even mean?"

Jaw clenched, he squeezed his eyes shut. "It means that you've got my head spinning, and it's turning me into an idiot." He opened his eyes and looked at me. "And you're right. You didn't deserve for me to snap at you. I'm sorry."

Surprise lit me from within.

"I've been playing Madelaine's games for years," he admitted softly. "We knew each other growing up. Our dads were best friends, so we were together a lot. Maybe seeing all the shit she pulled left me jaded, and when I thought you were keeping something from me, it made me remember all the times she fucked me over."

I moved closer to him. "This is about more than the thing with your coach, isn't it?"

His throat bobbed as he swallowed hard. "Yeah."

I reached out and linked my pinky with his. "You can tell me about it."

He gave me a wry smile. "In case you haven't noticed, I'm not big on sharing my feelings, Mads."

I feigned shock. "And here I thought you were an open book."

He smirked and tugged me the rest of the way to him. His fingers tangled in my hair. "I'm really sorry."

"Thank you," I said, leaning into his touch.

He lowered his head but kissed my forehead. I was still pouting a little when he pulled away. Enough so that he laughed.

"If I kiss you now," he said, his tone a gruff rumble that made my insides liquify, "I'll be dragging you back to the car and you won't make it inside the party."

I smiled brightly as I tipped my head back. "I'm okay with that."

He huffed another laugh and pulled me toward the house. "Later."

I was trying to figure out ways to entice him to make good on his idea when he opened the door and every head turned to me. The music stopped abruptly.

"Surprise!"

The entire room shouted the single word at me, and I almost screamed. As it was, I jolted in surprise and ducked behind Ryan with my heart pounding.

"Happy birthday," he told me with an amused smile.

My gaze roved around the room, taking in the balloons and streamers of the party.

The *birthday* party.

For me.

I stared at Ryan. "You did this?"

He grinned at me. "I thought you might like a birthday party. Besides, I'd be a shitty fiancé if I didn't throw you a huge party, right?"

I blinked back a sudden rush of emotional tears. "Jerk," I muttered as the crowd broke into "Happy Birthday" and a massive tray of cupcakes was wheeled into the center of the room.

Candles lit the beautifully decorated cakes. I floated to it, almost in a dream, as Bex and the guys grinned at us. Hayley and Kayleigh stood near the front of the crowd with the rest of our squad. Toward the back of the room, Brylee gave me a small wave.

"Make a wish, gorgeous," Ryan whispered in my ear as the song ended.

Sucking in a deep breath, I closed my eyes and made my wish.

A second later, I exhaled as hard as I could and managed to get all the candles out in one breath as everyone clapped.

Ryan wrapped his arms around me from behind, resting his chin on my shoulder. "Birthday girl gets the first one."

I selected a gorgeous pink and white vanilla cupcake. I peeled back the delicate paper around it and took a bite, smiling as sugar burst across my tongue.

Ryan leaned in and kissed me, licking frosting from my lips.

"Thank you," I whispered, touched, as people moved in to grab their own cupcakes and the music started playing again.

"Happy birthday, Maddie," Linc said, sneaking past Ryan for a hug.

I popped the rest of the cupcake in my mouth when he released me as Bex dove into my arms.

"I'm *so* glad you're here," she whispered fiercely.

I squeezed her back. "Me, too."

I coughed as I pulled away, and then tried to clear my throat.

That cake was drier than I'd anticipated.

"Is there any—" My question cut off in a coughing fit. I turned away, feeling like I was choking as I kept coughing.

"Are you okay?" Ryan asked, touching my back.

Court passed me a bottle of water. I tried to drink but couldn't stop coughing long enough to swallow.

"You good, Maddie?" Court asked, looking a little concerned.

I tried to nod, but something felt wrong. Totally wrong. I tried to pull in a breath, but it was like the air was being sucked from the room. I wheezed in a raspy breath and dropped the bottle of water.

It rolled across the floor as I went lightheaded, my vision going fuzzy around the edges.

"Maddie!" Ryan shouted, grabbing my arm as I started to sway.

"Shit," Bex whispered. "We need her purse. It's in the car."

"What—"

Bex grabbed my other arm. "Maddie, *breathe*, okay?" She turned her panicked eyes to Ryan as spots appeared in my vision. "She's having an allergic reaction. Her epi-pen is probably in her purse!"

Linc whirled and took off at a run. I watched him knock a guy down as he raced out the door.

"What can I do?" Ryan demanded, panic edging into his voice.

I struggled to breathe in again, but the air was simply *gone*.

And then everything faded to black.

CHAPTER 43

The rhythmic sound of beeping dragged me out of sleep. I blinked my eyes open, cringing against the fluorescent lighting. I sucked in a ragged breath, my throat raw and swollen.

Everything in me wanted to slip back into the oblivion of sleep, but the soft murmur of arguing voices snagged my attention.

"What the hell happened?"

"I don't know."

"I told you guys that she had a peanut allergy."

"And I told the bakery she was allergic!"

An uncomfortable silence settled, until a lethally cold tone cut in.

"I want fucking answers. Someone did this."

A quiet gasp. "You think someone wanted to *kill* her?"

"Ry, that's a big jump."

"I think I want answers," the same voice growled again.

"I already called the bakery and raised hell. It had to have been a mistake, bro."

I tried opening my eyes again, but my blurry vision couldn't make out the people standing in the corner. Everything was still unfocused and confusing.

I licked my dry lips, desperately needing water.

"Ryan, she's awake."

One of the people peeled away from the group and was by my side in an instant, grabbing my hand in his.

"R-Ryan?" I croaked out the word.

He sat on the edge of my bed, his blue eyes more serious and worried than I had ever witnessed. "Hey, Maddie." A hand smoothed my hair away from my forehead. "How are you?"

"I'll get the doctor," someone else said and left the room.

The others moved closer to the foot of my bed.

Ash, Bex, and Linc. All wore matching expressions of worry.

"What happened?" I asked, my voice barely above a whisper.

Ryan's hand kept stroking my hair. "You had an allergic reaction to the cupcakes. There must have been peanuts in them."

"Maddie, I swear I told the bakery you were allergic," Linc added vehemently.

I tried not to make a big deal out of my allergy. The school was aware of it, and since food allergies had become almost normal, there was an entire separate section of food prepared separately for those with allergies. Gluten, nut, dairy... A school like Pacific Cross employed enough cooks to make sure their elite clientele was perfectly catered to.

But I had gotten lax at the party. I hadn't even considered the vanilla cupcake I'd selected might have been cross-contaminated.

And then, to make things worse, I'd left my purse with my epi-pen in the car.

"It's my fault," I mumbled, closing my eyes and leaning back against the pillow.

"The hell it is," Ryan snarled.

"Ry," Ash said softly, a warning note in his tone that had me opening my eyes.

Bex sat on my other side and took my free hand. "Don't say that."

"I should've been more careful," I muttered. It had been years since I'd had a reaction like that.

Ryan's jaw tightened, but his shoulders relaxed. He focused his attention on me. "You just need to rest, okay, baby?"

I looked around the room. "Am I in the hospital?"

He nodded. "Bex gave you your epi shot and the ambulance brought you in."

I groaned. "So everyone at the party saw me lose it?"

"You had a medical emergency," Ash pointed out. "That's hardly losing it."

Ryan's eyes flashed. "And everyone at the party can fuck themselves. If they give you shit about it, I'll handle it."

"We'll handle it," Linc corrected firmly.

The door opened and a doctor came in, followed by Court. The doctor paused in the doorway, taking us all in. He cleared his throat and directed his attention to me.

"If you all will excuse us, I'll speak with Miss Cabot," he told us.

Bex squeezed my hand and got up to follow the guys out of the room, except for Ryan. He stayed by my side.

"I'm her fiancé," he said flatly, clearly refusing to leave. If anything, he held my hand a little tighter, daring the doctor to make him leave.

Wisely, the doctor gave in.

"Miss Cabot, I'm Dr. Andrews," he introduced himself before checking the tablet in his hands. "You're a lucky lady. Your friends were able to give you an epinephrine shot and get you in here so we could treat you."

"Can I go home?" I asked softly.

Ryan sucked in a sharp breath.

"I'd prefer you stay here overnight for observation," Dr. Andrews said apologetically. "We had to give you multiple shots of epinephrine to stabilize you. I'd rather we kept you under observation for a few more hours. If all goes well, you can go home in the morning."

"Okay," I agreed, feeling small and weak in the hospital bed. But at least I had my own room.

"Do you have any idea how you came into contact with the peanuts?" he asked me.

"I ate a cupcake at a party."

Sighing, he nodded and made a note on the tablet. "You really must be more careful. I don't need to remind you how potentially fatal an exposure can be."

I flinched and Ryan's chest vibrated with an irritated growl.

"She *was* careful," he gritted out defensively.

I squeezed his hand. "It's okay."

The icy look he shot back at me might have been enough to silence me if I didn't already feel like shit, but I was exhausted and ready to just rest.

"Thank you, Dr. Andrews," I said.

He nodded and glanced at Ryan. "Visiting hours are over, son."

Ryan bristled, the muscles in his shoulders visibly bunching. "I'm not leaving her, and unless you want me to have all supplemental funding vanish from this hospital, you won't ask again."

Eyes narrowed, Dr. Andrews glared at Ryan and turned and stalked out of the room.

"Was that really necessary?" I asked softly.

He turned his icy stare to me. "Fuck yes it was. I'm not going anywhere, Maddie."

I swallowed roughly, still wishing I had that water to quench my thirst. "Did you call my... Did you call Gary?"

If it was possible, Ryan's face hardened even more. He gave a terse nod. "He's in Germany. He has important meetings lined up all week, and since you're technically an adult and he doesn't have to be here... The hospital called him since he's your emergency contact, but he asked me to make sure you were okay."

"Oh." I looked down at the white blanket covering my legs as pain splintered my heart.

"Aw, hell," Ryan muttered. A second later, he lifted me enough to crawl into the bed with me and pull me against his chest.

I sniffled, hating myself for being weak and vulnerable. "I'm sorry I'm a mess."

"I'm not," he whispered against my hair as the door opened and my friends came back inside.

"Everything okay?" Bex asked hesitantly, coming over beside me. Her hazel eyes were huge on her pale face.

"The dickface doctor said we have to go, but I can make Court punch him if that'll help," Linc offered.

I smiled at that, especially when Court nodded like he was agreeing to the plan.

"I have to stay overnight," I replied, trying to be brave, but my voice cracked a little. "But I'll be fine. You guys should go."

Ryan rested his chin on top of my head. "I'm staying with Maddie tonight. Can you guys grab us a change of clothes?"

Ash nodded. "Yeah. Anything you need, man."

I coughed a little. "Would someone mind getting me some water?" I looked at Ryan and pushed myself up a bit. "Or let me up so I can—"

"You're not moving," Ryan scolded as Court moved to grab some water from the pitcher on the counter. He passed the glass to me, and they all watched me drink until it was gone.

I handed the empty cup back to Court with a "Thank you."

"I can stay if you don't want to," Bex offered, giving Ryan an out.

My heart pounded a little, wondering if he would take the chance to bail. Part of me braced for it.

"I'm not leaving Maddie," he said firmly, his fingers tangling with mine. My breath caught as he drew them to his lips and kissed the back of my hand.

Bex flashed me a supportive smile. "Okay. I'll grab some stuff from your room and we'll bring it back in a little bit." She reached over and gave me an awkward hug, since Ryan didn't seem inclined to move over.

Linc grinned at me, tugging a lock of my hair. "We'll see you soon, Maddie."

"But call if you need anything else," Court added, practically demanding. His dark eyes were full of worry.

Ash and Ryan simply exchanged a wordless look. "Get some rest, Maddie," he told me before opening the door so everyone could leave.

Once the door was closed, I let out a breath I hadn't realized I was holding.

"How are you really?" Ryan asked quietly, the low rumble of his voice soothing.

I did a mental inventory. "Tired," I admitted. "Annoyed with myself."

He did that annoyed growly thing in his throat that usually meant he was about to argue.

"I've had this allergy since I was a kid, Ry," I explained gently, meeting his gaze. "I know to be careful."

He shook his head, clearly not ready to let me shoulder some of the blame. "I should've—"

"Should have what? Had each cupcake tested to make sure it wasn't cross contaminated? It happens," I told him.

"You could have died," he whispered.

I tried to smile. "Then you'd be a free man."

He scowled at me. "Haven't I made it fucking clear? I like you. And I have zero plans of letting you go."

My mouth went dry again for a whole new reason.

His hand cupped the side of my face. "Tonight scared the shit out of me, Maddie. I felt so goddamn helpless."

"I'm sorry for that," I said.

He huffed. "You almost died and you're apologizing to *me*?"

I smiled a little. "I'm sorry you worried."

"I'm not," he answered honestly, leaning his forehead against mine. "I've never cared about anyone the way I care about you."

"Not even Ash?" I teased. "He's your best friend."

"I don't plan to fuck Ash," he replied evenly.

I sucked in a gasp, my eyes going wide.

His smile was a thing of beauty and danger, and he leveled the full weight of it at me. "I owe you a lot of apologies, Madison. For the way I first treated you, for some of the shit I've said and done since we met. And I plan on spending a long time showing you that I'm not that guy. That I can be better."

"You can?" I whispered.

He nodded slowly. "Yeah. You make me want to try to be better." His gaze dropped to my left hand and reached out to turn the diamond ring on my finger. "I know I never really gave you a choice about this."

My eyebrows flew up. "Are you trying to propose to me?"

He laughed. "No. But I don't hate seeing my ring on your finger. I like looking at it and knowing that you're mine."

"How very caveman of you," I muttered sarcastically.

He smirked. "I guess you bring out that side of me."

I rolled my eyes. "Lucky me."

"I guess my point is," he finished, taking in a deep breath, "we have a chance here. Whatever this is between us, I don't want it to stop."

"Me neither," I admitted breathlessly. Saying it out loud felt like stepping off a cliff and freefalling with no bottom in sight. The sensation was utterly terrifying and hopelessly addictive.

"Okay," he said with a small smile. "Let's see where this goes, Madison Porter."

I pressed my lips together but was unable to hide my grin. "Okay, Ryan Cain."

CHAPTER 44

Between Ryan and Bex hovering and the guys watching me like hawks, it was a miracle I was able to go to the bathroom by myself over the next few days. Ryan had even gotten me excused from classes and had Bex bring me my missed assignments.

They took shifts so I wasn't alone, and Ryan spent every night in my bed. The doctor had insisted I take it easy over the next several days so as not to trigger another reaction, specifically I had to avoid activities where I would get overheated, like cheerleading. But Ryan took it a step farther and had set up a rotation of people to make sure I didn't lift a finger.

With nothing else to do, I had tried calling Mom a few more times, but the rehab center kept telling me that she was busy or sleeping. I even texted Gary about it. He said he would look into it, but I still hadn't heard anything.

Even tonight, everyone had ordered pizza and was currently in my dorm hanging out. My dorm was a good size, but the living area wasn't built for four massive football players. That became especially apparent when we started playing cards.

"Stop looking at my cards!" Bex snapped, shoving Linc's shoulder so he backed off.

He gave her an innocent look. "I wasn't trying to see your cards, B."

She narrowed her eyes in suspicion. "Oh, no? Then what?"

"I was looking down your shirt," he replied nonchalantly with a shrug.

She glanced down at her shirt. The collar was barely an inch below her throat. "You can't see anything, idiot."

"Then how do I know your bra is pink?"

Bex snorted. "Nice try. It's black." Then she blanched. "I just admitted that, didn't I?"

Linc burst into laughter as Court and Ash shook their heads. I kicked Linc from across the circle, nearly scattering the cards.

Ryan's hands pulled me back between his legs as he rested his chin on my shoulder, looking at our cards.

Yes, *our* cards. Because when I pointed out the floor didn't have much space for six people to play *Uno*, Ryan simply declared we would be on the same team and I could sit on his lap. Since we were on the floor, that quickly translated to between his legs.

It had felt awkward at first, but when I realized none of our friends seemed to care, I stopped caring, too. I finally let myself relax against the world's most solid chair.

Court glared at Linc from where he sat on Bex's left. "You're such an ass."

Linc winked at him. "Am I? Or am I the best wingman ever?"

Ash dropped his last card into the pile. "I'm out."

"Seriously?" I demanded, throwing my remaining six cards down.

"Cheater," Linc muttered.

"How the hell does someone cheat at *Uno*?" Court snorted.

Linc started collecting the cards. "I don't know, but if anyone can, it's spy-boy."

Ash rolled his eyes. "You're such a sore loser."

"Only when you cheat." Linc scowled at his friend. "I demand a rematch."

Bex yawned and leaned back. "Not me. I'm tired. It's after midnight."

"Okay, so Cinderella's out," Linc said, shuffling the cards. "Anyone else?"

"I want to get back and check on Maddie's phone," Ash declined, standing up. "The program I was running it through might have something now." He shot me an apologetic look. "I'm sorry it's taking so long. That app is no joke."

"It's okay," I answered. I didn't miss the phone, especially since Ryan had given me a brand new one before I even checked out of the hospital.

"Maddie needs her rest," Ryan agreed, getting up and then pulling me to my feet. He tucked a lock of hair behind my ear.

"Oh, *I* need my rest?" I snorted, shaking my head. "I've been resting all week, Ry."

"And one more night won't kill you," he countered firmly.

Linc put the cards back in the carton. "You're leaving early in the morning, right?"

I blinked in surprise as Ryan nodded tersely.

"Where are you going?" I asked, feeling a little stung I didn't know he was leaving. Not that he needed to run his weekly itinerary by me, but I had gotten used to seeing him every day.

Okay, fine. I looked forward to seeing him every day. A lot more than I probably should have.

"I'll catch up with you guys, okay?" Ryan said to his friends, not taking his eyes off me.

"Night, Maddie," they called.

Bex lingered, her eyes on me. "Do you want me to stay?"

I gave her a smile, grateful that she cared enough to offer. "I'm good. Thanks, Bex."

She gave me a tiny nod and went to the door where Court was waiting for her. Once the door shut, I turned back to Ryan.

"Why the secrecy?" I asked softly.

"It wasn't meant to be a secret," he admitted. "Cori's birthday is tomorrow. I always go home and spend the day with her."

"Oh." I turned away from him and started picking up the throw pillows on the floor we had used as cushions. "That's cool."

"Maddie," he started.

I held up a hand. "It's fine, Ryan. I know your sister means a lot to you."

And clearly you don't want me near her.

Why did that hurt so much?

"So do you," he returned quietly. "With everything that happened when you—"

"Almost died?" I cracked weakly, tossing a pillow back onto the couch.

"Don't joke about that," he ordered, a muscle in his jaw ticking.

I shrugged and started toward the kitchen to clean up the remaining dishes from dinner. "It's either laugh about or cry about it, and honestly? I'm so over crying, Ryan."

"Would you stop?" He grabbed my shoulders and turned me around to face him. "I want you to come with me."

I paused. "To meet your sister?"

He swallowed audibly and then gave a slow nod. "Cori's the most important person in my life. For years it's just been me and her."

"What about your dad?"

He scoffed. "I stand by my first statement."

"Ouch," I murmured. I had seen him with Beckett only a few times, but they seemed to have a good relationship.

"My point is," he went on, pulling me back into the moment, "you're important to me, too."

A small smile crept across my face. "I am?"

He sighed, his face softening with affection as he rolled his eyes a little. "Yeah. If I haven't made that clear, I'm worse at this boyfriend thing than I thought."

My heart sped up. "Boyfriend?"

An unexpected look of unease, almost vulnerability, flickered across his face. "I mean, yeah. I just assumed..."

"We never really talked about it," I said quietly. "You told me I had to ride the celibacy train while you did whatever, or *who*ever, you want. Discreetly, of course."

He cleared his throat. "Yeah, I was an asshole."

"You really were," I murmured, but smiled.

He grinned ruefully. "Yeah, well, I'm trying to make up for it. And for the record? I haven't been with anyone since I found out who you were, Mads."

"Really?" Surprise and hope warred for dominance in me.

"Really," he replied, sliding a hand up to sift through my hair. "So if I fuck up this boyfriend thing, it's because I'm pretty new at it."

I pressed my lips together. "I'm pretty new at being a girlfriend, so I guess we're even."

Chuckling, he dragged my body to his and hugged me. His powerful arms wrapped around me, and I snuggled my cheek against his chest, listening to the soothing rhythm of his heartbeat.

"I'll pick you up around nine, okay? I usually spend the day with Cori and head back to campus after dinner," he told me, letting me go.

I looked up at him. "That sounds great. Do you think she'll like me?"

"She's met Madelaine a few times," Ryan answered. "Cori... Cori's not what you expect."

"She hated Madelaine?" Worry churned in my gut.

He shook his head. "No. Cori loves everyone. Madelaine couldn't be bothered with Cori."

My nose wrinkled as I frowned. "Why?"

"Cori has autism," he replied honestly, watching me for any reaction. I could see him bracing himself for whatever reaction that emotional revelation usually yielded. "I mean, she's fairly high functioning, but she has some quirks."

"Okay," I said, not caring if she was autistic or had eleven toes. She was important to Ryan, so she had to be important to me. "Should I bring a gift?"

The smile that broke across Ryan's face, with full dimples, was absolutely stunning. "No. I think you'll be present enough for her."

That sounded cryptic, but I went with it. I rolled to my toes and kissed his lips quickly. "I can't wait to meet her."

His hand tightened on my hip. "Where the hell did you come from, Madison Porter?"

"Cliftown," I answered with a shrug.

Chuckling, he gave me another kiss. This one was slower and lingering. His hand moved from my hip to grab my ass and squeeze. I gasped into his mouth as a horn honked below.

"Fucking, Linc," he grumbled, breaking the kiss. "He has the patience of a five year old."

I giggled as he stepped away. "Should I wear something in particular?"

He shook his head. "We'll mostly be at the house, so whatever you want is fine. Be comfortable."

I nodded in agreement as I followed him to the door. "I just hope she likes me."

Ryan turned and looked down at me, his expression unreadable. "I think she'll love you."

I closed the door as he turned away, but I could've sworn I heard him add, "It's hard not to."

As it turned out, Ryan's house wasn't far from Gary's. Or, I guessed, my house now. We chatted and listened to music during the two-hour drive, and time flew by quickly.

He turned his car into the long drive leading up to a three-story limestone house, and I craned my neck to look out the window.

"Wow," I breathed, amazed at how spectacular it was.

Ryan's gaze was hidden behind aviator shades. "I guess."

I slapped his shoulder with the back of my hand. "You live in a castle."

"Does that make me a prince?" he teased, kissing my bare shoulder.

I shot him a suspicious look. "I'm not sure yet." With that, I pushed open the door and got out of the car, glad I had opted for jeans and a simple tank top. California weather was warm even in fall.

I turned in time to see the front door thrown open and a blonde girl come barreling out. Ryan barely had time to get out of the car before she was hurtling through the air at him with a shriek of glee.

"You came! You really came!" Her thin arms wrapped around his neck and squeezed with all she had.

Ryan easily carried her weight around the car, her gangly legs wrapping around his waist as she buried her face against his neck with a happy sigh.

Corinne's head lifted, her pale blue eyes finding me. A crooked smile bloomed across her face. "Hi, Madelaine!" She pushed until Ryan let her go, and then she was flying at me.

I caught her with an *oomph* and saw Ryan's eyes widen with concern.

Laughing, I wrapped my arms around Corinne, surprised when she wrapped her arms around my neck. Going with it, I picked her up in a giant hug. She squealed and giggled in response, and I saw Ryan's shoulders sag with relief.

Like he had worried I would reject this little girl's obvious love.

I set Cori down. "I heard it's someone's birthday."

"It's mine," she announced with a grin. "I'm eleven. It's a special birthday because the numbers are the same."

I clicked my tongue, thinking about it. "You are right. So what are we doing for this extra special birthday?"

"I got a new puppy!" Her blue eyes went comically wide. "Want to meet her?"

"Sure," I agreed, holding out my hand.

Cori didn't hesitate to slip her hand into mine and drag me into the house.

"Cor," Ryan called.

She paused halfway up the stairs. "Yeah?"

"I'll be up in a minute, okay? I need to talk to Dad."

Corinne made a face. "Okay, but he's super grumpy today."

A shadow crossed Ryan's face. "Thanks, kiddo."

Corinne giggled. "I'm *eleven*. Dad says that's not a kid anymore."

I got the impression Ryan was grinding his teeth now, annoyed at

Beckett's assessment. Smiling, I looked at Corinne. "I thought we were going to see a puppy?"

"Yes!" She practically screeched the word and pulled me up the stairs, chattering about the new puppy.

I glanced back and winked at Ryan. That seemed to relax him a bit as he watched us go.

"Ryan's room is at the end of the hall," Corinne informed me, speed-walking to her room. She pushed open the double doors with a flourish. "*This* is my room!"

She let go of my hand to walk into the center of a very pink room so she could twirl in the middle. The skirt of the dress flared out adorably.

"I love it," I told her, looking around the big room and noting she had every size and color stuffed dog imaginable.

Scrambling to her bed, Corinne grabbed one that was fluffy, white, and had pink tinsel in its fur.

"This is Majesty," Cori said seriously, handing me the dog carefully. "She's new. Ms. Hoffen gave her to me for my birthday. But, *shhh*." She held a finger to her lips. "We can't tell Daddy."

"Okay," I whispered back, stroking the dog's soft fur. "Why not?"

Her face fell, and I felt like shit for asking.

"Daddy says I'm not supposed to act like a stupid little kid," she answered quietly, the hurt in her tone heartbreaking. "Little kids have stuffed animals."

Fucking Beckett Cain. What a dick.

I knelt down. "You know, I always wanted a dog."

Her eyes lifted to me. "You did?"

I nodded, handing Majesty back. "Yeah. My mom was... she was sick, so I never could."

"Like the flu?"

"Kind of," I hedged.

"I can't have real dogs," Corinne said, placing Majesty back in her place on the bed. "Daddy's got allergies. And he says dogs are stupid."

Daddy needed to stop using the word *stupid* around this awesome little girl before I slapped him.

"I don't think dogs are stupid," I announced. "In fact, I think I'm going to get one."

"Today?" Corinne's eyes went huge.

I shook my head. "I can't have one at school. But maybe when I'm done."

She nodded sagely. "Yeah, dogs need a lot of love. You can't do that if you're in school."

"Plus, I have cheerleading," I added with a sigh. "No time for a dog."

"I wish I was a cheerleader," Corinne said wistfully.

"Why can't you be?" I asked, standing up.

She scuffed her toe into the carpet. "Because I can't do tricks."

"Says who?" I challenged. "Can you do a cartwheel?"

She shrugged a small shoulder. "Kinda. I'm not good."

"Want me to practice with you?"

Her mouth fell open. "You'd do that?"

"Anything for the birthday girl," I promised. "But you need to change out of your pretty dress. Do you have something else? Maybe shorts?"

"Yes!"

"Okay, you change and I'll meet you downstairs, all right?" I asked.

She threw her arms around my waist. "Thank you, Madelaine!"

I stroked her hair and hugged her back. "Anytime, Cori. Get changed, okay? I'll grab Ryan."

I left her in her room, already starting to pull off her dress, and made my way back downstairs. Once in the foyer, I looked around, but the house was eerily quiet.

Quiet, except for the angry voices I heard coming from deeper in the house.

Against my better judgement, I followed the voices, hoping to find Ryan. When I turned down the end of a long corridor, the noise led me to a partially open door at the end of the hall.

Good news? Ryan's voice was definitely one of them.

Bad news? He sounded pissed as hell.

Wincing, I turned to go when I heard Beckett's angry voice announce, "I mean it, Ryan. Fuck things up and I'll do it."

Something crashed into a wall and shattered. "What the fuck is wrong with you? She's a kid," Ryan hissed.

"Corinne's fucking useless," Beckett spat. "She's a halfwit, but she can access that trust fund with a ring on her finger as easily as you can."

"And you're the monster who's planning to sell his own daughter," Ryan's disgusted voice echoed my thoughts exactly.

What the fuck?

"Yes," Beckett said flatly. "You know what needs to happen. Handle things with Madelaine, or I'll make other arrangements."

The door wrenched open and Ryan came flying out, his face a mottled red with fury. He froze as he realized I was standing there, listening.

"Ryan." I held up a hand and took a step back, his wrath unnerving.

Stalking forward, he grabbed my arm and yanked me around the corner before pressing me against the wall.

"What the *fuck* do you think you're doing?" he demanded.

CHAPTER 45

Sucking in a shocked breath, I placed my hands on his chest. "I was looking for you."

He sneered at me with a coldness I hadn't witnessed in weeks. He pushed my hands away. "You fucking found me."

I let that slide. For now.

"Cori and I wanted you to come outside with us," I said softly, trying to keep calm even though I was reeling from what I'd heard Beckett say and the fact that Ryan was beyond furious.

"Are you spying on me?" he demanded, his hot breath fanning across my face.

"Why would I do that?" I tried to laugh it off, but the deadly serious look on his face quickly killed it. I forced myself to take a breath and not just immediately react to his accusation.

"No," I said honestly. "I told Cori that I would show her some cheer moves. She's upstairs changing while I came to find you."

His hard eyes narrowed. "And you just happened to walk in on us arguing?"

"It's not like you were being quiet about it," I pointed out. "I heard your voices and followed them here to you." I hesitated as my pulse raced, my chest heaving between us. "Are you okay?"

His head jerked back. "Do you actually care?"

Ouch. That felt like a slap.

Irritation crawled up my back. "Well, I did, but now I'm not so sure." Planting my hands on his chest, I shoved him back a step. "I don't know what's happening between you and your dad, but I'm not the bad guy here."

His jaw ticked with irritation as he stared at me. All I could do was stare back because I was right; I wasn't the bad guy in this situation.

"Is everything okay?" Corinne's soft voice asked.

Ryan and I turned in unison to see her standing in the hallway, a brown stuffed dog under one arm and her blue eyes wide with worry.

"Totally fine, Cori," Ryan said, instantly smiling at her like nothing was wrong. "Maddie and I were just having a conversation." He lowered his voice. "One we'll finish later."

"Can't wait," I hissed back, still pissed and a little annoyed I couldn't swallow my emotions down the way he so clearly could.

Asshole.

Ryan reached out a hand for Corinne, leaving me to trail after them. Once we were outside, Corinne broke away from Ryan to stand expectantly in front of me.

"All right, show me what you've got," I encouraged.

Nodding, Cori danced away and hurled herself into an awkward cartwheel that left her in a heap on the ground.

"See?" she said from where she sat, folding her arms. "I told you. I can't."

"But you did," I pointed out, ignoring the way Ryan watched me as I focused my attention solely on his sister. "We just need to work on sticking the landing and straightening your arms and legs."

Jumping to her feet, she asked, "Can you show me?"

I executed a couple of cartwheels back to back. I loved the feeling of twisting my body around as my fingers dug into the ground. It made me miss the time I had spent in the garden during summer. There was something utterly satisfying about feeling the earth on your palms.

"You make it look pretty," Cori breathed when I turned back to her.

I smiled back. "You'll make it pretty, too."

A few more tries with me correcting her, and she turned out a nearly flawless cartwheel of her own.

"I did it!" Cori shouted with a laugh and a squeal, running up and hugging me.

I hugged her back, grinning like an idiot. "Yeah, you did!"

"Did you see, Ryan?" Corinne asked, seeking his approval.

His smile was blinding. "You did amazing, Cori. I'm proud of you."

"Can I do more?" she asked me.

"Go for it," I encouraged, releasing her to cartwheel her way across the large lawn.

I felt Ryan walk up beside me before he spoke, but I refused to acknowledge him. My feelings were still hurt from the shit he'd said earlier.

"You're good with her," he admitted gruffly.

I shrugged. "I used to help out with a camp for younger kids who wanted to cheer in the summers. I wish they'd all been as eager to learn as Cori."

He sighed softly behind me. "I worry about her with me being at school and her being alone here. Dad sure as shit doesn't understand her, so she's mostly been raised by nannies."

"What did he mean? About Corinne?" I asked quietly, daring to look at him. I held my breath as I waited for the answer.

Ryan didn't look at me. His eyes simply watched Corinne as she played and tumbled around the yard.

"My mom's family came from a lot of money," he finally began. "When she died, she left all her family's money in a trust fund. Her dad —my grandfather—has more money than that, but he's dying. And Mom convinced him to add his money that she would have inherited to the trust she set up."

"For you and Cori?" I guessed.

He shook his head grimly. "No. For her grandchildren."

I jerked my head around to look at him.

"I think she knew my father would use whatever inheritance we got for his business or other shit," Ryan admitted hoarsely. "She left it to be given to her grandchildren."

Horror slammed into me as I looked at Corinne. "So your dad—"

"Would sell Cori to one of his disgusting old friends to get her knocked up so he has access to the money? And Cori would agree to it to make my dad happy," Ryan finished coldly. "Yeah."

Disgust left a bitter taste in my mouth. "That's why you agreed to marry Madelaine."

He gave a curt nod. "We were both as trapped as possible by our families. Ironically, all these trusts and rules were set up to protect people from greed. Our dads are just master manipulators who figured out a few immoral loopholes."

"I'm so sorry," I whispered.

His blue eyes flashed like lightning as he looked at me. "Now do you get it? If I don't get married and have a kid before Cori turns eighteen, he'll use her. He'll barter his own daughter off to one of his friends. Fuck, I wouldn't put it past him to even sign a goddamn waiver or some shit to have her married at sixteen."

I pressed a hand over my mouth, like that would contain the horror I felt. "How the hell can your dad *do* this?"

"How could your mom pick drugs over *you*?" he pointed out. The words hit like a barb, but his tone was almost apathetic. He was just stating a fact.

"Our parents suck," he muttered, rubbing a hand across the back of his neck. "But I'll be damned if I let that little girl be broken because our father's a sadistic bastard."

I watched Cori run to a patch of flowers and bend over them intently.

A surge of protective ferocity swelled in me at the idea of some guy like Adam Kindell getting his pervy hands on her.

"I don't care what it takes," I murmured, looking at Ryan. "We have to protect her."

"It might take us getting married," he pointed out, his gaze beyond intense as it bored into me.

I shrugged a shoulder. "I guess it's a good thing I don't hate you anymore."

"I'm sorry," he said softly, touching my hand. "I jumped to the wrong conclusions earlier and acted like a jerk."

"You did," I agreed, not quite willing to let him off the hook yet. Did I understand why he freaked about Corinne? Absolutely. But if we were going to be partners in this, then he needed to trust me.

"Madelaine used to spy on people," he admitted. "That was her thing. I caught her listening in on conversations my dad or others were having. She usually reported back to her dad. I don't know. When I saw you standing outside the door... It felt too much like *her*."

"I'm not my sister," I reminded him, my tone gentler than before.

His fingers laced with mine and he pulled me around to face him. "I'd like to say it won't happen again, but it probably will. I don't trust many people."

I squeezed his hand and reached up to cradle his jaw with the other. "You can trust *me*."

He turned his head and kissed my open palm, nuzzling against it for a second. My heart stuttered in my chest, and I barely held back a gasp at the intimacy of the moment.

Which was shattered quickly by Corinne cooing at us with a long, "Awww!"

Rolling his eyes at being caught by his little sister, Ryan let me go and took off after Corinne with a roar. She shrieked and ran as fast as her legs could take her.

Ryan caught her, swinging her up into his arms and tickling her mercilessly.

Corinne twisted in his arms and looked at me. "Maddie! Save me!" she cried before dissolving into giggles.

Laughing, I ran over to save the birthday girl.

We spent the rest of the day playing with Corinne until it was time for a family dinner that, thankfully, Beckett made only a brief appearance at. His jaw tightened when he saw Corinne's shorts and how mussed her hair was, but he wisely didn't say anything.

Especially when I made a point of leaning over and kissing Ryan's cheek, playing up our happy couple facade for him.

By the time we left, Corinne was asleep from all the excitement of the day and after crashing from the sugar high of cake and ice cream. But I could tell Ryan was still reluctant to leave her.

We started the drive back to Pacific Cross in silence. He was brooding, and I was happy to give him his space as the radio played quietly. I stared out the window as the coastline zipped by in the dark. Occasionally I could make out the white caps of cresting waves lit from the full moon, but the road leading from Pac City up to the school was nearly empty.

Ryan pulled the car up in front of my dorm and cut the engine.

"I'll walk you in," he announced, getting out before I could tell him it wasn't necessary.

He came around to my side and opened the door for me, then helped me out and kept hold of my hand as we walked inside and I used my keycard to access my floor.

When I unlocked my door, I hesitated in the entryway. "I had fun. Cori's great."

"She is," he replied with a nod. His gaze darted past me into the open room before he pushed the door open wider and went inside.

"Sure, come on in," I muttered to myself before following him in and closing the door. I sighed and rubbed my forehead, tired and not sure I wanted to engage in another round of What the Hell is Ryan Cain Thinking?

"Ry—"

He whirled and pressed me against the door with his body, his mouth crashing against mine with the force of a hurricane making landfall.

I gasped, opening my mouth for a whole new kind of assault as his tongue attacked mine, stroking it into submission as my pulse raced and throbbed.

His lips moved with mine, hard and soft, fast and slow. Just as I got used to one type of kiss, he changed it up until I could only cling to the front of his shirt and hold on for the ride.

Ryan's hands found my hips and lifted me up, my long legs wrapping around his body and notching my center against his erection. I hissed out a breath as I instinctively ground down onto it, desperate for any kind of friction to relieve the pulsing between my legs.

He grunted as he carried me into my bedroom, hitting the light switch with his elbow before lowering me onto the edge of the bed.

I stared up at him as he loomed over me, bracing a hand on either side of my head. I could only imagine how I looked sprawled under him like some breathless virgin sacrifice ready to take whatever he decided to give.

His lips twisted into a grin as he seemed to read my mind.

"I owe you an apology for today," he murmured, lifting one hand from the bed to drag it from the base of my throat, between the valley of my breasts, and toward the edge of my jeans.

My breath caught. "You already apologized."

"With words," he agreed, his fingers tracing the edge of the denim and making my stomach dip and swoop. He snuck the tips of his fingers under the fabric, his nails dragging deliciously along my flesh.

"But I've always been a firm believer that actions speak louder than words," he went on, his eyes finding mine. "Don't you agree?"

My head was spinning.

Didn't I agree with *what*?

At that point, I would have agreed to whatever he wanted as long as he stopped torturing me and moved his fingers *lower*.

He stopped altogether, and I groaned in protest. My eyes squeezed shut for a second of agony.

"I asked you a question, Mads," he reminded me, smirking like the asshole he was.

"I agree," I said in a quick rush of breathy words, nodding my head furiously. "Whatever you want."

Those dimples I loved appeared. "I thought you might say that." He removed his hand and rested it on my hip. "Madison, look at me."

MAD WORLD

I gave him my irritated attention because my body wanted things he had wordlessly insinuated were about to happen.

He smiled wider at my annoyance and dipped his head to kiss me quickly before retreating once more. "Do I have your attention?"

"Wholly and undividedly," I gritted out, wanting to whine.

"Good. Anytime you want me to stop, I will. Just say the word," he said, his thumb stroking the bare skin above my hip.

I blinked. "That's sort of the problem."

He cocked his head curiously, confusion wrinkling his forehead.

"I don't want you to stop," I whispered with a wink.

Snorting, he shook his head with a wry smile. "I'm not fucking you tonight."

And all blood simultaneously drained from my body and then flashed through my veins like fire. I was burning up and suddenly ice cold in the same heartbeat. But overwhelmingly, I was disappointed.

"*When* I fuck you," he added slowly, his knuckles dragging across my abdomen and to the button of my jeans, "I don't plan on having to leave you when it's over, and I have an early morning practice."

I gulped. "Okay."

"But I still owe you that apology," he murmured, slowly lowering the zipper on my pants. I felt each click of the teeth pulling apart as he worked it down.

His hands worked the denim over my hips and down my legs as he knelt on the floor, taking the time to remove my shoes and socks before tossing the jeans over one shoulder. When he looked up, his eyes were level with the plain blue cotton covering my pussy, and it was the most exposed I had ever felt.

Vulnerability crept in as I stupidly started to wonder a million things. As the doubts became chaos in my head, I tried to draw my legs together.

He stopped me with a light slap to the inside of my thigh. The sting made me gasp and knocked the doubts away for the moment.

"I'm enjoying my view," he told me, his voice heavy and thick as the hand on my thigh slid up to the curve where my leg and hip joined.

I bit the insides of my cheeks to keep from saying anything else, wondering what he was thinking. He seemed content to simply trace the edge of my underwear like he was studying cartography and needed to map all these new lands he was finding.

When his fingertips brushed the center of my panties, I gasped and rocked my hips, chasing his touch as it ghosted away.

"Dammit, Ryan," I swore, squeezing my eyes shut.

"Problem, Maddie?" He sounded so innocent asking that, his blue eyes lifting to mine in amusement.

I ground my teeth together. "Yes."

His eyebrows rose slightly, his other hand rubbing the inside of my thigh. "If you need something, just say so."

"I thought you were apologizing," I practically snarled, panting a little as the pads of his fingers drew closer to the apex of my thighs and then drifted away once more.

He hummed under his breath in agreement. "Apologies take time. I have to make sure you know I'm truly repentant."

I was about to tell him where he could shove his repentance when he splayed a hand right above my pelvis and ground the heel of his hand on my clit. I cried out in frustration when the pressure was gone as soon as it appeared.

"Please," I begged, my tone fracturing on the word. "I want..."

"What? Tell me what you want, Maddie," he encouraged softly, kissing my knee and opening my legs wider.

I was sure my panties were soaked by now, and he had a front row seat to my arousal. Somehow, I was beyond caring about that. My body had been reduced to one singular, base train of thought.

"I want you to touch me," I whispered.

Another cocky smile. "I *am* touching you."

My hands fisted in the comforter. "No... Touch me *there*."

He made a soft tsking sound. "Maddie, you've got to use your words. I'm not a mind reader."

My patience snapped like a rubber band being stretched beyond its limits. All my defenses fell as I lifted myself up on one elbow to glare at him down the length of my body.

"I want your fingers inside of me *now*," I demanded even as my cheeks flamed.

He gave a low laugh. "God, I'm going to love corrupting you, baby." He slipped my panties to the side and glided a finger through my slick folds, circling my clit once.

Twice.

And then dipping down to bury his finger inside of me as deep as it would go.

My hips bucked off the bed as I cried out, the invasion of his thick finger sharply erotic and more than I was ready for.

I sucked in a breath through my teeth as he started pumping the finger in and out of me slowly.

"Fuck, you're tight," he said, his voice strained.

I managed a weak laugh. "Told you I was a virgin."

That grabbed his attention and he slowed his movements. "You need to tell me if I'm hurting you, Mads."

"If you don't start moving, *I* might hurt *you*," I replied with a soft moan, wriggling my hips a little.

A crease appeared in his cheek from a dimple, and then his finger started moving again. "You're fucking perfect," he muttered, pressing a kiss to the inside of my thigh as his finger slipped easily from me and circled around my clit again.

He traced my opening once more. "You're sure you're okay?"

I nodded, almost mindlessly as I focused solely on where he was touching me and waking up nerve endings I'd never known about.

"Okay if I try something else?" he asked.

"No screwdrivers," I blurted out.

He stopped abruptly. "What the fuck?"

I felt my cheeks heat. "I was reading a book. This girl was with her boyfriends and there was a screwdriver handle... I'm not ready for that."

The shock on his face was comical. "I don't even know what to say to that. Did you say *boyfriends*? Plural?"

I nodded, embarrassed as hell now. "Yeah. It's a reverse harem book."

"And you like that?"

"Hey, no judging," I said indignantly, wishing like hell we weren't having this conversation while his head was between my legs, but here we were and I wasn't okay with him shaming my lit game.

"Zero judgement," he assured me with a laugh. "But I draw the line at sharing, so keep your reverse harem fantasies to your books. Linc and Court might be into that shit, but I'm not."

"Wait, they are?" I felt my eyes go wide. I wondered if Bex knew that. I knew she liked Court, but she was also always flirting with Linc.

Ryan sighed. "Can we maybe stop talking about my best friends when I want to fuck you with my tongue?"

"Sh-sure," I stammered, pulling in a shaky breath.

He grinned. "Awesome." Then he peeled my panties away from my body and used his thumbs to spread me wide as his tongue made one long pass from my opening to my clit.

"Fuck," I hissed, squeezing my eyes shut as ecstasy ricocheted through my body hard enough to curl my toes. Unable to help myself, I tangled my fingers in his hair and rolled my hips up to meet his mouth.

His finger returned, slipping inside of me and then being joined by a second that stretched me wider as his tongue played with my clit.

I whimpered as his fingers hooked inside of me, hitting a spot that had pops of light bursting behind my eyelids as my back arched off the mattress. I clenched my teeth to keep from crying out too loudly.

"Don't do that," Ryan ordered, nipping at the delicate skin inside my thigh. "I love hearing you scream. Don't you ever hold back with me, Madison."

He sucked my clit between his lips with a firm, steady pull as his fingers curled again. I cried out loudly, my hands fisting in his hair hard enough to start ripping it out by the roots as pleasure crashed over me like a tsunami that destroyed everything in its wake.

That was Ryan Cain.

He was my own personal tsunami, wrecking all the walls and security I had built up with devastating force. In weeks he had dismantled what I had spent a lifetime creating, and I wasn't sure I could ever be the same.

My pulse thundered in my ears as I slowly fell back down to earth. The only sounds in the room were my heavy panting and the soft kisses and licks Ryan was still giving my overstimulated pussy. Each brush of his lips sent off another shockwave until the pleasure spiked so sharp it bordered on hurting.

Sensing I'd had enough, Ryan kissed his way up my body until his mouth found mine. I opened willingly, wantonly, as he teased my tongue with his. The taste of me in our kiss was a whole new level of intimacy I hadn't expected.

Breathing hard, I let my body go boneless as Ryan chuckled into my neck, peppering more kisses across my skin. I could feel the hard length of him pressing against my hip.

Uncertainty made me nervous once more. "Um, should I... I mean, you're still—"

He silenced me with a kiss that fried what was left of my brain function. "This was my apology, remember? You can worry about that when it's your turn to apologize."

"God, I hope you screw up a lot more," I muttered without censoring myself.

His chest shook with laughter. "Me, too, Mads. Me, too."

CHAPTER 46

"Okay, ladies, that's it for today!" Coach called, and blew her whistle, ending practice the following Thursday. "Madelaine, looking good! I'm liking this new routine."

"Thanks!" I called back as I gasped in a breath and reached for my water bottle.

"See you at dinner, right, Maddie?" Claudia asked as a few of the girls paused collecting their gear to ask me.

I shrugged. "I'm having dinner at Ryan's."

"Lucky girl," Sandi said with a grin. "We'll see you tomorrow then, right?"

I nodded and watched them leave. Thankfully, Hayley and Kayleigh bounced away with them. It seemed like they'd gotten the hint in the last few days that I wasn't crazy about them, and I had found myself with space to actually breathe.

"I do love the new routine," Brylee agreed softly, coming up behind me.

I turned and flashed her a quick smile, still not ready to lower my guard around the girl who could potentially overthrow Satan one day. "Thanks."

"Can I make a suggestion?"

Surprise flew across my face. "Uh, sure."

"Maybe end the routine with a back layout instead of the twist? It might give the end a little more flair," she offered, then blushed. "I mean, if you want."

I ran through the change in routine in my head. "No, it's a good idea. I like it."

"Really?" Brylee looked stunned. "You've never liked my ideas before."

"People change," I said simply. That was the party line I fed everyone when they commented on how un-Madelaine-like I acted.

I had to believe in my heart that people *could* change. Look at Ryan. A month ago, I'd hated him. Now I looked forward to seeing him every day. It had sucked that since the night of Corinne's birthday we hadn't been able to be alone because of his practice schedule, but he and I always had dinner together, and then he walked me back to my dorm.

At least tonight he had a break. They were leaving for an away game tomorrow afternoon, and since the academy team had a home game I was expected to cheer at, I wouldn't be going. Hence why Ryan had decided I should spend the night tonight.

I ignored the anxious butterflies (okay, more like pterodactyls) that took flight in my tummy at the idea of spending a night completely alone with him.

"You really have," Brylee murmured. "At first I thought it was just an act to get people to like you after the shit you pulled last year, but you're, like, a whole different person."

I grabbed my bag and gave her a tight smile. "You have no idea."

"Hey, you'll be at the frat tonight, right?" she asked as I started walking away.

That made me pause and slowly turn. "Yeah. I'm hanging with Ryan and the guys tonight."

She smiled. "Then I guess I'll see you there."

I frowned a little, confused. "They're not having a party."

In fact, Ryan had been adamant that it *not* be a party. I think he was still rattled by what had happened to me at the last party I'd attended, even though it had been almost two weeks now.

I also had a feeling that he'd talked to the kitchen staff at school, because my food was always handed to me with an assurance that it was "nut-free."

His overprotective streak was adorable and a little freaky.

"I'm dating Dean," Brylee told me. "I mean, it's casual, but our families are old friends, so it makes sense, you know?"

The smile fell from my face like ice cream melting in the California sun. "Brylee, you can't date Dean."

She paused and gave me a strange look. "Why not?"

"Because he isn't a good guy," I answered honestly. "You saw the shit he did to Bex at the party before school started. He drugged her."

Brylee's shoulders stiffened. "He did that because she's a vapor."

"A what?" I asked, genuinely confused.

"A vapor," she repeated smugly. "You know, something that disappears in the wind? As in something that doesn't really matter."

"What the hell is wrong with you?" I demanded. Why had I ever tried being nice to this girl? "You know what? You and Dean have fun."

"Oh, we will," she assured me, a calculating glint in her eye. "But try to stay off my boyfriend's dick this time, okay, Laine?"

"I promise it won't be a problem," I assured her coldly, wondering why the hell I had thought she had changed.

Her eyes narrowed. "Good. I gave you a pass last time, but I won't again."

"Brave words for someone who doesn't seem to have a friend left in this school," I replied archly, pointing out that she was still on the bottom of the social ladder thanks to Ryan.

"You can't hide behind Ryan forever," she sneered. "It's fucking pathetic that you can't be happy for anyone except yourself."

"Excuse me?" I spluttered. "Because I'm not jumping for joy that you're hooking up with a guy who's casually cool with date rape?"

"Oh, please," she scoffed, tossing her hair over one shoulder. "He wouldn't have actually done anything to her except maybe take a few pictures to keep her in line with all the other plebs that belong in their place in this school."

"You're fucking insane," I said bluntly, as plainly as I could.

She stepped toward me. "And you're a fucking hypocrite. You might have everyone around here fooled, *Maddie*, but I know who you really are. I've seen the videos. Talk about sick shit? Jesus. You're the fucking ringleader of the twisted circus this school is."

I shook my head.

Her brows flew up. "What? Are you going to deny it? Because I've *seen* your little stash of blackmail. I'm just telling you that your time is almost up."

"Duly noted," I said drolly, ignoring the way my heart thundered in my chest like an ominous warning. "Anything else?"

She hitched her gym bag higher on her shoulder. "Yeah. And, honey? I'd avoid the cupcakes from now on. We wouldn't want you to have another *accident*."

She turned away with a swish of her ponytail, leaving me reeling. All I could do was stand there and try to process what she had said.

Had she been implying that she was behind the cupcake incident?

I lost track of how long I stood in the middle of the grass, my mind chaotically full and frustratingly blank at the same time. It wasn't until someone nudged me that I realized I was acting like a total zombie.

"Hey, you okay?" Linc asked as he appeared by my side, breathless and sweaty from his run. He motioned for the other guys on his team to keep going, but I noticed Ash and Court also stopped with us.

"Um, yeah," I stammered distractedly.

"You want to try saying that in a way we'll believe?" Court asked, his dark brows lifting.

I shook my head. "Yeah. Sorry. It's just... Brylee said something."

"Ugh," Linc groaned. "I hate that bitch."

"She's dating Dean now," Ash remarked quietly.

"You knew?" I asked, surprised.

He shrugged. "He was bragging about her sucking his dick the other day to some of the younger guys, and I saw them making out a few days ago."

"You didn't say anything," I muttered.

He gave me a careful look. "I wasn't aware you cared where Dean got his dick wet or what pipe Brylee was guzzling."

I grimaced at that mental image. "I don't. I just... Brylee apologized to me right before my birthday."

Now Linc was the one giving me a strange look. "She did what?"

"I thought she was feeling regret for being iced out," I explained with a little shrug. "I kind of felt bad for her."

"Felt bad for the girl who was tormenting Bex?" Court cut in sharply, his dark eyes getting even darker.

I threw my hands up. "Sorry, guys, but I can't just stop feeling human, okay? She apologized and it felt genuine. That's why I warned her about Dean when she told me she was dating him."

"How'd that go?" Link asked.

"Not great," I admitted. "I think she thought I was jealous or something? But then she warned me not to eat any more cupcakes."

"She did *what*?" Linc demanded while Ash and Court exchanged looks.

"It's weird, right?" I asked, rubbing my arms, suddenly cold. Fall was definitely in the air, but it was still Southern California and the sun was bright above our heads.

"You're sure she said that?" Ash pressed, his green eyes narrowed in thought.

I nodded. "Yeah. You don't think that she did something to them, do you?"

"Do I think she's petty enough to do something like that? Yes," Ash replied without hesitation.

"Remember when she dumped a bottle of that laxative shit into the swim team's Gatorade?" Court pointed out.

My jaw dropped. "No way."

"They had to close the pool for two weeks to clean that mess out," he confirmed grimly.

"But everyone knows Maddie's allergic to nuts," Linc said stonily. "That's not a stupid prank where people shit their pants. That's attempted murder."

I stepped back. "You think she was trying to kill me?"

"I think we're making a lot of assumptions," Ash said softly, cutting us off. "Let me see what I can figure out."

"I thought you looked into the cupcakes." I frowned, remembering he had told Ryan that the bakery swore they hadn't made a mistake. Even still, Ryan reported them to the health department and had inspectors crawling all over their place for almost a week.

"I looked into the bakery," Ash confirmed, "but I didn't really think someone might've switched them out at the party before we showed up. We assumed it was a stupid accident, not something deliberate."

"Fuck," Court growled, the muscles of his impressive biceps tightening.

"I guess I should go shower," I muttered, shaking my head. I wasn't quite ready to deal with the attempted-murder speculation right now.

"You should come with us," Linc said, touching my wrist.

Ash nodded. "Yeah, I'll take you to the house now. Ryan wouldn't want you to be by yourself after Brylee basically threatened you."

"Where is Ryan?" I asked, confused as to why he wasn't running with the team.

"Coach called a meeting with the QBs," Court explained. "We ran over here to tell you Ryan would be late. He said for you to just wait for him at the house."

"I was going to walk over with Bex," I told him. Rarely was Bex not included in our group, and I had noticed it had caused some jealousy with some of the other girls who noticed Court and Linc following her around when we weren't in class.

"I'll grab her," Court assured me.

"And I'll take you back to the house," Ash stated. They both looked at Linc.

Linc glowered at them both. "I guess that means I'm on Ryan-detail?"

"Godspeed, brother," Court said, clapping him on the shoulder.

"Fuck," Linc swore. "He's going to lose his shit."

"Why?" I asked. Angry Ryan was unsettling, and I hadn't seen him appear since he'd argued with Beckett nearly a week earlier.

Ash laughed a little and wrapped a sweaty arm around my shoulders. "Oh, Maddie, if you haven't figured out why yet, you're not as smart as I know you are."

I ducked out from under him. "You stink."

"You don't exactly smell like roses either, Mads," he replied, grabbing my bag and shouldering it for me. He looked at Court and Linc. "We'll meet you guys back at the house, okay?"

They nodded and took off in different directions while I fell into step with Ash. It was nearly half a mile to their frat house from this part of campus, but I could use the cool down after practice.

"I didn't have a chance to tell you," he started suddenly, "but I unlocked part of the phone."

"You did? What did you find out?"

Ash gave me a look. "I didn't look, Maddie. It's your business."

"Oh. I guess I just assumed..." I trailed off.

"That because I helped Ryan spy on you in the beginning that I still would?" He shook his head. "Nah. You're one of us now. If Ryan trusts you, that speaks volumes."

"It does?"

He nodded. "I know you know about Corinne and Beckett."

I scowled. "Beckett's a dickface."

He snorted and nodded. "He is. But Ryan's only told five people that secret."

"To be fair, he didn't tell me." Why I felt it necessary to point that out, I had no idea.

"He trusts you," Ash told me firmly. "He gave you a key to his room. He let you meet Cori. That's fucking huge. He's protective as fuck about her. Hell, I don't think half the people at this school even know he has a sister because he's so worried people will hurt her to get to him."

"This world is fucked up," I muttered darkly as we stepped off the grass and onto the paved path that led to the Greek houses on campus.

"Bet you sometimes wish you could go back, huh?" He nudged my shoulder as he walked.

I shrugged. "Honestly? The methods and faces change, but it's still the same shit. Instead of dodging literal bullets, now I dodge emotional ones, I guess. But sometimes I think actual bullets do less damage than some of the shit I've seen happen around here. At least where I'm from, you usually know who people are. The bad guys are the bad guys and don't apologize for it. Here, the bad guys pretend to be the good guys while doing evil shit everyone's expected to be okay with because it makes money."

"Ouch," he murmured, rubbing his chest. "Why do I feel like that barb was aimed at me?"

I sighed and shook my head. "It wasn't. Not exactly. I'm just having a hard time reconciling what I believe with what I've seen."

"Like?" he pressed.

I bit my lower lip. "You're Ryan's best friend, right?"

He gave a short nod. "Yup."

"So you know about Shutterfield?" I asked slowly.

His face went carefully neutral. "Do *you* know about Shutterfield?"

My lips flattened in annoyance at his sidestepping. "I heard them talk about how Ryan sealed that deal. How he knew the CEO or whatever was visiting little boys in brothels."

Ash's jaw tightened. "Yeah. That's some fucked up shit."

"But Ryan seems totally okay with it!" I exclaimed, my irritation bubbling over. "I'm having a hard time reconciling the guy who is so casual about that with the guy who is insanely protective of me and his sister. Hell, he even looks out for Bex."

"Why can't he be the same guy?" Ash inquired, his brow furrowed.

"Because he *can't*," I argued. "He can't be the devil and the savior."

"Pretty sure he's neither," Ash remarked. "But he's probably closer to the devil, if you really want to know."

I stopped abruptly, feeling the annoying bite of angry tears pricking my eyes. "Dammit, Ash, this isn't helping."

Ash gave me a steady, unflinching look. "Maddie, you're asking me to share secrets that aren't mine to share. I won't betray my best friend even if I think you should have answers. If you have questions, you need to ask Ryan."

"Do you think he'll be honest with me?" I asked, having serious doubts.

"Trust goes both ways," he said simply. "You know Ryan trusts you. Do you trust *him*?"

That stopped me cold. Did I trust Ryan?

"I think so," I said slowly, my eyes meeting Ash's.

"Be sure, Maddie," he said, pressing his lips together. "If you're in, you need to be all in."

"Like the mafia?" I teased weakly.

"Fuck no," he replied with a grin. "The mafia is child's play compared to the world you're in now."

CHAPTER 47

I let myself into Ryan's room with my key, taking the time to glare at Dean's door before closing Ryan's and locking it again. I didn't know if his nasty ass was even here, but I didn't want to chance running into him.

I dropped my bag on Ryan's floor, glad I had brought a change of clothes with me, but I would be sleeping in another of Ryan's shirts since I hadn't been able to go home and pack an overnight bag first.

Grabbing my clothes, I walked into Ryan's massive bathroom and flicked on the light before closing the door and stripping out of my cheer clothes. I opened the glass door to the massive shower and paused.

I could see all of Ryan's stuff laid out on the built-in shelf, but there were also a few bottles of the stuff that I routinely used in my shower. Shampoo, body wash, conditioner, a new razor...

Because he knew I would be here and did that for me.

I laughed a little, amazed at how thoughtful he could be.

The spray of the dual shower heads felt great on my aching muscles. I'd missed over a week of cheer practice after the peanut incident. Since then I'd been pushing myself to make up for lost time with the squad. Homecoming was only a few weeks away now, and my routine had to be perfect.

I was mentally running through the choreography *again*, and legit considering Brylee's suggestion, when I felt a cool draft on the backs of my legs. A moment later, two arms wrapped around my waist and pulled me into a very hard, very *naked*, body.

I jolted, but it only took me a moment to realize it was Ryan when he kissed the side of my neck.

"Mmm," he rumbled appreciatively against me with a sigh. "You're a fucking wet dream."

"Because I'm *wet*?" I deadpanned, resisting the urge to tilt my head to give him total access. "Not very original, Mr. Cain. Maybe you've taken too many hits to the head recently."

He growled, his teeth nipping sharply at my shoulder as he pressed his cock against the small of my back.

My mouth dried so suddenly it was like I was trying to swallow sand. I hadn't pictured my first time being in a shower, but the flash of heat through my blood had me realizing I wasn't against it, either.

"Is this weird?" Ryan asked quietly. "I can go if you want."

Taking a deep breath, I turned around and prayed he would think the pink in my cheeks was from the steamy shower. Yeah, Ryan had gotten my pants off and gotten all up close and personal with my lady bits, but I hadn't been *totally* naked and the room had been a little shadowed.

There was no hiding in this space. Then again, Ryan had been stripping me naked long before any clothes actually came off. This was simply one more layer he was exposing.

"You should stay," I said, my voice a little throaty as I forced the words out.

He kept his bright blue eyes on mine as he smiled and watched me. One hand slipped down to my ass and squeezed the fleshiest part before delving gently between my legs.

My lips fell open on a gasp as I kept my eyes locked on his. My breaths came in short pants, my vision going unfocused, when he slipped the tip of his finger inside me and then swirled it around my clit.

I bit down on my lip to keep from crying out, and his gaze heated when he watched my teeth catch my bottom lip.

His finger pushed in deeper and the groan I was trying to stifle broke free. It echoed wantonly off the glass walls around us. Unable to bear the sensation, my eyes fluttered shut and my knees buckled a little.

"So responsive," Ryan murmured, almost to himself as his finger was joined by another and he pumped them into me as he rocked his cock against my clit. Our bodies slid together easily as the water sluiced down our skin.

"Shit," I swore as starbursts sparkled behind my vision when the head of his cock hit me just right.

"Look at me, Madison," he ordered quietly.

I blinked my eyes open, barely able to focus on him as he maneuvered us out of the direct spray and pressed my upper back to the marble wall, my breasts smashed against his hard chest. My nipples pebbled, and I wished there was a way for them to join in the party. I wondered what it would feel like if he wrapped his mouth around...

"Fuck," he hissed. "What was that thought?"

"What?" I asked back.

"Whatever you just thought had you clamping down on my fingers like a fucking vise, and your pupils dilated."

Fuck it. If I was doing this, I was *doing* this.

"Just imagining how great it would feel if your mouth was on me," I admitted.

His eyes flared. "You want me sucking on your clit again while I fuck you with my hand? That can be arranged."

I caught his jaw with my hand before he could lower to his knees on the tiles. "Actually? It's another part of me that wants your mouth." I used my hands to push his head down so his face was level with my chest.

He didn't hesitate to suck a nipple into his mouth with a firm tug.

I cried out, my head falling back against the marble as he worked me over with his mouth and hands. Occasionally his dick would hit my clit and send shockwaves rippling through my system.

It only took him minutes, maybe seconds really, to work me up and over the edge of an earth-shattering climax. He wrapped an arm around my waist at the last second when my knees finally gave out as my body jerked uncontrollably.

I dropped my forehead to his chest as I came back down from the high. With a stuttering laugh, I pulled back and peered up at him.

"What were you apologizing for this time?" I managed.

He grinned. "Just banking a few extra orgasms for the next time I fuck up."

I licked my lips, my hands coasting down his sides. "That's smart. I think I like your version of a savings plan."

"I hear it has great returns," he added with a smirk.

"Use this investment plan a lot, huh?" I tried to keep my words light, but it still kind of stung.

"First time," he replied.

I paused, my gaze flying to him. "Really?"

"Guess I never really cared about investing in my future before," he said quietly, pushing some of my hair back.

I nodded slowly, letting my hands continue on their path and working between us until I brushed against the hot, hard length of him. I wrapped one hand around the base of him and gave an exploratory squeeze. "It sounds like a *solid* plan."

He braced a hand on the wall above my head, his forehead dropping to mine. "What are you doing, Mads?"

I gave an indifferent shrug as I moved my hand down to his tip, taking the bead of moisture I found there and massaging it into the crown of his dick. "Opening up my own account?"

His bicep flexed by my head, the tattooed numbers jerking as I jerked *him*.

"I'm not sure what I'm doing," I admitted awkwardly, still moving my hand up and down his shaft and contemplating if I was ready to try and use my mouth, too. I was insanely curious about his taste, but also knew he was a guy who'd likely had his dick routinely sucked by the strongest mouths at Pacific Cross.

I didn't want to worry the whole time if he was picturing someone else doing it better.

"Funny, you're pretty natural," he told me with a grunt, his jaw clenching.

"Is this the part of the story when you tell me anything I do is perfect because it's me?" I asked, my mind flashing back to countless virginal first times I'd read. I mean, seriously. What girl came ready made with no gag reflex and a Hoover for cheeks?

His eyes snapped open. "I don't lie to make anyone feel better. But if you want some pointers?" His hand closed over mine with more pressure and he pulled harder on his cock. "Harder is better. If I was inside your tight pussy, it would be squeezing my dick just like *this*."

Oh, hell. My heart slammed against my ribs.

"Okay," I said breathlessly.

"Better," he told me with a smirk, letting my hand go. "But you have two hands, baby."

Again, Ryan reached down and guided my hand past his shaft and to his balls. "See? Can't leave the boys out."

"Of course not," I replied, snorting a little. My amusement died when he groaned loudly as I worked his other friends into the moment. I added a little more pressure to his shaft as I squeezed and his abs flexed.

I got caught up watching his body for cues. What seemed to set him off or didn't really do much. Learning his body was a subject I was determined to excel at. I grinned to myself as I felt his body start to shake.

"Shit, Maddie," he moaned, leaning down and pressing his mouth to mine as he jerked in my hands, a hot liquid splashing onto my stomach.

I kissed him back until he reached down and removed my hands from him. He lifted them above my head and pinned my wrists together with one large hand.

His other hand stroked down my arm and palmed one breast before pinching the tip.

I gasped into his mouth as a new streak of arousal shot through me.

He chuckled against my mouth. "We should probably get out of the shower soon."

"Define soon," I mumbled, arching my back and trying to get him to keep touching me.

"I think I created a monster," he chuckled, shaking his head.

I looked him in the eye and smiled slowly. "Maybe I was always a monster. Maybe I just needed another monster to show me the way."

Judging by the wide grin Bex flashed me when I came down the stairs, it was no mystery what Ryan and I had been up to.

I rolled my eyes and shook my head, going for the tacos that had been delivered and snagging a tortilla chip before taking a big bite.

Linc grinned at me. "Maddie, you almost fit that whole thing in your mouth. Have you been practicing?"

Ryan slapped him on the back of the head on his way to grab a container. "Don't be an asshole."

Linc rubbed the back of his head. "Don't be so touchy." He turned to me. "Was that it? Was he too touchy, Maddie?"

This time Bex was the one who hit him when he dodged out of Ryan's reach.

"Don't be a dick," she admonished.

Linc watched her grab her own food before muttering, "I'll give you a dick." He caught me watching and winked.

All I could do was roll my eyes and follow the others outside to the patio area where Court and Ash were already waiting.

Ash stood up as I approached, my old phone in his hand. "Here you go."

I set my food down on the table and took the phone, staring at it like it might attack.

"Like I said, it only pulled back the first layer of encryption, so it's a lot of older stuff, I think. Stuff she copied over before the program updates that offered more security." He shoved his hands in his pockets and watched me.

They were *all* watching me.

"Maddie? Are you okay?" Bex asked softly, getting up from her seat next to Court.

My head snapped up. "Um, yeah." My eyes found Ryan.

I *always* found Ryan.

He looked at me patiently, which I knew had to be driving the alpha side of him crazy. He was used to taking and demanding, and his newfound patience with me was still in its infancy. I was a little amazed he hadn't had Ash look through the phone before giving it to me.

"I don't think I'm that hungry anymore," I admitted. "Is it okay if I..."

Ryan nodded. "Yeah. You can go into my room if you want to be alone."

I shook my head and pointed to the stairs a few feet away. "I think I'll hang out here, if that's okay."

I couldn't explain it, but I needed to be close to my friends if anything happened. I needed the security of knowing they were literally at my back.

Ironic how I had spent my entire life being as self-sufficient as possible and now I was hopelessly addicted to being part of a group.

"Of course," Ryan said. "We're here if you need us."

I wandered to the edge of the deck and sat down on the stairs, my back to them as I unlocked the phone and opened the app.

There were still a lot of locked icons next to files indicating Ash hadn't been able to open them, but there were several that were available. I tapped on the first video file and smiled as a young Madelaine literally tumbled into view.

"Tada!" she exclaimed, throwing her hands above her head as she got up with a grin. One of her front teeth was missing and her hair was in messy pigtails.

"Very good, Lainey," Mrs. Delancey's voice said from behind the phone. "Want to try again?"

"Yes!" She clapped her hands and turned to start all over.

Mrs. Delancey cheered Madelaine on until the screen went dark.

I frowned, not sure why that would need to be kept on an encrypted app, but whatever.

The next video was dark and grainy. It was a recording of another recording, whoever was holding the phone was shaking as they zoomed in on a set of security cameras.

I squinted. I knew that hallway that was being filmed. The wall colors were different, but it was still the same layout. I glanced at the blurry timestamp in the corner.

I watched as Madelaine's door opened, not sure why someone would be creeping out of her bedroom at two a.m. the day after, what would have then been, our thirteenth birthday.

The man slipped through her door and quietly shut it before tucking his shirt into his pants.

"No way," I whispered in horror as Uncle Adam turned and walked right in front of the camera.

"Motherfucker," I breathed, my insides shriveling and dying as the video jumped to a new timestamp a week later.

Same motherfucking pervert left my sister's bedroom.

It happened again the next week. And the next.

My stomach roiled with nausea. What other fucking reason could there be for a grown man to be in a thirteen-year-old's bedroom at two in the goddamn morning? It went on until just before Christmas and then the videos stopped and the file ended.

The phone slipped from my fingers and clattered onto the bricks. It probably would have shattered if not for the protective case that was clearly worth its money.

"Maddie?"

I heard several chairs scrape back as people stood up, but it was Ryan who reached me first. I felt his eyes staring intently at me, but I was too lost in my own thoughts to really pay any attention.

MAD WORLD

"Madison?" Bex whispered from my other side, touching my wrist gently as she sat beside me.

I jolted and turned to her, grabbing her arm so hard she gasped.

"What did you say?" I asked desperately.

"About what?" she asked, her gray eyes wide.

I squeezed my eyes shut, trying to think and trying to unsee those tapes. "When she... The *scar*."

"Shit," Ryan muttered, rubbing my back. He had heard my conversation with Bex, so he knew what Madelaine had tried to do.

I ignored him as I fixated on Bex. "You said everything changed after she turned thirteen."

She nodded quickly. "Yeah. She was more withdrawn and erratic. She never let me come over. And then, after Christmas..."

"She tried to kill herself," I whispered.

"Whoa, whoa," Linc said, coming around to stand in front of me. "She did *what*?"

"I know why," I told Bex, my eyes filling with tears and spilling over before I realized I was crying. "Why she wanted to file for emancipation, why she slit her wrist."

Bex's face screwed up in confusion. "Maddie—"

I reached down and picked up the phone, opening it and cueing up the video to hand to her.

"Maddie, what's going on?" Ryan asked, reaching for my other hand as Bex started the video.

Court leaned over her shoulder with Ash. "Is that a security camera?"

I knew the second Bex realized what I had when she jumped to her feet and tossed the phone back at me. "I'm going to be sick," she said and stalked away taking deep breaths as Linc followed her.

I handed the phone to Ryan as the video kept playing.

"It's Adam," I said quietly, brokenly, as he watched.

His jaw dropped open.

"Your dad's business partner?" Ash pressed, grabbing the phone from Ryan so he and Court could watch.

"Look at the date," I added, rubbing my head as my temples started

377

to pound. "It started the night we turned thirteen and kept going until Christmas. Bex said that's when she tried to kill herself."

Ryan reached over and lifted me up to settle in his lap. All I could do was bury my face against the side of his neck as tears fell.

It was no wonder Madelaine was so messed up. She'd been abused for years by that monster. Say what you wanted about my mom, but I never had to deal with *that*. The one boyfriend she'd had who dared look at me a little too long she beat over the head with a frying pan.

Literally slammed the skillet over his head with a *crack* that still haunted my dreams.

Did Gary know one of his closest friends, the guy he had entrusted his daughter to, was abusing her?

My heart felt sick over it.

Ryan's hand smoothed up and down my back as he cradled me to him like I was the most precious thing in the world. Like I was worthy of protecting and he was planning to shoulder that burden.

My tears gave way to a couple of soft hiccups as I got myself under control. When I peeked out from Ryan's neck, I noticed Linc and Bex had rejoined us. At some point, Bex had sat beside Ryan and taken my hand.

"He has to pay," I said, my voice trembling with emotion, mostly rage. I wanted Adam Kindell dead or worse.

"He will," Ryan vowed.

Court, Linc, and Ash all nodded in agreement.

I swallowed the last of my tears and looked at Ash. "I can't... Can you see what else you can get off her phone?"

"Of course," he promised, pocketing the phone.

Ryan's nose brushed against my cheek. "Want me to take you home?"

I turned and met his gaze. My heart twisted a little more at the concern and worry in his eyes.

"I'd rather stay, if that's okay?" I whispered, afraid he might reject me. Everything was shifting under my feet like quicksand.

He nodded slowly. "Of course you can stay."

"Okay," I mumbled, glad that it was settled. My heart was more than a little bruised and I hated the idea of being alone. Sure, Bex would've stayed the night if I'd wanted, but right now? My heart wanted Ryan. He made me feel less alone. He silenced the chaos in my head.

"Are you hungry?" Bex asked gently.

"Starving," Brylee declared loudly as she and Dean came around the back of the house.

I turned my head so they wouldn't see the remnants of my crying, but I knew Dean spotted it by the way he smiled. No doubt guessing Ryan and I were fighting or some shit. His arm tightened around me reflexively.

"Trouble in paradise, Lainey?" Brylee cooed.

"Not today, Satan," Linc muttered, jerking a finger at the back door. "Be gone."

"I'm Dean's guest," she hissed. "Or does only Lainey get to spend the night with her boyfriend?"

"You know the rules, Dean," Court gritted out. "No skanks upstairs."

"Excuse me?" Brylee shrieked indignantly.

Dean glared at Court. "She's my girl."

"I stand by my statement." Court shrugged indifferently.

Brylee's gaze landed on me, and I could see her gearing up for an argument.

"Not to-fucking-night." Ryan's cold voice cut through the tension between us. "Take her and go, Dean."

"You're not the boss, Cain," Dean spat.

Ryan stared up at him with flat eyes, somehow still seeming more in charge of the moment, sitting with me curled on his lap, than the frat president did standing. "I'm not saying it again. Fucking walk."

Scoffing, Dean moved around us and up the steps. Brylee followed, the pointed toe of her shoe connecting with Bex's knee.

"Oops," she giggled, glancing down. "I totally didn't even see you there, Becky."

She gasped as Court upended his beer over her head.

"Oops," he said mockingly, shaking out the last droplets onto her stunned face. "I totally didn't even see you there, bitchy."

Brylee blanched and looked at Dean, who—like the true knight in shining armor he wasn't—looked away.

Linc started laughing as he pulled Bex to her feet and wrapped an arm around her in a show of affection that made Brylee pale even more.

So much for her crush on Linc.

Bex blushed but didn't flinch away from Brylee's accusatory stare. *Good for her.*

I watched Dean and Brylee go into the house and slam the door.

With a squeak, Bex pushed away from Linc. "What the hell was that?"

"I wanted to cuddle," Linc said innocently. "Ryan would've punched me in the nuts if I tried to cuddle with Mads."

Bex looked at me, her cheeks still flaming.

"To be fair, he's right," Ryan replied. His arms tightened around me once more. "I don't share."

My gaze instinctively flicked from Linc to Court and then to Bex. Both of them were watching her with interest.

"Whatever," Bex sighed. "Next time, cuddle with Ash if you need a buddy."

"Hard pass," Ash said firmly, walking away from us. "I vote we move the food into the theater room and watch a movie."

"Movie sound good to you?" Ryan asked me quietly.

I nodded. "Something funny, please."

He kissed the tip of my nose. "Got it."

Thank God someone did, because I sure as hell didn't.

CHAPTER 48

One movie turned into three somehow, and we finally stopped when Linc's snoring kept waking everyone up between naps. Court offered to take Bex home, and she blushed as she agreed. She hugged me with a quick promise that we would get together tomorrow when the guys were on the bus headed for their away game.

Ryan let me use the bathroom first, giving me another one of his shirts to sleep in. I changed and brushed my teeth quickly, staring at myself in the mirror and wondering how different my life would be if Madelaine were standing here instead of me.

I must've taken too long because Ryan knocked on the door and cracked it open. When he saw I was just standing in front of the mirror, he pushed the door open and leaned against the frame to watch me.

"What's on your mind, pretty girl?" he asked softly, his azure gaze curious as he studied me.

I smiled at the compliment. "I was wondering how different things would be if my sister was standing here right now."

His mouth flattened. "She wouldn't be."

"She would be your fiancée," I pointed out, holding up my hand where his diamond still perched atop it.

"She would be," he agreed, "but I never would have had her spend the night."

I looked at him in surprise. "But you said we needed to for the optics."

He smirked and looked away. "Maddie, do you really think I give a shit about what people think of me?"

"No," I finally answered with a laugh. "So, why insist I stay the night that first time?"

"Because you're hot," he replied bluntly, "and why the hell wouldn't I want you in my bed?"

I rolled my eyes and laughed as he came into the room and stood behind me. His hands found their place on my hips, and I leaned back against him with a heavy sigh.

"I never would've trusted Madelaine enough to let her into my life this much," he confessed quietly.

I watched him in the mirror. "I know you hated her."

He snorted in agreement. "Understatement of the year, Mads."

"I need you to mean what you said, though," I went on, my tone dropping seriously. "Adam has to pay for what he's done. Not to me, but to my sister."

"I know," he replied.

I sucked in a breath between my teeth. "I mean really pay, Ry. Not that shit like you did with that prick from Indonesia or Dean. I don't care if he goes bankrupt. I care if he's in prison or..."

"Or?" he tempted darkly.

"Dead," I answered. "I want him dead."

"So, do I." A muscle popped in his jaw. "Your sister wasn't one of my favorite people, Mads, you know that. But she was barely older than Cori when Adam started whatever the fuck happened in her room."

Frustrated, I turned and leaned against the counter so we weren't touching. "Ash told me I should talk to you."

His eyes narrowed. "About?"

"About how I'm having a hard time matching up the guy who wants to kill a pedophile for me but didn't lift a finger to help those kids in another country," I said plainly, folding my arms protectively around my torso. "Or why Dean is *still here*. Bex should never have to see him again."

He watched me for a long time before nodding. "You're right."

My hands fell to my sides with a slap. "Then why haven't you done anything?"

"It's complicated," he said softly. "There's a lot you don't understand."

"Then *make* me understand," I begged. "Because... Shit." I looked away with a heavy sigh and ran a hand through my hair.

"Because what, Madison?" He caught my chin between his thumb and index finger and turned me to look at him.

I took a deep breath and jumped off the cliff my heart was teetering on.

"Because I need to know that the guy I'm falling for isn't one of the bad guys," I told him, laying it all out there.

His gaze softened. "I'm not one of the bad guys, baby."

"I really want to believe you," I whispered, tears gathering in my eyes again.

He pressed a gentle kiss to my lips. "I can't explain everything to you right now."

I stiffened and tried to pull away.

"But I will," he finished, not letting me retreat. "Give me until the engagement party."

Two weeks.

Could I give him two weeks?

"I need to sort some things out, but I'll tell you everything," he said, his eyes searching mine intently. "I promise."

"You promise?" I echoed.

He nodded and thumbed away one of the tears that fell. "I hate when you cry."

I sniffled. "Then maybe you should stop making me."

"I intend to. But I need you to trust me for right now. Can you do that, Maddie? Can you just... trust me?" He seemed to hold his breath, waiting for my answer.

This was it. This was the moment.

I knew I was falling in love with Ryan Cain, but could I really trust him?

A piece of my armor fractured and broke away, falling as helplessly into the unknown as I was. "I trust you," I said quietly.

He pulled me into a hug, crushing my body against his. "Thank you."

I lost track of how long I stayed in his arms, my ear pressed to his chest as he held me.

But eventually I pulled away. "I'll let you finish getting ready for bed."

"Want me to sleep on the floor?" he called to my retreating back.

I shot him a look over my shoulder. "Hell no," I laughed before pulling the door shut to the sound of his chuckling.

I pulled back the covers on the bed and hesitated before getting in.

When I had come into the house tonight, I'd had a pretty good idea of where tonight would end up. I snorted to myself when I realized it sure as hell wasn't finding out my sister had been molested and Ryan spending most of the night like a helicopter parent waiting for me to crack.

I sank onto the soft sheets as the sink stopped running in the bathroom. A moment later, Ryan emerged in only his boxer-briefs. He paused when he realized my head was somewhere else.

"What's going on?" he asked cautiously.

Those fucking tears returned once more with a biting pinch. "It's not right."

"What isn't?" His patience seemed endless as he waited for me to explain.

I met his gaze. "Your first time should be special. Hers was with... *him*. She was a kid, and he took it from her."

Anger darkened his face. "Madison."

I shook my head. "My sister didn't get that." My gaze snapped to him. "But I want that."

He froze, clearly unsure with what to do with my announcement.

"I want *you*," I clarified as my heart thundered in my chest.

His jaw clenched. "Maddie, I'm trying to be the good guy here. Tonight's been a mess for you, and I don't want you waking up tomorrow with regrets."

"I won't," I replied, knowing in my heart it was the truth. "I came here wanting to be with you. What happened to Madelaine? It just proves how out of control life can be. I don't want to wait anymore."

His hands clenched at his sides. "There isn't a clock on us, baby. We don't *have* to do anything tonight. I know you still have doubts—"

"I trust you," I cut in. "Yes, I still have questions, but I trust you, Ryan. Completely. Totally. I'm... God, I'm in fucking love with you, okay? I lied earlier. I'm not falling for you—I fell. Like off a freaking skyscraper."

His eyes widened and he rocked back.

My heart was hammering so loud now that he *had* to hear it. "Tell me I'm not alone here, Ryan. Tell me I'm not the only one who feels this between us?"

He licked his lips slowly. "You're not. I feel it, too. I..." He exhaled hard, his throat working as he tried to find a way to say what he felt.

Even if he couldn't say the words, I knew.

I felt them in his touch, I lived them in his kiss.

Ryan Cain loved me as much as I loved him.

"You need to know exactly what you're getting into with me, Maddie," he rasped, his eyes dangerously wild as he raked a hand through his hair. "I'm an asshole most of the time. I'll do stuff you hate because I think I know what's best."

A laugh bubbled out of me. "I'm *well* aware."

He held up a hand to stop me. "If you think I'm a possessive ass now, you haven't seen shit. If you're really mine, I'm not letting you go. Ever, baby. That ring won't just be a sparkly accessory on your finger. It will mean you're *mine*. Completely. Totally."

He threw my words back at me like a challenge, daring me to accept him. Tempting me to submit to his light and his demons.

"I want it all," I told him honestly.

"Okay," he agreed quietly.

He moved so fast, I didn't see him coming. One second he was next to the bed, and the next he had yanked me to the edge by my feet and was looming over me.

His hand snaked under the hem of the shirt, stroking me over my panties.

"Last chance to call me off before I'm buried inside *my* pussy," he warned, a finger finding my clit through the fabric with unerring accuracy. "You say the word and I'll stop."

I lifted my hips, my body already trying to find a rhythm to chase him with as I gasped.

"One word, Maddie," he teased darkly, slipping his finger under the elastic and groaning when he found me already soaked for him.

"All you have to say is no." He was practically choking on his own words now.

My head was spinning as he circled my clit and then dragged his finger to my opening.

"I say *yes*," I hissed defiantly, staring straight into his eyes.

His lips curved into a devastating grin. "I was hoping you would."

He tore my panties down my legs then knocked them open wide with his hips as he shoved my shirt up under my chin. His tongue lashed against my center as his fingers tweaked and stroked my nipples.

I cried out at the sudden onslaught of pleasure that spiked through my body like an electric current. My back bowed over the bed, my hips jerking to meet him.

His tongue thrust into my core as he dropped a hand to play with my clit.

I reached out blindly, my fingers twisting in his hair as he forced a splintering orgasm from my body.

I was still riding that wave when he pulled my shirt off over my head and positioned himself. The head of his cock pushed inside of my body, and the new pressure burned and stretched.

I flinched at the intrusion, and Ryan hesitated before linking our hands and pressing them to the mattress above my head.

"Eyes on me, Madison," he ordered, watching me carefully.

I nodded and steeled myself for the pain I was *sure* was coming.

First times sucked, and I was okay with getting this pain out of the way so we could move on to more fun things.

But that didn't mean I was looking forward to it.

"It's okay," I told him, knowing he was holding back for fear of hurting me.

I welcomed the hurt if it meant Ryan was mine.

His hips flexed into me, pushing into me with a sharper pinch than I'd expected. I cried out, my body tensed as I fought the urge to shove him off of me.

"I'm sorry," he whispered softly, lowering his mouth to kiss me slowly.

He didn't move as his mouth coaxed mine into a searing kiss, letting me adjust as much as I could before sliding out of me and rocking back in.

I hissed at the pain, trying to swallow my discomfort so he wouldn't worry.

Ryan transferred both of my hands into one of his and lowered the other between our bodies where we were joined. I gasped when his finger slid against the side of my clit and pleasure overrode the burning ache between my legs.

He let me go long enough to lift my hips a little off the bed as he dropped one knee to the mattress and thrust into me again.

This new angle hit that place in me that sent pops of light flashing behind my eyes.

"Fuck," I whimpered, hoping he would do that again.

"Like that?" Ryan murmured, repeating the motion.

I wrapped my arms around his shoulders, my nails clawing into the phoenix tattoo as pleasure curled in me.

"More," I begged, amazed the pain had burned away into something unexpectedly addictive.

I squirmed under him, writhing as I tried to figure out if this was agony or ecstasy.

His hips pumped into mine with deep, claiming thrusts as his lips captured mine once more, demanding I surrender everything to him.

My climax crushed me as it detonated in my body. I felt myself clench around Ryan as he released a guttural moan and jerked inside of me.

I was still twitching with the residual aftereffects of my orgasm as he pulled out of me.

"Shit," he muttered, his worried eyes going to me. "I didn't use anything. I've never *not*—"

I sloppily patted his lips with my fingers. "I have an IUD."

"Okay," he replied, still shaken. "I didn't even think."

"Neither of us did," I murmured, cracking an eye open.

He dropped a kiss to the side of my breast before standing up. "Let me get something to clean you up."

I waited for him to come back with a washcloth. I hissed when the damp fabric touched my sensitive folds.

"Sorry," he murmured, gently wiping away the mess we'd made. He grimaced as he tossed the rag into the hamper across the room.

"Are you okay?" he asked softly, sitting next to me.

I blinked slowly at him. "Do you usually ask all the girls you've screwed if they're okay afterward?"

"It wasn't their first time," he replied, shrugging one muscled shoulder. "And they weren't you."

I smiled at him. "That's a good answer."

"Are you?" he pressed.

I sat up. "Ryan, I'm okay. I swear."

"Good."

I poked his shoulder. "Look at you, being all concerned and adorable. I'm surprised."

He took my hand in his and met my eyes. "Yeah, well, I'm in love."

My lips parted in amazed shock, and he grinned, touching my lower lip. "Remember what I said about open mouths, baby?"

I dropped back with a laugh, happier than I had been in a long time.

CHAPTER 49

The bed was empty the next morning when I woke up. A little disappointed, I rolled onto my side and realized the door to the bathroom was shut and the shower was running. I snuggled a little deeper into my pillow, pulling the soft sheets around my still-naked body as I tried to decide whether or not to join Ryan.

I was about to get up when the water cut off, making up my mind for me. A few minutes later, Ryan opened the door with a towel slung low on his waist. I was so busy watching the way his muscles moved that I nearly missed the smile that lit up his face when he saw me.

He crossed the room and sat on the edge of the bed, reaching out to touch my shoulder and drag a finger down my arm.

"How are you feeling?" he asked.

"Good," I admitted. I was a little sore, but I sure as hell wasn't complaining. And it hadn't stopped me from straddling Ryan when I'd woken up in the middle of the night for more.

His eyes narrowed as my cheeks flushed at the memory. "Do I want to know what your brain is thinking?"

I licked my lips. "Depends. Do we have time?"

Sighing, he shook his head ruefully and looked at the clock. "I need to be on the bus in less than twenty minutes."

I pouted a little. "You're no fun."

"We both know that's not true," he snorted.

I pushed myself up onto one elbow as his hungry gaze took in the way the sheet slipped precariously. "My eyes are up here," I teased.

"Yeah, but your tits are down *there*," he replied wolfishly, reaching forward to tug the sheet down and bare my breasts to his gaze.

My nipples pebbled in the cool air as my center clenched, achy and wanting.

"Fuck, you're gorgeous," he murmured. "I wish I could stay."

Not as much as I wished he could.

With a groan, he got off the bed and walked to his closet and started pulling out a suit. He dropped his towel, the hard globes of his ass flexing as he pulled on his boxer-briefs and tucked his half-mast dick inside with a hiss.

"You're such a tease," I muttered as a wave of arousal heated my blood.

He glanced at me with a smirk as he pulled on his pants. "I'll be home Sunday night. I want you in my bed, waiting for me, when I get in."

I mockingly gasped. "On a school night?"

But seriously, I did have an English test first thing Monday morning that I needed to study for this weekend.

"Try every night," he answered smugly as he buttoned up his shirt and tucked it inside his pants. "I might even have to video chat with you tonight so I don't go to sleep rock hard."

A fist pounded on the door. "Ry! Fifteen-minute warning!" Linc shouted. "Hey, Maddie!"

I giggled and yelled back, "Hey, Linc!"

Rolling his eyes, Ryan grabbed his suit jacket and duffel bag from the floor. He paused next to my side of the bed, his gaze heating as it roved over me.

"Madison, last night was..." He trailed off and shook his head, before rubbing the back of his neck with an impish smirk.

"I know," I told him, grabbing his hand and smiling. "I'll see you tomorrow night, okay?"

He nodded and leaned down to kiss me. I groaned as he pulled away, not nearly satisfied by the simple kiss when I knew the magic his tongue and lips could conjure in my body.

"Have a good game," I called.

"Stay out of trouble," he warned me with a wink before leaving the room and closing the door.

I mean, I would do my best, but I wasn't making any promises.

I threw the covers off and headed for the bathroom, already knowing I couldn't wait to talk to Bex. I was hoping she would also have an idea about what kind of dress I needed for my engagement party in a couple weeks.

Finishing in the bathroom, I got dressed and made a mental note to ask Ryan if I could stash some of my stuff in a drawer here. It would be easier than packing overnight bags.

Then I freaked a little, realizing I was going to ask him for a *drawer*. Like a girlfriend or something. Which, okay, I knew I was (kind of) but everything still felt so new and sparkly with Ryan. I didn't want to rock the boat we were in, especially since we'd started our relationship in the middle of a freaking typhoon.

I liked just being with Ryan.

But the running back and forth across campus was exhausting.

I finished shoving my dirty clothes in my bag as my phone chirped with an incoming text message.

BEX: Breakfast off campus? My treat!

Smiling, I tapped back a quick reply.

ME: Sounds great, but I'm at Ryan's place.

BEX: Clearly I will need all the details. Pick you up in 5.

I tucked my phone into my pocket, grabbed my bag and opened the door.

"Jesus," I gasped when I saw Dean standing in front of me. Ryan's door slamming shut at my back made me jump. "Lurk much, asshole?"

"Cute," he sneered, crossing his arms and leaning a shoulder on the wall next to his bedroom. "You know, you and I used to be friends, Lainey."

I grimaced. "Yeah. And butterflies *used to be* worms. People change and grow." I gave him a disgusted look. "Some of us, I mean. Spread your wings and fly, Dean."

"Cute, Lainey," he snapped. "But we both know the only spreading you're capable of is with your legs. Gotta say—I miss being between them."

Oh, fucking gross.

Madelaine had zero standards, and part of me wanted to resurrect her just to slap some sense into her.

Unable to keep the revulsion off my face, I shuddered. "Yeah, well, I need to go."

Dean slapped a hand on the opposite wall as I tried to pass, barring me from leaving.

"Move," I ordered.

"I don't get it," he said softly. "I've tried figuring out what the fuck your game is this time, but it's like you had a freaking lobotomy since spring. Like you're a totally different person."

My heart thundered in my chest. "Maybe I am."

His eyes narrowed. "We had fun last year, didn't we? You were supposed to help me put Cain in his place once and for all. Instead you're all over him? If I didn't know any better, I'd think you actually liked the fucker."

I tried to keep my face impassive, but something must have slipped.

He reared back. "Fuck me. You actually *like* him?"

"Why do you even care?" I demanded, throwing my hands up in the air.

He stepped closer, looming over me. "Because you spent nights in *my* bed, screaming *my* name. Now I have to listen to you fucking *him* at night?"

I tilted my chin up, refusing to cower. I gave him a smile full of sarcasm. "Get earplugs."

He grabbed my arm as I tried to walk by, swinging me back around.

"Get *off*!" I snapped, yanking at my arm, but he held tight.

He pulled me closer, his eyes searching mine. "What the hell happened to you?"

"Let me go, or I'll scream," I threatened through gritted teeth.

He shrugged. "I like it when you scream, remember? And most of my brothers are on the team, and they're gone."

Okay, that was unsettling, and a kernel of fear started forming in the pit of my stomach.

But I also knew that showing fear was one of the worst things I could do at this moment. I needed to stay calm.

I stopped fighting and forced myself to look bored as I glanced down at where his hand was on my arm. His knuckles were white from the effort.

Sighing loudly, I stared at him while channeling as much of my twin as I could. "I have plans for breakfast that don't include being annoyed by you. Can I go?"

He released me with a small push. "Get the fuck out of my face."

"Happily," I chirped, spinning on my heel and resisting the urge to rub my sore arm as I went. I stomped down the stairs and out the door, thankful when I saw Bex's car idling out front. I tossed my bag in the backseat and got in.

"Are you okay?" she asked curiously.

I exhaled hard. "Not really."

"Ryan?"

I shook my head. "No, but he's going to be pissed. Oh, fuck."

"What?"

I opened the door again. "I forgot to lock Ryan's door. Give me a second."

I dashed back into the house and thanked my lucky stars that Dean's door was shut when I went back and locked Ryan's door, twisting the handle to make sure it was secure before hurrying back outside.

Bex gave me a look as I clipped my seatbelt. "Everything okay?"

"Ugh," I muttered, shaking my head as I remembered Dean.

"Sounds like a conversation we need to have over a giant stack of waffles," Bex murmured, putting the car in gear.

Definitely. I needed caffeine, sugar, and carbs.

Maybe that would keep me satisfied until my heart got back what it really wanted.

After breakfast, where I spilled everything to Bex about my night with Ryan and my morning with Dean, she took me shopping for my engagement party dress. Standing on a platform in front of three mirrors, my breath hitched softly as the lights shimmered off the hand-sewn crystals on the bodice of the silver gown.

"You don't think this is too fancy?" I whispered, almost afraid to breathe for fear of messing up the dress.

Bex came up behind me with a smile. "It's your engagement, Maddie. Everyone will be in formal wear."

I kept staring at myself, and then I foolishly let my mind wander into the "what if this was real?" fantasy that kept popping up.

Sighing, I turned and gave Bex a thin smile. "I'm good with this dress."

Her eyes narrowed suspiciously. "Okay, a second ago you were in love with this dress, and suddenly you look like someone kicked your puppy. What gives?"

I walked to the elegant white sofa and sank onto the edge. "I guess I'm having a hard time reminding myself that this is all an act."

Bex sat beside me. "I thought you said you and Ryan were the real deal."

"We are," I said hesitantly. "I mean, we like each other."

She gave me a pointed look.

"Fine, I love him," I confessed. "But what kind of future can we have?"

"Whatever future you want," she replied.

"Gary is looking for a way out of this engagement for me," I reminded her. "And I don't want to spend the rest of my life being Madelaine Cabot. At some point? I want to be Madison Porter and live the life *I* want."

"And you can't do that with Ryan?" Her nose wrinkled in confusion.

"I'm not Susie Homemaker, Bex." I explained, shrugging my bare shoulders. "I want a career. I want to make a difference."

"Who the hell said you can't have a career and make a difference? Ryan?"

"No," I admitted. "Beckett and Gary both implied that—"

"Screw Beckett and your dad," she cut me off. "You're not marrying them. You'd be marrying Ryan."

"Am I?" I asked, frustrated.

"Are you what?"

"Marrying Ryan?"

She looked at my finger. "That rock is a pretty solid indicator, Maddie."

I held up my hand and twisted off the ring. I felt strangely naked without the familiar weight. "This is a ring he got for *her*. Do I want to marry someone where I'm just filling in for my dead twin?"

Bex folded her hands in her lap. "I don't have all the answers, Maddie, but this sounds like a conversation you need to have with Ryan. You guys don't have to put a timetable on anything. Do what you want."

Except there *was* a timetable. This giant clock was hanging over our heads—more like over my uterus—that affected Corinne. And I would marry Ryan to save Corinne, but I needed to make sure my heart wasn't going to be shattered in the process.

I hadn't told Bex about that part. As much as I trusted her, I didn't think Ryan would want me sharing that family secret, especially since I wasn't even supposed to know it.

"You're right," I finally said. "I need to talk to Ryan about it. I'm just afraid of messing things up since they're so good, you know?"

She held my hand. "I do, but I think it'll be worth it."

"Maybe," I allowed with a wry smile.

"Are you going to tell him about Dean?" she asked, wincing a little.

I made a face. "I know I should, but part of me wants to just let it go."

"Are you sure that's smart?" She tucked her dark hair behind her ear. "Dean is a snake."

"A snake that my sister was apparently screwing," I muttered darkly. I shuddered at the idea.

"Exactly," she said emphatically. "Ryan would want to know."

"Ryan would also lose his shit if he knew Dean grabbed me this morning," I added. Thankfully the only bruise I'd gotten from his hold was where his thumb had dug into the underside of my arm.

I shook away the memory and focused on my friend. "But enough about me. I'm curious to know how things are going with Court."

Her cheeks pinked. "We're friends."

"Right," I drawled. "Just like you're friends with Linc?"

Her hazel eyes went wide. "Yes."

"Your words say *yes*," I teased, "but the squeak in your voice says there's more to the story."

"Ugh," Bex groaned, falling back against the couch. "I mean, everyone knows the stories about those two."

I glanced around the store and raised my hand. "Uh, I don't know."

"They share. Girls, I mean." Her blush turned crimson.

"Oh! I thought you meant they shared a bathroom or something." I winked at her.

She slapped my leg. "Dammit, Maddie!"

I laughed. "Okay, okay. Ryan may have mentioned something about them sharing, but is that a bad thing?"

"It is when your uncle is making a run for the presidency on a wholesome family values platform that doesn't include anything but hetero-normative roles," she replied.

"And? That's your uncle."

"My parents tend to think the same way. I mean, they like to say they're more *liberal* than he is, but when push comes to shove? We're family, and I'm expected to fall in line." She picked a loose thread on the hem of her shirt.

I frowned. "That's *their* problem."

"And Gary marrying you off to Ryan is *his* problem, too, but here you sit."

She had a point, as much as I hated to admit it. At some point I had slipped the ring back onto my finger.

"We're a mess," I muttered, shaking my head. "We need to start acting like the badasses we are. Stop taking shit from all these adults who are clueless."

"Sounds like a plan," she agreed, but poked my shoulder. "You first."

"I was afraid you'd say that," I murmured.

"Great. And while you're making your plan to assert your inner female badass? We need shoes to go with this dress."

I groaned loudly. "I was even more afraid you'd say *that*."

CHAPTER 50

I yawned as I knocked on the front door of the frat house the following night. The academy team had won their game last night, but unfortunately Ryan's team had lost in a pretty stunning upset. He'd called me after the game, but he sounded frustrated and annoyed, so I agreed to see him Sunday night as he had requested and let him go.

Yes, Ryan Cain was actually capable of *requesting* things from me.

I'd spent most of Sunday in a study group for the English exam in the morning, and after having dinner with Bex in the cafeteria, I decided to go to the house to wait for Ryan, who was still an hour or so away.

I knew if I went back to my dorm, I'd crash and not wake up.

I waited for one of the guys to answer the door. I probably could've walked in, but it felt weird.

Josh, the guy I had seen in Dean's room the night he drugged Bex, stood there.

"Hey, Madelaine," he greeted, gnawing on a chicken drumstick. "Ryan isn't here."

"I know," I replied, trying to control the heat level my cheeks were projecting. "I'm meeting him."

"Oh." He wiped a greasy hand on the front of his shirt, and then his brown eyes widened knowingly. "*Oh.*"

"Yeah," I muttered, dipping my head so that my hair covered part of my face.

"Cain has all the fuckin' luck," Josh muttered.

"Thanks?" I wasn't sure exactly how to answer that.

"Come on in," he said, waving me in with the flourish of a chicken bone. "Hungry?"

"Just ate," I answered, thankful it was the truth because the smell of the chicken he was casually tossing around was a little nauseating.

"No worries," he mumbled. "We're watching the game if you want to join." He indicated to the large flatscreen where a bunch of guys, including Dean, were gathered. He glanced up at me as I paused in the doorway.

"Actually, I've got some studying to do, so I'll just hang in Ryan's room. But thanks," I added, making a quick getaway.

I should've known it was too easy when I made it to Ryan's floor and—*yet again*—Dean grabbed my arm.

This time, at least, he let me go.

"Madelaine, wait a sec," he said.

I whirled, annoyed. "Pass."

He held up his hands in surrender. "Can you just hear me out for a second?"

"What do you want?" I demanded, already regretting my decision to hear him out.

He shoved his hands in his pockets. "I wanted to apologize."

I scoffed, not believing a damn word of it. "Really?"

"Yeah," he said, frown lines appearing on his forehead. He looked genuinely perplexed. "Last year, I thought you and I had something good. I mean, I know you were with that coach or whatever, but we both knew you were using him to fuck with Cain. I thought I made it clear I was okay with that. I thought we were on the same page."

I clenched my teeth, trying to keep my face neutral.

"But I guess things changed this summer," he went on. "It just sucks you aren't moving on with me."

"Well, you have Brylee," I pointed out.

"Yeah, but we both know she's not you." Dean winked at me. "But I wanted to say sorry for yesterday."

"You're still a piece of shit," I felt compelled to say.

He shrugged. "I know. Wait, shit. I have something of yours."

"You do?" My brows rose skeptically.

"Yeah." He opened the door to his room. "You left it here last year. I never had a chance to give it back to you. I forgot about it until I was cleaning my closet."

Curiously, I followed him to the doorway and stood outside his room. I watched as he went to his closet and rummaged around.

Steps on the landing made me turn, and I wrinkled my nose to see Josh with his bucket of chicken. He waved a thigh at me with a grin.

"Lainey?" Dean looked at me expectantly as he held a sweater out to me, making me come inside to get it. I left the door open, not entirely sure if Josh would care if Dean did something douchey, but at least I would be able to exit the room quickly.

I took the soft cashmere from his hands and turned it over in my hands. It wasn't mine, which meant it was my sister's.

An unexpected wave of regret threatened to topple me as I held something that had once belonged to her in my hands. It had sat here, just waiting for its owner to reclaim it.

And she never would.

"Thanks," I mumbled and hurried out of the room, blinking back tears. I turned and unlocked Ryan's door and got inside before leaning against the wood and letting out a soft sob.

I knew my sister was less than perfect. She was a category five hurricane that had no problem leveling anything in her path. But my heart still ached and grieved for the other half of me that I'd never gotten to know.

I gave in to the stupid wave of emotion and let it take me away until I was cried out. Once I got up from the floor, I went to the bathroom to clean up and change.

When I sat down to use the toilet, I swore.

MAD WORLD

Great. No wonder I was so stupidly hormonal and weepy today; my period was early.

That definitely nixed my plans with Ryan tonight. Instead of pulling on one of his shirts, I pulled on Madelaine's sweater and a pair of yoga pants before climbing into Ryan's bed and snuggling under the sheets.

I turned on the TV across the room to a documentary about a haunted prison, but felt my eyes drooping shut before the first commercial rolled.

I woke up to the feeling of lips on mine as my mouth was slowly coaxed open. A small flutter of panic rippled through my chest before I realized I knew this mouth and this taste.

Groaning, I rolled to my back as Ryan settled over me, one hand tangled in my hair to position my mouth exactly where he wanted.

"Hi," I murmured when he let me up for air.

He chuckled, his nose bumping mine. "Hi."

"I'm sorry about the game," I told him.

His jaw tightened in frustration. "I don't get it, Maddie. They're the worst team in our division. We should have had this game locked down. It was like..."

"Like what?" I pressed curiously.

His conflicted gaze searched mine, and he huffed a wry laugh. "Like they knew our plays before we did? I don't know."

"I'm sorry," I whispered, knowing he took the loss personally and hating that for him. "Is there anything I can do?"

His hand played flat on my belly and then lowered to the edge of my pants. "Take my mind off it?"

I winced and grabbed his wrist to stop him. "I... Can we not?"

He pulled back, looking confused and surprised. "Yeah. Of course."

I blinked the last parts of sleep from my eyes. "Sorry. I got my period and..."

He gave me a steady look. "You don't owe me an explanation, Mads. A simple 'no' works."

I touched his jaw. "And that makes me want you even more."

He smirked. "Really?"

"Mmhmm," I hummed. "Consent is sexy as fuck."

"I mean, I can have you sign a waiver if you really want to make sure consent is documented," he added.

I burst into laughter. "You're such a dork."

He dropped his forehead to my shoulder with a chuckle. "I'm not usually."

Sobering, I watched as he sat up. "I'm sorry. I just have cramps from hell and feel anything but sexy."

He paused and looked back at me. "Do you need anything?"

I gave him an amused look. "Why? If I say yes, are you going to get me a heating pad? Chocolate?"

"I have a heating pad in my closet for when I pull a muscle," he informed me. "The chocolate I can send a pledge out for."

I looked at the clock on his bedside table. "It's after midnight."

"And?" He truly wasn't concerned by this at all.

"Let the pledges sleep," I said, rolling my eyes. "Right now that's all I want."

He nodded and stripped off his shirt and jeans before getting in beside me and gently maneuvering me into his arms.

"Is this okay? Are you comfortable?"

I snuggled back into his chest with a contented sigh, hiding a smile at how sweet he was being. "This is perfect."

"Are you ready for your exam tomorrow?"

I twisted my head around to see him. "Are you seriously asking me about my test?"

"You said you had to study," he reminded me. "I'm just trying to..."

"To what?" I giggled, watching as he seemed to squirm.

"Show an interest in your life?" He groaned at how corny it sounded. "Fuck."

I laughed. "What the hell are you talking about?"

He rubbed a hand over his face. "Fucking Linc."

"You're talking about fucking Linc?" I teased, acting like I was going to get up. "I can go if you two need to be alone."

"Brat," he snarled, pulling me back down and rolling me onto my back so he was over me. "No, Linc mentioned that I needed to start doing shit like this if we were going to be together."

"You're taking dating advice from *Linc*? I haven't been here very long, but even I know he's PC's resident man-whore." I shook my head in amusement.

"I know, you're right," he agreed, resting a hand on my hip. "I just don't want to fuck this up."

I covered his hand with mine. "I said almost the exact same thing to Bex yesterday."

"You did?"

I nodded. "Yeah. She said that we can take our time, but we both know we can't."

Worry flashed in his eyes.

"I didn't say anything to her about Cori," I assured him.

"I'd be okay if you did," he said quietly. "You trust her, and the way Court and Linc are obsessing? I don't see Bex going anywhere anytime soon."

"It's your secret to tell," I answered gently.

"Technically it's our secret," he corrected. "You're just as tangled up in this as I am."

I was silent for several beats as I gathered my thoughts. "I found a dress for the engagement party."

"I can't wait to see it," he murmured, nuzzling my cheek.

I took a deep breath and turned my head so our faces were an inch apart. "Ryan?"

"Hmm?"

"I want a new ring," I said softly, unsure how he'd react.

He sighed. "I thought you might."

"You did?"

He nodded. "Yeah. I didn't even pick that ring out. My dad's assistant did. It was something flashy and opulent. Fuck, I didn't even put it on Madelaine's finger. I think I threw the box at her before I grabbed a drink."

"Romantic," I deadpanned.

"I hated her," he said honestly, his blue eyes startling open and clear. "I think we both need a fresh start, and a new ring would help. Do you want to pick it out?"

My nose wrinkled. "You probably don't want me to."

"Planning on breaking the bank?"

"More like I would probably buy a tiny little diamond with a silver band and barely spend a hundred dollars," I replied with a smirk. "Bex had to hide the price tag of the dress I bought yesterday, or I probably wouldn't have gotten it."

He snorted, bemused. "Okay, I'll pick out the ring then."

Happy with that, I nodded. "Sounds good."

"You know, I won't make you marry me." His hesitant voice made me pause. "I know you're doing this for Corinne, and you don't know what that means to me—"

I pressed my fingers over his mouth to silence him. "*When* I marry you, it'll be because it's what *I* want. Helping Cori is just an added incentive, okay?"

Relief shone in his eyes a second before he kissed me soundly.

"How the hell did I ever think you were her?" he wondered quietly, tracing my lips when he lifted his head.

I smiled. "It doesn't matter now."

He brushed my hair from my cheek and kissed me again before pulling me to his chest. "Get some sleep, Maddie."

I was asleep again within seconds.

CHAPTER 51

The following Sunday, I picked up a fallen leaf on the quad, watching as Ryan and his friends and some of their teammates played a pickup game of football even though they had just played a game last night.

A game they had damn near lost. Ryan had saved it, running in the final touchdown in overtime to clinch the victory. He was hoping a playful game today would snap the team out of their funk.

Someone had decided the teams should be shirts versus skins, and I was happy that Ryan had landed on the skins team.

The last week, outside of the game, had been sweet and amazing. Ryan was, in a word, incredible. We ate dinner together with our friends every night and then either went back to his room or mine. Most of the time we wound up sleeping in the same bed, and I was becoming stupidly addicted to having him around.

Thankfully my period had done its thing, and we'd been able to do more than just sleep and cuddle together.

Even now my cheeks heated as I remembered the way Ryan had woken me up three times last night until my body was absolutely spent. I hated that his team had nearly lost yet another game, but I wasn't complaining about being a distraction to lessen his stress.

Even now, when he threw the ball and his sweaty muscles glistened in the sun, I licked my lips, remembering the way he tasted. A second later Court got to him, but it was too late and the pass sailed neatly through the air. Linc caught it effortlessly and took off down the makeshift field toward the tree that served as the goalpost.

"That's game!" One of the guys from Ryan's team yelled, throwing his arms in the air at their victory.

I clapped along with the rest of the student body that had filtered out to watch the unofficial game. Unsurprisingly, the audience was mostly female, and as soon as the game stopped, they strutted onto the field.

"Yuck," Bex muttered next to me, her nose wrinkling. "It smells like pheromones and desperation."

I laughed, tipping my head back as the sun's rays warmed me.

"It's a shame Ryan isn't going pro," Bex remarked, pushing her sunglasses higher on her nose.

"He definitely has skills," I murmured, watching him barely acknowledge his fan base as it grew around him. His clear blue eyes found me, and he rolled them in annoyance.

An NFL scout had been at the game last night, but when I'd asked Ryan about it, he shut me down. Going pro wasn't an option; he was expected to step into his role as the heir to Cain Global. Beckett let him play football because Ryan was amazing at it, and it looked good for Beckett to have such a star for a son.

Ryan had admitted the one time he'd considered going pro, Beckett had casually mentioned something about sending Corinne away to boarding school.

He was such a manipulative asshole.

A shadow fell across us, and I looked up to see Charles standing over us. In a sleeveless shirt and gym shorts, he had clearly been out for a run.

"Hey," he greeted with a smile and that fabulous accent. "Maddie, right?"

"Yeah, hey." I grinned and gestured to the woman next to me. "This is my friend, Bex. Bex, this is Charles. The *fourth*."

"Hello," he said to her, nodding politely, but grimacing a little at the title.

Bex waved back and gave me a curious look. "You're the duke, right? You transferred in at the start of the semester?"

"Yes," he agreed warmly.

Her nose wrinkled as she shaded her eyes with her hand to peer up at him. "I bet that's fun."

He smiled ruefully. "Rather boring, actually. Mostly stuffy old men who haven't realized the monarchy is simply an antiquated institution that causes more harm than good."

I slowly blinked at him. "Tell us how you really feel."

Blushing a little, Charles rubbed the back of his neck sheepishly. "I suppose that was a bit forward of me, wasn't it." His eyes focused on me. "I was hoping I'd see you again."

"Here I am," I replied with a shrug.

He grinned adorably. "Yes, well, I've seen you around, but you've always been with some other bloke."

"My fiancé." I smiled at him, my lips automatically turning up at the thought of Ryan.

"Right. I suppose that means it's serious then?"

Holy shit, was this guy hitting on me?

My eyes snapped to Ryan... who was currently on his way over to us. And judging by the cold look he had fixed on Charles, this wasn't going to be the start of a new bromance.

I jumped to my feet, Bex joining me, as Ryan bore down on us.

"It is," I told Charles.

"All the good ones are taken," Charles mused with a soft laugh.

I laughed awkwardly with him, my eyes on Ryan as he came up behind Charles and then moved around him to pull me into his arms. The kiss he gave me was a total show of alpha-male dominance, and if it hadn't made my head spin, I might've been pissed off or embarrassed.

"Hey, baby," Ryan said, completely ignoring Charles as he rubbed his sweaty body against mine.

I shivered, recalling the last time his sweaty body had pressed against mine as he thrust into me.

I shook my head to clear the fog of hormones. "Um, Ryan, this is Charles."

"Nice to meet you, mate. I saw your game last night. Looked like you were going to lose it all in the last half, but that final score was bloody brilliant," Charles said with an easygoing smile as he held out a hand to Ryan.

Ryan glanced at the hand in disdain before taking it. "Thanks."

Then he turned his back on Charles, effectively cutting him out of our conversation as he faced me.

"Ryan!" I hissed, annoyed that he was acting so ridiculous.

He arched a brow at me.

"No, worries, Maddie," Charles said, but I could hear the strain in his tone. "I'll see you later."

Ryan's shoulders tensed and he barely glanced back over his shoulder as he muttered, "She's busy later."

I reached out and grabbed Ryan's wrist, squeezing it warningly.

"I think Maddie can speak for herself," Charles uttered, not bothering to hide his contempt. He looked at me over Ryan's shoulder between us. "If you ever need help—"

Ryan whirled with a snarl. "What the fuck would she need your help with?"

Charles was nearly as tall as Ryan but didn't have his bulk. He was all lean muscle where Ryan clearly spent a lot of hours in the gym. But Charles didn't back down. He straightened his spine and glared at Ryan.

"Simply offering my services to the lady," Charles ground out. "In my experience men who have a habit of forcing their women into submission are the most insecure out there."

"He's not forcing me into anything," I said quickly, coming around Ryan to push myself between them. "He's just protective."

Charles looked at me before his gaze cut back to Ryan. "What some women call protective, police might call abusive."

"Who the fuck do you think you are?" Ryan demanded, trying to move me out of the way. "Stay away from my fiancée."

"Or what?" Charles gave him an unimpressed look. "You don't scare me, Cain."

"Then that's your mistake," Ryan spat venomously, sending chills up my spine.

"Okay, can we all just settle down?" I asked evenly, my unease turning into full blown worry as I realized we had caught the attention of most of the people on the quad.

Ash, Court, and Linc had edged closer to us, and while I knew Ryan didn't need the backup, the four of them were a unit on campus. Mess with one, mess with all.

Charles looked at me. "Apologies, Maddie. I didn't mean to cause any issue. My offer stands, however. Should you need anything..."

"I'm good," I said swiftly before Ryan could interject on my behalf. "Thank you."

He nodded at me and turned, breaking in a light jog as he resumed his workout.

I spun around and glared at Ryan. "What the hell?"

He glared at me.

At *me*.

Like I was in the wrong here. I immediately bristled, ready for a fight.

"I could ask you the same question," he replied coolly.

I felt my eyes go wide with incredulity. "Please tell me you're joking."

Ash moved to Ryan's shoulder. "If you two are going to do this, take it somewhere private. People are watching."

"Let's go," Ryan told me, holding out a hand like I was a child he needed to guide along.

Fuming, I grabbed his hand, digging my nails into his flesh. I smirked when he grunted a little, but then snarled at him when he pulled me fast enough that I tripped on the grass.

He slowed a little, but not much, as he headed for my dorm, which was the closest one to the quad.

By the time we made the silent trek to my room, I was beyond furious. I unlocked the door and whirled around, ready to lay into him.

But Ryan, being freaking Ryan, had to go first.

He slammed the door and glared at me. "Are you fucking kidding me? Charles fucking Winthrope?"

"Are *you* kidding *me*?" I snapped. "He was saying hi and you went off like an asshole!"

"Oh, please," Ryan sneered bitterly. "He was fucking into you."

"So what?" I threw my hands in the air.

He made a face. "Oh, sorry. I didn't mean to interrupt you being fawned over by some pretentious prick."

"The only pretentious prick out there was you," I fired back. "And I don't give a shit about Charles."

"Then why were you talking to him?"

"Because he stopped and said hello? Is that a crime?" I demanded.

Ryan's eyes narrowed. "When it's my fiancée? Hell yes."

"Wow," I muttered, turning away from him to put space between us. "Are you seriously that possessive? I can't talk to a guy unless he's on your pre-approved friend list?"

A muscle in his jaw flexed with annoyance. "In case you've forgotten, you don't know how shit works around here. And he's definitely into you."

"Okay, first? Don't throw the fact that I'm not from your twisted world in my face," I snapped, holding up a finger. I ticked up another. "And second? It doesn't matter if he likes me or hates me, Ryan. I'm with *you*!"

"Then maybe act like it," he said frostily, folding his arms over his chest.

That made me pause.

"Are you being serious right now?" I asked softly, hurt and confused.

He simply shrugged his shoulders.

"The only reason I was out there was to be with you," I reminded him. "I planned on spending the day in my room, writing my ethics paper, but you wanted me to come along, so I did. Which I enjoyed very much... right up until the end."

He stared back at me in stony silence.

"You realize you sound exactly like what Charles said, right? Like an abusive boyfriend trying to gaslight me into thinking I did something wrong?"

His brow furrowed as his impassive facade cracked. "Maddie—"

I held up a hand. "No. My mom had a boyfriend who flew off the handle any time he caught her talking to another guy. Didn't matter if it was my teacher or a freaking bill collector. He went off every time that she was a tease. And when words weren't enough to make her change her behavior? Then he started hitting her."

Ryan paled a little. "I would *never* hurt you."

"What do you think you're doing now?" I kept my voice low and even. "You're acting like a possessive caveman because a guy talked to me. So fucking what? Did you see me losing my shit at all the girls who flocked around you after the game? Or last night's game? Or the ones who hover around the table in the cafeteria trying to get your attention every single night?"

He pressed his lips together, but wisely didn't say anything.

"Exactly. Because you asked me to trust you, and that's what I'm doing," I pointed out. "I told you that I *love* you. In what world does that mean I'm interested in other guys?"

He slowly walked to me and reached for my hands. "Maddie, I trust *you*. It's other guys that I don't trust."

I shrugged out of his touch and backed up. "I think you need to leave."

He frowned. "Madison, come on."

"No, you need to go, Ryan," I said, firming up my resolve. "We can talk later, but right now? Right now I need a break."

He swore under his breath and rubbed a hand over the back of his neck. "Mads, I'm sorry."

"And I appreciate that, but you still need to go," I insisted, looking pointedly at the door.

I loved Ryan, I truly did, but I wasn't going to just take his accusations and not react. I wasn't his doormat, and I could think for myself.

He sighed and dropped his head with a short nod. "Okay. We'll talk later."

"Fine," I mumbled, standing on the other side of the room until he left. Then I sat on the couch and let myself cry.

CHAPTER 52

"You guys have to talk," Bex told me later that evening after I avoided dinner. I hadn't been a total chicken; I'd sent Ryan a text saying Bex and I were eating in my room.

And then I turned off my phone.

It sat on the coffee table while Bex and I dug into the tacos that we had ordered. I drank the rest of my soda and sighed. "I know I have to talk to him."

"Then why are we hiding in your room?" she asked, popping a nacho into her mouth. "Not that I don't enjoy the change of scenery, but your engagement party is in less than a week."

"It's not real," I muttered, not sure if I was trying to convince Bex or myself.

She gave me a look, her dark hair falling over one eye. "Mads, we both know shit got real weeks ago with you two."

"He was out of line today," I said sharply, not ready to concede that point.

"Agreed," she replied quickly. "But..."

"But what?"

She pursed her lips. "But, in his defense, he's a guy who's used to getting what he wants, and he's not used to people challenging that. And he clearly wants *you*."

"He can want all he wants," I sniped. "But right now? He isn't getting it. And I'm not okay with how Ryan acted."

"Nor should you be," she told me wryly, "All I'm saying is to also weigh current events. Court told me their coach has been up Ryan's ass about the last two games. Most of his plays have been messed up or inter-whatevered."

"Intercepted," I corrected grumpily.

She rolled her eyes. "Yeah, that. Also? Ryan hasn't had a serious girlfriend because, in his entire life, there's been no shortage of women willing to undress at the snap of a finger."

Ugh, I didn't need that reminder. I *humph*ed unhappily.

"My point is," she went on, nudging my leg with her foot, "Ryan's not used to having to try or be accountable. He's figuring this whole relationship thing out. Add on top of that the stress with the team? I'm not saying he gets a pass for what he did, but I'm also saying you might want to give him the benefit of the doubt."

I drew my knees up to my chest and rested my chin atop them. "And if he does it again?"

"I'll help you cut his balls off," she said, completely straight-faced.

I started to laugh.

"I'm serious. We'll knock him out and castrate him," she added, this time with a small grin.

I leaned back against the couch as I dissolved into giggles. I didn't stop until someone knocked on the door. Sobering, I sat up and looked at Bex expectantly.

"Did we invite someone else?" I asked, starting to get up. I paused when I saw the guilty expression on her face. "What?"

"Court might have texted me that Ryan was on his way over," she admitted, holding up the phone she'd had in her lap most of the night.

"Traitor!" I hissed in mock-outrage.

Groaning, Bex nodded. "I know. I'm the worst." She wiped her hands on her jeans and quickly gathered our trash. "I'll throw this in the garbage chute on my way to my room."

"You could always stay and... mediate?" I offered weakly.

She shook her head. "You're on your own, Mads. But call me in the morning if you're up for it. Or tonight if things go bad."

"Thanks," I mumbled as she opened the door.

"Hey," Ryan greeted her, but his gaze was solely focused on me.

"You two play nice," Bex said seriously before walking past Ryan.

He came inside and closed the door but didn't move toward me. "So, now you're avoiding me?"

"Probably not my most mature decision," I conceded with a grimace. I sat down on the couch and pulled my legs up again.

"I guess we're pretty perfectly matched, since I definitely acted like a kid who got his favorite toy taken away earlier," he agreed, coming to join me. "Not that you're a toy, it's just an analogy."

A smile ghosted over my mouth. "Noted."

"I am sorry, Maddie," he said sincerely. "I got jealous, and I took it out on you. And that's not okay."

"I appreciate your apology," I replied. "But I'm not going to apologize for just talking to someone, Ry."

"I don't expect you to," he answered, steepling his fingers in front of his face. "I'm not going to pick your friends for you."

"I wouldn't even call us friends," I said a little helplessly as I was still struggling to make sense of his anger earlier. "We've talked twice, and you've gotten pissed both times. I mean, I get it at first because you thought I was Madelaine and I was messing with you."

He winced.

I stopped abruptly, my eyes narrowing as I looked at him closer. "Is that it? Do you think I'm like my sister?"

"No," he answered, but maybe it was a little too quick. His gaze skirted away from me for a second.

"Oh, my God," I whispered, my fingers covering my mouth. "You do."

"I know you aren't Madelaine," he said sharply. "I hated your sister, remember?"

"But you still think I'm like her," I concluded quietly.

"No," he replied earnestly. "But I'll admit it felt like something she would do, and I just reacted."

"Something she would do?" I echoed.

He frowned and licked his lips. "Okay, I guess it's time I told you the truth."

Anxiety rolled in like the tide. My body tensed, waiting to be dragged out with the waves. "Okay. Tell me."

"When our dads first told us about the engagement, I didn't *hate* the idea," he confessed, looking at the ground.

I sucked in a breath. "Seriously? But I thought—"

"No." He cut me off, shaking his head. His ice blue eyes met mine. "Did I know Madelaine was a spoiled brat? Absolutely. But I also was a little relieved that I wouldn't have to spend time trying to sort out if a woman wanted me or my bank account."

I winced a little. That would suck.

"And I genuinely wanted us to try and make things work," he added. "I tried dating her last year. We kept things casual, and honestly, it wasn't much. But then that thing with my coach happened... I mean, we never said we were exclusive, but when I found out exactly how far she was willing to go to hurt me? And I'm sure there were other guys."

I sighed, wanting to reach for him but also not wanting to exacerbate the situation by confirming what he suspected. I knew Lainey had also been sleeping with Dean. And she had been with Evan over the summer and alluded to the fact that they were fuck buddies before then.

Dredging up Lainey's twisted history might only hurt him more, so I kept quiet about that.

"I'm sorry she did that." I felt compelled to say it. Madelaine wasn't here to apologize for herself, but the words needed to be said.

"And I'm sorry I let my past with her cloud my present with you," he said gently, taking one of my hands in his. He linked our fingers. "I told you I would mess this up at some point."

I smiled weakly. "No one's perfect, Ryan, and I don't expect you to be."

He exhaled hard, puffing out his cheeks. "You'd be the only one."

"That's not true," I reminded him. "You have amazing friends who have your back, and you have me."

"Do I?" he asked quietly. "Do I have you?"

"Yes," I told him, squeezing his fingers. "Just because I got pissed at you doesn't change how I feel about you."

His gaze heated. "Say it."

My tongue darted out to wet my lips, his eyes dropping to track the movement.

"I love you," I breathed.

He smiled at me. A full blown, genuine smile with those dimples I adored. "I don't deserve you. But I love you, too."

Those three little words did more for my heart than all the money in the world could. I wasn't sure what happened next, if I reached for him or he grabbed for me, but then I was straddling Ryan's lap as I kissed him.

His fingers flexed around my hips as I ground down against him. I whimpered, my mouth falling open as his tongue swept inside and devoured me.

He sucked and licked while coaxing my tongue into submission, until my lips were simply reacting to the strength and power of his intoxicating kiss. One hand slipped under my shirt and past my ribs to palm my breast. Fingertips tweaked my nipple into a hard pebble inside the lace of my bra.

I pressed my aching center against him, needing more pressure to relieve the throbbing between my legs. It wasn't enough. I rolled my hips in jerky, frantic movements, cursing the layers of clothes between us.

With a laugh, Ryan stopped kissing me and halted my grinding by holding me still. "We have all night, Mads."

"Great," I murmured breathlessly, tossing my hair over my shoulder. "Then let's get started now." I reached down and pulled my shirt off over my head and tossed it to the far corner of the room.

Ryan's eyes lit up like a kid at Christmas as his hands came up to knead and pet my breasts a second before his lips lowered over one, sucking the tight bud into his mouth through the fabric.

My head fell back in wanton abandon as I let the sensations crash against me.

One hand came up and deftly unclasped my bra, pulling the scrap of lace away so his mouth could greedily suck my other nipple into his mouth. His other hand pinched my nipple lightly, tugging gently before he switched his mouth to that one.

My fingers tangled in his hair, my nails scraping his scalp as I rocked my hips against his.

His teeth nipped at the side of my breast as he kissed his way back to my mouth. When his lips found mine, he groaned at the contact and I felt that down to my toes.

My hands dropped between us, snaking under his shirt and tracing the ridges of abdominal muscles I found. My nails scratched across his chest, pushing up his shirt until he stopped kissing me long enough to rip it off.

His hand came up to cradle my jaw. "I fucked up tonight."

"But now you get to fuck me," I said smugly.

His eyes flared. "I plan to. But I think I owe you another apology."

Heat washed over me. "I love how you apologize," I admitted huskily.

"Since I messed up and I owe you, ladies' choice."

I arched a brow quizzically as he kissed under my jaw.

"I can make you come on my fingers," he kissed my shoulder, "my tongue," he kissed my other shoulder, "or my cock." He kissed the valley between my breasts.

I gasped, my mind quickly playing out the options. I knew my underwear was soaked, and Ryan's proposition was throwing my hormones into overload.

He chuckled. "Can't decide?" He tweaked my nipple.

I groaned softly, closing my eyes to brace against the spike of pleasure. "Cock," I managed.

His hand fisted in my hair, forcing my eyes open to look at him. "Say it again."

My lips fell open as my chest heaved. "I want your cock."

"Good girl," he murmured, his voice practically a purr that rippled through me. "If you want it, come and get it."

He released me so I could scramble off his lap. I reached for his jeans, working open the button and zipper to tug them down his powerful legs. He lifted his hips to help me, and I paused long enough to strip off his shoes and socks. He wasn't wearing any underwear.

"Confident in how tonight was going to go, huh?" I teased from my position between his legs. I braced my hands on his knees as his cock bobbed up to hit his abs.

He reached down and gave himself a firm stroke and something about that was dizzyingly erotic.

"I had a pretty good feeling," he admitted, his voice a deep rasp that warmed my skin.

"Cocky," I muttered, shaking my head.

He glanced down at his impressive length. "Obviously."

Narrowing my eyes, I leaned forward, licking him from root to tip before sucking him into my mouth and hollowing my cheeks.

"Fuck!" He shouted the curse, his hand landing on my head and pulling my hair back so he could see me swallowing him down.

I slipped my hand between us to toy with his balls as I took my time driving him crazy with my mouth. I gagged a little when he thrust too deep, but he retreated quickly. I relaxed only to have him repeat the motion.

"Too much?" he asked, his tone a dark thing that sent shivers skittering down my spine to curl my toes.

I shook my head, desperate to take as much of him as possible. Somehow what had begun as *my* blowjob turned into *him* fucking my mouth. He held my hair, and my head, firmly so he could use me as he wanted, and there was something decidedly dirty and almost decadent about being used for *his* pleasure.

"Enough," he finally panted, pulling my mouth off him and dragging me up his body to kiss. "Your mouth is too fucking amazing."

"Just my mouth?" I whispered against him.

His hand slid down my front and into my jeans. He cupped my pussy possessively, pulling me back by my hair to look in my eyes as he swirled a finger over my clit. My core clenched at nothing, desperate for him inside of me.

"Not just your mouth," he assured me with a wicked grin. He pulled his hand out of my pants only to undo them and jerk them over my hips. My panties went with them, and then he pressed a finger inside of me. "I'm pretty into this pussy, too."

I released a shaky breath as he added a second, then a third finger, thrusting them in and out of me. Occasionally he curled them, and I cried out, my body jerking every time.

Finally I pushed his hand away and moved myself over him before sinking onto his cock with a throaty groan as he filled and stretched me. I panted, catching my breath for a second as I adjusted to his invasion.

I rolled my hips experimentally, finding a grinding rhythm as his thumb slipped along the side of my clit. It took less than a minute before my orgasm slammed into me. I fell limply against Ryan's chest as he chuckled.

He gently gathered me up in his arms and stood. With a slow kiss, he lowered me to my feet and slipped out of me. I whined in protest until he turned me around. He pressed a hand between my shoulder blades, bending me over the arm of the couch.

I was still kind of loopy and sluggish from my climax, but everything came roaring back into focus when he slammed into me from behind. I splayed my hands flat on the cushion under me as he snaked a hand between us to play with my clit.

I whimpered as a second, more intense, climax built. I squirmed, trying to get away from a pleasure so bright that lights popped in my vision. Every place I tried to move was useless; Ryan held me steady by my hips as he pistoned in and out of me with low grunts.

I arched up to my tiptoes in a last-ditch effort to outrun the impending tornado of sensations as they ripped through me, my blood thrumming with electricity under my flesh as he kept going.

For a brief moment in time, I hovered on the edge of some impossible precipice, and then I was freefalling into oblivion with a hoarse cry as my body contracted and pulsed around him. Ryan shouted something unintelligible as he jerked inside of me.

His weight fell against my back as his chest heaved. I could feel the galloping of his pulse as he pressed against me.

"I hate fighting with you," I half-mumbled into the cushions. "But, God, this feels amazing."

He laughed and pulled me upright, turning me in his arms. "We have all night."

I smiled, knowing I probably looked a little drunk. "Sounds perfect."

CHAPTER 53

I smoothed my hands down the front of my dress as I stared into the mirror in Lainey's bedroom at home. The silver dress was even more spectacular with the right makeup and hair, courtesy of the team Gary hired to help me get ready for the evening.

The evening of my engagement party.

I glanced at the vanity in front of me and lifted Madelaine's engagement ring before sliding it onto my finger. I wished Bex was here to talk to, but she was getting ready for the party herself.

Everyone in Gary Cabot's orbit had been invited to the party where he would announce the engagement of his only daughter to his best friend's son.

Except I was the wrong daughter.

The sounds of the string quartet that was playing for the evening drifted up through the vents, providing a soothing background to my thoughts.

"Wow," I murmured, unable to tear my eyes away from the woman in the mirror.

My hair had been twisted up into an elaborate knot with softly curled tendrils framing my face. The sweetheart neckline of the gown left my neck exposed and elegant looking. My makeup was artfully applied; just the right amount of sparkle and a healthy pink glow on my cheeks that matched my lips.

I looked amazing.

And I looked like my sister.

This was a far cry from the girl in the trailer park.

With a pang of regret, I eyed my phone and contemplated trying to reach Mom again. We hadn't spoken in weeks now. Anytime I called, she was either in group sessions, solo sessions, or in a meditative session where speaking was forbidden. To make matters worse, Gary was *still* brushing me off about it.

A knock on my door had me turning. "Come in."

The door opened and Gary stepped inside, dressed in a formal tuxedo that made him look handsome.

He smiled softly at me. "You look beautiful, sweetheart."

"Thank you," I said. I glanced down at my dress. "I'm terrified I'll spill something on it tonight."

"If you do, you'll just have a... what is it you young ladies call it? A wardrobe change," he finished, snapping his fingers as the phrase clicked. Something flashed in his eyes. "But you won't disappoint me, will you?"

"No," I answered slowly.

He clasped his hands in front of him. "Wonderful. So, I'll make the announcement about the new merger with Shutterfield, and then Beckett and I will announce your engagement to Ryan with plans for an early summer wedding. Have you spoken with the wedding planner about finalizing the date at the venue?"

I tilted my head curiously. I knew he had hired a planner for Beckett's sake, but she hadn't actually contacted me. Then again, I didn't answer numbers I didn't know. "No."

Something like irritation crossed his face, but then disappeared just as fast. "Well, make sure you do. We can't have anyone stealing your big day."

"I thought this was all a ruse," I reminded him. "You said I wouldn't actually have to marry Ryan."

He blinked at me, his mouth flattening. "I thought you and Ryan were happy together."

"Yeah, I mean, we are, but..." Ryan and I had discussed getting married to save Corinne, but suddenly it felt like everything was moving super fast.

"But what?" His tone had a bit more bite than I had expected.

"I haven't heard from Mom in weeks," I said suddenly, watching him closely.

His face gave nothing away. "Have you tried calling her?"

"I told you that I have. That facility always says she's busy," I answered, letting frustration seep into my tone. "I was thinking maybe I could fly out and see her? I'm sure wherever she is allows family to visit."

Gary gave a heavy sigh, his shoulders slumping. "I'm sorry, but I directed the staff not to connect your calls to your mother."

Alarm bells started going off in my head. "Why the hell would you do that?"

"Your mother relapsed," he informed me quietly.

I gasped, staggering back a step.

"I didn't want to interrupt your studies or your new relationship—"

"You thought that me going out with Ryan meant I wouldn't want to know about my *mother*?" I cut him off angrily. "I've been asking you about her for weeks!"

His gaze hardened. "I wanted your focus where it needed to be."

"That wasn't your call to make!" I cried.

"I'm your father, and it was absolutely my call to make," he snapped, glaring at me. "Stop acting like a child."

My jaw dropped open. "I want to see my mom."

He tugged at the cuffs of his jacket. "Let's see how tonight goes and then we'll talk."

Everything in me went cold. "Are you telling me that if I don't go along with your plan that you'll, what? Not let me see her?"

He snorted and shook his head. "Honestly, I'm so over the theatrics, Lainey."

"Madison," I corrected softly, stunned by his slip.

He paused and stared at me. "What?"

My insides twisted anxiously. "My name is *Madison*. You called me Lainey."

"You know what I meant," he said dismissively, waving a hand as he checked his phone. "It would appear your fiancé is here. I need to speak with Beckett before guests begin arriving. You look amazing, my dear."

And then he was gone, and I was still reeling. I was still sifting through our conversation when Ryan appeared in the open doorway.

"Damn," he whispered, awe in his voice as he came inside and closed the door. His eyes raked over me, lingering at the way the corseted bodice hugged my figure. "You look gorgeous, Mads." His eyes narrowed shrewdly. "But not happy. What's wrong?"

I gave him a confused look. "I don't know."

"Are you okay?" He came to me, reaching for me like he was unable to be in the same room without touching me.

"I don't know," I repeated, still a little thunderstruck. "Gary said that my mom relapsed."

Ryan's brows slammed down in concern. "What? When?"

"I'm not sure. Weeks ago? I've been trying to reach her, and he had all of my calls fielded by the staff," I murmured, touching my lips absently. "Why would he do that?"

"Did he give you a reason?"

"He said so I wouldn't be distracted." I frowned. "But that makes no sense. He knows one of the biggest reasons I agreed to this was to help my mom."

Ryan stilled. "But that's not the *only* reason you're doing it, right?"

The note of vulnerability in his voice made me pause. "Of course not. I'm just saying it's weird because *he* doesn't know that. As far as Gary knows, I'm still playing by the terms I agreed to at the end of summer."

"Maddie." His hands spanned my waist as he looked in my eyes. "I promise that I'll help you figure out what's going on with your mom. Screw Gary. You and I can figure this out."

I laid my palms against his chest, wishing he wasn't covered up by a stiff white shirt and thick tux jacket. I wanted my hands on his bare skin where they belonged.

"You know, when you say that, I believe it," I told him, tilting my head back as relief sank into my bones. Ryan was right; he and I could handle anything together.

He grinned, dimples flashing. "Because it's true. I love you, Maddie. I'll do whatever it takes to make you happy."

I slipped my arms up and around his neck. With my heels, I was only a couple inches shorter. "*You* make me happy."

He kissed me softly. "I'm going to enjoy stripping this dress off of you tonight," he murmured against my lips. "But I definitely think I'll fuck you with the heels on."

I laughed and pulled away to make sure he hadn't smeared my lipstick. I swiped my thumb under my bottom lip, cleaning up the edge of my lipstick before I glanced at the clock.

"I guess we should go down. People should be here any minute," I said, making sure everything still looked perfectly in place before turning around.

My heart stopped at the sight of Ryan kneeling on one knee.

"What are you doing?" I whispered, stunned.

He smiled at me and pulled a small black velvet box from inside his jacket. He opened the box to reveal a stunning diamond solitaire. It was brilliantly blinding and beautiful in its simplicity. The stone was smaller than the one currently adorning my left hand, but it was perfect.

It was *me*.

"I think it's time we do this the right way, don't you?" Ryan started with a small smile. "Madison Porter, will you marry me?"

Tears made my vision blurry as I let out a wobbly breath. "Yes, Ryan Cain. I will marry you."

With a smile bright enough to rival the sun, he got up and pulled me into his arms. His lips found mine, and I stopped giving a shit about my makeup as I kissed him back in earnest.

"We need to stop," he said with a warning chuckle.

"Do we, though?" I challenged, trying to drag his mouth back to mine.

He pressed his hips against me and I could feel him starting to harden. "Yes, because I'm not walking down there and saying hi to a bunch of my dad's business associates with my dick trying to jailbreak my pants. Not all of us can discreetly hide our arousal between our legs in a pair of panties."

I gave him an odd look. "Who said I was wearing panties?"

He sucked in a sharp breath through his teeth. "Maddie."

"What?" I feigned innocence. "Does it look like this dress would let me wear any kind of undergarments?"

He groaned, his eyes squeezing shut. "You fight dirty."

"But you love it," I teased lightly.

His piercing blue eyes opened to take me in. "I love *you*."

"I love you, too," I told him softly before kissing him again.

Downstairs, the bell chimed to announce someone's arrival.

"I guess it's showtime," Ryan remarked. He lifted my hand and twisted off the old ring before sliding on the new one.

I admired it on my hand. "I love this."

"Good," he said, bending to kiss the side of my neck. "Let's just have fun tonight, okay? Enjoy our engagement party. Tomorrow we'll figure out what to do about your mom and everything else."

I smiled up at him, my heart feeling three sizes too big for my chest. "Deal."

CHAPTER 54

I wasn't aware facial muscles could get fatigued until I used them to smile for nearly thirty minutes straight.

Apparently a big part of this evening was standing beside my father as he received our guests for the party. I had a front row seat to his colleagues and associates as they kissed his ass and praised him for everything from his beautiful home to his beautiful daughter.

"Thank you," I said with as much sincerity as I could muster as another of his cronies shook my hand, his lecherous gaze lingering on my exposed cleavage.

He reminded me a lot of Uncle Adam, who thankfully was unable to attend the party due to some last-minute business issue that needed to be handled personally. Gary had informed me of his absence like he thought I would do anything less than celebrate.

Gary placed a hand at the small of my back as a new car pulled up to the curb. My smile turned genuine when I saw Bex exit the car after a couple who must be her parents.

They walked up the stairs as a unit, her father pausing to allow his wife and daughter to enter first.

"Hi, Mr. Cabot," Bex greeted softly, but then she turned to me and grinned before hugging me. "You look amazing."

"Thanks," I replied, hugging her back before taking in her red and gold gown. "You look stunning."

"Absolutely beautiful, Rebecca," Gary added. "I'm so glad you and Lainey have rekindled your friendship. I heard that you've been seen with Jasper Woods' son."

"Court?" Bex looked surprised he knew that. "Yeah, we're all friends."

Gary gave me a knowing smile before turning to Bex's parents. "Malcolm, Betty. Thank you for joining us."

Betty was an older but just as pretty version of Bex with long dark hair. She gave Gary a tight smile. "Of course. Thank you for inviting us." She turned her cool eyes, the same hazel as Bex's, to me. "Madelaine."

I almost flinched at the way she said my name. Disdain dripped in her tone, and she immediately moved past me.

Bex winced. "Yeah, Mom's not your biggest fan. Every time I came home crying about something *she* did, Mom would pick up the pieces. She's actually kind of pissed at me for being friends with you."

"Sorry," I murmured, thankful I was able to force a smile back onto my lips as Malcolm shook my hand and went to find his wife.

"Lainey," Gary began, "why don't you go and find Ryan? I'll see you in a bit."

Happy to be relieved of hostess duties, I grabbed Bex's hand and dragged her into the crowd of people, ducking between servers with trays of food I couldn't pronounce. I did snag a glass of champagne from one, giggling as Bex did the same, before we made it to a safe space practically under the stairs.

Bex looked around with a strange smile. "Lainey and I used to hide here when we were kids. We always wanted to see what was happening, and all the pretty dresses."

I glanced around the space. It was a good vantage point to watch people mingle. The foyer opened to a large dining area that had been cleared, with the makeshift stage erected for the band. A bar had been set up in the parlor room across from it, and guests roamed freely around the space.

I downed the champagne like a shot and set the flute on the sideboard table behind us.

"One of our nannies would always find us and drag us back to her room, though," Bex finished.

I felt like an absolute outsider as people talked and laughed together in all their fancy clothing. It was like I was a little girl playing dress up, and I was waiting for a nanny to come and shoo me away.

Bex's hand touched mine. "Are you nervous?"

"A little," I admitted, not entirely sure what to expect when Gary made his announcement. I wasn't a fan of people staring at me, but I had a feeling that's exactly what would happen.

I grimaced as Dean and Brylee walked by, arm in arm. "I can't believe they're here."

"Dean's dad is one of Beckett's attorneys, and Brylee's parents have known Gary since they were all at PC together." Bex shrugged apologetically. "It's one of the reasons Lainey and Brylee got along so well."

"Are you okay with this?" I asked Bex softly. I would grab one of the overly muscled security guards my dad had walking around to escort Dean's skeevy ass out if she wanted.

She turned to me with a genuine smile. "I am."

The crowd parted a little and I could see Ryan on the other side of the room, a tumbler of something in one hand as he smiled and chatted with an older couple, the man in a wheelchair. Without fail, his icy gaze found me and warmed. He lifted his chin, beckoning me forward.

"Go," Bex told me. "I see Court and Linc over there. I'll hang out with them."

I nodded and stepped back into the party, carefully threading my way through the crowd. I paused a few times as people stopped me to compliment my dress or ask about my father.

Ryan's face lit up as I finally made it to him. He wound an arm around my waist and tucked me against his side. "Maddie, I don't know if you remember my grandfather or not, Michael Harris?"

Of course I didn't, but I understood that meant he had met my sister before.

MAD WORLD

I smiled down at Ryan's grandfather, amused to see Ryan had gotten his pale blue eyes from his mother's side.

"Hello, Mr. Harris," I said politely.

Michael Harris was mostly skin and bones, but if you looked closely, you could see hints of the man he used to be. The strong jaw under the sagging skin, the fierce intelligence behind the bleary film over his eyes.

He stared up at me, and I wasn't sure if he remembered my sister or was genuinely confused about where he was.

"Miss Cabot," he said with enough frost in his tone that I knew that he definitely remembered Madelaine.

"Maddie, please," I corrected him, still maintaining my smile.

Ryan shot me a perplexed look. "I was just telling grandfather about how I proposed."

I glanced down at the ring on my finger and bit my lip. A curl of warmth spread in my belly and suffused out.

"Is that..." Michael's question gave way to a hacking cough. The woman behind him immediately produced a handkerchief.

My eyes widened when it came away with specks of blood. The woman gently wiped his mouth before straightening.

"Can I get you some water?" I inquired, wanting to help but not sure how I could.

The woman gave me a gentle smile as she shook her head.

"I'm Eloise," she said in a sweetly cultured French accent. She tucked the cloth away as if nothing had happened.

"Maddie," I replied instantly, offering my hand.

Michael caught my other hand with trembling fingers as he lifted the ring close to his eyes before turning to Ryan.

Ryan gave him a slow nod as something passed between them that I wasn't in the loop on.

"Is everything okay?" I asked hesitantly, wanting to snatch my hand back but afraid it would be rude.

Michael let me go. "Yes. Yes, everything is just fine, my dear." He gave me a thin smile before tilting his head toward Eloise. "Eloise? I believe I'm ready to retire."

"But you just got here," Ryan protested. "I was hoping—"

"Hush, my boy," Michael chided him. "I'm an old man with weeks left. I know what you wanted, and you have it."

I glanced at Ryan curiously as he stilled beside me. "Have what?"

Ryan's fingers dug into my side as he looked at his grandfather. "You're sure?"

Michael nodded and patted his grandson's hand. "I know what that ring means, and so do you. I trust your judgement, my boy. I'll have it sent to you in the morning. I wish you everything I had with my Clara." His eyes met mine. "Good night, Maddie. I hope we see each other again."

"Good night," I mumbled back, still confused as Eloise wheeled Michael away.

"What just happened?" I asked Ryan softly, turning toward him.

He swallowed, his throat working as he inhaled. "Your ring."

I couldn't help but look at it. "What about it?"

"It's glass," he said slowly. "The stone is glass."

I laughed a little. "You gave me an engagement ring made of glass?" I wasn't offended, just confused.

His cheeks puffed out as he looked around before meeting my gaze. "When my grandfather was young, his parents arranged for him to marry a girl. But by the time the wedding came around, my grandfather was already in love with one of the maids. When he told his father, he was given a choice."

My breath caught as I waited.

"Do what the family ordered or be disinherited. My grandfather chose the maid. My grandmother, Clara." He cleared his throat. "When they got married, he had nothing. All he could afford was a glass ring. When he made his fortune, several times over, he bought her a new ring, but she only ever wanted the glass one, so he had the glass taken out of the cheap silver band and put in a platinum setting. That ring."

His hand caught mine, lifting the glass to the light as my lips parted in surprise.

"There's another ring that goes with it. It's covered in diamonds, and this one sits inside of it, but my grandmother always wanted a visible reminder that he chose love over money. When she passed, she left me the ring."

My breath hitched and tears burned my eyes as I realized the significance of the ring his thumb stroked over. It was humbling that Ryan trusted me with it.

"My grandmother made me promise to marry someone I loved." A sad smile crossed his face. "I didn't think I'd be able to keep that promise... until you."

The lump of emotion in my throat was making it impossible for me to speak, let alone breathe. I tried to swallow around it. "Ryan."

His blue eyes met mine, clear and sure. "I can get you another ring if you want—"

I covered his mouth with my fingers. "No. It's perfect. I love it."

I had been so invested in what Ryan was saying, that I had missed the band silencing and our fathers taking the stage. People had gathered in the room where they were to hear Gary tell them all about the newly arranged deal with Shutterfield.

A scattered applause broke out.

"But no business merger can compare to the news Beckett and I have truly brought you here to share," Gary boomed, his voice carrying above the crowd. "Where is my girl? Madelaine?"

Eyes turned toward me, and I considered ducking behind Ryan.

"Here we go," he muttered, using the hand on the small of my back to guide me forward to the stage.

I slowly marched up to the dais, trying not to blush.

Gary made a show of coming over to kiss my cheeks. "I'm proud of you, sweetheart."

I smiled back, not sure how to respond. Thankfully, I didn't have to. He stepped back and grinned at Beckett before turning his megawatt smile to the audience.

"Tonight, Beckett and I couldn't be more thrilled than to announce the union of our families, as Ryan has asked Madelaine to marry him!"

The announcement set off a flurry of gasps and whispers. I was wondering if people were genuinely surprised or acting, since the ring

I'd been wearing for weeks wasn't exactly low-key and these people gossiped like they never left middle school.

Another round of applause roared through the room as I felt Ryan kiss my temple before reaching over to shake Gary's hand. Beckett came over to squeeze my hand and flash Ryan a loaded glance before grinning at their audience.

A soft buzz buffered the dying applause, and then a few chirps and dings as phones went off. I heard Ryan's phone vibrate in his pocket as people started to pull them out, probably worried a stock had crashed or something.

It wasn't until several loud gasps rang out in the sudden silence that I felt an inkling of something being very wrong.

"What's going on?" I murmured to Ryan, but he looked just as confused as I was.

I found Bex in the crowd, and knew when her stricken gaze met mine that I wasn't going to like whatever came next.

Beckett pulled his phone from his pocket as Gary glared at him, annoyed he would do something so rude as looking at his cellphone during their big moment. But Beckett's face blanched, and then his accusing eyes snapped to me and narrowed.

I took an instinctive step back.

"Holy shit," someone in the crowd whispered.

"Is that..."

"It's *her*."

Frowning, Ryan pulled out his phone, where a message from an unknown sender waited. He tapped it open... and a video started rolling.

It was hard to make out the occupants at first, but the breathy moans gave away exactly what was happening in that room, on that bed.

I narrowed my eyes.

Wait, I *knew* that room.

The woman tossed her long mane of blonde hair back as she rode the man under her.

"Fuck, yes, Dean. Just like that," she moaned like a pornstar as she peeled her sweater off her head. When she shook out her hair again, bringing the man's hands up to squeeze her breasts, her head tipped back again for the camera.

It was *my* face.

I watched in horror as a girl with my face and body rode Dean like he was a fucking prize stallion at the Triple Crown.

Madelaine. Madelaine really had been sleeping with Dean, and the proof had been sent to every phone at the party. Maybe in the world, for all I knew.

It was too much of a train wreck to stop watching.

She finished with a heady moan that sounded way too much like me, and then she sagged onto Dean's chest.

"Tell me again," Dean demanded, fisting her hair in his hand and wrenching her neck back. "I want to hear it one more time from your sexy mouth."

Madelaine giggled in response. "Ryan is such a fucking pussy. I'm so glad I have a real man like you."

Disgusted, I flinched away from the screen and looked at Ryan. But he wasn't watching the screen. He was watching *me* and the look of pain was quickly eclipsed by something darker as he gaped at me.

And that was how my world exploded.

CHAPTER 55

"Are you *fucking* kidding me?" Ryan seethed, jerking away so that my body wasn't touching any single part of him.

Surprise lit through me. Wait, he didn't actually think that was *me*, did he?

"Ryan—"

"Shut up," he hissed. "Just shut the fuck up."

Okay, now *I* was pissed. What the hell? He wasn't even going to give me a chance to explain? What happened to all his promises of love and us figuring stuff out together?

With a grimace, he took my hand and pulled me down off the stage. I didn't have to look back to know our fathers were following. We were pushing through the crowd to the back of the room, when Dean stepped in front of us.

Ryan pulled up short.

Dean flashed Ryan a pitying smile. "Sorry, man. I didn't want you to find out like this."

Ryan glared from Dean to me and back.

"You're a *liar*," I snapped, my cheeks on fire as people around us watched and whispered.

"Am I?" Dean gave me a pained look. "Lainey, let's just be open about everything, okay? I feel bad enough that we've been betraying my brother. I can't do this anymore."

"Ryan, you *have* to listen to me," I insisted quietly, squeezing his hand.

I may as well have been holding a brick in my hand for all the warmth and support he gave back.

"It's true, man." Josh materialized from behind Dean with a grim face. "I saw her going into Dean's room the night you were coming home. She came to the house early to be with him."

My jaw dropped open.

"You were wearing that sweater when I found you," Ryan mused woodenly, his jaw clenched so hard I was afraid it would shatter.

"Because Dean *gave* it to me!" Shit, that didn't sound good when I heard it out loud.

Ryan's eyes drifted closed.

"Ryan." I could feel the distance between us growing, stretching like a rubber band being pulled close to its snapping point.

"If you'll excuse us," Ryan said with rigid formality, "I need to speak with Madelaine."

"Aw, hell," Dean muttered, looking genuinely pained. "There's something else, Ry."

Ryan froze, waiting.

I was trapped in some sick car wreck I couldn't get away from.

Dean reached into his pocket and handed Ryan a notebook.

All the color leached from Ryan's face as he took it with a shaking hand. "Where did you get this?"

I stared in horror at Ryan's *playbook*. The team's playbook. The reason he had lost his away game and nearly lost the other game last week. The reason his coaches were furious and his team was stressed out.

"Lainey took it," Dean answered with a shrug. "She thought it would be fun to feed your plays to the other teams. It's how it almost cost you a game. Shit, almost two, right? She told me about it that night. I kind of feel like a jerk for letting her do it, but when she said she wanted to see your ass knocked down a few pegs... Well, I couldn't help myself. She left the book in my room.

"Truth be told," he added with a disgustingly smug glint in his eyes, as he leaned in with a loud stage-whisper, "I can't believe you used the same trick to mess with him again, Laine. I'm not sure if you're losing your imagination or if Ryan's too blinded by your pussy to see the truth. Though, it is a sweet pussy, so I'll give him that."

Ryan let me go like I was made of fire, and I might have been for as much as my chest blazed with burning agony.

I turned to Dean, my hand balling into a fist as I realized what he was doing. What he had *done*. "You asshole."

He gave me a withering look, his cold eyes dead and flat. "I don't like Ryan either, Lainey, but someone's going to get hurt if you keep playing these sick games."

I lunged forward, but a hand clamped painfully on my wrist as Gary started pulling me toward the back part of the house where the kitchen was. We stormed past the surprised catering staff, up the rear staircase, and down the hall to my room.

He shoved my door open and pushed me inside.

I had been too stunned to fight back, my mind still reeling from the video and the depth of Dean's deception, but now I was furious. My arm ached from how hard he'd held me, and I rubbed it as I turned on him.

Ryan and Beckett stepped into the room, matching expressions of fury on their faces, before the door closed all four of us into my room.

"What the fuck was that?" Beckett roared, storming toward me.

I scrambled out of the way, my gaze instinctively going to Ryan for support or protection or *anything*, but he seemed completely out of fucks to give. He folded his arms over his chest and watched his father back me into a corner of the room.

"Do you have any idea what you've done, you stupid little slut?" Spittle droplets hit my face as Beckett screamed at me, his face a dangerous shade of ruddy purple as a vein in his forehead throbbed.

"It wasn't *me*," I insisted desperately, looking from Gary to Ryan. They had to know what that meant even if Beckett didn't.

Beckett scoffed in derision, but it was Ryan who spoke up.

"Give us a minute," he said in a flat tone.

Beckett glanced over his shoulder at his son.

"Give us the fucking room," Ryan ordered darkly.

Surprisingly, Gary and Beckett did just that. They stalked out into the hallway and slammed the door.

I gasped as the gravity of what was going on started to settle. "Ryan, you have to listen to me. That wasn't me, it was Madelaine."

"Was it?" he asked stoically, icy cold in his eyes. "The timestamp on the video is from two weeks ago. The night I came home from the game."

"Then you know it wasn't me!" I cried. "I was in *your bed* when you came home."

"Wearing the same fucking sweater in *my bed* that you wore in Dean's," he hissed.

"No..." I whispered, my mind spinning back in time. "Dean *gave* me that sweater that night. He said I left it in his room, but—"

He cut me off with a sardonic chuckle. "So, he gave you back the sweater you left in his room."

"No, *Madelaine* left it in his room!" I exclaimed.

"And you conveniently got your period so I wouldn't sleep with you right after you'd fucked him?" He sneered at me, disgusted. "I guess I should thank you for not letting me shove me dick where his had just been."

"Ryan!" I was too stunned to do more than gape at him, my heart breaking at the hate in his tone.

"Do you think I'm fucking stupid?"

My spine welded to steel as I glared at him. "Honestly? Yes, if you can't see the truth in front of you."

"Oh, I see the truth in front of me," he murmured, stepping closer. "I see that you're even more manipulative than Madelaine was. You really had me fucking going. I actually bought into all the shit you were selling."

I sucked in a deep breath.

"And the playbook? Did Madelaine steal that, too?" He gave a scornful laugh. "Except she *couldn't* have. That's this year's book. So how the fuck did Dean get it?"

"Maybe he broke in?" I suggested wildly.

"You don't think I would've noticed if the lock was fucked with?"

Oh, shit.

"I left the door unlocked," I whispered, the truth crashing over me with dizzying clarity. "It was only for a minute. I forgot to lock it when Bex came to get me, but I ran back inside and—"

"Just fucking stop, Maddie!" He roared.

I shook my head as I stared in open horror at him. I could feel my heart shredding into a mangled wreck in my chest.

"So, this is it? One video and you're done? You don't believe me?" I snorted as I blinked back tears. "Great, Ryan."

He stared at me with so much contempt that it was hard to remember the way he'd loved me for the last several weeks. This was like before when he didn't know who I was.

No, this was *worse*.

He might have hated Madelaine, but he'd never loved her. The betrayal in his eyes made everything so much worse, cut so much deeper.

He was in pain and lashing out, looking to cause maximum damage. And I had let him into my heart, so he had all he needed to destroy me now.

And he would use that information mercilessly.

"Did Josh really see you go into Dean's room that night?"

I clenched my teeth. "Yes—"

"Were you wearing the same sweater in the video and in my bed?"

My hands started to tremble. "Yes, but—"

"I'm fucking *done*," he cut me off cruelly. "We're *done*."

I felt his words like a physical blow and squeezed my eyes shut against the pain that blasted through my chest. When I looked up, I saw him walking for the door.

"If you leave, then *I'm* done," I said woodenly.

Ryan paused and glanced back at me with narrowed eyes.

"I mean it," I added, gathering what was left of my pride. "If you leave, you've lost me for good. I forgave you for the way you treated me when I got here, I agreed to help you with Corinne and your dad. I told you I *love you* because I meant it. You were my first, Ryan. You know that."

He lifted a callous brow. "I didn't see you bleed, so maybe you're just as good of an actress as your sister."

Humiliated tears spilled over my cheeks. "You bastard," I whispered. "Newsflash, asshole—not all virgins bleed."

"Noted. I'll keep that in mind for the next virgin I fuck," he remarked dryly. "Can I go?"

"I'm serious, Ryan. If you leave like this, then everything we had is done."

"It was done the minute you climbed into Dean's bed and sold me out," he spat venomously.

I yanked his ring off my finger and tossed it at him. Only his quick reflexes saved it from hitting the floor.

"Get the hell out," I told him.

There was a moment of hesitance in his eyes. I saw it. The conflict where he was doubting himself for just a heartbeat.

And then it was gone. He jerked the door open to reveal our fathers, still looking just as pissed.

Beckett looked at Gary. "I'm enacting the morality clause of our agreement, Gary."

Gary flinched. "I expected as much."

"Expected *what*?" I demanded, sick to death of being in the dark.

No one spared me a second look.

"Let's go," Ryan told his father flatly, brushing past him and walking away.

I leaned against the wall as my legs threatened to give out. This couldn't be happening. How had we been standing in this room hours ago, totally in love and in sync, and now it was just *over*?

I swallowed a sob as Gary walked back into the room and closed the door.

Heavy silence hovered between us like a toxic cloud, thick and cloying and suffocating.

"I can't believe you did this," he finally said.

"I *didn't*," I insisted. "That wasn't *me* on that video!"

He sneered at me. "You're just as much of a slut as your sister and your mother. I don't know why I'm surprised."

God, that hurt more than it should have.

"After everything I've done for you," he railed. "I gave you everything you wanted. Every chance. And then you went and fucked me over. Do you know what your indiscretion just cost?"

"Does it look like I care?" I gritted out, over Gary and over this world. I would take a gang war in the streets over this.

His blazing eyes fixed on me. "Oh, you'll care, because that morality clause Beckett just invoked cost me ten million dollars."

I threw my hands up. "I don't know what the hell you're even talking about!"

"When your sister fucked around on Ryan, Beckett had that clause added to our agreement to prevent another scandal. I never expected you to behave as your sister did." He rubbed his jaw. "And in front of all my fucking friends? Do you realize what you've done to my business?"

I stared at him. "That sounds like *your* problem. Not mine. Not anymore."

"Excuse me?" he hissed.

"I'm leaving. I'm going back home. Kick Mom out of the treatment center. Do whatever. I'll work my ass off to pay you back, but I'm done playing in your sick world." Hopefully Bex was still here and she would give me a ride to the airport or a bus station.

I went to storm past him, but he caught my arm in a death grip. I cried out at the pain as it shot down my arm.

"Let *go*," I demanded, trying to jerk free.

"Selfish brat," he boomed. His hand lifted and cracked across my face.

I fell down, fire licking under my skin as it swelled from where he'd struck me. I looked up at him, at his maniacal eyes and heaving chest, and did the only thing left.

I ran.

I made it into the hallway, but he caught up with me easily. Stupidly, I realized I could still hear the music playing downstairs as the party apparently went on without us.

"You stupid *bitch*!"

His voice cracked through the empty hallway as I scrambled back several steps, as if I could actually outrun his fury.

I had seen him angry, but never directed at me. And never this out of control. His rage was its own entity as it swallowed up the air in the space and pressed around me from every side.

Terror dried my mouth to ashes, and I struggled to form words to calm him down.

"Just... take it easy, okay? We can talk about this." I held up my hands between us, but he lunged forward and grabbed me, hauling me toward his powerful body.

He wrenched my wrist to the side, and I cried out at the sharp sting of pain that blasted up my arm. My eyes flooded with tears, but I wasn't sure if it was from fear, frustration, or physical agony.

"I'm done talking."

I tried to pull away, but that only made him angrier. The haze of rage in his eyes was chilling.

"I can expl—"

He cut my words off with a backhanded slap that sent me stumbling into the side table and knocking it to the ground. Glass shattered as a picture fell.

A picture of *us*. Or, more accurately, what should have been us.

I raised a hand to my jaw, feeling the pulse of blood as it swelled and throbbed.

Fuck.

Someone had hit me before, but never with that much power or strength.

Maybe because I had never been hit by someone who truly *hated* me. Hated me in a way that I hadn't seen until it was too late.

Way too late.

I had made a mistake. A horrible mistake.

Believing him was going to cost me everything. The same way it had cost my twin.

I closed my eyes as the next punch he threw sailed toward my face.

Pain exploded in a riot of white pops of light behind my eyes as my legs gave out and I fell to the floor.

See you soon, Madelaine, my brain whispered as I surrendered to the dark.

∽

A SOFT HAND touched my shoulder, gently shaking me back to consciousness.

"Maddie? Maddie, wake up," Bex begged softly.

I groaned, my face on fire as I tried to open my eyes. My pulse pounded in my temples as I came to. I was still in the hallway, but Gary was gone. Only Bex was here now.

And that music was still fucking playing.

"Jesus, Maddie," Bex whispered, "I should get my mom. I think you need a doctor."

"No," I managed. "No. I need to leave."

"But—"

"No." I started to push myself up into a sitting position. "Where's Ryan?"

It was a reflex to ask for him. If I was hurting, I wanted the one who made the hurt go away.

Except this time? He'd caused the worst of the hurt.

The bruises Gary had left on my face were nothing compared to the way Ryan had eviscerated my heart.

She bit her lower lip. "He left with Beckett. When Gary came back down, I came looking for you to see if you were okay."

At least I still had one person I could count on.

"Should I call the police?" Bex asked.

I shook my head, instantly regretting it when black spots formed in my vision. "No. I just need to go. I need to get out of here."

"Okay," she agreed, helping me stand up.

I braced a hand on the wall as a wave of dizziness rocked me.

"You can come to my house," she offered.

"No, I'm going home," I said firmly.

Her gray eyes widened. "Are you sure?"

"Yeah." It was the only play I had left. I would get back to Michigan. Marge would probably let me crash on her couch until I figured things out.

"I get it," she mumbled, looking hurt.

"I'm sorry, Bex. I can't stay here. It wasn't me in that video," I insisted.

She blinked at me, her face open and guileless. "I know. You would *never* do that, and with Dean of all people?"

"The video has to be of Madelaine and him. He set me up," I realized, thinking of how he'd gotten me into his room and given me *that* sweater. Hell, he'd probably even arranged to have Josh see me leaving his bedroom.

"I figured," Bex admitted.

"But the video was timestamped," I mused.

Bex shrugged. "It's easy to fabricate, Mads. I bet Ash could figure it out."

I gave her an incredulous look. "You really think any of Ryan's friends will help me now?"

"Court and Linc were pissed," she confessed softly, "but Ash didn't say anything. They all left after Ryan."

A shadow flickered over her eyes.

"What?" I pressed.

"It's nothing." She shrugged and looked away.

I leaned against the wall. "Bex, please, just tell me."

"How did Dean get Ryan's playbook, Maddie? That only would have been in Ryan's room and everyone knows he always keeps it locked," she pointed out softly, a thin tendril of doubt creeping into her tone.

I closed my eyes, a wave of regret rolling through me. "Remember when I left the door unlocked, the morning we went to breakfast?"

"But you went back in and locked it," she exclaimed.

"Yeah, but Dean was in the hall when I left to meet you. He could have easily walked into Ryan's room and grabbed the book." I was an idiot. A total idiot.

"The team lost their game after that."

"And almost lost another," I finished with an almost detached whisper. I hadn't given the playbook to Dean, but I had sure as hell given him access to it.

"This still isn't your fault," Bex told me fiercely, grabbing my hand and squeezing. "Dean did this. Ryan and the guys are assholes for believing him. Giant assholes."

She must have read the question in my eyes.

"Linc told me I was an idiot when I said I was going to talk to you." She wrapped her arms around her thin frame, hugging herself. Tears sparkled in her eyes. "Court wouldn't even look at me."

"I'm sorry," I whispered.

She sniffled. "Screw them, right?"

"Yeah," I agreed, knowing neither of us really meant it.

"If you're leaving, you should do it now. While Gary's still downstairs trying to smooth things over with people," she told me.

I nodded resolutely. "Okay. I just need to change."

I went back into my room—

Fuck that.

This was *Madelaine's* room.

I yanked open the first drawer I found and pulled out a pair of yoga pants and a t-shirt. Bex helped me out of my dress, and I glared at the beautiful gown as it pooled into a sparkly puddle of fabric.

I kicked it aside with a growl before jerking on my clothes and then turning to the mirror to see what a mess my face was.

My makeup was trashed, and the left half of my face was seriously swollen. I'd also gotten a good view of the bruises Gary had left on my arm as he dragged me around.

I considered using makeup to try and cover some of the bruises but decided I didn't care. I gently removed what was left of my makeup. When I glanced down at the vanity, Madelaine's engagement ring reflected back at me.

I picked it up and tossed it in the garbage can.

"Let's go," I told Bex. I didn't bother grabbing anything except my purse. My box of belongings I'd brought from Michigan was back at Pacific Cross; maybe I could get Bex to mail them to me.

But I wasn't taking a single thing from Madelaine's life with me.

"We'll go down the back stairs and leave through the kitchen," Bex said quietly as she opened the door. "The only people in there will be the caterers. But, shit. I came here with my parents' driver. I don't know if he'll take us without them."

"Gary has a fleet of cars in his garage," I muttered, following her into the hallway. "We'll take one of those."

"Steal it?" she hissed.

"Borrow," I clarified. "You'll bring it back after you drop me off at the bus station."

"Airport would be faster," she told me as we came to the stairs.

I shook my head. "I have enough cash for a bus ticket. I'd have to use a credit card to get on a plane. I don't want to owe Gary any more than I already do."

"I can give you the money," she offered.

"You're an amazing friend, Bex. Madelaine didn't deserve you," I murmured as we stepped into the kitchen.

It was still busy enough that no one noticed us leaving out the back door. We walked along through the pool area until we came around the garage. I opened the side door and flicked on the lights to illuminate Gary's fleet of expensive cars.

"Pick your poison," I told Bex.

"The SUV," she said, pointing to the giant black monstrosity at the end. "I'm not trying to drive a sports car in this dress with these heels."

I grabbed the keys and tossed them to her. The garage was on the far side of the property, set away from the house, so we easily got inside and left through the open front gates.

"You're going to have to look up the bus station," Bex told me as she drove. "I'm not sure where it is."

I took the phone out of my purse to search for the location, and paused when I saw Madelaine's encrypted app.

I sighed. "Can we make a stop first?"

She glanced at me. "Okay."

I tapped in a new address. The route took less than fifteen minutes, and thankfully, the gates were open when we arrived.

"This is creepy," Bex muttered, looking around at the gravestones while we drove through the cemetery.

"There," I said suddenly, pointing when I spotted the mausoleum.

Bex pulled the car to a stop, and I unbuckled my seat belt. "I just need a minute."

She nodded. "No problem."

I got out of the car and headed for the crypt. The yellow light cast an eerie pall around the door as I punched in the code I had seen Gary use to unlock it. The code was my birthday. Madelaine's birthday.

I had thought it was sweet, but now I realized it was just a convenient set of numbers to him. It was the day his cash cow was born.

When I stepped inside, motion-activated lights flickered on. I slowly walked to the end where Madelaine was.

It was time to say goodbye and close this part of my life.

My sister had been far from perfect, but tonight had given me a glimpse into more of her world. A world full of terrible secrets and loathsome monsters. A world where she was simply a commodity to be traded around.

I couldn't blame her for wanting out.

In the end, we'd both run from this world, but only one of us had lived to tell the story.

With a heavy sigh, I paused in front of her tomb.

"I'm sorry, Lainey," I whispered, laying my hand on the cool marble front. "I'm so sorry for everything that happened to you, and I'm sorry I couldn't make it right. I hope you're at peace."

I turned to go and froze when I saw that the tile beside her compartment had been put in. The generic **M. Cabot** was gone, replaced by the formal one to match all the others.

My heart pounded in my chest as I traced the engraved letters. Horror curled in my belly as I tried to make sense of what I was seeing.

MADISON PORTER-CABOT

"No," I whispered, my hand coming up to cover my lips. Underneath it was my birthday and the day Madelaine had died in the fire.

But that was *my* name.

I jerked around as Bex honked the horn several times. I stumbled forward as I hurried out of the crypt... and right into two men who grabbed me from either side.

"Maddie!" Bex yelled, but I could see she'd been pulled from the car by another man.

"Let me go!" I demanded, fighting as hard as I could. "Bex!"

I lost sight of her as I was pushed into the back of a car. Both men got in with me, bracketing me on either side, and a third drove the car into the night.

CHAPTER 56

The men pushed me into the now-empty foyer of Gary's home. The sound of the door slamming open echoed in the vacant space.

I fell to my hands and knees, my bones jarring as I landed in a heap on the marble floor. My teeth clacked together, and I sucked in a deep breath to ready myself for whatever was going to happen next.

I lifted my head and looked around, surprised to see the house had been put back together as if the party had never happened.

Gary's shoes clicked against the floor as he walked slowly to me, his mouth set in a grim line.

"Thank you, gentlemen," he told the goons who had dragged me back as he came to a stop less than a foot from where I was sprawled.

They nodded at him and stepped back but didn't go far. One closed the front door, but then they simply waited for their boss' orders.

I pushed myself up. "Where the hell is Bex?"

Gary swirled the drink in his hand. "With her parents, of course. Don't worry—I assured them I won't press charges for her stealing my car."

"She didn't steal it, asshole," I hissed. "I told you, I'm done and I'm leaving. You can't keep me here."

"Can't I?" He challenged me curiously, like this was a game.

I shook my head. "I saw the tomb. You can't do this."

"I've already done this," he informed me coolly. "Now it's time to renegotiate our arrangement."

"Fuck you," I seethed. "I'm not negotiating shit. I'm leaving. If you want to take me to court for whatever money Mom's rehab cost or whatever money I spent, go for it. I'll work the rest of my *life* to get out from under you."

He snorted in amusement. "I can't exactly sue a dead girl."

"I'm not dead."

"I beg to differ," he said softly, calculatingly. "I have the death certificate to prove it in the safe." All of his fury had melted into what seemed like indifference now. Like we were discussing the weather.

"You're insane," I told him flatly, my gaze darting around the room as I looked for an escape.

"Can we stop with the theatrics?" Gary gave me a long-suffering look. "I'd rather not have to tie you down for this conversation."

I clenched my jaw, my insides trembling with fear. I tried not to show it, but I'm sure he could see it in my eyes.

"Madison is dead," he said flatly.

I flinched at his tone but kept quiet.

"I realize now that I was too lenient with you," he added. "I apologize for that."

"Just for that?" I couldn't help but ask as I felt my face still throbbing.

His lips twitched. "Are you finished interrupting?"

My hands balled into fists at my sides.

"Good girl," he said patronizingly. "As I said, I was too lenient. I thought you would eventually step in and fulfill your duties as your sister obviously couldn't. I was even a little bit proud when you got Ryan to fall in love with you."

He chuckled darkly. "I hate paying Beckett that ten million dollars, but it was worth it to see his son break. But it can't happen again. The wedding will happen this June, regardless."

"Ryan hates me," I reminded him coldly. "He won't marry me."

"He will if he wants to save his sister," Gary replied, smirking.

I stared at him in horror.

"Oh, you think I didn't know about Beckett's plans for Corinne if Ryan doesn't play by the rules?" The mocking glint in his eyes burned through me.

"What the fuck is wrong with you?" I cried, rage cresting like a tidal wave in me and nearly spilling as tears threatened.

He frowned. "Nothing. It's just business. Which is why I'm making this deal with you."

"Pass," I shot back.

"But you haven't even heard my terms." He *tsk*ed and wagged an annoyed finger at me. "It's quite simple: You continue living as Madelaine. I realize now you had too much free rein, so we're going to cut that back. When you go back to school, you will attend classes and meals and whatever functions Ryan deems necessary, but you are confined to your room beyond that."

"So, I'm a prisoner?" I snarled, wondering what his henchmen would do if I walked over and punched his arrogant face.

He shrugged. "See it how you like. I'm also not a fan of the way you've looked recently, so I'll put you on the same food regimen Madelaine had. All meals will be prepared for you by staff either here or at school. Hopefully you'll shed the weight before the wedding."

He snapped his fingers. "Which brings me to the wedding—the planner I hired will handle everything. You'll simply have to show up, say your vows, and spread your legs the night of the wedding to consummate it. Although, after tonight's video, it doesn't seem like that particular part should be a problem for you."

My mouth dropped open. "No. Not fucking happening."

"But I haven't told you what you'll get if you agree," Gary said with an amused smile. He snapped his fingers once more, and one of the men who had brought me in peeled away and headed up the stairs.

"There's nothing you can give me to make me agree to this shit," I told him. "You're out of your mind."

He simply kept smiling until a soft moan dragged my attention to the top of the stairs.

MAD WORLD

I looked up in confusion... and my heart sank like a rock. "Mom?"

The man who had gone upstairs was holding her up as her head lolled to the side, a hazy smile on her face as she swayed.

She was high. I knew that look.

My gaze snapped to Gary. "*What did you do?*"

He shrugged indifferently. "See something you want?"

I could only stare in horror as she was dragged back deeper into the house.

"I'll keep your mother alive and happily blitzed out of her fucking brain in exchange for you doing what I say," Gary told me with a smug smile. "But another disaster like tonight? And your mother will be found in an alley with a needle in her arm."

My vision blurred as I struggled to breathe.

"I'm sure the police will assume she lost whatever will she had to live when her daughter died," he concluded, hammering the last nail into my coffin.

I closed my eyes and felt the tears fall. I hated crying in front of this monster, but I was truly alone now. I had no one left.

Gary's shoes clicked as he came closer. "Now, go upstairs. I'll let the school know you won't be returning this week. That should give you time to heal and accept your circumstances."

I opened my eyes. "I hate you." I put all my pain, fear, and rage into those three words, feeling them vibrate in my bones with truth.

He smiled, openly mocking me. "I don't care. Do you plan to walk upstairs by yourself? Or shall I have my men assist you?"

Sucking in a ragged breath, I turned and went up the stairs, going down the hallway to my room. When I got to my door, the man who had held up my mother waited. Once I went inside, he locked the door behind me.

I sank to the floor, my back pressed against the door, and drew my knees up to my chest. I looked around the room. This room that I had fallen in love with. The beautiful furniture, the space, the buttery soft sheets. At some point, I had started to think of Madelaine's room as my own.

Ryan had asked me to marry him in here, and I had agreed. How could I have fallen so far, so fast?

I wondered if Madelaine had once done the same thing. If she had once sat in this very spot and tried to figure out when it had all gone wrong. When she realized this room was her prison, and everything was a lie.

My sister had been born into her cage. She'd never had a chance. But I had built the walls of my own cell.

And I would tear them down with my bare hands until I was free.

COMING WINTER 2022

The Blackwater Pack series will continue with Addie & Nikolai's story, SCARS, will be out in Winter 2022. You can pre-order it now on Amazon: SCARS by Hannah McBride

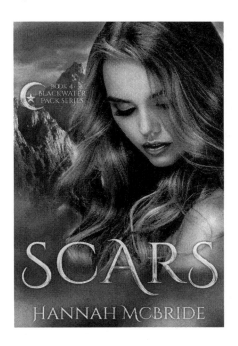

COMING SPRING 2022

Ryan & Maddie will be back in Spring 2022!

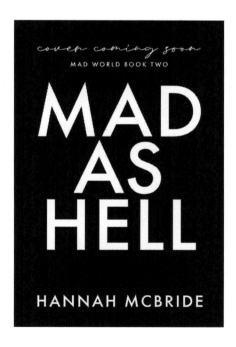

ACKNOWLEDGMENTS

This is honestly my favorite part of finishing a book; looking back at all the people who helped make this a reality. And trust me, there are a *lot* of people.

I have to start with the two women who made this book possible: Krista Davis & Nicole Sanchez. You two had my back this entire book, and your feedback and help is as invaluable as your friendship.

The other person who made this book so much better than I ever imagined is my editor, Natashya Wilson. It's been a dream for nearly a decade to write that sentence in the acknowledgments section of my own book, and there simply aren't word to express how much I love you and what you've done for me.

Quirah Casey for this *insane* cover. Your talent is mind-blowing.

My Alpha team: Vonetta Young, Kayleigh Gore, Ricarda Berger, Tracy Kirby, Katie Akers, Asis Gonzalez, & Lisa Carina Gaibler.

All my Inner Sanctum friends! You guys rock my world on a daily basis.

My family: Mom & Dad, Micah & Lauren, Sherry & Tricia, and especially Aria & Nora.

Anyone who is reading this right now: thank you for letting me tell you a story.

ABOUT THE AUTHOR

Hannah McBride has been many things in her life: a restaurant manager, a clinical research coordinator, a dreamer, a makeup brand ambassador, an event coordinator, a blogger, and more. But at heart, she's always been a writer, and in 2020 she decided to make it official. Good luck stopping her now.

ALSO BY HANNAH MCBRIDE

Blackwater Pack Series:

SANCTUM

BROKEN

PREY

LEGACY

SCARS (coming Winter 2022)

For giveaways, teasers, and everything else about books, join my Facebook Group:

THE INNER SANCTUM

Mad World Series:

MAD WORLD

MAD AS HELL (coming Spring 2022)

Printed in Germany
by Amazon Distribution
GmbH, Leipzig